AMONG MEN AND HORSES

BY

M. HORACE HAYES, F.R.C.V.S.

Late Captain 'The Buffs'

AUTHOR OF

'THE POINTS OF THE HORSE,' 'ILLUSTRATED HORSE-BREAKING'
'VETERINARY NOTES FOR HORSE OWNERS,' ETC.

Illustrated
by Reproductions from
Photographs

PREFACE.

THIS book is an account of the way in which I gained whatever knowledge I may possess about horses. Horse-lore is an extremely difficult science to acquire, owing, I believe, to its immense extent, and to the difficulty in finding out the schools in which its various branches are taught. If this story of my life among horses in many lands fails to be amusing, it may serve the useful purpose of a guide book to others who know less about horses than I do, though equally interested in them. In the teaching books which I have written on Veterinary Work, Riding, Breaking, Training, etc., I have had so much to say pertinent to the matter in hand, that I have had in them little or no opportunity of illustrating principles by the narration of my own personal experience. The good opinion of my publisher gives me the happy chance of 'holding forth' about myself; but instead of doing so with an air of superiority and assumed infallibility, I find that I have written as a student ever seeking for more light by which to acquire knowledge of the subject to which he has devoted the best years of his life. As I have often found mistakes to be more enlightening than inspiration, I relate them both, heedless of the fact that instead of posing as a prophet, I 'give myself away' as one who not long ago was just as ignorant about my own pet study, as anyone else. I believe that the Public and the Press are inclined to receive reminiscences with a lenient and forgiving spirit, as a sort of dying speech by those whose active life is finished. I beg, however, to disclaim such a concession; for my wife and I look forward to having many more adventures in foreign lands among men and horses. The sad part of the thing is that by the time one acquires a large amount of insight into any difficult subject, one is too old to put it into practice. Happily, my stock of equine lore is far from being complete.

M. H. HAYES.

Woodbine Cottage,
Melton Mowbray, 1st June 1894.

CONTENTS.

———o———

CHAPTER I.

Early Days in Ireland—George Hawks—Slack-rein Riding—The Irish Famine—Old Style of Stable Management—Putting the Corn into them—Lord Fermoy—James Hayes, the Privateersman—Gentleman Riders—Dick Barry—Sir John Astley—Captain Machell—Dr Tanner—Mr Dan Horgan—Billiards—Colonel Warburton—The Dutchman—Captain John Bayly—General 'Begorra' Brown, - - - - - - - page 1

CHAPTER II.

The Royal Military Academy—School Riding—Baucher—Pugilism—Bill Richardson—Joe Nolan—Rowing—Joe Sadler—Jim Pudney—Fairplay in England—Mitchell—Bat Mullins, - - - - - - - 26

CHAPTER III.

India—Sport as a Training—Cultivation of Pluck—Conscience—Swadharm—My First Book—Literary Style—Life in India—Riding Buckjumpers—Steve Margarett—Lord Lansdowne—Buckjumping defined—Buffalo Bill—Accidents—Fear of Death—Sir Lyon Playfair—Livingstone—Rustem Pasha—Sir Edward Bradford—Sanson—Madame Dubarry—De Thou—Cartouche—Durman Dakoits—Balthazar Gérard—Effect of Nervous Shock on Animals and on Prize-fighters, - - - - - - - 34

CHAPTER IV.

Training Horses for Racing—Watering Horses—Stable Management—Wasting—Charlie Bailey—Colonel Locke Elliott—Ben Roberts—East Indian Horses—Australian Horses—Arab Horses—Sheikh Esa bin Curtas—Veterinary Work—How Ideas come to Authors—Professor Williams—Salmon Fishing—Professor Dick—Dr Fleming—Veterinary Surgeons—'The Buffs'—Leaving the Service, - - - - - 51

x   *Contents.*

CHAPTER V.

A Horse Registry—Captain Lynx—A Book on Riding—Mr Stanley Berkeley—Mr Alfred Watson—The Old Castilian—Mr Joe Radcliffe—Mr Phil. Robinson—Mr Sinnett—Poker—Mr Allen—*The Field*—Mr Comyns Cole—Mr William Martin—Mr Edwin Martin—Dalmeny and Ferkun, page 66

CHAPTER VI.

Cramming—Militia Subalterns—A Book on Tactics—Mr John Hubert Moore—Horse Breaking—Writing New Editions—Mr John Sturgess—A Book on the Shape and Make of Horses—Newmarket—Mr John Hammond—St Gatien—Mr John Corlett—*The Sporting Times*—'Gubbins'—'Shifter'—The Earnings of Jockeys and Trainers—Irish Horses in England—Touting—Mr Townsend, the Horse Painter—Mr Oswald Brown—Mr Allan Sealy—Mr Sam Waller—Mr Briton Rivière—Mr Haywood Hardy—Mr John Charlton,   -   -   -   -   -   -   -   76

CHAPTER VII.

Horsebreaking—'Professor' Sample and his System—Quackery in Horsetaming—'Professor' Galvayne—Sample's Show in London—Originality in Horse Taming—Frank and Joe,   -   -   -   -   -   98

CHAPTER VIII.

Colonel Dudley Sampson—Return to India—Bombay—A Free Show—Poona—Colonel Morton and the 14th Hussars—The 17th Lancers—General Wardropp Calcutta—Horsebreaking in a Class and in a Public Performance—Causes of Success—Learning as I went on—Horse Taming and Horsebreaking—Show at Simla—Lord and Lady Dufferin—Lord Roberts—The Duke of Bedford—Sir George White—Mr Rudyard Kipling—'The Guides'—Hyderabad and its Native Noblemen—Improvements in Horsebreaking—Mr Jimmy M'Leod and Britomarte—Racing—'The Treasure,'   -   111

CHAPTER IX.

Nellie Reid—Sample and his Machine—A Class at Woolwich—Mr Hermann Vezin—Ormonde—Mr John Porter—Breaking at Kingsclere—Schoolwork for Race-horses—Captain Fitzgerald,   -   -   -   -   128

Contents.

CHAPTER X.

Gibraltar—Malta—Duke of York—Duke and Duchess of Edinburgh—Cairo—Colonel Valentine Baker—General Grenfell—Horses in Egypt—Ceylon and its Planters—Breaking a Jibber—The Spanish Mail—Tubbing—Singapore—Mr Harry Abrams—Horses from Western Australia—Horse-breaking—Savage Horses—Wood Flooring for Stables, · · page 137

CHAPTER XI.

The Blue Funnel Line—'We have never lost a Passenger'—Lascar Crews—Steering on Land—Chinese Boatmen—Hong Kong—China Ponies—Racing in China—Buckstone and Tim Whiffler—Mr Fraser Smith—Bandmann—Shanghai—Mongolian Ponies—Mr Kelly Maitland—Small Feet—Society in Shanghai—Shanghai Race Club—Horsebreaking at Shanghai—Rickshaws—Gambling for Food—Tientsin—Mr Butler—Mafoos—The French Mail—Japan—Hotels and Food, · · · · 150

CHAPTER XII.

Return to India—Starting a Newspaper—Society in India—The Counter Test—Planters—Life in Calcutta—Public Opinion in India—Indian Officials—Amateur Actors—Miss Amy Sherwin—Mr Rudyard Kipling as a Flatterer, · · · · · · · · · 178

CHAPTER XIII.

Importation of Colonial Horses into India—Horse Dealing at Calcutta—The Saddle selling the Horse—Horses on Board Ship—Mr More on Lord Combermere—Saddles—Colonial Horse Dealers—Mr John Stevens—Maoris—Teddy Weekes—Treatment of Sprains in Horses—Racing in India—The Apcars—Lord William Beresford—Paper-Chasing—A Jingle—India as a School for Riding, · · · · · 186

CHAPTER XIV.

Frank Fillis—Bill Hayes—Mickey Miley—Horse Photography—Journalism in India—Shows in India—Mr Woodyear—Arthur Hancock—Captain Astley 'The Mates'' Brother. · · · · · · · · · · 201

Contents.

CHAPTER XV.

Dan Kingsland—Argentine Horses—Sample's Second Show in London—Another Frost—Colonel Pole Carew—Taming Horses by Machinery—The Love of Englishmen for Horses—Lecturing at the Polytechnic—Mr Frank Haes—The Veterinary Fellowship Degree—Bound for South Africa—Mr Edwin Ashe—Mr W. W. Reade's Cricket Team—Miss Genevieve Ward and Mr Vernon, - - - - - - - - page 211

CHAPTER XVI.

Horsebreaking in Cape Town—Englishmen in South Africa—Social Equality —No Style—Sir Henry Loch—Port Elizabeth—A Stranded White Man —A Cockney and a Mule—A Real Showman—'Outside of the Ring, please'—Killing Horses—Rockwell—Driving Tandem without Reins or Traces—*A Café au lait* Funker—October, the Basuto Kafir—Mr Hilton Barber—South African Farmers—Cauliflowers Three Shillings a Piece —South African Horses—Horse Sickness—Defeated by a Mare—Bloemfontein—Orange Free State Boers—Colesberg—Candlemas and Belladrum —Roaring, - - - - - - - - - 220

CHAPTER XVII.

The Diamond Fields—Lecturing at Kimberley—Badly reported—The De Beers Company—'Squaring' Governments—'Trapping'—'I. D. B.'—Taking the 'Sulk' out of a Horse—The Horse and the Goat—Equine Friendships—'Wasters' and 'Remittance Men'—Captain Goodwood—Brokendown Officers—Manners and Customs in South Africa—The Kimberley Exhibition, - - - - - - - - - 235

CHAPTER XVIII.

Diamonds, - - - - - - - - - 248

CHAPTER XIX.

South African Railways—Coaching across the Veldt—Driving Twelve in Hand— Driver and Guard—Food for Horses—Oat Hay—Temper of South African Horses — South African Method of Horsebreaking — Horsemanship in South Africa and Australia—Tying Horses to Posts in the Streets— Knee Haltering—The Veldt, - - - - - - 252

Contents. xiii

CHAPTER XX.

Arrival at the Gold Fields—Clubs in South Africa—Johannesburg: its Jews, Englishmen, and Boers—Types of John Bull—A Public Performance under Difficulties—A Lady riding Buckjumpers—Performances at the Johannesburg Circus—Bad to Mount—The Farce of Horse Taming Shows in England—How to make a Good Impression—J. R. Couper, the South African Champion—Wolff Bendoff—'The Mates'' Son—Mr Grey Rattray—Eggs Sixpence a Piece—Dave Moss and the 'Tape'—Johannesburg 'Sharps'—The Ready Reckoner Story—Justice to 'Niggers' in the Transvaal—Vichy, the Winner of the Johannesburg Handicap —English Horses in South Africa, - - - - - - page 259

CHAPTER XXI.

Racing in South Africa—Polo—Performances at Pretoria — An Accident— Enthusiasm of the Boers—General Joubert—Breaking-in a Zebra—The Language of the Boers—A Journey by Coach—Prize Fighting in South Africa—Nickless and Kelly—Majuba Hill and Laing's Nek—Harrismith —Hendrik Truter—Maritzburg—Sir Charles Mitchell—Colonel Swaine and the 11th Hussars—Horsebreaking at Durban—Farewell to October— The Climate of South Africa—Return to England, - - - - 279

CHAPTER XXII.

Homeward Bound—Blazing Weather—'Professor' Norton Smith—The Dublin Horse Show — Jumping — Paris — High School Riding—Baucher — M. Auguste Raux—Gustave—Teaching a Horse to Jump—Horse Taming Competition between Sample and Leon, - - - - - 296

CHAPTER XXIII.

The Horsewoman—Practical Lectures on Side-Saddle Riding—The Wards— Fred. Allen—Teaching Ladies to Ride—Riding Masters—Learning from Teaching—Improvements in Side-Saddles—Safety Skirts—The Danger of being 'Dragged'—Saddlers—Walsall—Effect of Cast-iron on the Franco-German War—The Row—Lady Dilke. - - - - - - 318

xiv *Contents.*

CHAPTER XXIV.

Accident to Gustave — Ranelagh — Richmond — The Duke of Cambridge — Management of Horse Shows—Apathy of Londoners to Horse Shows— A Libel Action—Berlin—Berliner Tattersall—German Riding and Breaking—The Thiergarten—Riding in Berlin—*The Points of the Horse*—Fillis and Germinal — Circus Renz — Lectures — Rugby — Yorkshire — Melton Mowbray—End,   -   -   -   -   -   -   -   -   - page 338

LIST OF ILLUSTRATIONS.

———o———

CAPTAIN M. H. HAYES, AND MRS HAYES.	*Frontispiece*
	PAGE
SIR J. D. ASTLEY,	13
MR JOHN CORLETT,	85
'NATHANIEL GUBBINS,'	89
MR JOHN PORTER,	133
MR J. MORAY BROWN,	299
MR F. V. GOOCH,	323
DUKE OF RUTLAND,	349

Also, Illustrations on pp. 1. 26. 34. 51, 66, 76. 97, 98, 111, 128, 137, 150. 178, 186, 201, 211, 220. 235, 248, 252. 259, 279. 296. 318. 338.

Photo by M. H. Hayes.

AMONG MEN AND HORSES.

CHAPTER I.

Early Days in Ireland—George Hawkes—Slack-rein Riding—The Irish Famine—Old Style of Stable Management—Putting the Corn into them—Lord Fermoy—James Hayes, the Privateersman—Gentleman Riders—Dick Barry—Sir John Astley—Captain Machell—Dr Tanner—Mr Dan Horgan—Billiards—Colonel Warburton—The Dutchman—Captain John Bayly—General ' Begorra ' Brown.

NOT long ago I casually told an experienced journalistic friend that my publishers had asked me to write for them a book on dogs. 'Do nothing of the kind,' he replied. ' The public regard you as an authority on horses. If it finds that you take up other subjects, it will imagine that you cannot know as much about horses as it thought you did ; and it will hate you under the idea that you won its regard too

A

easily.' The words I knew were wise; so I went home to repeat them to my partner. She, with a woman's keen sense of the practical, remarked that she had been waiting 'ever so long' for a windfall to buy a new dress; that Gustave's livery bill had not been paid for the last five months; that there was nothing like having something to 'go on' with; and that I really ought to get half-a-dozen new shirt collars for myself, as the old ones were hopelessly frayed out at the edges. Necessity prevailing over sentiment, I produced the 'copy,' sent it in, and cashed the cheque. Having done the deed, I feel more or less brazen about its accomplishment, and shall henceforth insist that the study of many subjects is imperative for the thorough acquisition of one. Hardened in my revolt, I have included among the illustrations of *The Points of the Horse*, photographs of an antelope, cheetah, lynx, bullock, buffalo, and a rhinoceros. I shall now go a great deal further, and say that although I have always been fond of horses, and have lived more or less among them, I have devoted myself specially to them only for the last five-and-twenty years.

I was born and bred in the county of Cork, which is a very horsey part of the world. My father, who had flour mills at Ovens, near Ballincollig, and afterwards at Bellgooley, near Kinsale, kept a miscellaneous lot of animals for cart-work, driving and riding; but he took so little interest in them, that he was never able to recognise any of his own. Probably the reason for his apathy to the topic which absorbed all the attention of his neighbours, was that he was a singularly honest man, and would never believe ill of anyone until too late. The story had its usual ending: he made the fortune of others and lost his own. My step-brother was devoted to horses. He read Youatt instead of the Bible. He rode well out hunting on any horse he wanted to sell. He went to Australia, and is now very rich. The earliest incident of my childhood which I can remember is that of catching hold of the hot bars of the old-fashioned fireplace, in order to steady my uncertain steps, while toddling, contrary to orders, through the kitchen on a voyage of discovery. I remember how I yelled, and how my distracted mother, the nurse and maids, with kisses and jam for my lips, and flour out of the dredger for my blistered hands, strove to comfort me. Although I have often repeated many other follies, I have never, since that memorable morning, caught hold of the bars of a grate in which the coals were burning. The punishment of the disobedience came so quickly after the offence, that the very sight of an old-time fireplace recalls to me the pain of burned fingers. This was my first lesson in horse-breaking, and one by which I have greatly profited; for it admirably illustrated the sound principle of rendering a rebellious horse amenable to discipline, by making him connect in his mind the idea of pain with that of disobedience. By it I have made many a 'difficult' horse quiet to handle and ride. Baron de Curnieu, in his *Leçons Hippiques,* tells us how the owner of a vicious biter, acting on the same principle, cured the animal, when it rushed open-mouthed at him, by presenting to it a hot leg of roast mutton, which it grasped in its teeth, and accordingly burned its gums and lips. Ever after, the horse seemed to think that its master was red-hot; for it made no further attempt to devour him. Next to the kitchen, my favourite place of resort was the stables. My pet groom used to put me on the back of one of the horses, where I used to remain while he told me highly-coloured stories of hunting and steeplechasing. Throughout the Muskerry country, in which lay the little village of Ovens on the banks of the river Bride, the only amusements of the gentlemen and farmers were those in connection with horses. That fine old Irish sporting family of Hawkes lived next to us. One of the brothers, George, a one-armed man, used to hunt the Muskerry hounds, and was considered one of the best men who had ever crossed that big country which lies between Cork and Macroom. He, like many of the old style, rode with a loose rein, and trusted everything to the honour of his horse to carry him safely. Needless to say that animals trained in that school, had their cleverness and intelligence developed to an extraordinary degree, and that they were trustworthy to an extent which horses that are taught to rely on their riders for direction, can never attain. They had only one fault—a grave one, I admit, as far as indifferent riders are concerned—and that was that any interference with their mouths when they were in the act of jumping, would be liable to make them fall. The fact of his hunter going at a fence, no matter how big it was, never made George Hawkes catch hold of the reins with his only hand, when he wanted to blow the horn or put a lash on the thong of his whip, an operation which he used to do with his fingers and teeth, while he kept the reins hooked on his arm. One of his brothers, Mr Quail Hawkes, has been a well-known coursing judge for many years, and still follows the hounds, whose music first charmed his fancy considerably over sixty years ago.

Men *talk* of lifting horses over fences and of making them take-off where they like. They even accuse their best friends of throwing horses down. That reminds me of a story which is not quite new, but which is perhaps fresh enough to serve its turn here. A man once brought a horse with a pair of broken knees to a veterinary surgeon, and told him that his groom, being a bad rider, had thrown the animal down. 'You'll do me a great favour,' replied the veterinary surgeon, 'if you'll let me have that groom. I'll be a kind master to him, and will pay him a bit extra; for he'll save me a lot of money. I have often to get horses thrown for operations, and this strong fellow will be able to do what it now takes three men to perform for me.' Whatever ideas we may have about regulating a horse's speed when he is coming up to a fence, it is incontrovertible that the less we interfere with his mouth when he is in the act of jumping, the less chance will there be of an accident. The great difficulty most men have in giving, as they ought to do, a horse the free use of his head at that critical moment, is, that if they have not the reins to hang on by, they would probably fall off. If any of my readers wish to test the correctness of this opinion of mine, they should put one of these rein-grippers on a clever jumper in a riding-school, so that the animal may not run out; erect a fence say, four feet and a half high; take off the bridle; drive the horse over the obstacle; and then they will see who is right. I may mention, in order to harden the heart of any waverer, that my wife, and ladies she has taught to ride, have done this feat scores of times without making the slightest movement in the saddle. The serious part of the evil of hanging on by the reins when a horse is jumping, is not that it is apt to make him blunder by interfering with him; but that, by punishing his mouth, it is liable to convert him into a confirmed refuser, or into a dangerous rusher.

Another point of good riding which was early impressed upon me by experienced cross-country men, was that, when going over a fence, one should draw back the feet, so as to avoid the shock which, if the knees were kept straight, would be transmitted, on landing, from the stirrup irons to the pelvis, through the legs, and which, being in a direction behind the centre of gravity, would tend to make it rotate forwards.

My mother was a Scotch-woman of broad-minded charity, and of refined and educated tastes, which did not include horses and hunting. She loved flowers, animals, and scenery, and was delighted to have the opportunity of showing those friends of ours who came to stay with us, from time to time, the beauties of stream and woodland by the banks of the Bride and Lee. On one occasion she took a couple of English ladies, who were on a visit with us, close to the kennels, in order to obtain a particularly pretty view of the country. On hearing one of the ladies exclaim, 'How beautiful!' the old huntsman, who happened to be standing by, replied, pointing to a fox's brush which was nailed to the door, and which he supposed was the object of admiration, 'True for you, ma'am, it is a beautiful one; but if you will come round to the stables, I will show you one twice as handsome.' And thus men and women go through the world, thinking that the subjects which fill their minds are interesting to other people. When the terrible famine and pestilence of 1847-8 afflicted Ireland, my parents had wooden sheds constructed in the grounds near our house for the accommodation of the starving and fever-stricken poor, and aided by our servants, tended and fed them with their own hands. Our part of the country was very sorely stricken. Helpless women and children and gaunt men would drag themselves, cold and weary, to our door, and when quickly taken down into the kitchen and given a bowl of soup or warm milk, would, after saying a word or two of grateful thanks, often stretch themselves in front of the comforting fire, and with a smile of peace and relief on their wan faces would gently pass away out of a world of pain and misery. I can just remember those terrible scenes of uncomplaining suffering on one hand, and unselfish devotion on the other. The famine fever was so virulent, and help so feeble, that the dead lay rotting by the sides of the roads, and the burials in the churchyard had to be conducted so hastily, that many of the corpses were only partially covered with earth. The calamity was so widespread and sudden, that much of the generous aid which came from England and elsewhere was woefully misapplied. Immense quantities of Indian corn meal were imported and distributed among the starving Irish, who, being entirely unacquainted with its use, tried to cook it in the way they had been accustomed to prepare their familiar diet of oatmeal. As the amount of boiling suitable to the latter was altogether insufficient for the former; the new kind of porridge, instead of proving nutritious, acted as a direct irritant to the poor, weakened stomachs of the people, and killed more than it saved. After the distress had passed away, we left Ovens and went to Bellgooley.

Our new abode at Bellgooley was about four miles from Kinsale, and about thirteen from Cork. Mr Tom Knolles of Oaklands hunted the country, until he was nearly ninety years of age; and his brother, an old retired naval

Shoeing Horses.

officer, used to rattle 'puss' out of her form with a musical pack of beagles, which he followed on foot. I often went with my father, who was accustomed to drive every week day to and from his office in Cork; though my proper work was going to school with my sister in an old 'inside outside' car to Kinsale. The amusements of my childhood were trout-fishing and riding every horse upon which I could get a leg up. Being a good deal on the road, I saw something of the evil effects of the old system of shoeing. At that time, shoeing smiths liked to lower the heels of the horses' feet as much as they could, in order to get frog pressure; but did not think it necessary, also, to lower the toes, so as to equalise the work between the respective muscles which bend and straighten the joints of the legs. They thinned the sole until it would yield to the pressure of the thumb, and to show their skill at carving, they pared away the frog. To further aid in the softening of the sole and frog, the grooms and 'strappers' used to keep the feet of the horses during the night stuffed with cow-dung, or some other favourite filth. The result of such practice was, I need hardly say, that the majority of the cart and harness horses were more or less footsore; that they were liable to fall if they happened to tread on a stone; that they frequently 'picked up' stones; and that their feet were hardly ever free from thrush. The evil effects of this bad method of shoeing were not so apparent in hunters, whose work was on softer ground than that over which animals in shafts had to travel. This pernicious system was less the outcome of ignorance than of an endeavour to shoe horses according to wrong principles laid down by veterinary surgeons. The gross faults in the construction of the shoes were slurred over, as much as possible, by the free use of the rasp on the outside of the hoof, and by making the heated iron burn a bed for itself in the 'wall.' The real trouble and danger began when the smith proceeded to 'drive' the nails, which, being hand-made, were of various patterns, sizes and textures.

As the foot had been pared down to its utmost limit of safety, the ill-constructed nails, which were not infrequently made of defective and unsuitable iron, were liable under the blows of the hammer, to take unexpected directions; to split in two, one part coming out in correct position to be clinched, the other penetrating the sensitive tissues; and to perform other eccentric and hurtful feats. The careful smith had therefore to drive the nails in fear, if not in trembling, and to anxiously listen to the fall of the hammer on the nail head, ready to stay his hand and draw the nail, if a dull sound, which would indicate the entrance of the nail into soft tissue, were emitted. The necessity for the detection of this dull sound was the first and only useful hint I received about shoeing in the village smithy. The general adoption during late years of machine-made nails, to say nothing of machine-made shoes, has immensely improved the shoeing of horses, which now leaves but little to be desired. The arbitrary and often unjust law of making forge-masters responsible for the 'pricking' of horses shod at their smithies, despite the proof that there had been no neglect in skill or care, no doubt works well in the advancement of this art. Another point of veterinary science in which we have greatly improved on the practice of our ancestors, is the treatment of wounds, which they were wont to bathe, poultice and stimulate by the application of various 'oils,' with the object of producing what they were pleased to call 'laudable pus.' We, on the contrary, have learned that suppuration, being accompanied by the destruction of valuable tissue, is the very thing which we ought to try to prevent in such cases, and accordingly we adopt as a rule, 'dry dressing.'

At the time of which I am writing, eye diseases and consequently blindness were very common among Irish horses, owing to the horribly unsanitary conditions under which they were kept. In many instances, the horse's bed was a dung heap, and in all, special precautions were taken to prevent the existence of free ventilation. Not alone was

Stable Management. 9

the chronic disease of the eyes which is popularly known as moon-blindness, engendered by the evolved ammonia and vitiated air; but the mares and sires so afflicted, conferred on their offspring a hereditary tendency to this complaint. Under such stable conditions, it was not to be wondered at that chest troubles, asthma and chronic bronchitis, for instance, were rife among these horses. Besides, the germs of 'stable fever' were permanent residents in these abodes, into which, no young horse fresh from grass, could be put without his becoming afflicted by this disease. The principles of proper stable sanitation require no special study; for we have in ourselves a sufficient guide to their just comprehension. If a stable be so clean, well-drained, and properly ventilated, that an ordinary, cleanly, healthy man or woman could, without well-founded repugnance, eat their meals and sleep in a stall, we may feel fairly confident that it is good enough for a horse to live in. But if, after personal experience, we find that the air is close and there are bad smells in it, we may be equally certain that it is no place in which to house a horse. Ventilation with horses, as with men, should be obtained (except in the tropics) without draughts, which, in cold and temperate climates, are apt to give rise to coughs and colds. The worst kept stables as far as neglect of proper ventilation went, were those in which the old Irish post-horses lived. I remember one four-horse coach in which there was only one eye capable of seeing with, and that belonged to the one-eyed driver. Much of the coaching was done with Bianconi's quaint-looking conveyances, which were long and large four-wheeled outside cars. The horses of all these coaches were terrible cripples with hardly a sound leg among twenty of them; and yet when they were warmed up with a mile or two's travel, they would face their collars, stride along, and stay their distance in gallant style. I remember asking an old coachman, by whose side I often sat on the box seat and whose utterances I treasured in my youthful memory, how it was that such ancient and apparently used-up 'crocks,' had such fire and bottom. 'It's the five or six years' corn they have in them that does it,' he replied. This answer has been one of the most useful hints about horses I have ever received; for its application to horses I have trained, has enabled me to win many races I would otherwise have lost. Instead of 'throwing horses by,' 'letting them down,' and allowing them to convert the most of their muscle into fat, which would have to be subsequently worked off with probably disastrous effects to the suspensory ligaments and back tendons, I tried as far as possible to keep the corn in them. Without attempting any physiological discussion, I may broadly say that different kinds of food produce different qualities of tissue. Of this fact I had a good practical proof on seeing the manner in which bacon produced from pigs which had been fed principally on horse flesh, conducted itself on being fried or boiled; for the fat all turned into grease, and the lean into sodden strings. I may mention that these hogs had been kept in the yard of a knacker who thought he might thus economically use the stuff which was not good enough for the manufacture of saveloys. If people knew how much horse offal is given to pigs, they would be more chary than they are of the promiscuous eating of pork, bacon, sausages and hams.

In those days, as at the present time, people in Ireland regarded horses almost entirely from a jumping point of view; and horsemanship, as riding. In these two branches, they had every reason to be proud of their animals and of themselves; although in other and equally important points of horse knowledge, they were singularly ignorant. They despised driving, except when they were drunk and going at full gallop down a hill as steep as the side of a house. If a farmer had a young hunter for sale, and one asked, as an Englishman would naturally do, if he went in harness, the farmer would feel grossly insulted. Their shoeing was a mutilation; their veterinary practice, a relic of barbarism; their ideas on 'make and shape,' a contradiction based on

Lord Fermoy.

the idiotic aphorism that 'horses run in all shapes'; and their breaking, an implicit reliance on the dispensations of a fickle Providence. When I was about twelve years old, we left the country and went to live in the suburbs of Cork, where I devoted more of my time to running, rowing and other athletic sports than to horses; although I went out from time to time with Lord Fermoy's hounds, and the Duhallows. Lord Fermoy was a fine fellow and a rare good judge of a horse. As he was not rich, he seldom gave more than a hundred pounds for a hunter, at which price his eighteen stone of bone and muscle was carried in a manner that it would take five or six times that amount to do at the present time. In those days in the county of Cork, £60 was regarded as a price that ought to buy a first flight hunter which could jump, gallop, stay and carry weight—£200, now, is nearer the figure. I remember a particularly fine hunter which Lord Fermoy had, called Bullagaun, and named after a small place that belonged to him, near Monkestown, 'on the pleasant waters of the River Lee,' in the county of Cork. Strange to say, after an interval of thirty years, that name fell on my ears one morning by the Calcutta racecourse when I was looking at a smart racing pony being measured. 'Bullagaun,' I muttered, half to myself, 'was the name of a great horse I once knew.' 'And he belonged to Lord Fermoy,' added, greatly to my surprise, a tall, fine-looking young fellow who was standing near, and who happened to be the owner of the pony. Mutual explanations followed, and I learned that the gentleman to whom I was speaking was Captain The Honourable Ulick Roche, who was Lord Fermoy's son. He told me that the original Bullagaun was bought by his father for £200, sold by him for 1500 guineas, and subsequently fetched in Paris 2500 guineas, which is the highest price I have ever heard that has been given for a *bona fide* hunter. Lord Fermoy used to encourage horse-breeding among his tenants, and was always ready to buy from them any likely colt or filly they bred. Writing about

Lord Fermoy and his son reminds me that I am a sort of a
'thirty-first cousin' of theirs; for my great-great-grandfather,
George Hayes of Ballivooher, married a Miss Johanna Roche
of that family. Her son, James Hayes, belonged to a *letter
of marque* during the French War of his time; was taken
by the enemy after a long privateering career, and kept in a
French prison for seven years. He and a fellow-prisoner, the
father of an old doctor in Bandon, were liberated through the
influence, at the Court of France, of his maternal cousins.

In my early days, the Gentleman Rider was sternly re-
pressed by the professional, who, like the Cusacks, Carols,
Noble and others, regarded gratuitous chase riding as an
unwarrantable attempt to take the bread, or rather the whisky,
out of their mouths. Poor Captain Barnard Shaw, who was
so fond of getting a mount, that he would have gone a hundred miles to ride even a loser, got killed by a couple of
jockeys, who closed in on him at a fence, and who had vowed
that unless he would stop riding they would 'do' for him.
A stronger executive than that which ruled the Irish turf in
those days, has knocked that monstrous idea out of the heads
of the Irish pros., who have often now to resign their pride of
place to such amateurs as the Moores and Beasleys. At the
time about which I am writing, the best G. R. of the South
of Ireland was Mr Dick Barry of Carrigtwohill, who used to
ride his own horses and those of his father. He had extraordinary bad luck at Punchestown with that fine chaser,
Bounceaway, who, in the run-in, after having jumped all the
fences and was coming in alone, put its foot in an old wheel-
rut in the middle of the field, fell down and lost the race.
The chief fault of my countrymen, I may remark, is their too
ready submission to the dictates of scoundrels, especially
those of their own kith and kin. Those of us who have
studied history, know that the sympathy of Irishmen for
criminals is a legacy handed down from the time when
English law meant, to them, injustice. Although it takes
many years to entirely efface from the minds of a people

Photo by H. R. Sherborn, Newmarket.

the evil effects of oppressive legislation, the traditions of which continue to be handed down from father to son for several generations; we may be confident that the national sentiment which rebelled against injustice, will become devoted to laws, the working of which is found to ensure to the people justice and order. With all their faults, the Corkonians of those days had one strong claim to be considered sportsmen, namely, they paid their debts of honour. Although I have already told in *The Pink 'Un* a story about Sir John Astley in this connection; I trust I may be pardoned for repeating it here. 'The Mate,' who had proved himself the champion sprinter of the British Army in the Crimea, made, in the spring of 1858, a match, which he won, with a Mr Taylor, who had beaten Captain Machell, and who, as a pedestrian, was the pride of the County of Cork. The race came off in the Barrack Square, and the course, 100 yards, was roped in. Before the men toed the line, Captain Astley, with an overcoat covering his tights, walked up and down the enclosure, round the sides of which were thronged hundreds of Cork sportsmen, taking all the bets he could get on; and he would not 'peel' as long as there was anyone left to answer his challenge: 'Who'll back the Irishman?' In his usual impetuous way, he omitted to book any of his bets; but his trust in the honour of his opponents was not misplaced; for everyone of them came up after the event had been decided and 'weighed in.' Little Jimmy Paterson, 'the Flying Tailor,' used to train The Mate and give him his gallops. Eight years later, I helped to avenge the honour of Cork by training a young farmer, whom I matched to run 110 yards against Captain Marryatt of the 65th Regiment, who at that time was one of the fastest amateur sprinters in England. With a novice who was a yard better than 'even time' for 100 yards, I had a good thing against a $10\frac{1}{4}$ second man. Our side won over this match more money from the Sassenach, than The Mate and his friends had carried away.

Captain Machell, who was in the 14th Regiment, and who

was stationed in Ireland at the time about which I am writing, was a fast runner; although his chief forte was hopping, at which accomplishment he had no equal in England. I have often heard people talk of his hopping on to the chimney-piece of the Kildare Street Club, which, if I remember rightly, was about 5 feet from the ground. He was also known to have hopped over a billiard table. The 14th Regiment also possessed a very good all-round man in Captain Aubrey Patton.

In the late Fifties and early Sixties there was keen rivalry between the Cork athletes and English visitors. The arrival of the celebrated London Rowing Club four-oared crew, of which Playfair was stroke and Cassamajor bow, was an event which stirred into excitement every man, woman and child of our sporting city. As might have been expected, the unconquered strangers were too good for the local men. The visit was justly regarded as a high compliment; and the defeat, as a stimulant to increased exertion. During the seven years which followed, the River Lee in the summer time was the busy scene of hard training and well-contested boat races, in some of which I rowed. There were two great rival clubs: the Glenbrook and the City. The members of the former, of which I was one, regarded themselves as gentlemen amateurs, and the latter, as amateurs without the prefix; for our rivals —and worthy ones they frequently proved themselves to be— were chiefly recruited from shop assistants; while we considered ourselves to be untainted by trade, in contra-distinction to commerce. The City men, not to be behindhand in a vice which has been castigated by Thackeray, drew the 'line' between themselves and the members of a mechanics' rowing club. The fact of the beautiful situation of our club on the river, close to Queenstown, prompted its committee to enlarge and improve the club-house, until they had made it a very pleasant resort for social meetings, with the result that its luxurious surroundings killed love of rowing, which needs for its highest development, self-denial and hard work. The question of the difference between amateurs and professionals has now no further interest to me, so I can afford to laugh at it. In art, literature, and science there is no distinction between the two. The amateur actor, the amateur photographer, the amateur cricketer, or the amateur athlete who thinks he is socially superior to his professional rivals, because he is an amateur according to certain arbitrary rules, either values his social position—generally, a miserably poor one at best—more than his art, or by deliberately sailing under false colours tries to make more money out of it than he could do as a professional. The instances at hand are so numerous that mention of some would be invidious to others. When Sir John Astley and Captain Machell used to run, it was rightly considered that amateur peds. might contest money matches against each other, so long as they 'found' their own coin; just as an amateur billiard player of the present day would incur no social ban on account of having a bet on a game.

What villanies have been perpetrated on the cinder path! When I was 'cramming,' as a boy, in Dublin for the army, I entered for a 150 yards handicap, which had been organised by Jack Levitt, the old ten-mile champion. Being unknown, I got 14 yards start and won easily. When I came next day to run in the second round, I found that I had been put back 10 yards, and that a very smart Englishman who had run the previous day in faultless style and had won his heat in a trot, had been moved forward the same distance. I lost, and thought no more about the affair, until about a couple of years afterwards I found myself in the Bow Running Grounds, looking at the decision of a sprint handicap. Thinking that I had seen on some previous occasion the scratch man, who was giving long starts to the other professionals, I asked one of my running acquaintances who he was. 'That's So-and-So,' he replied; 'he is about an even-timer and is a great pall of Jack Levitt.' And then I went away proud and happy with the consciousness that at least one man had a good opinion of me, and that was Jack Levitt, who, in case of accidents, had made me concede 5 yards to one of the fastest sprinters in England. Although the old champion and his friend, no doubt, divided what ought to have been my handicap money, as well as the bets; still Levitt was a man of real 'grit,' which he nobly proved by losing his life, in a heroic attempt to save some persons from drowning. Levitt's chief rival in the Fifties was Jackson, who got the name of the American Deer, from the great race of 20 miles which he ran about the year 1847, in the States, against a large number of famous American-Indian runners. Some of the Redskins kept the lead up to 15 miles, when Jackson went to the front and won under two hours. He is still alive and is about seventy-five years old. He continued running in fine form until he was well over forty. I do not think that there was ever a better long-distance runner (not even excepting Hazael or Cummings) than he was when at his best. An immense impetus was given to pedestrianism in about the year 1860, when George Martin, the great hurdle race professional, brought over Deerfoot *alias* Louis Bennett, the Canadian half-breed. Martin was a fine showman, and used to 'kid' the public by equipping Deerfoot in paint, feathers, mocassins, and tights. He used to then let him loose on some public running ground, like that of Hackney Wick, when the supposed Redskin would whoop and yell in the manner described by Fenimore Cooper, while he bounded along. When Martin thought he had exercised his legs enough, he used to run into the middle of the course, stretch out his arms, shout out some gibberish, which passed for Cherokee or Iroquois, and try to stop the 'wild man,' who used to act the part to perfection and take a lot of catching and holding. After running him at various public grounds, Martin took him round the country with a large tent and a 'stable' of several of the great runners of the time, such as Bill Lang, Teddy Mills, Jackson, Mackinstray, and Richards. This tour paid well, until

Jackson being dissatisfied with his treatment, went to law, and told in Court how Martin 'worked' the supposed matches. Pedestrianism is a poor game now. I remember C. Smith, an American, getting on a good mark, and winning a big Sheffield handicap in 1880. Having been put back a long way, he bided his time for eight years, until he got so placed, that he thought he was certain of winning. He came in first, right enough; but the judge, for reasons best known to himself, awarded the race to the second man. Smith being then thirty-one years old, and having a comfortable business of his own, thought it best to stick to it, and to give up sprinting.

About a year after Sir John Astley's visit there were some open foot races held at Passage near Cork, at which assembled all the local fleet of foot; the only stranger being the late General Fred. Brine, who was then a captain in the Royal Engineers, and who was fond of sprinting. In the 100 yards race, Quain, a Mallow man of great local celebrity as a runner, was winning easily; but making the fatal mistake of turning round to laugh at Captain Brine, who was close behind him, he slipped, fell close to the winning-post, and let the sapper win. All the County of Cork looked upon the next event, the 150 yards race as the one by which justice would be done to Ireland, and especially to Mallow. As I was a young lad, and had never taken part before in such an important affair, I was very much excited when I toed the scratch, with Quain on my right and five or six other competitors on my left. I got a little the best of the start and won by several yards, with Quain second, and Brine, who afterwards warmly congratulated me on my success, third. So Cork was avenged; though not by the one she expected.

The young men of the class from which officers of the army and members of the various professions are recruited, in the present day, owing to the improved sanitary conditions under which they exist, are undoubtedly bigger and stronger than those of thirty years ago; but I cannot help thinking they are 'softer.' They appear to have left the cultivation of athletics almost entirely to the class below them, which is chiefly represented by shop assistants and the sons of small shopkeepers, who furnish a large proportion of the cycling, football, running, boxing, and swimming champions. I grant that these amateurs and promateurs (to borrow the expression of poor Sampson of the *Referee*) are a good deal 'mixed'; but the fact remains that for every five hundred lawn tennis players who get their commissions in the Army, there is not one who can box, or ten who can ride across country. My old friend 'Young Reid,' who used to keep a room for teaching boxing in Lower John Street, off Golden Square, and who died not long ago, often bewailed to me the decadence of 'the noble art' among the youth of the wealthier classes. He had been one of the cleverest light-weights who had ever fought within a 24-foot ring, and by his civility, tact and honesty had had a very large connection, as a teacher, among the nobility and gentry of England. Though many of his old pupils continued their practice with Reid, few of their sons cared to put on the gloves. As the old man was growing feeble, he was always glad to see me at his room, so that I might spar with any of his pupils who wished to have some 'loose play,' which in this case was generally a one-sided affair; for Reid made me promise never to hit one of them, except on the shoulder where they could not get hurt. 'If you hurt them,' he used to say with a solemn shake of the head, 'they'll go away and I'll never see them again.' His prophecy was proved to be correct on two occasions, when irritated by chaff from a pupil with whom I was sparring, he asked me to hit hard. I do not think that this objection to getting knocked about with the gloves arose in the slightest from fear of 'punishment'; but from disinclination to get marked about the face. The more civilised we become, the more averse are we from incurring risks of personal injury. Take for instance the Irishmen and Highlanders of sixty years ago and compare their pugnacity with that of their descendants of the present day. Fighting is undoubtedly one of the greatest pleasures some men and many animals have. Under the softening influences of culture the quarrelsome instinct will in time be lost, and the 'rapture of the strife' will no longer stir the human breast. Although it is true that as our intellectual faculties become stronger, our instinctive ones diminish in power; it is by no means certain that we do not get more amusement out of the latter than out of the former. Personally, I prefer a judicious mixture of the two, with which to beguile my hours of relaxation.

I have said so much about my own athletic doings, that I must explain that although I won a lot of events in that line, my success was due not to my being particularly good, but to the fact of my opponents being rather moderate. I was about equally proficient at all the various sports I took up; but was not first-class at any of them.

One of our best friends in Cork was Dr Tanner, father of the present Member of Parliament. He was a fine, generous-hearted man and a grand operator, whose skill with the knife earned him the name, among his admiring medical students, of The Butcher. He made up for any lack in knowledge of minute anatomy, by extraordinary 'nerve' and ready resource. He, like his eldest son, Major Kenny Tanner, an old 99th man, was a staunch Tory. Politics, I may remark, have no attraction for me. If I turn to the history of sixty years ago, I find that the views of the then Liberals, say, on the Reform Bill, were not as advanced as those of the Conservatives of the present day. I am an evolutionist. From the history of nations I see the working of evolution in politics and religion, as clearly as I can trace it from books of stone, in the descent of the one-toed horse or in the two-toed chamois.

Billiards was a favourite game of the Cork sportsmen. There were several fine players among the markers, notably, Tom Chudleigh, George Dunovan, and Dan Horgan. The last mentioned was a bright exception to his predecessors; for he was not alone the best player we have had in Ireland, but was steady, honourable, gentlemanly and masterful. He soon abandoned the *rôle* of scoring and handing the rest, for that of manager; and when his old employer, Paddy Farrel, retired, he took over the billiard rooms and wine cellars. The last time, not long ago, I had the pleasure of meeting him, he had been twice Mayor of Cork, and was one of its most respected citizens. He is unspoiled by prosperity, and is the same pleasant good fellow whom I knew twenty-five years ago. *Il ira loin*, if he choses to plunge deeply in the not very reputable game of politics; for he is capable and is possessed of infinite tact in the management of men. I may mention that Mr 'Tay Pay' O'Connor's father was also a famous billiard professional in Athlone. In those days, an immense amount of gambling was carried on at billiards; more at public rooms probably than at clubs. The Dawson Lane Billiard Rooms, Dublin, were particularly well patronised. Every afternoon, the chief room, which was reserved for good players, was crowded by spectators who backed their respective fancies in silver, gold and paper money as freely as they would have done on a racecourse. The best local gentlemen players were Mr Gard and Mr Paulett. In 1866-7, Captain (now Colonel) Fred. Warburton of the Royal Engineers was a long way the best amateur in Ireland. His skill brought him bad luck; for happening to win about £1500, at single pool from an English officer in the club to which I belonged, he, thinking that the 'scrip' which he had received was as good as ready money, had a dash at sovereign unlimited loo, and lost £1200, which of course he paid up out of his own pocket, as his opponent of the previous evening did not 'part.' Captain Warburton had imperturbable nerves, and was a remarkably fine hazard player. There was a billiard sharp, nicknamed The Dutchman, who used to pay Ireland periodical visits with much profit to himself. His game was pyramids, at which I have never seen a better player, not even Jack Roberts or Mr Mayhew. No matter what odds

Billiards.

he gave, our Irish players were no use with him when he had backed himself heavily. His long and successful career with fifteen red balls and one white one, was summarily stopped one day when he was crossing a London street by a careless cab driver who accidentally destroyed the sight of one of his eyes by a flick of his whip.

Five-and-twenty or thirty years ago, there was a great deal of swindling carried on at public rooms by billiard sharps, whose occupation has now entirely departed. Few gentlemen at present devote their talents to it. Taken all round, I am inclined to think that amateur play is much inferior to what it was when Roberts had rooms in Brighton ; and poor Bill Cook had rooms on both sides of Regent Street. The best gentleman player I have ever seen was Mr Myers, who used to strike terror into the hearts of the Brighton pool players. He handled his opponents with great tact, and seldom ventured to take a whole pool ; but when tempted by fair odds, he would lay himself down to work and clear the table in a manner I have never seen equalled. Despite his forbearance, which was mere policy without a taint of deception, his skill became so dreaded that Roberts had at last to choose between pool or Mr Myers, with the result that he asked this gentleman to retire for a season. The frequenters of the rooms did not mind the professionals, such as poor Fred. Shorter or Stanley ; but they felt that they had no chance with the amateur. Good players as Mr Rogers, Captain Warburton, Mr Douglas Lane, and Dr Galway were, they were a long way inferior to the Brighton gentlemen. The best player we ever had in the army was Captain John Bayly, of whom my friend Captain Astley, 'The Mate's' brother, writes to me as follows :—
'John Bayly was a left-handed bowler in the Eton eleven. Shortly after joining my old regiment, the 11th Foot, he used to grumble when confined to barracks on duty the whole day. He took my advice to practise billiards on these days, and he soon became extraordinarily good at the game. As

he then adopted my further suggestion to take trips to London for instruction from John Roberts, it was not long before he became the best billiard player in the army. In Dublin in 1883 we backed him to give the marker of the Army Club 100 points out of 500, and then we 'kidded' that we had played the fool, and appeared downright sorry that we had made the match. This was swallowed by the 'clever division,' who to a man backed Pat the marker. This astute lot, among whom were three or four generals (one a terrible Wolseyite), was told by Pat that he could not lose, as he was able to beat John Bayly level. The match came off and John Bayly won. There was tremendous consternation in the ranks of the clever division. By far the worst loser was the Wolseyite, who is still alive, I much regret to say. One, and only one, loser, namely, General "Begorra" Brown, took his licking gracefully and paid up without a murmur. "Begorra" has, I am sorry to say, left this planet—what a fine man he was! Six feet two inches high; grave and sedate; only one arm; and a well-known figure in Rotten Row. The day after the match, "Begorra" came up to me and said : " If it had not been for you, sir, John Bayly would have lost. You know what I mean, sir!" The stately figure then withdrew. I am fond of all thoroughbreds. "Begorra" was a thoroughbred Irishman from Galway, and had all the good points, with very few of the bad ones of the Hibernian.'

The people in Cork were so devoted to amusement that, as a boy, I made little progress in study. My mother prayed that I would be famous in the world for goodness, wisdom and learning; my own aspirations were for billiards, riding, rowing, boxing and running. Her gentle admonitions had some small effect on youth's brutal selfishness; for after spending a year on the Continent, where I learned gymnastics, fencing, French and German, I worked hard and passed fairly high up on the list for the Royal Military Academy, which was then the only gate of entrance, by competition, to the army. As a set-off to my reluctantly rendered obedience, I devoted myself from that out entirely to sport. Though I failed to get 'Sappers' and succeeded in obtaining only a commission in the 'Gunners,' I had the fleeting glory (remembered now only by myself) of obtaining the winner's prize for winning the greatest number of events each time I competed at the annual foot races for the cadets.

Photo. by M. H. Hayes.

CHAPTER II.

The Royal Military Academy—School Riding—Baucher—Pugilism—Bill Richardson—Joe Nolan—Rowing—Joe Sadler—Jim Pudney—Fairplay in England—Mitchell—Bat Mullins.

THE Royal Military Academy at Woolwich was an admirable school for 'knocking the nonsense' out of young fellows and for teaching them discipline. It was better at that than in teaching riding, the system of which in the army was the same then as it is now, with a total absence of 'why?' in it. Certain hard and fast rules were and are laid down, and no reasons given. It is easy to find fault with this apparently strange omission; but we must remember that a reasoned-out system of equitation and horsebreaking is a growth of modern culture which germinated in the minds of men long after that part of the *Cavalry Regulations* had been stereotyped. The literature of the subject did not, practically, touch on it until Raabe, Barroil, Dr Le Bon, *mois qui vous parle*, and other modern writers broke through the conventional train of thought. This is strange as regards England, considering how greatly instruction in the theory of musketry has improved the shooting of our army. And yet some of the teachers of musketry were highly finished rule-of-thumb gentlemen, if we may judge by their reported questions and answers; as, for instance, 'What should always be kept in the butts?' Answer: 'Silence.' And 'With what should you clean a rifle?' Answer: 'Care.' From my very short list of reasoners, I have purposely omitted the name of Baucher; not because I am in any way unwilling to withhold reverence to the *grand français* as an *écuyer* (a riding-school horseman); but because his attempted reasoning was hopelessly obscure. When we add to this, change of front after the regrettable accident which deprived him to a great extent of the use of his legs, the student may be pardoned for giving him up in despair. Although Baucher was unsurpassed in the practical part of his work; no one could become a Baucheriste from a perusal of his books. Baron de Vaux in his charming book, *Écuyers et Écuyères*, gives a very appreciative account of this high priest of *l'équitation savante*. '*Un élève de Baucher*' describes his system in detail, without illustrations, but with an abuse of technical phrases, which would have charmed his master, had the old man been alive; but which do little to enlighten the reader. It is possible that in mentioning M. Barroil's name, I may do injustice to his teacher, Captain Raabe: but from reading that admirable work, *L'Art Équestre*, it is impossible to say how much there is of *le maître*, and how much of *l'élève*. I may mention that when I was in F Battery 19th Brigade Royal Artillery at Kamptee, our riding-master was a Mr Wilkinson, who was an enthusiastic Baucheriste. He tried to introduce the various 'flexions' of the French reformer; but because those exercises were not in the drill-book, the officers, as well as the 'non-com.'s' and drivers did not support him in this endeavour, and Baucher's name was held up to derision without a fair trial having been given to his methods. The fundamental error—which it took me many years to find out, and which has been corrected by Fillis, Barroil, and Count de Montigny—in the lateral flexions of the head and neck, is that the principal of these 'suppling' lessons is opposed to the fact that a horse, on receiving an indication of the reins to turn to one side or the other, ought to obey it with his hind quarters, as well as with his head, though in an opposite direction. I may well ask, what good, if a horse refuses a jump or bolts off to one side, say, to the left, is it for him to bring his head round to the right, on that rein being pulled, if he does not bring his hind quarters, at the same time, round to the left, and then put himself straight in the desired direction? When a horse understands the indications of the hand and foot properly, he will turn on his centre either by the 'feel' of the rein, or by the pressure of the drawn back foot. If the latter be strong enough to check the rotation of the hind quarters, then, and then only, should it be possible, by the former, to bring the head round without influencing the position of the hind limbs.

As soon as my fellow 'last joined' cadets and myself were sent to the riding-school, those of us who were Irish, had the proud satisfaction of seeing that a far larger proportion of our number could ride than that of the English. Nationality, contrary to what we flattered ourselves, had no influence in that fact, which was naturally caused by the greater concentration of the well-to-do classes in towns in England, than in Ireland. Almost all of us Irish lads had been brought up in the country; and had had far more facilities for learning to ride than which fell to the lot of boys brought up in large cities.

During the three years I spent as a cadet at Woolwich, I generally got leave on Saturdays, and spent the afternoons on the river, or at some running grounds, and my evenings at some boxing saloon such as that of Nat Langham, Ben Caunt, Bill Richardson, Bob Travers, Jack Hicks, or Jem Mace. Fond as I am of 'the noble art,' I am glad the P. R.

is dead; for it disgusted its supporters and destroyed its finest exponents. 'Ramps' and 'crosses' were frequent at actual fights. Visitors to the sparring rooms were constantly importuned to take tickets for 'benefits' which never came off, and to contribute to the collections at the end of each set-to. I ought not to grumble much at the last-mentioned custom; for after having had a spar with some professional whom I had intended to 'tip,' my opponent, on different occasions, offered me the half share of the coppers, and few bits of silver which had been chucked into the ring after the bout. I need hardly say that I always refused the kind and flattering offer, and that I invariably contributed half-a-crown or so to the amount. Many prize-fighters when they were asked to give lessons, insisted on being paid in advance for a dozen, and then gave their pupil such a 'doing' in the first one, that he seldom returned for a repetition of ill treatment. This was a favourite trick of the once peerless Joe Nolan. And thus the goose gradually forsook its old haunts and now deposits its golden eggs for the support of such admirable institutions as the German Gymnastic Club, The Orion, West London, etc. The cleverest of the clever and bravest of the brave were, as a rule, *exploité*'d by rascally (ironically called 'sporting') publicans who used them as mere 'draws' to the house, for 'the good' of which they were supposed to take all the drinks offered or cadged for. A short course of this prostitution of manhood soon made the clear eyes blurred; the dauntless heart 'jumpy'; and the hard athletic frame, a mass of diseased fat. Even now, the whisky bottle is the champion knocker-out. Among the unsavoury crew of gaffers,' the portly, if not bloated figure of Bill Richardson, the king of the East, stands boldly out. His place at the Blue Anchor, which is off Church Street, Shoreditch, is now well filled by my good friend Tom Symonds, who is as decent a fellow as ever knocked a man down, opened a bottle of champagne, or layed you the favourite. The stories I could tell about Bill Richardson, who had a very strongly marked personality, would furnish ample material for a novel; but unless disguised in some such way, would be too plain writing for print. He ruled his rough pack like a despot; though he kept faith with them as long as their interests were identical with his own. It happened that the police, being in search of the hiding-place of the proceeds of a large jewelry robbery in the city, knocked at the door of the Blue Anchor at two o'clock one morning and demanded instant admittance. They succeeded in getting in, but were stopped on the staircase by Richardson, who, revolver in hand, threatened to shoot the first man that advanced, until he had seen the authority for the raid. When the paper had been produced, a light procured, the old man's spectacles adjusted on his nose, and much valuable time wasted, Richardson's indignation at the invasion of his hearth and home subsided, and he gave the police permission to search his premises, in which, of course, nothing was found. His prey sometimes escaped him. For instance, the incomparable fighter and drunkard, Joe Nolan, the night before his great match with that stout-hearted Welshman, Dan Thomas, got leave for five minutes to go out of the bedroom in which Richardson had locked him up with himself, and did not return until he was brought back, about midday, dead drunk after having been run over by a cab. Though the fight came off, Thomas was robbed of his victory; for the Blue Anchor gang would tolerate no greater disaster than a 'draw.' This murderous following, which was similar to the pack of scoundrels that was imported to Bruges for the protection of the cowardly Smith against the gallant Slavin, was well utilised by Richardson. Mine host of the Blue Anchor was the early patron of Jem Mace, who, he always affirmed, was a better man than Tom Sayers, which is a statement contrary to the weight of historical evidence. When he and Mace fell out, he produced Tom King to beat him, but the honours were divided. Mace, in those days, kept a public house in John Street, Shoreditch. A man who has been badly treated by fame is Bob Travers, the black, who had the Twelve Cantons in Castle Street, Leicester Square. As his battles with Mace proved, there was little to choose between the two, and yet his name is in no one's mouth. I believe he is still alive and that he 'follows' racing. I often sparred with Joe Goss, who seemed to enjoy so much the pleasure of knocking me about, which he well could do, that I readily forgave him. He was an unlucky man to keep encountering Mace, who was just a little the better of the two. The cleverest light-weight I have ever seen was Jack Lead, who defeated George Holden. Like most of the others, he died from dissipation. The last prize fight I saw was between Woolf, the black, and Joe Warmold. Although Woolf was utterly out of training, he managed to make a draw after fighting for four hours and a-half in the Dartford marshes. On this form I never could see what pretensions Warmold had to be considered a champion.

My chief rowing mentor was Tom Pocock, who, as well as Tom Grant, young Harry Clasper and Jack Mackinney, used to come over to train the amateurs at Cork. When I was at 'The Shop,' I often met the Claspers, Bob Chambers, Harry Kelly, and Joe Sadler. An old rowing friend, whom Sadler used to train, tells me that Joe was wont to impress on him the necessity, when he felt 'bad' while rowing a match, of not thinking about himself, but of the terrible 'gruelling' the other fellow must be having. He says that was the only good wrinkle Joe ever gave him; but that it was well worth all the money he paid his professional coach. We would all be brave in every contest through life, if, instead of bewailing our own knocked-about condition, we were to congratulate ourselves on the amount of punishment we were giving that 'other fellow.' Among the peds., I liked Jim Pudney, the old four-mile champion, best. He was not only a very graceful runner, but was also a nice, gentlemanly fellow. His most pleasant reminiscence was that of his first big ten-mile race, in which he encountered Jackson the American Deer, Frost the Suffolk Stag, Jack Levitt, and others. His mother, hearing of her lad's doings, went down to the running grounds, and when she saw her boy dash off with his beautiful lengthy stride to the front, being unable to contain her feelings, she called out, to the astonishment of the motley crowd of roughs, 'Look at my Jim! They'll never catch him.' Nor did they; for he won from start to finish.

The popular idea among people who have not had much experience of 'taking their own part' in a row, is that when two Englishmen come to blows in an impromptu manner, they observe as nearly as possible the rules of the London P.R. My experience, which can be amply corroborated by the police reports, is that they kick, bite, scratch, stab, strike with lethal weapons, throw any missile within reach at, or otherwise unfairly assault each other; but that, except in very rare cases, they don't 'put up their hands' and fight in the supposed orthodox manner, which can in no way be regarded as a national method for settling disputes. In Lancashire, for instance, kicking is the recognised style, as we may see if we observe the sharp-pointed, and steel-tipped boots of the young sporting men of Wigan, Oldham, and Manchester. Irishmen are fairly consistent in sticking to the shillalegh, which not infrequently takes the form of spade, or is supplemented by a lump of lead, or heavy iron ferule.

When that *soi-disant* Champion of England, Mitchell, whose last victory was over a decrepid old man in the Strand, had an impromptu turn-up with Bill Goode, he was careful to use a poker! Could anyone who knew them imagine Tom Sayers or Nat Langham doing such things? Most certainly one could not. We have no 'line' by which we can compare the best prize-fighter of the present day, namely, Jackson the black, with those of bygone times; but we have one by which we may guage the pretensions of Mitchell. When he was first launched on the world for exhibition purposes, prior to his going to America. Bat Mullins, who was then close upon forty, in the sere and yellow leaf of a not over careful life, offered to fight him; but those 'behind' Mitchell were wise enough to avoid a match, which, if it had come off, would not have been won by their man. Bat, in his best days, though 'game' and very 'clever,' was far too light to be within measurable distance of championship form. No one would ridicule the idea of his having been the equal of Sayers, Heenan or King more than himself. Bat is, I think, the last of the old-time pugilists who teaches boxing. Any of my readers who wishes to learn the noble art of self-defence could not do better than to employ him; for he is as civil and decent a fellow as ever threw his cap into a 24-foot ring. I first knew him when he was a lad at Nat Langham's place, The Mitre, in St Martin's Lane. Although individual Englishmen, as a rule, have very vague views of fair play during the heat of a personal rough-and-tumble fight, they are collectively sound on this subject, especially when they have backed the right horse or man.

Photo. by M. H. Hayes.

CHAPTER III.

India—Sport as a Training—Cultivation of Pluck—Conscience—Swadharm
—My First Book—Literary Style—Life in India—Riding Buckjumpers
—Steve Margarett—Lord Lansdowne—Buckjumping defined—Buffalo
Bill—Accidents—Fear of Death—Sir Lyon Playfair—Livingstone—
Rustem Pasha—Sir Edward Bradford—Sanson—Madame Dubarry—
De Thou—Cartouche—Burman Dakoits—Balthazar Gérard—Effect of
Nervous Shock on Animals and on Prize fighters.

AFTER I got my commission in the Royal Artillery, I stayed six months at the depôt in Sheerness, then exchanged into a field battery which was at Kamptee, and went out to India to join it. The voyage out and back has been so frequently described that I need not allude to it further than to say that I have been three times round the Cape and seven times overland.

India. 35

The monotony of the long homeward-bound voyage from India by a sailing ship used to be very pleasantly broken by a day or two's stay at St Helena, at which there was stationed a wing of an infantry regiment, and a battery of Garrison Artillery. Of course, the officers used to have races on this rock, as the French are pleased to call it; in fact, one or two winners were pointed out to me among the crowd of scarecrow ponies which took passengers from the port, James Town, to Le Tombeau, where Napoleon's body was laid for some time, and Longwood, which had been his residence. The native grooms always accompanied their fare for the three or four-mile journey, and kept up, no matter how fast the pace, by hanging on to their animal's tail, the hair of which was of course purposely kept long. The only travellers who now go to St Helena are passengers by the intermediate steamers of the Castle and Union lines. The island is well worth a visit.

India is an admirable training ground for youngsters, who get, there, chances of learning to ride and shoot which those in the army would very seldom obtain in England. Besides, the fact of, practically, everyone in India owning a horse or pony, and of having, to a great extent, to superintend the stable management of one's own animals, and to conduct one's own shooting expeditions, gives one every opportunity of acquiring a good insight into the nature of horses and guns, by whose aid we are able to enjoy the best forms of sport the world can afford. Without India, English officers would be little if anything better than those of continental armies. Few of them, except in the mounted branches, would be able to ride, and still fewer to shoot, except at a target. Lawn tennis would be more cultivated than ever, and cycling would no doubt be adopted as a substitute for horse exercise. The difficulty of getting into the army, and the hard work demanded from its officers deter the sons of monied men from entering it—a fact which is amply proved by the fewness of the candidates for cavalry commissions, which, formerly, were the coveted prizes for the Sandhurst cadets. As the keeping of 'pleasure horses' means the possession of money; knowledge of riding and of horses is becoming rarer and rarer among the last joined officers, who, if they be wise, should try their best to go out to India.

Admirable as cricket, lawn tennis, golf, and other kindred games may be, I must confess that I am rather prejudiced in favour of those which have a fair share of danger in them, such as hunting, pig-sticking, chasing, and big game shooting, as a means of taking the softness out of young men. Were pluck a common human attribute, its possession, as has often been said, would be accepted as a matter of course, and would not be held up for universal admiration. Of the many meanings embraced in the term 'sportsman,' one of the most essential, to my thinking, is that of a good loser—of a man who will face danger and will bear physical or mental pain without flinching; in fact, a good plucked 'un, to use a colloquialism which is more expressive than elegant. The strain of a desperate struggle to be first in a race, whether on foot, boat or bicycle, demands quite as much pluck as a a prize fight. I may remark that courage, like other mental qualities, requires practice for its high development, and is shared by beast as well as man; by black as well as white. My experience of the world, of which I have seen a great deal, has made me regard the people in it as 'much of a muchness'; one nation not being greatly superior to the other, except by reason of its opportunities. In my young days, we thought Britons and Irishmen could box, row, and play any game which demanded strength, activity, skill and pluck, better than anyone else; because they were Britons and Paddies. Jack Heenan, J. L. Sullivan, Murdoch and his fellow-cricketers, Hanlon, and other Colonials and Americans, to say nothing of Frenchmen and Dutchmen, have of late knocked a good deal of this nonsense out of our heads. We were boastful about our horses until Gladiateur, Fille de l'Air,

Foxhall, Iroquois, and a host of others, made us more humble minded. The lesson to be learned from this not altogether pleasing experience, is that men excel best in what they practise most. If we have at present no pugilist or oarsman, like Tom Sayers or Jem Mace, like Bob Chambers or Harry Kelly, worthy of upholding the honour and glory of England in the 24-foot ring, or on the river, we have the best football players in the world, some of the best bicycle riders, and the finest jockeys. Though we have done more than any other nation in the advancement of athletics, and of a love for horses, we have no monopoly either of the vices or of the virtues of the human race. If at times we soar to extraordinary heights of heroism; on other occasions we descend to an equal distance into the depths of baseness. The records of our naval, military, and civilian life bristle with feats to be expected more from gods than men; and yet the columns of our newspapers publish a chronicle of cowardly brutality as dark as the other is light. As I turn over the papers of this month, I read that 'an inquiry was held with reference to the death of John Thomas Bonner, aged six years, the son of a labourer. The deceased began playing by a pond in the Potteries. Shortly afterwards a scream was heard, and when Mrs Bonner ran out she found her boy in the water. The mother's sister followed to the pond, and there saw the woman tearing her hair and screaming for assistance. Four men were also at the spot, but none of them made any attempt to rescue the boy, who was drowned in front of his mother's eyes. Witness said to the men, "Why don't you try and save the boy?" and one of them replied, "It's no good trying; the child has gone down for the last time. I am not going to drown myself; the little —— had no business there." The man was not called, and the jury returned a verdict of accidental death.' Within a fortnight there have been two diabolical attempts, by bodies of miners on strike, to upset railway trains filled with men, women and children. At an inquest on the body of a boy who was drowned in the

Grand Surrey Canal, a juryman asks: 'Was there no one near when deceased first sank?—Witness: Yes, I saw at least twenty young men standing on the towing-path.—A juryman: What were they doing?—Witness: Looking on, like a lot of cowards. Any one of them could have saved the lad had they tried.' At a similar inquest held on the same day, we learn from a witness that 'When he got there there was a mob of people looking on, but "not a solitary soul" tried to save the lad.' On reading such cases, which are no isolated ones, we might be justified in thinking that these people were devils, not men. And yet the fault is more from lack of ability to take the initiative and from want of training, than from badness of heart; for such dastards of circumstances are recruited from the same class that gave us the heroes of Balaclava, of the *Birkenhead*, and of the *Victoria*. However much we may talk of free will, we cannot get over the fact that men are gregarious animals, and that the proportion, among them, of bell-wethers is extremely small. Bravery *en masse* comes almost as easy to us as wholesale cowardice. Some men of the masterful kind are not gregarious and take their own 'line' without effort. Others, by dint of strenuous effort, succeed in freeing themselves from the trammels imposed upon them by the nature of their being. I once knew a ship's captain who, on the occasion of the vessel of which he was in command being wrecked, behaved with conspicuous and brutal cowardice. By an extraordinary piece of luck he got another ship, which also was wrecked; but instead of repeating his former conduct, in this instance, he was the means, by his self-sacrificing heroism, of saving many lives. The owners of the lost craft, to mark their gratitude, put him in command of a third ship, which, in course of time, followed the fate of its predecessors. Again the captain courted death in heroic efforts to save others, and acted so nobly and unselfishly that the entire English press rang with the praises of his bravery.

To get a proper estimate of people, we ought, I think, to

Conscience. 39

judge them by their standards and not by our own. Take for instance the wild tribes on the northern frontier of India, who believe in the principle of a tribal vendetta, and who think that they are not alone justified, but are fulfilling a sacred duty, in slaying an absolutely innocent man who has never done them the slightest harm, on the sole plea that he happens to belong to a tribe of which some other member had killed one of their clan. We, from our standpoint, sententiously assert that conscience is an infallible guide; but here we have thousands of men who are ready at any moment to *conscientiously* commit murder. The conscience of the Hindus is quite as susceptible to the influence of training as is that of the Kybarees. They are governed to a great extent by the principle of *swadharm*, which signifies in Sanskrit that each one has his own particular work to do, the performance of which is a virtue in him, although it might be a vice in others. Thus the man who replied, 'I am a thief,' to the rajah who, in one of the stories of the *Baital Pucheesee*, asked him who he was, simply stated, without either shame or bravado, the nature of his vocation. The women of certain tribes regard the exercise of professional 'gaiety,' as the work for which Providence brought them into being; in the same manner as their brothers look upon themselves, with a clear conscience, as robbers and poisoners. This belief in *swadharm* saves Hindus, and all who acknowledge Hindu authority, from the snobbishness of wishing to pose as belonging to a caste superior to their own. The Dom, Dhobi, or Mehter, the mere touch of whom would be pollution to a Brahmin, is as contented in his sphere of life as a 'twice born.' Hence, among Hindus we find castes, to the men of whom death has no terror; and others, like the Bengalees, who are not ashamed to admit that they belong to a nation of cowards. It is unfortunate that the chief leaders of native thought in India, should be recruited from this pusillanimous race. The Parsees, also, know all about trade; but nothing about fighting. Our system of selection, by competitive examination, for official posts, is not well suited to India.

At Kamptee, which was my first station in India, I was well 'entered' to Eastern sport; as there was capital pig-sticking and shooting within easy reach, with occasional racing. After two years of the Madras side, I got transferred to the livelier one of Bengal, and gradually took up the training of race-horses and chasers, for which, my previous intimate acquaintance with the training of men, was an admirable introduction. With experience to test and modify my theories, I acquired in time a good deal of skill in the art of bringing a horse fit to the post, and introduced many improvements and innovations which have since been accepted by Indian racing men. My first contributions to the local press in about the year 1869, were reports of race meetings which I attended. This practice with the pen appears to have given me confidence; for five years afterwards I brought out a book on *Training and Horse Management in India*, which has run into five large editions, and which is accepted as the standard authority on the subject. Although I was well educated, according to the usual acceptation of the term, and had 'passed' creditably in French, German, Latin, Greek, Hindi and Urdu, I found extreme difficulty in expressing my ideas in fairly presentable English. Even after twenty years' work, I am well aware that I have attained comparatively little skill in this literary art, to which I have found no royal road. The branch of literature to which I have chiefly devoted myself is that of teaching, in which I candidly think that my success has been owing more to my method of explanation than to my knowledge of the respective subjects. It would be mere affectation in me to deny that I have a fair measure of the gift of explaining to others things which I know. On the other hand, I can frankly disclaim the possession of vast stores of knowledge which I have been unable to transfer to paper. In my 'line,' namely, that of teaching, the great essential to success is, I think, the ability to keep the reader's attention fixed as much as possible on the subject matter, without allowing it to wander to the consideration of the words used. Hence, I try, as far as I am able, to write plain and correct English; and to avoid any words, phrases, ambiguities or tricks of style which might arrest the attention of the reader, whose train of thought might thus be broken by my meddlesome interference. Writers of 'pure literature' are, of course, free to pay more attention to words than to facts or ideas. In many Persian and Urdu books (take the *Fasan-i-Ajaib* for instance) the authors display their literary skill solely by the manner in which they manipulate the actual words.

I liked the life in India and the facilities for sport to be found there, so much, that I got transferred, after passing the requisite language examination, from the Royal Artillery into the Bengal Staff Corps, in which I had more pay and far less work to do. During the nine years I remained in the Staff Corps and the one in 'The Buffs,' I devoted myself almost entirely to the training of horses for racing and chasing, and had a remarkably 'good time,' which was but little broken in upon by military duty; for my different commanding officers liked my sporting ways, and gave me as much leave to go racing as they possibly could. I must not inflict an account of these ten years on my readers; for its interest would principally be local. Besides, I have already committed it to paper in *Indian Racing Reminiscences*.

With usually ten or twelve horses in my stable, I had always something to ride, and I profited greatly by the able teaching of poor Jack Irving, the jockey, who often came and stayed with me. Jack, who was the finest jockey we have ever had in India, had graduated in John Scott's stable, and was a thorough workman. I won some steeplechases, and a few welter flat races; but had, later on, to give up the game I dearly loved, as my health would not stand the strain of wasting. I had, however, quite enough to do, training, schooling and teaching my stable boys to ride.

I have been lucky in escaping from accidents with horses. Of course I have often got hurt when there has been a good deal of 'bone' in the ground, as there usually is in India; but I have never been more seriously injured than getting my elbow dislocated from a fall off a buckjumping Australian. The theory that a good horseman should never get a fall except *with* a horse, does not stand the test of practice. There are many different kinds of fine horsemanship. In racing, chasing and hunting, the capable rider adopts the seat which, while having a sufficiency of adhesiveness for the object in view, is the best possible one for enabling the horse to exert his powers to the greatest advantage. In rough-riding, on the contrary, the main consideration is ability to stick on. I have seen some of the finest riders in England shot off a horse's back from the slight provocation of a mere 'pig's jump,' which is a mishap that should cause no adverse reflection to be cast on the deposed one's capacity to ride brilliantly on the flat or over a country. As Colonial horses for ordinary riding work are, as a rule, allowed to run wild until they are about four years old, they are at first very difficult to ride, and often retain during the remainder of their lives, a tendency to 'put their backs up' and buck, especially after having had a few days' rest. Although horses in the Antipodes, year by year, receive greater attention and earlier handling; still the proportion of 'difficult' ones remains so large, that young Colonials, almost all of whom ride, diligently cultivate the art of sticking on, and are inclined to ridicule the pretensions to horsemanship of any 'new chum' who may have less 'gum' in the saddle than they. Such a claim to superiority is not altogether valid; for Australian jockeys are quite as indifferent rough-riders as are English ones. In fact, the former would be as little inclined as the latter to, knowingly, get on the back of a buckjumper. I may here explain that although I have never been in Australia, I have met and intimately known for years so many scores of Colonial jockeys, rough-riders and dealers, and have owned, ridden and broken so many hundreds of Australian and New Zealand animals, that I venture to speak of the horses and riders in those countries as if I had lived my life there. I fail to see much merit in the mere sticking on to a buckjumper in the Colonial style; for the success of such a feat depends more on the saddle than on the rider. Although any ordinary lad could learn, in a month, to sit a buckjumper by the aid of a Colonial saddle; there are very few of the best professional buckjumping riders who would even attempt to do so, in an ordinary English hunting saddle. Steve Margarett is the only one I have ever seen able to do this. Although he has spent most of his life in Australia, with frequent visits to India, where I knew him; he was born and bred in Gloucestershire. I may remark that he is as good over a country as on the back of a buckjumper. In Australia he has frequently defeated all comers in buckjumping competitions, in which the aspirants to fame have to ride each other's horses, and consequently bring the worst they can find. In one of these contests, when Steve was mounting a terribly vicious brute, he pulled off the bridle, the throatlash of which he had purposely left unbuckled; so that the animal, while he was on its back, was free to do everything it possibly could to unseat him. As Steve stuck on to the horse, without having any reins to steady himself during the desperate plunges made by his mount, he won the prize amid the frenzied plaudits of the delighted spectators. Steve won the buckjumping prize at a horsebreaking performance I gave in aid of the Jockeys' Benevolent Fund, a few years ago at the Calcutta Grand Stand before the Viceroy, Lord Lansdowne, and an immense audience. The illustration on page 34 is a photograph of an Australian rough-rider in a regular buckjumping saddle, and mounted on a half-broken, underbred Colonial horse. My readers will observe that the 'rolls' on the saddle flaps are made to afford a bearing to the lower part of the thighs, and not to the knees.

I may mention that if the rider of a buckjumper holds on

tightly to the reins, he will, almost to a certainty, become displaced in his seat by being pulled forward, the moment the horse throws his head down. A well-timed buck will then scarcely fail to catapult the rider into space. To ride a buckjumper properly, one ought to try as far as practicable to prevent him getting his head down; but at the same time one ought to be ready to let the reins slip through the fingers, the moment one feels that one cannot resist the downward pull of the animal's head.

I think I may best define buckjumping as one or more consecutive standing leaps by the more or less simultaneous action of both fore and hind legs, executed by the horse in the same direction or to either side, with a minimum amount of forward progression, and with the greatest possible elevation of the hindquarters and depression of the head and neck. The check given to forward movement may be so well marked, that the leap, more or less *sur place*, may be converted into a backward spring. The more forward movement is given to the jumps, the more has the forehand to be raised, and the easier will they be to sit. When the action has a good deal of forward movement in it, it is usually called in the Colonies pigjumping. If the horse, instead of landing on both fore legs at the same time, alights on one and then on the other, as in the ordinary leap, the pigjumping is converted into the more familiar and still less discomposing act of plunging. I may remark that the higher a horse bucks, the less he goes forward; and that the more he twists himself round, the higher he cants up his quarters, the more he depresses his head, and the more uniform is the respective action of the fore and hind legs; the more difficult will he be to sit. It sometimes happens that a horse throws his hindquarters so high and puts his head so low down, that he 'comes right over,' with serious if not fatal effect to his helpless rider. It is much easier to ride a buckjumper in a small enclosed space, than in the open, where he would be able to get up a great deal of forward impetus, which, on being suddenly checked, would materially assist in throwing the rider forward. As it is impossible to practically make a rigid distinction between buckjumping and what I have called pigjumping for want of a more elegant expression; I do not like to speak authoritatively about the occurrence or absence of buckjumping among certain breeds of horses. I have seen many undoubted instances of it among Australians, New Zealanders, South Americans, Cape horses and Basuto ponies; but have never seen any attempt at buckjumping by East Indian horses, Arabs, Barbs or Persians. I cannot recall any case, within my own knowledge, of English or Irish horses bucking; although I do not see any reason against their being possessed of that vice, which is generally confined to animals that are 'taken up' at a comparatively late age. My readers may wish to know my opinion of Buffalo Bill's so-called buckjumpers and of the riding of his cowboys. Although I have frequently witnessed their performances at Earl's Court, I must say that if any of these animals really did buck, which I rather doubt, it was in the feeble manner which might have been expected from 'trick' horses which had to do their 'turn' twice a day for months, if not for years. Besides, buckjumping is a vice which no horse will continually practise, unless he receives the frequent encouragement of throwing his man off. The cowboys seem hard, active, fearless fellows, with whom it would be more pleasant to drink than to fight. No comparison can be drawn between their riding and ours, as the two styles are entirely different. Whether their bronchos buck or only pigjump, the feat of sticking on them is not very difficult when it is allowable to use a saddle of about 50 lbs. in weight and to hold on to it with one or both hands. The size and shape of their saddle are no doubt regulated to attain comfort in their hard work, and not merely to enable them to stick on. Had they practice in our saddles and in our methods, they would no doubt acquit themselves creditably, like the fine fellows they are.

As far as I can remember, I have been only twice nearly being killed by accident. On one occasion, I was carelessly sitting on the bulwarks of a sailing ship in which I was bound for India, one dark night, when the ship gave a sudden lurch and I fell backwards. As I turned over, I caught a projecting piece of wood, and being a good gymnast, I swung myself up and was on board in a second or two. As the ship was running free before a fresh breeze with all sails set, I would not have had a million to one chance of being picked up in the pitch darkness, had I fallen overboard. Another time I got a still worse jar to my feelings when riding in a five-furlong race, a very impetuous horse, who always buckjumped when much excited. A few false starts, as we were all anxious to be off, set him mad. On turning him round to get him to join his horses, he gave three or four desperate plunges, if not actual buckjumps, with such a jerk at the end of each one, that my racing stirrup-irons gave to the pressure, and caught my feet as tightly as if they were in a vice. Luckily the starter's flag fell and the pace was good enough to steady him. Had we been kept longer at the post, I should have had a trial of my ability to ride a buckjumper in a two-pound saddle, with the penalty of a horrible death in the event of my losing.

Although I was in a dreadful fright when I felt my feet caught in the stirrups when on the buckjumper, I believe if I had fallen off and got dragged, my senses, as long as I kept alive, would have been too numbed for me to have felt either pain or fear. I remember once walking unarmed through a part of the great Nirmul jungle in India, when suddenly a tiger sprung up almost at my feet. For probably ten seconds, which seemed as many years, he raced round me while I stood stock still, wondering why I could not put out my hand and catch him by the tail, which was the only thought that occupied my mind during these eventful moments, until with a bound and growl the tiger disappeared into the thick underwood. Sir Lyon Playfair says :—

Fear of Death.

'Having represented a large medical constituency (the University of Edinburgh) for seventeen years as a member of Parliament, I naturally came in contact with the most eminent medical men in England. I have put the question to most of them, " Did you in your extensive practice ever know a patient who was afraid to die?" With two exceptions they answered "No." One of these exceptions was Sir Benjamin Brodie, who said he had seen one case. The other was Sir Robert Christison who had also seen one case—that of a young girl of bad character who had had a sudden accident. I have known three friends who were partially devoured by wild beasts under apparently hopeless circumstances of escape. The first was Livingstone, the great African traveller, who was knocked on his back by a lion, which began to munch his arm. He assured me that he felt no fear or pain, and that his only feeling was one of intense curiosity as to which part of his body the lion would take next. The next was Rustem Pasha, now Turkish Ambassador in London. A bear attacked him and tore off part of his hand and part of his arm and shoulder. He also assured me that he had neither a sense of pain nor fear, but that he felt excessively angry because the bear grunted with so much satisfaction in munching him. The third case is that of Sir Edward Bradford, an Indian officer now occupying a high position in the India Office. He was seized in a solitary place by a tiger which held him firmly behind his shoulders with one paw and then deliberately devoured the whole of his arm, beginning at the end and ending at the shoulder. He was positive that he had no sensation of fear, and thinks that he felt a little pain when the fangs went through his hand, but he is certain that he felt none during the munching of his arm. Christians, however good they may be, seem more afraid of death than Mahamadans, Hindus, and other so-called heathen. Dr Johnson, who had much less reason than most of us to dread a future life, was constantly haunted by such fears; but Vespasian died with a coarse jest on his lips. Even on the scaffold men face death boldly. Nothing astonished Sanson, the hereditary headsman of France, who plied his ghastly trade throughout the Reign of Terror, than the patience with which his thousands of victims met their doom. Madame Dubarry, the pampered mistress of Louis XV., was almost the only exception. She struggled desperately with the executioner and his assistants, and her frantic entreaties for "one little minute more" rang in the ears of the spectators for months. The learned and virtuous De Thou, the innocent victim of the malice of the dying Cardinal Richelieu, insisted on having his eyes bandaged when he mounted the scaffold at Lyons. "Yes, gentlemen," he said, "I own I am a coward. When I think of death I shudder; my hair stands on end! The unhappy man had better reason than he wot of to dread the divorce of soul and body; for he was terribly mangled by the bungling mechanic who had replaced the regular headsman. A violent shock, as well as nervous tension, deadens the sense of pain. When the highwayman Cartouche was brought to the Place de Grève to expiate his countless crimes on the terrible wheel, he greeted the first blow of the executioner's crowbar which smashed his leg, with a howl of anguish. But the second stroke on the other leg was followed by a loud laugh. In reply to the confessor's surprised query, Cartouche said, "I was laughing, my father, at the folly and cruelty of men. They suppose they are giving me prolonged torture; but after the first blow I can feel nothing."'

Motley tells us, in the *Rise of the Dutch Republic*, about the marvellous fortitude with which Balthazar Gérard, who assassinated the Prince of Orange, sustained the most horrible tortures. 'During the intervals of repose from the rack, he conversed with ease and even eloquence. The constancy in suffering so astonished his judges that they believed him supported by witchcraft. . . . It was decreed that the right hand of Gérard should be burned off with a hot iron, that his flesh should be torn from his bones with pincers in six different places, and that he should be quartered and dis-

Fear of Death. 49

embowelled alive, that his heart should be torn from his bosom and flung in his face and that, finally, his head should be taken off. The sentence was literally executed on the 14th July, the criminal supporting its horrors with the same astonishing fortitude. So calm were his nerves, crippled and half roasted as he was ere he mounted the scaffold, that when one of the executioners was slightly injured in the ear by the flying from the handle of the hammer with which he was breaking the fatal pistol in pieces, as the first step in the execution—a circumstance which produced a general laugh in the crowd—a smile was observed upon Balthazar's face in sympathy with the general hilarity.'

A friend of mine who was a police officer in Burma, shortly after the occupation of that country, tells me that he was present at the execution of four dakoits who had been sentenced to be shot. All were tied up ready for their turn. One of the bullets of the volley that was directed on the first man, struck him on the forehead, at the junction of hair and skin, and lifted the top of his head off as clean as one would slice off the top of a turnip with a knife. Seeing this unexpected effect, the remaining three burst into shrieks of laughter; in fact, the occurrence amused the second man so much, that death alone restrained his merriment. His last words were: 'I wonder, will the top of *my* head be blown off?' The same gentleman tells me of another Burman who was on the scaffold waiting to be hanged. He first of all held up his hands and swore an oath a Burman is supposed never to break, that he was innocent. Then he asked to be allowed to make one last request. In reply, he was told that it would be granted, if at all reasonable. 'Then,' said he, 'hang my brother, who is in jail under sentence ; for I would like someone to keep me company when I am dead.' This was promised. 'But,' he continued, with a humorous twinkle in his eye, 'don't hang him immediately after me, if he wants to live a little longer.' And with a smile he passed into eternity.

I am afraid it will be seen from a perusal of the foregoing incidents, that the claim often made on behalf of Christian martyrs for a monopoly of indifference to torture and of fearlessness of death, is not altogether valid.

The fact that a violent, nervous shock deadens the sense of pain seems to hold good with the lower animals as it does with men, if we may judge by the behaviour of big game which die fighting after having received several serious wounds. In such cases, as those of tigers and wild boar, all experienced sportsmen are unanimous in declaring that the first bullet or spear-thrust produces a far greater comparative effect than any of the subsequent ones in stopping the animal. That peerless old-time fighter, Owen Swift, and also Young Reid, have often told me that when fighting according to the rules of the London Prize Ring, it was better, after hitting one's opponent hard, to wait until he had time to feel its effects before repeating the dose, than to expend one's strength in giving him a rapid succession of punches. Their conclusions on this subject were derived from long practical experience.

Photo. by M. H. Hayes.

CHAPTER IV.

Training Horses for Racing—Watering Horses—Stable Management - Wasting—Charlie Bailey—Colonel Locke Elliot—Ben Roberts—East Indian Horses—Australian Horses—Arab Horses—Sheikh Esa bin Curtas—Veterinary Work—How Ideas come to Authors—Professor Williams—Salmon Fishing—Professor Dick—Dr Fleming—Veterinary Surgeons—'The Buffs'—Leaving the Service.

I HAVE had so much to do with training horses that I cannot resist making a few observations about this, my favourite occupation. When training a horse for racing, we want his muscles to become abnormally strong and to acquire the ability of acting quickly. Under healthy conditions, the strength of a muscle varies according to the amount of its blood supply, from which it obtains the elements for its development. The less exercise is taken the slower is the circulation of blood, and the muscles tend, so to speak, to become starved and weak. When the amount of exercise is increased, more blood is brought to the muscles, which consequently become proportionately stronger. As the circulation of the blood through the tissues quickly resumes its normal rate, after exercise has been stopped ; it follows, that for the highest development of muscle, the exercise should be of long duration. The healthy effect of exercise, however, can be obtained only as long as it can be continued without fatigue, which produces an injuriously depressing influence on the nerves. To save the animal from the ill effects of fatigue, and to give him as much beneficial exercise as possible, we should divide the work by frequent intervals of rest. Thus, instead of giving all the work in the morning, we might give, say, a third of it in the afternoon. We should also allow the horse on which our solicitude is bestowed, a roomy loose-box, so that he might move about at will, instead of being cooped up in a narrow stall. Instead of giving him all his work, ' in once,' as betting men say, we might send him three short spins, with half-an-hour's walking exercise between each. As he gets on in his training, he will now and then require a strong gallop approaching in length the distance over which he has to compete. To win races, horses have to be galloped, not cantered only ; for speed in galloping can be cultivated only by practice, just in the same way as speed in boxing—but always with the saving clause of 'no fatigue.' Applying the golden rule of treating a horse as I would wish myself to be treated, I introduced in India many years ago, the practice of giving a horse in training a fairly liberal drink of water, immediately after he had done his work, before sending him back to his stable—and with the happiest results. By my example and writings, I destroyed, in India, the old and cruel myth of a drink of water being dangerous to the health of a heated horse ; supposing, of course, that the water was not too cold. Take, for instance, a man who is exhausted and streaming with perspiration after doing some violent work : What, may I ask, is the first thing that he does? 'Takes a drink, if he can get it,' you naturally reply. 'And after he has had his whisky and soda, glass of beer or shandy-gaff, cup of tea, or glass of water, what does he say?' 'By Jove! that has done me a power of good,' or words to that effect, you answer. Right again, my reader, and so would your horse say, under similar circumstances, were he able to speak. But I fancy I hear you observe that even horses have been known to drop dead from taking a drink when they were hot. Such instances, I admit, have undoubtedly occurred; but only when the imbibed fluid was comparatively cold, in which cases it caused death by nervous shock. The precaution of slightly warming the water, or of giving it only in small and repeated quantities, is not difficult to adopt. In a field artillery battery to which I belonged, it was the custom to water the horses after they were fed. Our farrier-major, luckily, had provided himself with the recipe of Professor Dick's admirable anti-spasmodic drench (an ounce of laudanum, an ounce-and-a-half of turpentine, and a pint of linseed oil), and accordingly made himself locally famous for his ability to cure colic! I need hardly say that the best practice in giving water to horses is to allow them a constant supply in their stalls. If that cannot conveniently be done, they should be watered each time before being fed.

Much of the routine work of training is carried on in such an unavoidably mechanical manner, that trainers are apt to accept facts without analysing the causes of the results. In most cases, whether in England or abroad, race horses in training get their gallops at such a distance from their stables, that they have the opportunity of becoming cooled down, during their walk home, which, if we come to reflect on it, is a potent means of keeping them in health. This fact was often prominently brought to my mind in India during stage journeys, on which the carriages, either light four-wheelers or *tongas* (a kind of curricle) are drawn by ponies. The intelligent native horse-owners, recognising the immense importance of walking a horse which is heated from work, about until he has cooled down, not alone give orders to their servants to this effect, but sometimes purposely have the stables a couple of miles or so distant from the stage halting-places, so as to ensure the observance of this rule. As the scientific discussion of this question is outside the province of this book, I may content myself with saying that all horses, and especially hard-working ones, will last much longer if, instead of being put into their stalls when they return heated from work, they be walked about until their circulation has resumed its normal condition. The observance of this precaution is even more important for the preservation of the soundness of an animal's feet than for shielding him from the evil effects of chill. If we consider for a moment the mechanism of the blood supply to the feet, we shall see how liable the neglect of the simple precaution I am advocating is to be followed by an attack of laminitis, or navicular disease. It would well repay the shareholders of omnibus and tramway companies to insist that this rule should be observed with their animals.

Among other improved methods of stable management which I introduced into India, I taught that horses should be cleaned by being hand-rubbed, whisped and brushed down, and not by washing them, as was formerly the usual practice; and that hay or dried grass should be given at the same time as the corn. Withholding the hay until the animal has eaten his oats, is like making a man who is at dinner, finish his allowance of meat before giving him any bread or vegetebles. The practice now common in England of giving 'chop' with the oats is an excellent one. The bad custom of washing horses in order to clean them is practised in many English livery stables, in which the grooms may be well excused for 'slurring over' their work by the fact that, as a rule, each of them are supposed to 'do' from six to nine horses. Washing the legs is a fruitful cause of cracked heels and serves no useful purpose. During the half hour which is the least por-

Wasting.

tion of time which should be devoted to the cleaning of a horse's head, neck and body, the legs, unless they are very hairy, will have had full time to dry, and the earth and dust which had previously been mud, can be easily brushed off. A pricker and rubber will serve to clean the hoofs.

A short way back I mentioned the subject of wasting, which is a weighty one to many people besides jockeys and G. R.'s. To do it properly a man has to get thin while observing the rules of health. This procedure can be carried out in only one way, and that is to take a maximum amount of exercise and a minimum quantity of ordinary food. I have met crowds of such fat people that they weren't able to see their toes, and yet there was not a single one of them who did not insist that he or she was a remarkably small eater. This is a harmless delusion which has no truth in it. Who, I may well ask, has ever seen an under-fed horse, especially if he be hard-worked, inordinately fat? Although we are not horses, our bodies obey the same laws as theirs. As exercise increases the appetite; the process of healthy wasting demands self-denial, which is the one virtue of all others that the ordinary man or woman finds difficult to practise. It is also unfortunate that the delicacies after which we most longingly crave, are the very ones the consumption of which adds most seriously to our weight. That scrape of butter, that spoonful of apricot jam just to finish up breakfast with, the sugar in our tea or toddy that glass of beer which goes well with the harmless horse-radish, that bit of fat which is necessary to bring out the flavour of the *filet de bœuf*, that *pâté de fois gras* which makes capital sandwiches, that trifle or Queen Mab pudding without which dinner is incomplete, and fifty other things are the very ones which must be eschewed by the person who aspires to be thin. I may point out that a food capable of keeping the body in a state of health must have a certain amount of vegetables or fruit, and starchy elements, such as those contained in bread, potatoes and rice. Although starch is a fat producer, it is not as bad, in this connection, as fat or sugar, and is a necessity to health in our diet. My advice to a person who wants to get down weight and retain health at the same time, would be to give up all fat and sugar, reduce the amount of the daily ration by a half or two-thirds as the case might require, and double, treble or quadruple the amount of the daily exercise. Getting down weight by Banting, Epsom salts or other medicines, Turkish baths, and 'sweating,' ruins the health. I may mention that the famous jockey, John Osborne, continued, till he was well over fifty, to ride about two stone under his ordinary weight and to keep his health, simply by self-denial in the matter of eating and drinking, and hard exercise in the form of daily walks of about twenty-five miles in length. In applying the adjective 'healthy' to a man who has wasted a great deal below his ordinary weight, I do so, comparatively. Although the functions of the body of a man who has 'got off' a lot of weight, may be in the best possible condition for undergoing violent and prolonged exertion, it is far less able to resist an attack of disease, than if it were in its normal state. I had a very sad instance of this in the death of a great friend of mine who, abhorring the idea of getting fat, kept himself light merely by hard exercise and by restricting his food and drink within very moderate limits. Happening to receive a chill during a wet day's shooting, he got congestion of the lungs and died in a few days. The doctors who attended him were convinced that had he had more fat in his system, he would have pulled through all right. Poor Charlie Bailey of the 20th Hussars, who was one of the finest cross-country riders we have ever had in the army, was a victim to wasting. On his return to England, after serving with his regiment several years in India, he got some illness which, under ordinary circumstances would not have been attended with any serious results, and died right off; his system appearing to have no recuperative power left in it.

'Ben' Roberts of the R.H.A. was another good man on

Colonel Ben. Roberts.

a horse who did a deal of wasting, but had the sense to give it up. Colonel Roberts is now Chief Constable of the Metropolitan Police. No better could be got; for he is one of the few men who have been born to command, and yet is possessed of infinite tact and charm of manner. No doubt he learned something about 'putting the comehether' on them while he was stationed with his battery at Ballincollig. I was then a cadet at the R. M. A., and during my holidays over in Cork, I used to hear extraordinary stories of the brilliant style in which the young gunner, Mr Roberts, used to 'pound' out hunting, some of the best men in the county. The last time I met 'Ben' Roberts was a short time ago in Piccadilly. He told me that he could ride over a country as well as ever, but the task of keeping two sons in the army, and the performance of his official duties obliged him to give up the old game. He looked just as hard and fit as the first time I saw him, more than thirty years ago, on board an Irish Channel steamer, when he was bringing over a County Cork mare with which to win the Royal Artillery Gold Cup at Woolwich.

The easiest way to get down weight—without resorting to the continued use of medicine, which cannot help being injurious to the health—is that of abstaining from taking any fluid during meals and for, say, an hour and a-half after meals; no restriction being placed on its consumption before meals, so long as the one and a-half hour's interval after them is observed. This I found very efficacious; but could not continue it, as it brought on rheumatism, on account, I presume, of the food being presented to the organs of digestion in too concentrated a form. A large amount of fluid is certainly required by the systems of most persons, to, so to speak, wash out the tissues and thus to prevent the deposition in them of deleterious products, the presence of which is apt to give rise to rheumatism and other untoward results. Acting on the fact that the weight of the bodily tissues is largely dependent on the amount of water consumed, Colonel Locke Elliott kept down his normal weight of about 10 stone to 8 stone 7 lbs. for several years by limiting the quantity of fluid he drank to one pint, but made no restriction as to its nature. Under this privation, he kept his health, strength, and 'nerve'; but then he is a very exceptionally 'hard man.' Had he done the most of his riding in England, instead of in India, I am confident that the public would consider him, as I do, as good a horseman, whether jockey or gentleman, as ever rode a race.

An untravelled Englishman or Irishman is apt to think that horses are more or less the same all over the world; though of course, in his opinion, nowhere so good as in his native country. Horses, however, are so greatly modified by the effects of climate, that each country, independently of the influence of selection, has its own particular type of animal, just as it has its own particular type of man. We see that European children born and bred in the tropics, acquire the small bones and delicate physique of the natives, in the same manner as the produce of imported stock loses to a great extent the characteristics of its sires and dams, even in the first generation. After three or four generations, almost all trace of the home blood will have disappeared. The type of Indian horse, taking it all round, is that of an under-sized, hardy 'weed,' capable of standing a great deal of hardship, so long as its small amount of strength is not overtaxed. At best it is capable of making an excellent light cavalry trooper up to, say, 13st. 7lb. At that limit of weight, its use, of course, would have to be limited to natives of India. For many years and at an immense expenditure of money, the Indian Government studs fought the climate by the constant importation of English sires, which were chiefly imported by Mr Phillips the once well known London dealer. The costly exotics thus produced, yielded only a small percentage of animals up to remount standard; but no permanent effect was made or could be made, on the native breed of horses, which, however much stimulated for the time being, quickly reverted, on the relaxation of the forcing process, to its original type. The good effects of the English and Arab blood are to be traced only among the native ponies. This policy of trying to establish in India, a breed of horses fit for English cavalry and artillery requirements is still spasmodically carried on, and with the same unsatisfactory results. Contrary to what many would suppose, the Arab cross in India does not, as a rule, confer increased size of bone. The unfortunate Indian taxpayer, who always remains unspoiled by the flattery of being consulted on any such subjects, has borne a great deal of provocation from costly experiments on his horses. The most glaring of these stupid and ignorant failures has been that of importing cart and half-bred blood to give 'bone' to the native breed. The Indian Government, made wiser by the stern logic of facts, now obtains from Australia its remounts for its English troops, and for many of its native cavalry.

At the time when I first went to the East, the Australasian remounts were, for the most part, coarse, fiddle-headed, flat-footed, three-cornered looking brutes, which contrasted unfavourably with the neater, though smaller, Arabs, Persians and country breeds with which the Indian army was formerly horsed. The cause of this lack of symmetry in the Colonials was the too free use of cart blood, which was utilised with the erroneous idea of quickly getting the required bone and substance. The Australian breeders, however, readily recognised the fact that 'quality' meant money, and they soon discovered that their admirable climate and virgin soil, by a marvellous piece of good fortune, would, with careful selection among thoroughbreds, give the necessary strength without their having to resort to the admixture of common strains. Since then they have never 'looked back'; but have gone on, until now they can produce for army and ordinary purposes, horses at a third of the price at which they can be got, equally good, in any other part of the world, with the exception, perhaps, of South America.

Arabs, which at one time were the chief racers, hacks, and

troopers of India, have been gradually more or less displaced by Colonial importations. Up to the height of 13.1 an Arab is not, speaking generally, inferior to any other pony as a galloper. At 14 hands, he is about equal to a 13.3 English pony; but at no height is an Arab as good as a smart English racing pony of 14 hands. I am taking these heights from a racing point of view, at which they would be, respectively, about an inch less than measurements made of unshod horses under ordinary conditions. From this we may see that Arabs have no racing pretensions. With few exceptions, they are poor jumpers and bad trotters. For their height, they are good weight carriers, fine stayers, and easy canterers. They are sound, have strong constitutions, and are capable of standing a great deal of work and privation. They are generally quiet, have wonderfully good 'manners,' and are light hearted plucky animals. They are the perfection of light, irregular cavalry horses. The one useful point in which the Arab excels all others is in the shape of his barrel, the roundness of which, and the length of his back ribs, give him unrivalled breathing power. I love them for their associations. Most of the Arab dealers, like what Sheikh Esa bin Curtas and Abdool Rayman were, and Ali bin Abdoola is, are very fine fellows. Esa always dressed in his national costume, was a rigid Mussulman, and was one of the most dignified, honourable and courteous gentlemen I have ever met. In late years, after he had left Calcutta and had settled in Bombay, I used greatly to enjoy paying him a visit at his stables, and was always received by the old chief with a smile of welcome and a kindly greeting, principally I think because he looked upon me as one of the few links between a happy past and an insignificant present. After cigarettes and coffee had been brought, he would always ask for news about our mutual and dear friends, General and Mrs Monty Turnbull; and then he would talk of Lord Mayo, Lord Ulick Brown, and others of the old Calcutta supporters of racing, whom we both knew. The last time he returned to the scene of his former joys,

Sheikh Esa bin Curtas. 61

which were all connected with horses, was at Christmas 1888, when he won the Calcutta Arab Derby with Fancy; the second being a horse which I had trained. After he returned to Bombay, he wrote me a letter in which he deplored the preference accorded to Australian horses (Walers) over Arabs. 'It is a well-known fact,' he said, 'that the blood of the Arab horse has spread through the world, and has improved the breed of horses from the time of the Prophet Soloman. There are, I hear, some officers who disapprove of Arab horses as chargers and for cavalry, and consequently give preference to Walers. We ought not to forget that it was the Arab horses which were in requisition in former years for the conquest of India and Kabul when Walers were not in existence. It is a thousand pities that Calcutta, being the centre of the sporting community, has neglected to give in the races a portion in the share of justice to the Arabs; but, on the contrary, gives all advantage and benefits to the wild Walers and country breds who have legs like unto the stem of a hookah.' 'The Walers,' he added in delightfully quaint style, 'are too big and wild for the status of men of the present day, and the Lord has not created man to the present time equal for them.' I could not help thinking, as I read my dear old friend's letter, that I would have had a very poor show during my breaking tour through India, if the Lord had made the average man equal unto the untamed Waler.

Although I acquired from practice and from the advice of more experienced men than myself, a good knowledge of training and riding; I felt that I was greatly handicapped by my ignorance of veterinary matters. To somewhat remedy this deficiency I spent a year's furlough at Professor Williams' Veterinary College in Edinburgh. The principal and his professors were kindness itself in answering the constant 'Why?' which was on my lips. Having obtained the solution of a sufficiency large number of questions, I wrote a book which I knew would have been of great use to me twelve months previously, and which I concluded would be helpful to persons who were in search of reasoned-out knowledge on horses. I wrote as a man who had not had time to forget how ignorant he had been. The work was an echo of my few student days, and I accordingly called it *Veterinary Notes for Horse Owners*. The only bit of originality about this first edition was the fact of its having been written by a confessedly ignorant man for others who were more ignorant than himself. We can judge correctly of the requirements of other people, only by our own wants, or by our own lately remembered wants. Had I delayed writing it until now, it would not have proved the success it has been. I have made it, in each succeeding edition, the repository of all the useful veterinary information (as regards horses) which I have acquired from time to time, and am certain that none of my readers consult it with so much benefit as I do myself.

I may here make a brief personal statement with reference to the oft asked question : How do authors write books ? As Balzac happily puts it, ideas spring up in the mind like truffles in the plains of Périgord. They come, but cannot be forced : at least, I find it so. I have only once sat down to write a book, and having finished it, not at all to my satisfaction, I took good care not to accept its paternity as the author. The first hint I receive of having to write a book, is a gradually developed feeling that my mind, unconsciously to myself, has produced a number of mental *fungi* (I do not venture to term them truffles), which retard the growth in me of other forms of brain produce. When this cerebral harvest is complete, I find that the only way to get rid of it, is to collect it together, and cook it into a literary *plat*, called a book, which I give to the public to consume. Or I might liken it to the germination, development, and birth of an *accident d'amour*, the delivery of which relieves me from an intolerable mental load. . And, then, what I am pleased to call my mind, remains fallow, until, perchance, again unconsciously stimulated to production. So you see that I am an absolutely irresponsible agent.

Veterinary Surgeons.

Professor Williams is a man for whom I have a great admiration; for he is original. Had it not been for that love of originality with which I have been troubled during all my life, I would have remained in the army and would have become a colonel or perhaps a major-general. But originality is the antithesis of routine, by the practice of which, our actions become automatic, and we ourselves are converted into machines. Professor Williams is a man of keen observation, independent action, enthusiastic, and has the rare gift of explaining to others what he knows. When he has once said a thing, he sticks to it, which is adorable when it takes the form of saying that one—no matter who—will give either of us a fiver ; but is liable to lead to complications in laying down the law on scientific subjects which have not been thoroughly thrashed out. The founder of the great Scotch school of veterinary surgeons was Professor Dick, who was a man of fine natural parts, and was also 'infallible.' Of his many clever students, Williams was undoubtedly the most original; Fleming, the hardest working; and 'Joe' Anderson, the best judge of a horse. Professor Robertson was thoroughly sound ; but he would write English à la Herbert Spencer, and consequently his *Equine Medicine* is a sealed book to those of us who must read fast, or not at all. Dr Fleming worked his way up with rare pluck, and placed a large amount of valuable French veterinary literature within the reach of a profession among whom there are few linguists. He did yeoman service in getting an Act of Parliament for R.C.V.S. ; and he improved the official status of army veterinary surgeons, so that they are now received at Court. His share of the Jubilee honours was only a C.B. It should at least have been a K.C.B. The clamour for cheap veterinary education has greatly retarded the advancement of the veterinary profession. Fees of £13 a year were thought to be sufficient to pay for the instruction in the art of healing animals ! The old timers, who had been chiefly recruited from the sons of blacksmiths and of small shopkeepers, were wont to exclaim when the inadequacy of such a payment was pointed out to them: 'If the fees are raised, how can the sons of poor men get into the profession?' —as if the profession was to be maintained solely for the benefit of the male offspring of indigent parents! On the contrary, the determination of the fees should solely depend on the amount requisite for obtaining adequate instruction. This view is now in the ascendant, and I may safely say that in the near future, veterinary surgeons will have just reason to consider that they belong to a learned profession.

In veterinary literature, Professor Williams is a worthy successor of Professor Percivall, who, not alone understood his subject from a scientific point of view, but was able to write correct and elegant English. Professor Williams, as a veterinary author, is unrivalled in the description of 'symptoms.' He, like a true artist, puts down only what he sees, and consequently the pages of his books are full of local colour, without a trace of that fatal gift of imagination which has made other horse and cattle pathologists spoil good pens, ink and paper in writing about non-existent diseases. To know him is indeed a liberal veterinary education. Contrary to the dishonest system of running up a bill or of doing 'something' to conceal one's ignorance of the true state of affairs, Professor Williams advised his pupils in all cases of doubt to adopt an expectant policy; to reserve their opinion; to put great trust in nursing; to give 'stimulants' only as long as the beer or whisky improved the patient's appetite: to be chary in administering medicine unless its employment was clearly indicated; and, if doing nothing acted well, to continue the treatment. I need hardly say that these admirable rules are as applicable to human beings as they are to horses. Professor Williams is a cheery companion, full of anecdote, and (as he has always told me) an enthusiastic salmon fisher. My old friend, Colonel 'Joe' Anderson, who sometimes accompanied Professor Williams with a long rod and a pocket-book of flies on his trips to the

'The Buffs.'

Tweed, says that salmon fishing is a delightful sport : beautiful scenery, charming company, delicious bannocks and haggises, and unrivalled whisky. But as the only 'sawmon fesh' Joe ever brought back from these expeditions was a kippered one, which he took home to show his friends that he had really been on the river ; I do not think that he knows very much about the gentle art.

Although my serious outdoor occupation during the cold months in India was racing and chasing. I did a good deal of race reporting for local papers. I also occupied myself with the study of Oriental languages, and was fortunate enough to obtain a Government grant of £300 for having passed the High Proficiency examinations in Hindi and Urdu. I made several shooting excursions into the Himalayas during the hot weather when there was no racing.

During the year which I spent in ' The Buffs,' I was very happy, and I parted with regret, on both sides. from Colonel Morley and his officers. My reason for leaving the service was that after I had exchanged into ' The Buffs ' from the Bengal Staff Corps, I found that I would have to retire on a pension of £200 on reaching the age of forty years, on account of not getting my majority before that time. This rule, I may remark, was introduced by Mr Cardwell to relieve the congestion in the junior ranks due to the abolition of the purchase system. As I had still three years to run, I thought it best to employ them to some good purpose and to take a bonus. than to wait until I got turned out.

Photo. by M. H. Hayes.

CHAPTER V.

A Horse Registry—Captain Lynx—A Book on Riding—Mr Stanley Berkeley—Mr Alfred Watson—The Old Castilian—Mr Joe Radcliffe—Mr Phil. Robinson—Mr Sinnett—Poker—Mr Allen—*The Field*—Mr Comyns Cole—Mr William Martin—Mr Edwin Martin—Dalmeny and Perkun.

HAVING left the Service, I returned in 1880 to London, where I met a strange character in a Captain Lynx, which was not his name, though it is near enough for the purpose. He was an Irishman, and had been in the army. He was mad upon getting up a horse registry, on very similar lines to the one which Lord Marcus Beresford at present manages. Having been talked over by Lynx, I got a major in the Bengal Cavalry to join in, and we three took an office and rooms in St. George's, Knightsbridge. I 'found' the money to start the campaign of saving people the trouble of buying and selling horses: *we* would do all that for them. Lynx was too hard up, and the Major and I knew too little of business to render success possible; but we had a very jolly time of it. Lynx was an amusing fellow. The world had gone dreadfully hard with him, and his name no doubt took some living up to. His heart and soul were in horse dealing; but, alas, without the money. In his direst straits, his only thought was to make a 'bit' by getting a horse for a man. He was a good judge, and knew how to 'show' a horse; but he was too hard up to go 'straight,' and had outlived or out-lasted his friends. The firm ate and drank of the best, amused itself, and kept a ledger and day-book unsoiled by ink. After three or four months' fooling I got sick of the game, and said I'd play no more. I was sorry for Lynx; though he would not or could not work for the firm. He had an inexhaustible fund of yarns, and talk about horses and men he had met, and like a true Irishman, bore his misfortunes with a light heart. He was getting old and losing his nerve; yet his spirit was always buoyed up with day-dreams of a house in the country, and a stable full of hunters. I wondered, while I listened to his hopeful words; for I knew his 'friends' would have nothing to do with him—one's 'friends' are always that way inclined when one's boots imperfectly keep one's feet off the pavement. At the time of our parting, my relations with him were strained; because, the day before, he had appeared in a new suit of clothes, and with the air of having done himself particularly 'well,' and I knew that his statement about a remittance from his 'friends' was figurative. I naturally thought that he had 'done a deal' which had not passed through the firm; yet, I believe, I wronged him. A year passed by and I had almost forgotten all about my whilom partner, when I suddenly met him at Tattersall's looking dreadfully ill in a magnificent fur coat and got up regardless of expense. You could have knocked me down—well, not quite with a feather; but with a small-sized pillow. His day-dreams had at last come true. He had a nice house in the country, and a stable full of horses; but his fortune came too late. He was too sick to ride, and he had sent his well-chosen horses up to Tattersall's to be sold. The explanation, you ask? Well, it was the old story of the unalterable devotion of a woman, whose wealthy father would not hear of their union. She, all through his evil days, had remained his friend; and married him when her father died. By the irony of fate, the cup of happiness was hardly at his parched lips, before death dashed it aside, and poor Lynx's troubled life was ended at last in peace.

I did not much mind the collapse of our horse registry scheme; for about that time I became aware that a book on riding was becoming developed in my mind. I wrote it chiefly from a racing, chasing, and hunting point of view, and called it *Riding on the Flat and Across Country*. I met a young artist who at that time was chiefly engaged in making drawings and designs for 'process' work. Although his talent, of which he has lots, had not been directed to horses, he illustrated my book very creditably, considering that I, who acted as his teacher in this line, knew extremely little about the way in which horses ought to be drawn. I was steeped in empirical traditions of equine conformation. Had I known more, I might have helped him over many difficulties connected with the correct delineation of horses. Although my young friend, who is now the well-known artist, Mr Stanley Berkeley, has made his fame and money in other branches of painting, I trust that he will study *The Points of the Horse*, which I have lately published; for in it he will find the solution of many problems which puzzled us both in the year 1880. The success of *Riding on the Flat and Across Country* came quickly, thanks chiefly to the generous reception it obtained from the London press. I was fortunate to meet the editor of *The Illustrated Sporting and Dramatic News*, Mr Alfred Watson, who did me several good turns in his own columns and also in *The Standard*, of which he was the music critic before he joined Mr Webling. I used to see a good deal of him in those days, and contributed now and

The Old Castilian.

then to his paper. A brighter writer on sporting matters treated with a light touch, and a kinder-hearted man it would be impossible to find. He is a first-rate journalist and a very capable music critic. To his admirable judgment as editor, Mr Webling is indebted for the success of the *I. S. and D. N.* of which he is proprietor. That paper is to be seen everywhere in England and has an enormous foreign circulation. I know this from Thacker & Co., who are the chief suppliers of literature to India; from Cave & Co., to Ceylon; from Kelly & Walsh, to China and Japan; Darter Bros. & Walton, to South Africa; and from other caterers of books and journals to distant lands. The esteem in which it is held is well merited, thanks to Mr Watson, whose crisp 'circular notes' are eagerly looked forward to, week after week, by many a home-sick exile.

Captain Jones, 'The Old Castilian,' also helped to give my book on riding some friendly pushes. He was one of the pleasantest guests at a dinner party, and one of the most brilliant utterers of carefully planned impromptus ever known. Like many other men about town, his mode of life was an enigma. He worked as little as the proverbial lilies of the field, and though not quite as gaily arrayed as they, his attire was immaculate, his cigars of Havanna, and he habitually travelled in cabs. Professionally he was a journalist and would have made his fortune with his pen, if he could have written as well as he spoke. Besides, the manual labour of producing 'copy' carefully and punctually was too irksome a task for his easy-going nature. He was nominally on the staff of *The Pink 'Un*, whose sparkling columns were enlivened by many a droll tale of his doings and sayings, though by little contributed by himself. Poor Jones worked hard, by amusing the members and sampling the drink and suppers, to render the Lotus Club a success. By encouraging the others, he paid his way right royally, even if 'Fatty' Coleman went through the formality of entering the Old Castilian's name on the slate. Though 'paddocked' for life, he dearly loved the 'great game,' which he had once played as an owner. I spent many a pleasant hour with him at Newmarket and elsewhere, talking racing, and observing (not 'watching,' please) the form and shape of horses. He was full of good intentions to write a history of the last twenty-five years of racing, and many a time we discussed its outlines and contents. No one could have written it better than he; but he lacked the necessary determination to sit down and tackle his subject. He had many friends who kept him 'going'; and, though close on sixty, by his wonderful fascination of manner, was as 'dangerous' to pretty women as to a hero-worshipping boy. If he got a 'bit' to go on with, he always respected the debt, and liked to pay it back, though very rarely in coin. Looking through an old book of press notices, I see that I am more in his debt than he in mine. One day I missed him, and the next day I heard he was dead. He was a man of the present, without a future. A man to be loved, even if he could not be respected. A man to be more kindly remembered than regretted.

Another man who was about town in those days, was poor Joe Radcliffe. He was one of those men who should never have gone near a race-course. He started in life as a gentleman, scholar, owner of a large property, and a thorough sportsman; but he was impulsive, incapable of thinking evil of others, extravagant, and easily led. He was generous and kind-hearted to a fault, and would not, by word or deed, have hurt the feelings of his worst enemy, even if he had one. Instead of listening to the counsels of his trainer, before his horse, Salvanos, won the Cesarewitch, he took the advice of the parasites who surrounded him, and had the mortification of failing to back the winner. To atone for this neglect, he made such a desperate plunge, again, contrary to the opinion of his trainer, on Salvanos for the Cambridgeshire, that the defeat of his horse ruined him; for he parted with every penny he had, to settle his debts. He was always cheery, never complained, did not seem to feel his change of circumstances or the coldness of old friends who gradually drew away from him; but the iron no doubt had entered his soul; for he did not live long to point a moral.

I had also a friend in Mr Phil. Robinson, who, as we all know, has made his mark in English *belles lettres*. The father, 'Julian the Apostate,' as he was called—for he was once a clergyman in the Church of England, but gave the office up—was a very able journalist in India, where Phil. served his literary apprenticeship. I used to see a good deal of Phil. Robinson in the early Seventies when he was on the Allahabad *Pioneer* with Mr A. P. Sinnet as editor, and Mr Allen as proprietor. The staff of the *Pioneer*, both regular and outside, has always been strong, even admitting the fact that I used to write for it. The Indian Family Robinson was full of talent. Though strangely volatile, they neither drank nor gambled, but suffered from that restlessness and impatience of control with which the possessors of genius are ofttimes afflicted. Phil. was manifestly too good for provincial journalism; so he gravitated to London, and made his name as a leader writer on the *Daily Telegraph*, a war correspondent of the *Daily News*, and as an author. His brother Kay—a rare good sort—after serving his time on the *Globe*, went out to the *Pioneer*, and is now editor of the Lahore *Civil and Military Gazette*, which is a smart paper. While Phil. was yet 'under the punka,' I used often to go down from Cawnpore, where I am stationed, to play poker with the Allahabad sportsmen, of whom Mr Sinnet (that was before his Blavatsky craze) was a prominent member. He had learned poker in China, when he was editor of the Shanghai organ, the *North China Daily News* (if I remember rightly) in the good old tea-clipper days of Dent and Jardine, and had written a book on the game. I had not much respect for his method; for I thought it was too mechanical. It was, in fact, more adapted for a game of cards, than for one of human character, which poker undoubtedly is. A man who can play poker is bound to succeed in any calling. This reminds me of the Yankee story of a young poker player who asked the father of his sweetheart for permission to marry her. 'Never,' replied the indignant parent, 'shall I consent to allow my daughter to marry a man who plays poker.' 'You might do worse,' pleaded the young man. 'How so?' asked the father. 'You might,' retorted the lover, 'let her marry a man who thinks he can play poker.'

The Allahabad poker players all got 'broke' one hot season, when I was not present, thank goodness! A young gentleman of the Indian Currency Department hoped there was no harm at his looking on at the game of 'draw.' Though he couldn't afford to play it; still it interested him, and he had read all the papers from home, and there was no new literature with which he could kill the time. 'Why, certainly,' was the reply from the old stagers who shrewdly suspected that the youth could not long resist the temptation of joining in. They were right, though he held out longer than they thought he would have done; just long enough to know the exact style of game each of them played; and then after much pressing, he took a hand, and in a short time won all their money, and all the 'scrip' they were good for. He then purchased a comfortable annuity with his gains, and has since that time steadily refused to play anything more exciting than the violin.

Mr Sinnet, as editor of the *Pioneer*, used to draw over £200 a month. Think of that ye Fleet Street scribes! It was, however, not enough to induce him to keep his newly-found theosophy out of the paper; so the proprietor, Mr Allen, got another editor. Mr Allen is a man of great energy, and has the rare gift of organisation. He commenced business as a chemist and druggist in India, at a time when he could get a rupee (worth then 2s. 2d.) for what one could have obtained in London for the odd coppers. And quite right too; for I don't suppose he went to India for amusement or for the good of his health, any more than other people do. He made money fast, and when he found that the trade in pills, powders and lotions was not as good as it had been, he retired and bought the *Pioneer*, which he managed according to big, open-handed ideas. He *soigné*'d the Government and particularly the ladies who pulled all the loose official strings upon which they could put their pretty and unprincipled hands. He gave *le beau monde* at Simla picnics, presents, balls and *fêtes*, and was repaid in the usual way by information which helped to make the *Pioneer* the most valuable newspaper in India. Mr Allen panted for social and political advancement. Although at last he got decorated, it was only with a C.I.E. Indian society, though quite ready to eat his excellent dinners, drink his expensive wines, and accept his costly presents, would not fraternise with anyone who had been in trade. In this respect it is far more 'select' than royalty. I believe that its extraordinary exclusiveness is due to the fact that a considerable proportion of its members are sons of tradesmen or of shopkeepers. The only way a man like Mr Allen could gain the intimacy of Indian society is by keeping a strong racing stable, —*verb. sap.*

Phil. Robinson once gave me a piece of advice which I have found very useful. Speaking about the difficulty I often experienced in judging of the merits of my own literary work, he replied that if my writing, on reading it over, pleased me. the probability would be that it would please the public; but that if I did not feel satisfied with it, the best thing to do would be to tear it up. In other words, that an author should be his own most careful critic. Anyhow, an author cannot, in his heart, feel satisfied, or even pleased with work which he has in any way slurred over. The well-known and particularly wise remark that no one is strong enough to play tricks with one's public, is specially applicable to literature.

The Field has always been a very kind friend to me. Professor Brown, Principal of the Royal Veterinary College (Camden Town), who I believe is its veterinary editor, has frequently said a good word in its columns for my *Veterinary Notes*. Mr Comyns Cole, its chief racing reporter and 'Van Driver' of *Bailey*, has often given me a helping hand. He is a charming writer, accomplished scholar, and polished gentleman of the stately old school. Another able man on the splendid staff of *The Field* is Mr Blew, who is a capable horseman, as well as as a clever journalist.

A journalist for whom I had a sincere friendship, was poor William Martin, the late 'Special Commissioner' of *The Sporting Life*. His father was Mr Martin, the old Newmarket trainer who used to look after the famous Tim Whiffler. His brother, Edwin Martin, won the Cambridgeshire on Bathilde, and now trains for Mr John Corlett and 'Mr Morton,' who owned Dalmeny. Poor Bill Martin was as fine a fellow as ever walked in shoe leather; 'straight,' independent, and bright. He had been brought up among horses and knew their 'points' to perfection. I saw a great deal of him and his worthy brother Edwin, both of whom were kindness itself to us when we lived in Newmarket. In connection with Edwin, who is a careful and able trainer, I may mention the following incident which is illustrative of the way in which trials sometimes go wrong. Having Dalmeny ready for the Goodwood Stewards' Cup of 1885, and wishing to find out if his candidate was in form, he 'put him together' with the Russian-bred horse, Perkun. Between two animals there could hardly have been a greater difference. Dalmeny was a small horse, all wire and whipcord; while the foreigner was of great height and substance. In the trial over a short distance, the big horse so effectively 'smothered' the little one, that Mr Martin naturally advised the owner and Mr Corlett not to back him. 'Mr Morton' is one of those fine, stubborn Englishmen who would sooner lose money than have a horse of his run unbacked for a big race. He was rewarded for his pluck; for his 'got on' his £300 (I believe that was the amount he wagered) at a good price, and Dalmeny won cleverly. The explanation of the misleading trial

Perkun. 75

was that Mr Morton's horse was one of the game sort which require the stimulus of an actual race to make them put forth their full powers; while Perkun was a soft-hearted customer who ran much better in private, than he would do in public.

Photo. by M. H. Hayes.

CHAPTER VI.

Cramming Militia Subalterns—A Book on Tactics—Mr John Hubert Moore—Horse Breaking—Writing New Editions—Mr John Sturgess—A Book on the Shape and Make of Horses—Newmarket—Mr John Hammond—St Gatien—Mr John Corlett—*The Sporting Times*—'Gubbins'—'Shifter' The Earnings of Jockeys and Trainers—Irish Horses in England—Touting—Mr Townsend, the Horse Painter—Mr Oswald Brown—Mr Allan Sealy—Mr Sam Waller—Mr Briton Rivière—Mr Haywood Hardy—Mr John Charlton.

AFTER having brought out my book on *Riding*, and looked on at a season's racing in England, I began to feel that I would like a new sensation. Colonel Kinchant, who was an old racing friend and who afterwards commanded the 11th Hussars, on hearing my plaint (for we used to go about a great deal together), suggested that I should try my hand at army cramming! 'You are an old Gunner,' said he; 'and you are smart at mathematics, drawing and all that sort of things,' he was kind enough to add; 'so all you have got

76

Cramming. 77

to do,' he continued, 'is to come with me and I will introduce you to a man who will get you a job!' I expressed my grateful acquiescence and we went to Mr Orellana's agency, which is in Conduit Street. Mr Orellana, a charming man, received us most kindly, and having listened to my 'cherubim' friend's outrageously flattering 'patter' as to my teaching abilities, said that he could put me on to a good appointment right off. He was a man of his word, and in a few days after that I was installed as a teacher of fortification and military topography at the Rev. Mr Pritchard's army cramming (I really forget the exact title the worthy 'rector' applied to his place) establishment, on a comfortable salary. My dear reader, please do not indignantly exclaim : 'The fellow ought to have been had up for obtaining money under false pretences ; for how the mischief could he have managed to have kept himself *au courant* with the enormous advances made in those branches of military science, since he had left "The Shop"?' Very easily, I may reply ; for my pupils were young militia officers going up for 'The Army Competitive' examinations, by which they hoped to obtain commissions. Though the numbers entered for each event were enormous, the 'form' to contend against was moderate in the extreme. The dear boys in physique, manners, and sporting instincts, were the *beaux idéals* of what British subalterns should be. They knew how to fight, ride, row, play cricket, make love, and take their own part in anything that did not require the exercise of brains. They had usually commenced their 'cram' career by a resolution to enter the Indian Civil Service. Being unable to master the difficulties of dictation, they thought they would have a better chance of Woolwich, but found the gates of the Royal Military Academy closed against them, on account of their inability to understand the meaning of what a square root was. Their third hope was Sandhurst ; but here again want of ordinary education was a bar to their ambition. Happily for them, Government opens a little back door for militia subalterns who can learn up an extremely small amount of fortification, military topography, military law and tactics, none of which, as far as militia subalterns are concerned, requires any knowledge of literature, art or science. It is needless to say that neither the militia nor the country obtains any good by these army candidates being obliged to obtain commissions in the militia before they are eligible to compete for commissions in the army. It, however, limits that form of army competition to the sons of comparatively rich men, who can afford to pay for uniform, and for the expenses of the necessary number of 'trainings.'

Mr Pritchard, I must add, made his young men comfortable, and did his best to induce them to 'pass.' I remained with him some months, and then went to resume my veterinary studies at Edinburgh. In order to pay my way, I continued to 'coach' militia subalterns, and was very successful in getting them to pass. They liked me and I was fond of them. I tried to manœuvre them in the same way that Tom Cannon would handle a wayward two-year which had been spoiled in its breaking in; for they were almost all rank jibbers at book work. I kept on cramming for about three years, during which time I took out my veterinary diploma. At last that unfortunate propensity of writing books again seized hold of me, and I produced *The Student's Manual of Tactics*. It happened in this wise. Militia subalterns had got into such a habit of learning the official manual of tactics by heart, and then answering the questions they were set, by *verbatim* extracts from it, that although the examiners had to confine the contents of their papers to the subjects treated on in the official books, they would give but little credit for this mechanical method of answering. It being hopeless to expect that the dear boys would read up the literature of the subject; I did that for them, and compiled a work from which they could obtain all the information they required. I may mention that *The Times* and other papers said a lot of nice things about my new literary departure. Before I published this book, I delighted in the teaching of tactics ; for it required a certain amount of research and originality to collect the required facts and to combine them with the requisite amount of skill. When the book was printed, I realised for the first time that I had henceforth to employ a labour-saving machine, instead of working with my brains. Military law consisted of learning up 500 or 600 possible questions ; fortification was as bad ; military topography not much better ; and here was tactics, the one redeeming subject of the four, placed on a purely mechanical basis. This, as poor Artemus Ward used to say, was a darned sight too much, especially as a yearning to get back again among horses was growing on me more and more. The chance at last arrived. I threw away my military books, and I departed on my travels. In clearing off the account of my cramming experiences, I find I have run off the line, so shall now hark back to pick it up again.

During the winter months of 1876-77, which I spent in Edinburgh at Professor Williams' Veterinary College, I had made the acquaintance of Mr W. H. Moore, who was also studying at the same place, and who has since developed into a famous G.R., even as his brother Garratt did. Before we went to Edinburgh in 1881, we received an invitation from Willie Moore to come and stay with his father, who had a training stable at Jevington, near Eastbourne, and who had in his string, among others, Liberator, Theodora and Pompeia. The old man, John Hubert, was known all over Ireland, and through a good part of England, as an extraordinary 'character.' He might justly be called the Father of Irish Steeplechasing, and has had, probably, more to do with the cross-country game than any man alive. At that time he was a tall, gaunt, powerful-looking man of about seventy, and a terrible ' tyrant,' as they say in Ireland. When roused to anger (and faith it didn't take much to set him on), he had an effective way of clearing a room—generally after dinner in an hotel, during a race meeting or horse fair—by seizing a table, sideboard, or even a heavy chair, dashing it on the ground, and belabouring his opponents with its larger fragments. He taught his sons and stable lads to ride over the biggest country, by, as he used to boast, making them more afraid of him than of falling off. His favourite commentary on broken limbs and dislocated necks was :— 'They that take by the sword, shall perish with the sword.' He was the teacher of many great horsemen. Barring being a bit short in the temper, he was a fine trainer, and the best breaker in Ireland, which was a fact that I had treasured up in my mind ; for breaking was the subject connected with horses about which I was most ignorant, and on which I longed most for information. I, therefore, went to Jevington, determined to leave it wiser than I came. Mr Moore, like many other enthusiasts, invested his methods with a good deal of mystery, which had become more habitual to him than intentional. His system chiefly consisted of the use, on foot, of the long reins (see *Illustrated Horse-Breaking*), which he had been taught to handle, when a boy, by an old Irish breaker called Fallon. He liked, when breaking, to fix the position of a horse's head by means of a bearing-rein and standing martingale buckled on to the rings of the snaffle. He maintained, and very justly, that the great point in making a 'reluctant' horse jump, was to bring him up to the spot from which he ought to take off ; that the next thing was to make him more anxious to get to the other side than to remain where he was ; and that both these operations could be best done by the use of the long reins. Mr John Hubert Moore is a man impossible to 'pump,' and was far from communicative on the subject about which I was most interested. Up to that time, I knew no other way of breaking in horses than by riding them with patience and good hands. These excellent agents always took, in my case, a comparatively long time to effect their purpose, and often failed—for instance, with hard pullers and old refusers. Of course I knew Rarey's system; but acquaintance with it gave me no hint to cure any vice, except that of kicking, biting, or other outrageous conduct. The gospel of the long reins and standing martingale (I rejected that of the bearing-rein) was a revelation to me, in that it gave me some exact ideas on the proper way to give a horse a good mouth, and to make him jump. Though a 'tyrant' when thwarted, Mr Moore is a grand specimen of that almost extinct class, an Irish gentleman of the old school: hospitable, kind-hearted, generous, and fearless; but if you have the good fortune to meet him, take my advice, don't argue with him, and don't, in his hearing, air your sympathy with the Home Rulers, or there will be 'ructions' in which I would be very sorry to join. Mr Moore, I am glad to hear from his son Willie, still retains much of his old fire. Two years ago he claimed Viscount out of a selling steeplechase, which thoroughly legitimate proceeding so incensed the owner, who was accustomed to the usual family party arrangement, that he refused to lend Mr Moore a bridle or halter with which to take the horse to his stable. Ever ready for an emergency, Mr Moore put his brawny right arm round the animal's neck and thus led him away without anything on his head, amid the cheers of the bystanders. Garratt happened to tell this story to an English friend, who, not knowing the strength of the old man, protested that it would be impossible to thus master an impetuous thoroughbred. 'You'd think differently,' replied the famous horseman, who had not forgotten the discipline through which he had gone at the hands of his father in his young days, 'if he had his arm round *your* neck.'

As the first edition of *Riding on the Flat and Across Country* went off quickly, I carefully revised it and got Mr John Sturgess to illustrate it. I may explain that if I happen to read a book which I have had published for a few months, and have thus banished it from my mind for the time being; I find that I have left out much which I ought to have said, and said much which I ought to have expressed differently, if not actually omitted. Hence, when I have the fortunate opportunity of bringing out a new edition, I always feel compelled to re-write the entire work; for I never can satisfy myself by mere marginal corrections. I think it was Benjamin Franklin who said that the setting up of type was the most valuable instruction in English composition he had ever received; for during this tedious process he had full opportunities of analysing the 'copy,' and specially of noting faults of redundancy and ambiguity. As 'composing' was to Franklin, so re-writing has been to me the most efficient means of improvement in style, for which, I freely confess, there still remains ample room. Anyway, there is no such thing as finality in art. Pains at literary work are well spent; for, as it has been truly remarked, hard writing makes easy reading, and *vice versâ*. Another advantage, which an author has, of re-writing and re-illustrating a book for a new edition, is that the fact of its having been given a different garb, will induce many persons who already possess a copy of the old edition, to invest in one of the new issue. I have mentioned that Mr Sturgess illustrated the second edition of my book on riding. He did the work admirably, and carried out my ideas, which, by the light of more extended experience, now appear to me crude in many instances; but that, of course, was not his fault. His horses, or perhaps I might more correctly say, his horse, was so well known to the public by means of the *Illustrated Sporting and Dramatic News*, that, after the second edition had appeared, almost everyone who spoke about it to me, declared that they had previously seen the same illustrations in Mr Webling's paper. This, really, was not the case; for Mr Sturgess, in the most painstaking way, had made separate studies for each of the drawings he did for me. I fully grant that his horses in Mr Watson's paper have an extraordinary family likeness to each other: a fact which cannot be wondered at. A man who has to draw, week after week, for, say, twenty years, horses to illustrate constantly recurring subjects at so much a page, can scarcely escape becoming 'mannered' in his mode of pictorial expression. It is futile under the ordinary conditions of such commercial contracts to expect that he should or could make separate studies of the particular animals, which alone could enable him to give individuality to each of them. Hence, with the best intentions in the world, he gradually adopts the suicidal method of tracing his horses according to his mental stencil plate, instead of drawing their actual portraits. Then, again, what tricks that mischievous imp, imagination, plays with many artists who illustrate periodical literature. While leading the draughtsman down the smooth slopes of its own domain, it deprives him little by little of the ability of seeing things as they are, until at last his drawings are all on one plane, without any 'guts,' as picture-dealer term the rendering of the different 'values.'

After leaving Edinburgh, I stayed a short time in Cambridge, 'cramming' militia subalterns for the army, and then went on to Newmarket. I may explain that my reasons for going in regularly to become a member of the R.C.V.S., was to improve my knowledge and to strengthen, in the eyes of the public, my writings on horse subjects, and especially on veterinary matters. I arrived in Newmarket, full of a book I had in my head about equine conformation, or, to use a popular expression, the make and shape of horses, which had always been a subject of deep interest to me. I had, however, made no progress in it; for I could find no teacher, either oral or printed, from whom I could obtain satisfying instruction. Although I had a fair share of practical experience, I was utterly ignorant of the true principles of the science, and consequently did not attach any importance to them. I had waded through the literature of the subject without much benefit. The English books, such as those of Percival, Carson, Stonehenge and Fitzwygram, had no 'why?' in them at all. Bourgelat, Merche and Lecoq were better in this respect; but their view was directed to an animal on the dissecting table and not in action. I had yarned about the conformation of horses with my racing, hunting and veterinary friends for so many years, and had tried so hard to draw practical deductions about it, that, in my self-conceit, I considered I was capable of posing as an instructor, and accordingly wrote a book. It of course contained all the old silly platitudes about the desirability of a horse being 'long and low,' 'good to follow,' etc. Following the footsteps of my predecessors, I tried to gauge the merits of all horses, by comparing them with an ideal steed of my own conception. I wrote this book, added some illustrations, made all arrangements for its publication, gave the MS. to a friend to take to the printer, and, as I have explained in the preface of a recent work, never saw it again; for my friend luckily forgot it in a hansom, and cabby appears to have wisely considered that it was not worth the trouble of taking to the Scotland Yard lost property office, which I haunted for weeks in a state of desperation. I became soon consoled for my loss; for every day's experience gained at Newmarket, forced on me the conviction that the empirical conclusions which I had desired to commit to print, were crude and faulty in the extreme. About the same time I got an opportunity of reading Professor Marey's *Machine Animale*, and Dr Pettigrew's small work on the same subject. Light had at last come! I at once rejected all the rule-of-thumb fables; and set myself to seriously study the horse as a living locomotive, and to investigate the differences in construction demanded by the requirements, respectively, of speed and strength. To test my conclusions, I invested in a six-foot tape measure, which I placed in my pocket, ready to run the rule over any animal whose points I wished, and was permitted, to examine carefully. This rigid method soon convinced me that the more a horse approached the heavy cart type, the longer and lower did he become, and *vice versa*. I need not allude to this subject further; as it is fully discussed in *The*

Photo. by Dickinson & Foster, 114 New Bond Street, W.

MR JOHN CORLETT.

Newmarket.

Points of the Horse, which I was unable to complete, hard though I worked at it, until last year (1893).

The Newmarket society, which I principally frequented, was generally to be found in the evening at Mr Chenell's White Hart Hotel. The chief *habitués* were Mr Jack Hammond, Tom Brown, Bill Jarvis, 'Old Tom,' 'Young Tom,' Hunt, Alf. Sadler, Jim Goater, Mr Sabin, Harry Day, and a few casuals. They were a very pleasant lot of fellows, barring 'Old Waterworks.' Mr Hammond is a credit to Newmarket. Different from many who rise from the ranks, he never forgot old friends, of whom he had many, and he was continually doing kind and thoughtful actions in helping the poor and unfortunate. He, like Jarvis, has very charming manners and a smile that does one good to see. Every one who knew him was delighted with his luck in 1884, when, with the aid of that wonderful pair, St Gatien and Florence, he won the Manchester Cup, divided the Derby, won the Gold Cup at Ascot, the Cesarewitch and Cambridgeshire, and wound up by being presented to the Prince of Wales, who warmly shook him by the hand, and congratulated him on his good fortune. Regarding Mr Hammond merely as a professional racing man, one might have thought that his methods would have been tortuous and his actions veiled in mystery. Nothing of the kind. When he fancied one of his horses for a race, he made no secret of his hopes, and gave the tip straight enough with scarlet and white his colours) flowers in his button-hole. I remember making a remark to him on the day St Gatien won the Cesarewitch, about the greatness of the task his magnificent three-year old had with 8 st. 10 lbs. to carry, and his reply: 'The others have a bigger task to beat him.' On that day and over that distance, I think the son of Rotherhill or The Rover was the best horse I have ever seen. Of course you will think I 'went Nap.' No, I did not. Instead of putting on a 'monkey,' which I could easily have done 'on the nod,' I invested the only two sovereigns I had at the time in my pocket, and won £16. You see it is no use imparting a 'good thing' to a man who hasn't the pluck to bet more than he can pay.

Our chief amusement at the White Hart was pool; and it was a 'warm' one. Cards were limited to long whist. Tom Jennings generally managed to secure Jim Goater as his partner. He then had three to two the best of his adversaries—which was moderate for him. Young Tom is a well-educated, gentlemanly fellow.

During the race weeks, I used to see Mr John Corlett, and had often a talk with him about horses. As he was one of the family, having married a Miss Stebbings, he of course puts up at the Rutland Arms, which is the aristocratic hotel in Newmarket. The trainers divide their patronage between it and the White Hart, which is the chief place of call for the jockeys. The other sportsmen are principally to be found at the Greyhound, which is kept by Mr Riley of coursing celebrity. Many persons who are unacquainted with racing are wont to imagine that Mr Corlett's paper *The Sporting Times*, alias *The Pink 'Un*, is wholly given up to remarkably clever though slightly risky jokes and funny stories. It contains, on the contrary, an amount of turf erudition in its leading article —written by Mr Corlett—that is worth ten times the price asked for the entire paper. Although the pleasantry which sparkles through its columns is no doubt heightened by an acquaintance with the genial staff, and is veiled to a certain extent by an affected absence of polish, it is, frequently, of marvellously high merit from a literary point of view, and is always acceptable to men of the world as a producer of a hearty laugh.. The editor is wont to playfully assume that owing to the 'festive' tendencies of the staff, the *Pink 'Un* is in a chronic difficulty of being in time for publishing day. Although the office in 52 Fleet Street is not run on absolutely teetotal principles, the working and responsible editor performs his part in a business-like manner which leaves nothing to be desired My friend 'Gubbins' is a thorough worker, and puts in a lot of good 'copy' unfathered by his

Photo. by J. Robinson & Sons, 172 Regent Street, W.

'NATHANIEL GUBBINS.'

name. The first time I saw him was in the late Sixties at Umballa, when he was a handsome young officer in the army. He kept racehorses, was a first-rate gentleman rider and amateur trainer, and could hold his own with Sir Seymour Blaine, who was called on account of his good looks 'The Destroying Angel,' poor George Joy, Walter Harbord, 'Bobby' Soames, 'Ben' Roberts, and others who used to play 'the great game' in India long ago. He is a capital actor, and it is 'kind' for him, as we say in Ireland; for he is a descendant of Garrick; the last, I believe. He is a fine fellow in every way, and the best of good company. I also frequently saw 'The Shifter,' who is clever, intensely amusing, kind-hearted to a fault, and hasn't an enemy bar himself. A funny thing about Mr Corlett is that not content with the immense success which the *Sporting Times* has obtained, he loves to 'run' a second weekly paper which changes its name as well as its colour from time to time. The last alteration was that of *The Bird of Freedom* to *The Man of the World*.

While staying at Newmarket, one cannot help being struck by the immense amount of money earned by some of the trainers and jockeys. At first glance, the author, artist, or man of abstract science might be tempted to disclaim against the partiality of Dame Fortune, who rains gold on comparatively uneducated men, but leaves him parched and thirsty, with often not enough for a 'drink.' In this plaint there is no more justice than in one against the giving of a few large prizes in a lottery, in which there was an enormous number of low-priced tickets taken. Although men are not born equal; they are certainly born with equal rights, which they may or may not get. The few jockeys and trainers who can drink champagne, dress their wives in fashionable clothes and pay their way, form an extremely small percentage of men who have spent their lives, which was all they had to give, in the vain endeavour to obtain a sufficiency of bread, cheese, New Zealand mutton, 'four ale,' shag tobacco, five shillings a week for rent, and the price of a few second-hand 'duds' now and then. The envious one probably thinks himself superior to the man of horses on the score of education, as if that of books were the only kind. I, as one who has had experience of both, can say that there is more improving knowledge to be acquired from practical experience with men and horses than from books, the mere study of which affords but poor mental training. It has been well said that no man is wiser for his book knowledge. Besides, money is the concomitant of business, not of pleasure. Had my object in life been the making of money, I would, instead of devoting my time to horses and the writing of books about them, have taken up some lucrative trade, such as that of a butcher or draper. A wise man into whose soul the iron had entered, has said that literature is a good stick but a poor crutch. Philistines will inveigh against the wickedness of 'the boys' who will do anything but work. They'll hang about public houses in wintry weather till they get drenched to the skin; they'll tramp on foot scores of miles to attend a race meeting; they'll sleep on door steps; they'll bear the pangs of hunger and thirst, until they cut their throats or drown themselves; but they won't work. I have a very kind spot in my heart for men of this disposition; for I am 'given' that way myself. I love to 'mess' away my time with horses, photography, patents about saddles, mineralogy, books, or any of my other 'fads'; but having had in my old age to forsake all *mes folles amours*, I am just at present in the pursuit of some steady commercial undertaking which would bring in more money than amusement.

Newmarket is exceptionally well endowed in the matter of training grounds, both on the Bury side and the race side, as the two divisions of the Heath made by the Station Road and Exning Road are called. When the turf begins to get hard, the Limekilns, which are specially favoured by nature and which are on the Bury side, are utilised for work. The grass grown in the neighbourhood is admirably suited for horses, as we might judge from an inspection of the local butchers' shops, in which we shall find that the mutton is far better than the beef, which fact shows that the grass is of the fine quality relished by sheep and horses, and not of the coarse, rank kind with which cattle like to fill their enormous paunches. I may mention that when Irish racehorses are brought over to England to be trained, they generally show that the change has been of benefit to them from a galloping point of view: an improvement which I am inclined to put down to the superiority of English over Irish hay as a food for horses. The emerald hue of the grass in Ireland indicates that it is apt to be too rank for training requirements.

The disease of touting is endemic in Newmarket. From Rodney who had built himself an observatory from which he used to search out the country from the Limekilns to the July Course with a telescope that was able to bring Jupiter's satellites to within a mile of the Heath, to the child in arms, all who are not owners, trainers, jockeys, officials, or 'mugs' like myself, send or want to send 'winners' to clients. My washerwoman was a tout, who 'gave herself away' to me by handing me one day her circular of terms by mistake for the washing bill. In this circular, she posed as the father of one of the leading jockeys! The desire which possesses the British public of gaining information about the merits of race horses, so that they may back winners, is to me, the height of folly. What great advantage can it be to us to know that a certain horse is 'meant,' or that his owner fancies him; when the intentions and hopes of, say, a dozen owners in the same event have not been disclosed to us. Even if we did know them, how could we tell which to 'follow'? You may reply that if it is good enough for Mr Abledealer to back his animal, it is good enough for you or me to do so. Quite right, supposing Mr A. had truthfully unburdened his mind to us or to our tout, and also supposing that we could get a correct 'price.' Book-makers, like other folk, must live; to say nothing about the wearing of diamonds and the drinking of champagne. Their finger is on the pulse of the market, so they can tell from whence comes the money, and if they find that a genuine commission has issued from a dangerous quarter, they will lower the odds below their proper value. It is no good for me to know that in a field of twenty, a certain horse has a three to one chance, when the fielders will lay only three to two about him. No maxim is truer than that betting on other people's horses is a fool's game.

With the fear of being touted ever on them, the Newmarket trainers are, and quite rightly, shy of strangers; but placed at rest on that point, they are, like most lovers of horses, hospitable, kind-hearted, and sporting. While we lived a little off the station end of High Street, we saw a great deal of Mr Townsend, the horse painter. I believe he was the only man in the whole place who cared nothing for racing and, if possible, still less for betting. A pretty bit of colour on field or foliage, or a graceful attitude assumed by a colt or filly, would have been prized by him more than the 'straightest tip' which Mat Dawson or poor Fred. Archer could have given him. Nature was the book he loved and studied. He liked above all things to paint mares and foals amid green fields and leafy hedgerows. As regards colour, he was seldom at fault; for he put down on canvas only the tints he saw in front of him. He was not very careful about the actual drawing, as long as the 'feeling' was all right. As regards that, we had many a friendly dispute. Primed with facts proved by my constant companion, the six-foot tape measure, I criticised his faults of proportion with the self-sufficient brutality of a recent convert; while he retorted that I was mechanical in my ideas and had no soul for art. The influence of truth was so strong on him, that the moment he saw there was anything wrong in a painting of his, he took it out and began the work over again. I never knew anyone more devoted to art for its own sake, and consequently, he had not, respecting it, a trace of rivalry with, or jealousy of, his brother 'brushes.' I remember one day, he rushed into our house in a great state of excitement, seized hold of my arm, and said, 'Come along with me quickly; for I want to show you a man who can really paint horses.' I must say that this remark interested me immensely, and I started off in hot haste with him to seek the paragon.

My guide gave me a lead across The Severals into one of Ryan's paddocks in which a quiet, pleasant-looking young artist was painting the portrait of a horse that stood in front of him. At a glance I saw that Townsend was right, and that the stranger *could* paint a horse. Seeing us standing by, the artist ceased his labours for a moment to speak to us. He has singularly charming manners and not a particle of 'side.' His only fault seemed to be distrust in his own manifestly great powers. The sitting or, rather, standing was soon over, Mr Townsend went away to keep an appointment, and the stranger, whose name I learnt was Mr J. H. Oswald Brown, strolled over to the Rutland Arms with me to have a drink, a smoke and a talk. The conversation naturally turned on horses, and as he listened with flattering attention to what I said, I thought him delightful. I saw a great deal of him while I remained in England, and I lectured him incessantly on 'make and shape.' He had a comfortable property, kept his hunters, and was wholly devoted to painting and horses. Having diligently studied in the best schools of France and Holland, he was a thorough master of the technique of his art. He delighted me beyond measure by saying that in me he had at last found someone who could supply him with the special knowledge about horses, in the search of which he had been fruitlessly engaged for a long time. Failing to convince him that the opinion he had formed of me was far too flattering, I exerted every effort in my power to make myself worthy of it. Although I was far from successful in this endeavour, I believe that I was of some small help to him, and I had the extreme good fortune to secure his services for illustrating my books. The success they have obtained was to a great measure due to his admirable drawings. I can never be sufficiently grateful to him for the untiring patience and sympathetic interest with which he worked for me. The purified ghost of the lost book on the make and shape of horses now began to haunt my mind. I made a desperate effort to re-write it on greatly improved lines, and Mr Brown illustrated many of my ideas; but all in vain. I felt that I was lacking in knowledge and experience, and accordingly tore up the manuscript at which I had toiled; hoping that some day the true inspiration would come with more matured knowledge.

Mr Allen Sealy was another capable artist whom I met at Newmarket, when, if I remember rightly, he was taking the portraits of a couple of horses which were in Mr Alf. Sadler's stable. While in London during the early part of 1885, I was asked by Mr Sealy one day to give my opinion on a horse picture of his, which was in the gallery of Mr Mendoza. While there, Mr Sam Waller came in and Mr Sealy introduced me to him. He, I need hardly say, is the famous painter of whose works, like those of ''Twixt Love and Duty,' 'The Day of Reckoning,' and many others, are known and liked by everyone. I, of course, began to talk horse, which proved a very attractive subject to Mr Waller, whose paintings almost always contain one or more of these animals. As we were about to say 'goodbye' and part, he asked me why I did not teach artists the principles of equine conformation. I replied that nothing would please me better, if I had the chance. He said that he knew several animal painters who would be glad to join a class, if I would lecture to them; and that he would get up the class, if I liked. I warmly and gratefully thanked him for his kindness, and, a few days afterwards, commenced my lectures at his house in Circus Road. I was flattered and delighted to have such pupils as Mr Briton Rivière—who was so pleased with my teaching that he brought his son—Mr Waller, Mr John Charlton (of *The Graphic*), Mr Haywood Hardy, Mr Sealy and others, all of whom took

Mr J. H. Oswald Brown. 97

a warm interest in what I told them about the 'shape and make' of horses. In these lectures I was greatly helped by having a few horse photographs. The fact which I now recognised, that the photographs of horses carried far more weight than drawings, however carefully and well they might be done, determined me to utilise, as much as possible, 'the black art' for the portraits of all the representative animals I required in my proposed book. I may mention that when the book at last appeared, eight years later, it contained 77 photographs and 205 illustrations, chiefly by Mr Brown. Although the London trade were unanimous in declaring that it was the most beautifully illustrated horse book ever brought out, its publication was to me, as sad a happiness as the birth of a posthumous son would be to a widowed mother; for just before it went to press, my friend and fellow-worker, Mr Oswald Brown, died after a short illness.

Mr J. H. Oswald Brown.

Photo. by M. H. Hayes.

CHAPTER VII.

Horsebreaking—'Professor' Sample and his System—Quackery in Horse-taming—'Professor' Galvayne—Sample's Show in London—Originality in Horse Taming—Frank and Joe.

IN 1885, I took a new and unexpected departure in my horse studies. As I have already said, I used to rely, for the breaking-in of horses, solely on the usual English and Irish method of quiet riding and patient handling, until I met Mr Moore, from whom I learned the virtues of the long reins and standing martingale. I knew Rarey's method of horse taming; but did not understand the correct principles of its application. My Newmarket experience did not teach me much; for English trainers trouble themselves little about giving racehorses good mouths and manners. The breaking-in of their yearlings is a very simple matter. Having been more or less handled from the time they were foaled, the efforts of these youngsters to resist control, when they happen to rebel, are feeble, compared, for instance, to the maddening struggles for liberty made by a four or five year old who, for the first time in its life, has felt the restraining hand of man on it. Lunging the animal and tying it up, so as to make it champ the mouthing bit, are all that is generally done before putting up a stable lad, who, as a rule, hangs on to the head of the colt or filly, without attempting in any way to teach it to go in an easy and well-balanced style. Although ignorant of the true principles of breaking, I knew as much as my neighbours, and perhaps felt my deficiencies in this respect more keenly than they did. Lunging in the English way I always abominated; for I knew that by throwing too much weight on the horse's forehand, it was a fruitful cause of injury to back tendons and supensory ligaments, and by making his hind feet move in a larger circle than his fore feet describe, it forces him to go in an awkward manner. I may here remark that if an attempt be made to remedy these defects, as is done in Continental *manèges*, by side reins, the outward one of the two will have to be shortened more than the inward one, and the animal will have his head turned to the right when he is being circled to the left, and *vice versa*. This, I need hardly say, is wrong; for a horse should of course have his head in the direction he is proceeding. Up to this time I knew nothing of the further development—which I have since then worked out by myself—of long rein work in teaching a horse to circle, turn, rein back and passage in a well-balanced manner. Such improvements I acquired only after much practice in the breaking ring and after a careful study of high school riding. As I could get no reasoned-out explanation of the principles involved in tying up a horse with a mouthing bit, for the object of giving him a good mouth, I would not employ it; as I have always been averse from trying experiments in the dark. Thanks to Mr Moore, I had a fair idea of the best way to teach a horse to jump, before putting a rider up. From the foregoing observations, my readers will see that my weak points in breaking, at the time of which I am writing, were ignorance of school work and of reducing unruly horses to obedience. I had seen so many disobedient horses confirmed in their vices by the punitive application of whip and spur, that I had long distrusted the efficacy of such means of coercion; but I knew none better. Being ignorant, I was inclined to accept the principle that if a horse 'played up,' the rider or driver was bound, in justice to himself, to 'take the nonsense out of him'—if he could—by punishment. If the rebel's temper got spoiled during the operation, it was—in my opinion and in that of all my horsey friends—his fault, and not that of his would-be instructor. Everyone who has had experience of racing, can recall to mind numerous instances of jockeys, from the late Fred. Archer downwards, flogging and spurring a horse unmercifully, solely on account of the animal having refused to obey the behests of its rider; the usual consequence being that such punishment will have an injurious effect on the horse's disposition for the remainder of its life. Such conduct on the part of a jockey is wholly inexcusable; for he is supposed to be paid for riding the horse in the best possible manner to win; but not for venting upon it any personal annoyance it may cause him. The tolerance shown to these disgraceful exhibitions of temper on the part of many jockeys, is the best possible proof that our jockeys, trainers and owners, know extremely little about the true principles of horse control.

About this time there came to England a 'Professor' Sample, who advertised himself as 'the great American Horse Tamer,' and who, like Rarey, claimed to possess a system by which he could cure, and teach others to cure, all kinds of equine faults and vices. Here, at last, was a man who I hoped would be able to show me how to 'take the nonsense' out of horses without spoiling their temper, and I accordingly embraced the earliest opportunity of seeing him, which was at Hengler's Circus, Argyle Street, Oxford Street, where he gave his first lecture. He was an American of middle height and of well-nourished appearance. His discourse consisted of a strange medley of childish remarks about the physiology of the horse, droll stories, and singularly acute observations on 'the noble animal.' Though not well educated, he was full of humour, self-reliant, and had the gift of holding the attention of his audience. I was charmed with his originality, and felt that I was in the presence of a man who had something new to tell about my favourite study. After he had done speaking, a Mr Sydney Galvayne got up and began to hold forth in a style which made me feel sick; for he was very commonplace. He acknowledged that he had learned 'the system' from Sample in Australia, and told wonderful stories about his own horse-taming feats and powers. The two 'professors' did absolutely nothing except talk, and inform their audience that Professor Sample would impart 'the system' at five guineas a head. This, as might have been expected, did not 'draw' the London public. Contrary to the course mapped out for Rarey by his clever manager, Goodenough, Sample produced no reformed Cruiser, and yet he was incomparably superior to his predecessor in the line they both took up. The show had been widely advertised. The Professor's pleasant-looking portrait was hung out on both sides of nearly every omnibus in London, and yet the essential element of success, namely, the taming of a well-known vicious horse was neglected. Sample, with the true instinct of a born showman, gave a highly creditable taming performance with a quiet horse or two, and he showed such a number of smart breaking dodges to the members of his class, of which I was one, that he saved himself from being termed an impostor; although he lost about a thousand pounds by the venture. He stayed at the Langham Hotel; wore an immense diamond shirt-stud; carried a fifty-guinea watch which had been presented to him by an appreciative Australian 'class'; and fancied himself as one of the greatest men that had ever lived. We became acquainted, and I saw a good deal of him at our house and at my club, where he loved to get a game of draughts, at which he was an extraordinary fine player. He had a low opinion of my knowledge of horses; because I am not rich! Once or twice when he became too unbearable, for he would brook nothing but blind acceptance of his views, I mildly represented that I was a veterinary surgeon; had written successful books; had had some experience with horses; and that I was not altogether ignorant of the subject. 'When a man tries to make out to me,' he replied, 'that he knows something about horses, I ask him how much money he has made by his information, and if, like you, he happens to be hard up, I calculate that he has as little knowledge as he has cash.' This remark made me laugh; for, though uncomplimentary, it contained an evident truth which I had been silly enough to have ignored all my life. He had seen an immense amount of 'show' life, and I was never tired of listening to the account of his varied experiences; for it contained many shrewd and sound practical observations about horses and their training. Sample was not merely a horse tamer; but was also marvellously clever in teaching horses all kinds of tricks, particularly for circus work. His practical experience was limited entirely to harness work, and he had no idea of giving a horse what a hunting man would call a good mouth. About teaching a horse to jump in hunting or chasing style, he knew nothing. Almost everything he knew, I was ignorant of, and *vice versa*. As Sample would not acknowledge even to himself, that anyone could possibly know anything about horses which he did not, and as I am nothing, if not a learner, our talk and discussions proved far more beneficial to me, than they were to him.

His system, I may explain, was simple in the extreme, and could be fully explained in one lesson. One application of it would, so he said, cure all equine faults and vices; and its effects, so he also insisted, were permanent. To render the payer of the five guineas proof against forgetting his one

The Head and Tail Method.

lesson, and to enable him, so Sample declared, to tell a horse's age with accuracy up to the age of thirty years, supposing the animal lived so long, the pupil was presented with a book, in which a short description of the system was given. All that the writer of the five-pound-five cheque further required was belief.

Although, as my readers may guess, there was some nonsense mixed up in this 'system,' it had many good points. It was particularly useful to me; because it supplied me with one of the things which I most wanted, namely, knowledge of methods to make, in a very short time, a 'difficult' horse quiet and obedient. I had, however, no belief in a rule-of-thumb system. All I wanted was knowledge, and as much of it as I could possibly acquire.

The practical working of Sample's system was as follows:—
A cord was attached to the tail of the patient and fixed to the headstall (which had been previously put on the animal), at such a length that the only movement of which the horse was then capable, was that of following its tail in a circle. It required practice to regulate the length of this cord, so as to obtain the proper amount of restraint. When thus tied up, the animal was 'gentled' over with a long pole, while, in the event of its being nervous, it was induced to spin round and round, until it perceived that it was easier to allow itself to be touched all over, than to perform an involuntary waltz. Cracking a whip close to and over it, rattling tin cans about it, and applying other kinds of terrifying appliances, had the effect of rendering it quiet if it had been previously wild. This, like Rarey's plan of throwing a horse down, was admirable with savage or excitable horses; for it impressed on the former their powerlessness to do wrong, and, on the latter, the important fact that it was foolish for them to 'play up' without being hurt. An appliance called 'the Indian war bridle,' which had the same effect as a severe twitch, also belonged to the system, as a preparatory means of control. The third factor was driving the horse with a pair of long

reins, which the driver, according to Professor Sample, should violently jerk when he wanted to stop or turn the horse. He claimed that these three methods had been invented by him. He added a fourth, about which he made no claim to originality. It consisted of a very easy manner of throwing a horse by tying up one foreleg, and drawing his head round to the other side. He also showed the way horses are taught, in circuses, to come up to and follow one; and a device to cure horses of the habit of hanging on the rope or chain which secures them to their manger in a stall. His method, which was not original, of telling a horse's age up to thirty years, was based on the alteration of shape which occurs in the upper corner incisor tooth (on either side) from five years old and upwards. This, taken in conjunction with other dental indications not given by Sample, is useful up to, say, eight years of age. After that, it is much inferior to a method based on the conclusions drawn, on the same subject, by MM. Goubaux and Barrier, in *L'Exterieur de Cheval*. For ages under five years, Sample adopted the usual routine of deciding by the milk teeth and 'marks.' Not alone did he present to English horse lovers a large mass of useful knowledge which was absolutely new to them, but he worked his methods—even when one could not altogether agree with them—in such a capable manner, that it was worth a journey of a hundred miles to see him handle a quiet animal; to say nothing of vicious ones.

An admirable principle, to which Sample attached great importance in the breaking-in of a young horse, and which is directly opposed to the ideas of the majority of horse-owners in England, was that of forcing the pupil to 'stand' all kinds of terrifying sights and sounds, while proving to him that they did not hurt him. With quaint stories, Sample used to illustrate the folly of old-fashioned breakers who do everything in their power to prevent a youngster getting frightened; the result being that after he has been thus 'carefully' broken, he will be ready to 'play up' if anything untoward occurs. Considering the cost of labour, and the high price of hay and oats, it seems preposterous to spend months in gradually making a young horse steady, when the operation can be performed, according to Sample's principle, in a few lessons much more effectively, and without any risk of imparting to the animal the undesirable knowledge of his own power.

The chief faults of his 'system,' like those of all other horse tamers, were its supposed universal applicability and the assumed permanency of its effects. With the light of nine years' copious experience, I may explain that we cannot any more cure all forms of vice in the horse by one method, than a doctor can heal all his patients by the same drug. Rarey was careful to select only one type of vicious horse, namely, the savage, and having demonstrated his power to reduce such animals to submission, he wrongly argued, or lead his public to argue, that because the most violent form of vice could be cured by his system, that milder forms were equally amenable to its application. As well might be advanced the preposterous assertion that because ipecacuanha was valuable in the treatment of dysentery, it would cure a broken leg. All these 'professors,' Rarey, Sample, Rockwell, Hurlbert, Magner, Gleeson, Pratt and others, were patent medicine men who prided themselves on the exclusive possession of some secret remedy, which, however excellent it might be in some cases, could not possibly be effective in all. A doctor, I may point out, does not rest his fame on the fact of his having invented or discovered any particular medicine, but endeavours to attain success by the intelligent application of the agents he has at hand; and herein differs from the quack and the so-called horse tamer. The claim made for permanency in the effects of any 'system' is manifestly absurd. All that we can do in the education of man or beast is to produce on the creature's mind an effect which may or may not be lasting. Horse tamers ignore, either ignorantly or purposely, the great truth that repetition is one of the most powerful means of rendering an effect on the mind permanent. They, as a rule, insist that the effect of the application of their system is so wonderful, that it requires no repetition! And yet, with all the humbug which is mixed up in horse taming, lovers of horses in England owe a deep debt of gratitude to America, for having sent us these 'professors,' who, by teaching us ready and effective methods of horse-control, showed us how to take the first step in reducing 'difficult' animals to obedience. Having effected our purpose in the first lesson, we are certain to find our pupil more amenable to reason in the second, and so on; until, by repetition, the habit of obedience has been more or less established. Without the power of taking this first step, the desired result would often be unattainable.

The head and tail plan has but little good effect on stubborn or sulky horses, which are consequently to be avoided for 'show' purposes. The plan of jerking the reins, so as to make the pupil obey the pressure of the mouthpiece, appeared utterly wrong to me as a riding man; for I knew from experience that if a horse will not go up to his bridle on account of being afraid of getting a 'job' in the mouth, he will prove an unpleasant 'conveyance' in saddle, and as well as in harness. I need hardly say that horseman in England and the Continent like horses to 'bend' to the rein. An animal, when receiving its mouthing lesson, according to Sample's method, is directly stimulated to acquire the pernicious habit of chucking up its head, so as to transfer the painful pressure of the mouthpiece off the bars, and on to the corners of the mouth. I tried as far as I could to impress on him that granting I am utterly wrong in my theories of breaking, the fact remained that English and Irish horsemen detested the practice of jerking the reins, and that he would not gain their countenance unless he modified, in this respect, his method of taming. Not being willing to argue, he got excessively angry and indulged in his usual rodomontade about the money he had made at horse taming, the years he had spent at it, the enormous fame he had acquired, the stupidity and ignorance about horses displayed by Englishmen, and his own transcendent knowledge. We may see from the foregoing remarks that Sample, like Rarey, aimed only at rendering horses quiet—in other words taming them—and made no attempt at forming their paces, rendering them obedient to the 'aids,' and teaching them to jump. I need hardly point out that this horse taming was only a preliminary step, though a very useful one, in the breaking-in of a horse. Knowledge of any such system of horse taming was of value only to capable horsemen, who, after they had made their animal amenable to discipline, would be able to complete its education.

Later on I learnt the circumstances which gave rise to the fiasco at Hengler's, and which were as follows: After travelling for several years in the horse taming line through America, his native country, Sample went to Australia to teach his system. He had great success in those colonies; as he was undeniably clever, and his methods were new, and well adapted to the rough and ready style of breaking which is employed in the Antipodes. While he was making 'big' money there, someone suggested to him that he should go to England, and told him that instead of making a hundred or two a week in Australia, he could amass countless thousands in England and especially in London, where, the tempter said, nobody talked or dreamed of anything except horses, and where he would be hailed as the great American benefactor of humanity. Yankee shrewdness not being proof against flattery, Sample yielded to the glamour of the idea, and departed to London to gather the harvest of gold and fame which he thought was awaiting his arrival. He found the great city a more difficult place to attack than he had expected; especially as the ways and views of its inhabitants were new to him. Instead of finding himself, like in the Colonies, in the midst of men who bred, owned, or at least drove or rode horses, he encountered worthy citizens who loved horses only theoretically. News also came to him that he was not the first in the field; but that a Mr Osborn, who had learnt the system while in Australia from him, had preceded his instructor by about six months, and was, at the time of Sample's arrival in London, busily engaged teaching in Yorkshire, the patent system on his own account. I may explain that it was Sample's custom to get each of his pupils to sign a paper saying that he would not disclose the secrets of the system. Under threat, so Sample tells me, of 'showing up' Mr Osborn for this breach of faith, Sample made Professor Galvayne, as Osborn now called himself, come to London and help him in his first performances; the chief part allotted to him being the supply of ferocious horses. Whether Galvayne was unable to procure these equine demons, or whether he did not see the force of helping a former master and present rival, I cannot say. Anyhow, the wild horses were not produced, and the affair, as I have already described, turned out a terrible 'frost.'

Anxious to see as much as I possibly could of this new style of horse taming I accepted Mr Galvayne's invitation to attend a *séance* which he was going to hold at a riding-school in Islington. He asked me to say nothing about the matter to Sample. The performance came off, and was conducted in a precisely similar manner to those given by Sample; except that, in this instance, Galvayne claimed the head and tail trick, Indian war bridle, long rein driving, the determination of the age of the horse up to thirty years of age, and everything else that Sample had shown to his class, as inventions of his own original genius; and yet, about ten days before that, I heard him declare in Hengler's circus that he had learned them from Sample!

Mention of Galvayne's claim reminds me to make a few remarks on the originality of horse taming systems. Mr R. Jennings in his *Horse Training Made Easy*, which was published in America in 1866, describes the head and tail method, in a manner which leads me to believe that it was ancient nearly thirty years ago. Referring to the Indian war bridle, he says: 'It is mentioned in *The Veterinarian* of London in 1828 as used by the North American Indians in subduing their horses; hence it is known as the Indian war bridle.' The Irish breaker Fallon used the long reins in the eighteenth century. Galvayne evidently did not know these facts, or he thought it advisable to conceal them. Though I have not the books by me to give chapter and verse, I believe that Rockwell, Magner, Dudley, Hurlbert, and other tamers who performed prior to the appearance of Jenning's book, were acquainted with all the foregoing methods, which in 1885 constituted Sample's secret system. As to Rarey, we have historical proof that his 'original' system was practised long before the Christian era. The fact of my doubting the justness of Sample's claim to originality, in no way lessens the admiration with which I have always regarded the manner in which he handles horses and reduces unruly animals to obedience. I might as well—if I may be allowed to employ the same simile twice—try to depreciate the merits of an able and successful doctor, because he had not invented or discovered any of the surgical instruments or medicines he is accustomed to employ. A doctor or breaker is not clever, because he has invented remedial agents, but because he is able to intelligently apply those with which he is acquainted.

Besides Galvayne *alias* Osborn, who soon left him, Sample's *personnel* consisted of a clerk who called himself Franklin, but whose real name was Sexton, and who, later on, endeavoured to burst on the world as 'Professor Leon the celebrated Mexican Horse Tamer;' Frank, an Australian rough rider; and Joe, who had been a sailor. Sexton, who is a brother-in-law of Galvayne, acted, I believe, as his advance agent while Osborn was running his show in the north of England before Sample's arrival in this country. It appears that during that time Franklin learned 'the system' from Galvayne. Subsequently Osborn and Leon 'fell out,' and parted. I must do Sexton the justice of saying that he always gave the credit of his instructions to Sample, and not to Osborn. Frank, after a short time, quitted Sample's service, and went horse taming on his own account. Joe, with the proverbial honesty of a seafaring man, stuck to the ship, and did not leave her until the gallant craft got blown up by an infernal machine, as I shall relate further on. When his old skipper launched another argosy, which was also destroyed, the faithful Joe again found his way on board, ready to give a helping hand. Joe is a strong, sturdy fellow of about middle height. He has a pleasant, English-looking face, and an inexhaustible supply of good temper, which must, at times, have been sorely tried by his dictatorial master, who was as fond of Joe, as Joe was of him, and that is saying a great deal.

After the London fiasco, Galvayne returned to Yorkshire, or wherever else he had been performing, and Sample 'opened' at Norwich. He was full of confidence that he would do well as soon as he got among men of whose lives horses formed a large part. He was pleased with the interest I had taken in his work, and told me when I was saying good-bye to him that he hoped, if I went abroad again, I would utilise to my profit all that I had learned from him.

Photo. by H. R. Sherborn Newmarket.

CHAPTER VIII.

Colonel Dudley Sampson — Return to India—Bombay—A Free Show—Poona—Colonel Morton and the 14th Hussars—The 17th Lancers—General Wardropp—Calcutta—Horsebreaking in a Class and in a Public Performance—Causes of Success—Learning as I went on—Horse Taming and Horsebreaking—Show at Simla—Lord and Lady Dufferin—Lord Roberts—The Duke of Bedford—Sir George White—Mr Rudyard Kipling—'The Guides'—Hyderabad and its Native Noblemen—Improvements in Horsebreaking—Mr Jimmy M'Leod and Britomarte—Racing—'The Treasure.'

ON the Derby day of 1885, I strolled as usual through the Epsom Paddock to see the horses and to meet old friends and acquaintances, who have a way of turning up at that famous rendezvous, as unexpected as it is pleasant. Among others whom I saw was Colonel Dudley Sampson, who was once a famous gentleman rider in India, and who has since developed into a country gentlemen and a writer of Unionist songs. We fell into a conversation which naturally turned upon horses. He told me that he was troubled about a well-bred four-year-old which he had unsuccessfully tried to turn into a hunter. He had trusted its reformation to five successive breakers, who had effected nothing beyond pocketing their respective fees of five guineas. I asked what the animal did. 'That's the worst of him,' replied the owner, 'he'll do nothing. A child can mount him and remain on his back all day; but no power or stimulus which we have hitherto applied, has been able to make him move.' In fact, the animal was a rank jibber. Knowing that it was young and guessing that its instructors had not been particularly able, I volunteered to attempt its reduction to obedience. This I did, a few days afterwards, chiefly by means of the long reins. In about an hour, I made the colt so amenable to discipline that he allowed himself to be ridden all over the place in the kindest possible manner. He got another lesson next morning, and gave no further trouble. Some time after that I met Colonel Sampson, who remarked to me that had he known how to break-in horses, he would have been saved, during his old Indian days, from much loss and disappointment with animals which had proved to be beyond his power of control. I also remembered the many wild and stubborn ones that had got the best of me when I used to race and ride in the Punjab and North-West. No wonder, then, when he suggested that I ought to go to India and teach the people there how to break-in horses, that I replied: 'Good-bye, I'm off.' Full of this idea, I took my passage and arrived in Bombay in less than a month.

A day or two afterwards, I met at lunch in the Bombay Club, Mr Remington, Mr Cecil Gray, Mr Symonds, poor Harold King, and others whose grand passion in life was horses. Of course their first question was: What had brought me back to India? With an air of solemnity which was due to the subject, and which in truth was not unfitting to the serious financial strait in which I would have found myself had I been unsuccessful, I replied that I had come to teach the

Bombay.

sojourners in India new methods of breaking in young horses and of curing of their vices those that had been spoiled. My friends, all of whom had 'done themselves well' at lunch cried out as with one voice: 'That's the very thing we want, to learn. Tell us how it is done?' I replied that nothing would give me greater pleasure; that the information which I had to impart was of immense practical value; and that I would instruct them per head for the small sum of £5, which they would more than recoup themselves the first occasion on which they had an unruly horse to handle. My friends roared with laughter at what they termed my preposterous proposal. In their opinion I would be more than repaid by the pleasure I would receive in teaching them, and in reducing to obedience all their buckjumpers, rearers, runaways, jibbers and kickers. Finding that my remarks on 'business,' on the necessity of living and of paying one's 'ex's,' and on the fact that no one came to India for amusement, were in vain, and feeling that the situation was becoming really serious, I volunteered to give them a free show, on condition that they would get me the two worst horses they could find in Bombay. This they consented to with delight; the performance came off at the Kennels of the Bombay Fox Hounds; and the representatives of the local press attended. Of the two horses brought, one was a vicious kicker in harness if the rein happened to get under its tail; the other was a determined jibber like unto Colonel Sampson's colt, but would violently buck if struck or spurred. By a great piece of good luck, my success was as rapid as it was signal. In about an hour and a-half, the kicker took no notice of the rein when placed under its tail; and the jibbing mare became so quiet that her owner, an unpractised horseman, was able to ride her all over the place without the slightest trouble. Previous to that, all the professional rough-riders who had tried her, had failed to make her move, or to stick on her when they proceeded to punish her. I may anticipate events by saying that, eighteen months after her first and only lesson, I received a letter from her owner, saying that she had continued to remain perfectly quiet to ride, even after she had been kept in the stable for several days. I know nothing about the subsequent history of the kicker. I may add that the work I had mapped out for myself consisted in showing the members of my class how to make a horse obey in the first instance, so that they could do likewise, and could repeat the lesson as might be required. I must have made a good impression at this free show; for next morning the papers were full of my praises, and I got up a large paying class.

From Bombay I went on to Poona, where I arrived just in time for a ball given by the Western Indian Club, for which I had received an invitation. That incomparable gentleman rider, Captain (now Colonel) Locke Elliott being always on the look out to learn something new about horses, would brook no delay, so he went round (after supper of course) with paper and pencil in hand, and got me up a class of almost all the gentlemen present—the ladies being placed on the free list—and when the ball was over we all drove or rode over to the Horse Artillery riding-school at Kirkee, which is about three miles distant. The Gunners kindly lent a few supposed incorrigibles, who would go only in the 'off centre' or 'off lead.' The greatest interest was taken in their subjugation, and neither man nor woman would go to breakfast and then to bed until they had seen the buck-jumpers quietly ridden. I mention this incident to show what a keen interest people in India take in horses. Practically, everyone there owns horses and uses them as one's greatest pleasure in life. In England everyone theoretically loves horses; but not one in say, 500, either rides or drives. Even those who possess one or more horses, are not, owing to the masterful ways of English grooms and coachmen, brought into the same intimate relations with their horses, as are their brethren in the East. Men in India often have to teach their native grooms how to dress and feed their horses; their smiths how to shoe them; and their stable-

The XVII. Lancers.

lads how to ride. In this country, we dare not take such liberties. After Poona, my success in India was complete. During a twelve months' tour, I held large classes in almost every station from Peshawur to Trichinopoly, and from Quetta to Mandalay, and taught the officers of nearly every regiment and battery. Naturally, my most enthusiastic pupils belonged to horse and field batteries, and to English and Native cavalry regiments. Although there are some fine exceptions, which it would be invidious to particularise, infantry officers of the present day do not 'go in' for horses as keenly as those of former times, who had more money to spend and less duty to perform. On leaving Poona, I went to Trimulgherry where I was a guest of Colonel Morton and the officers of the 14th Hussars, who, with the other officers took a great interest in the horsebreaking work which I showed them. The most of the ten days which I stayed at Trimulgherry, was spent in the 14th Hussar riding-school, where we had in all the unbroken and spoiled horses we could find. On leaving, Colonel Morton and the officers of the 14th Hussars and several officers of the 3rd Madras Cavalry and Hyderabad Contingent gave me a very flattering testimonial about the soundness of my work.

The following kind expression of opinion given to me by Colonel Cooke and the officers of the 17th Lancers, and other members of my Lucknow class, will afford an idea of the sort of horses I had to take in hand.

'We, the undersigned, wish to place on record our appreciation of Captain M. H. Hayes' methods of breaking horses of all kinds. The methods are various, and are applicable to all sorts of unbroken or refractory horses : most simple in application, and thoroughly efficacious. Some of the subjects submitted to Captain Hayes to test his methods were as follows :—

'A chestnut Waler of E-A., R. H. A., would not allow itself to be mounted, being most violent if mounting it were attempted, in a short time allowed anyone to mount and dismount.

'An unbroken remount and bad buck-jumper of 17th Lancers, in the course of two hours, became quiet to ride and perfectly tractable. Ample proof was afforded of the complete control that could be quickly gained over any horse. A stubborn refuser of the 8th B. C. very soon took a delight in jumping ; and a confirmed jibber of the 17th Lancers was glad in a short time to move in any direction asked. These few instances we consider convincing proof of the great power of Captain Hayes's system.'

My most apt pupil in the 17th Lancers was Major (now Colonel) Benson, who afterwards commanded the regiment. At Mhow I stayed with my old friend 'Ding' MacDougal, who is one of the finest steeplechase riders and polo players in the service. His colonel and brother officers told me that they were greatly pleased with my breaking at the class which I held in their riding-school.

I taught the 12th Lancers, at Bangalore ; the Carabineers, in Sealkote ; the 8th Hussars, at Meerut ; the King's Dragoon Guards, at Rawul Pindee ; and 'The Bays,' at Umballa. The only English cavalry regiment which was in India at that time and which I did not meet, was the 2d Dragoon Guards, some of whose officers, of which Colonel (now General) Wardropp was one, came over to Umballa to join my class. General Wardropp, who is a thorough horseman, helped me in the breaking, and spared no pains to learn everything he possibly could about it. At Calcutta I had an immense class in the race-course paddock which was kindly lent me by the Stewards of the Calcutta Turf Club. I have especially to thank Sir John Lambert, the Commissioner of Police, for his help on that occasion.

Altogether, I held about fifty classes at different places in India. Except once for a charitable object, and on the special occasion of breaking in a zebra in Frank Fillis's Circus, I did not attempt to give a public breaking show ; because I thought (and think) I could give my public better value for their money by endeavouring to teach them, than by trying to amuse them. A mere breaking exhibition, besides being, under the most favourable circumstances, a 'thin' show to the ordinary sightseer, has the terrible drawback that, with every precaution taken by the showman, the performers, namely, the supposed vicious horses, may refuse to 'play up,' and then the innocent showman runs the chance of being branded as a fraud. In a class, the teacher meets only those who are horsemen, or who have proved their interest in the subject of horses by paying their money. Consequently, if he has new and sound things to show them, he will be certain of an attentive hearing, even if he has only quiet horses upon which to operate.

No doubt, my readers would wish to know if I was invariably successful with the bad horses I took in hand. Not always, I can reply, but nearly always. I remember only one or two animals—jibbers which nothing, apparently, could get out of a walk or very slow trot—that I found was too much for me. A breaker can work only with the material he has at hand, and cannot give pluck and high spirits to the cowardly and sullen; though he can always ensure docility; besides I sometimes had not time to finish those I took in hand. India is, socially, a small place; though, geographically, a vast continent. Had I bungled badly at one station, the news would have preceded me wherever I went, and I could not have continued my tour. On the contrary, my fame increased as I travelled through India, and I left behind me a good impression, if I may judge by the testimonials I received, and by the largely-increased sale of my books. 'The cause?' you ask? Not any extraordinary cleverness on my part, I can assure you, but the immense amount of experience I gained, which, as I shall explain, can never be equalled by that to be obtained by anyone who will come after me. In the course of instruction in the art of giving horses good manners and snaffle-bridle mouths, I used to show to the members of my class every method and dodge which I knew were useful in breaking, and illustrated their employment on the animals brought to me. Though I worked very hard, I enjoyed myself immensely; for I met some of the best fellows in the world, and I kept learning more about horses than I had ever dreamed it were possible to do. When I arrived in India, the knowledge of horse-breaking was very small in that country; consequently, there was a large number of vicious and unmanageable animals, most of whom I successfully handled. The majority of my pupils were owners and enthusiastic lovers of horses. They profited so much by my instruction that they have reduced the percentage of 'difficult' horses to a very small figure. The horses imported from Australasia, which used to supply by far the greatest proportion of vicious brutes, are, owing to improved management, becoming year by year quieter and more easy to handle. Hence, anyone who will follow in my footsteps in India, will find wild horses almost as scarce there, as in England. I went to India very ignorant; but each one of the hundreds of bad horses I handled taught me something. Wherever I went, I had in my classes the most experienced men among horses in the place. While showing them all I knew and trying to explain everything I could about breaking, I was certain to be told any wrinkle or device which any of my pupils had found useful. On learning anything of this kind, I tested it, and if it turned out good, I promptly shoved it into my metaphorical bag of tricks, to be utilised on future occasions. Consequently, I not alone amassed invaluable experience, but also acquired the most of the knowledge previously possessed by all the fine horsemen whom I had the privilege of meeting. Had I lived a thousand years working by the light of only my own experience, I would not have obtained half the knowledge, for the possession of which I am indebted to horse-loving friends whom I have met in many parts of Europe, Asia and Africa; to say nothing of books.

As my readers will understand from remarks I have already made, sulky, stubborn horses are infinitely more difficult to break than the wild, hot-headed, and hostile kind, but give practically no 'show.' Two hours' tuition would be enough to qualify an ordinary draper's assistant who had never previously placed his hand on a horse, to make the worst man-eater in the world quiet in far less time than Rarey took to subdue the historical Cruiser; and yet years of teaching and practice might not enable this supposititious young gentleman to win obedience from an obstinate refuser, or jibber in harness. In the former case, a mechanical routine is sufficient; in the latter, the operator requires patience, tact, experience, and inspiration. Knowing how brilliant is the result and how easy of accomplishment is the breaking of a mad buck-jumper or ferocious savage, we can hardly blame the showman for playing to the gallery with one of this sort; instead of giving with, say, a jibber, an exhibition which would be as dull, as it would be meritorious.

As I continued to gain experience, I rejected or improved old methods, and adopted new ones. I found that, for practical (not 'show') purposes, the voice and the reins should be the chief means employed in the preparatory breaking of the horse; for their application can be repeated (repetition being the grand means for confirming the desired habit of obedience) without inconvenience and with manifestly good effect, every time we either ride or drive the animal. However effective throwing a horse down or making him waltz round with his head tied to his tail, may be for 'taking the nonsense' out of him, neither of these methods come within the scope of the ordinary horse owner, especially if they have to be repeated on several occasions. I soon rejected the use of the Indian war bridle for a method by which I make a horse stand steady when I order him to do so.

The kindness and hospitality I received during this tour, were not more gratefully appreciated by me than the warm interest which was taken in my work. Thanks to the good offices of Lord William Beresford, the Military Secretary to the Viceroy, I held a large class at Simla under the patronage and presence of their Excellencies Lord and Lady Dufferin, and Lord and Lady Roberts. Knowing that there were only quiet horses to handle at the seat of Government in the hills, I brought all the way from Calcutta with me an Australian buck-jumper, which gave a fine and exciting show. Lord Dufferin being a good horseman and an Irishman, was foremost in wanting to learn, so that, as he laughingly told me he might break-in his own hunters when he got back to 'The Old Country.' Though England could badly spare her greatest and most honoured diplomatist, I feel certain that he would be happier in a good hunting county in Ireland, with a nice stable of horses and a well-selected pack or two of hounds, than he is now as Ambassador at Paris. The world knows him chiefly as a diplomatist of extraordinary tact and wisdom ; and yet he is quite as able in winning the love and respect of his fellow men, as he is in securing political victories. He and Lord Mayo, both fine Irish sportsmen, contrast very favourably indeed with other viceroys I might name. Lady Dufferin was a fit wife for a mighty ruler. She is a *grande dame*, sympathetic, and large minded. On the day I gave my first performance at Simla, the Commander-in-Chief—he was then Sir Frederick Roberts—very kindly asked me to lunch. Referring to the interest he took in my work, he drew my attention to the fact that he had in his library all my books. After acknowledging this very high compliment, I could not help saying in fun, after glancing at them, that he had not the book I wrote on military tactics. The implied suggestion that he should consult my ideas on tactics, of which he is the great past master, was received by the Commander-in-Chief and those of his staff who were present, as a great joke. Before the lunch, I gave Sir Frederick a private *séance* with a horse of his which would not jump for him. Twenty minutes with the long reins made the animal take in the kindest manner, the fence we had put up on the lawn. Lord Roberts is as good and resolute on horseback as any subaltern in the service. He is a remarkably nice weight, and is wonderfully fortunate in having kept his nerves in good order. He has a kind spot in his heart for horses and sport; although he is now altogether devoted to his military duties. His chief thought in life is how to improve the men under him in discipline and *morale*. Lord Herbrand Russell, who is now the Duke of Bedford, was also in my Simla horsebreaking class, and was kind enough to lend my wife his handsome pony, Countryman, to ride while she was in the hills. He was a good horseman, and used to take a great deal of interest in pony racing, which was the only form of racing that was possible on the small course in the hills.

During my tour through Burma, I had the honour of meeting the present Commander-in-Chief of India, Sir George White, at Mandalay, where he was commanding. As soon as I had seen him and had answered his kindly greeting, I thought his hard resolute face and tall athletic figure were strangely familiar to me. And then came gradually to me the memory of a summer's morning at Glenbrook, on the Cork River, twenty-three years gone by, when I was a Woolwich cadet, home for the holidays, which I was spending by getting into training for some rowing races. A young officer in a Highland regiment, who had been staying with a gentleman who resided close by, had backed himself to do a weight-lifting feat against any Irishman his host could produce. He selected me, with the result that I proved good enough for the task; although he might have got other men much better than I was to compete against the future Commander-in-Chief of India.

At Lahore, I had the pleasure of meeting for the first time, Mr Rudyard Kipling, who was then a clever lad of about nineteen, and as yet unknown to fame. He was on the staff of the *Civil and Military Gazette*, and was doing much to brighten its hitherto somewhat staid columns. Although his tastes were wholly literary, he wrote for his paper a graphic and interesting account of my horsebreaking performances, which he witnessed, and which seem to have impressed him, if I may judge by his mention of my name in one of his *Plain Tales from the Hills.* He, like Phil. Robinson, found that India was too small a place for a man of literary power, and soon left it.

I had so many pleasant experiences during my tour in India, that I would fain dwell on them; but as they would no doubt be more interesting to me than to my readers, I must pass by them with a few exceptions. I met a pleasing relic of old Indian hospitality on the road I was travelling by pony express between Nowshera and Hoti Murdan, on my way to meet that fine regiment, The Guides, the officers of which had invited me to come and teach them the art of horsebreaking. Having travelled about half of the thirty odd miles of the journey, I was beginning to feel the effects of the northern Punjab sun, whose rays were beating down on my *tonga* (Indian curricle), when I was stopped in the road by a Native, who carried on his shoulders a couple of large baskets slung on a pole. In reply to my query as to what he wanted, he handed me a well-worn card upon which was written: 'Weary and welcome traveller to Hoti Murdan, rest awhile and refresh yourself.' The Native, evidently well accustomed to his task, proceeded to a green and shady spot close by; laid down his baskets, and extracted from them a clean white tablecloth, upon which he laid out a delicious cold lunch, with a plentiful supply of liquor, soda water, and cigars. I very heartily drank the health of my generous-hearted, though yet unknown friends, and having done justice to the excellent fare, proceeded on to meet the fine fellows who ably guard our northern frontier. I may mention that when travelling by pony post in India, the stages are usually about five miles long, and are covered, when the roads are good, at a fast hand gallop. One of these ponies, which average about 13.1 high, when harnessed in a small two-wheeled cart, is capable, with ease to itself, of carrying two or three men sixty miles, from sunrise to sunset on a burning hot day, provided it is halted every five or six miles, and given about three quarts of water, in which about a pound of parched barley

Hyderabad. 123

meal is mixed. This is a fact, to which I have further alluded in *Training and Horse Management in India*, that persons who advocate the practice of withholding drinking water from a horse until he is quite cool, should lay to heart.

At Hyderabad I held a class consisting of over fifty of the Native noblemen, who are almost all fine horsemen. In fact, their polo team is second to none in India. The Mahamadan gentlemen are *viveurs*, fond of spending money, delight in owning horses and racing, hospitable, and are uncommonly good 'company.' The two I liked best were Sar Firaz Hussain (usually called 'Sir Francis' by the English residents) and Vikar ul Umra. The Nizam is not much of a sportsman, and appears to devote himself chiefly to his domestic duties. Missing the strong hand, over them, of a man like the old Salar Jung, it is little to be wondered at that the turbulent crew which surround this native throne, prove difficult to manage.

I always found that I could make the best 'show' with a horse which was merely difficult to mount; for by the voice, it was easy in four or five minutes to make the most unruly animal of this kind stand like a statue to be mounted. Experienced horsemen know how terribly annoying the practice of this vice may be, and how frequently it spoils the sale of an animal intended for a lady (who, however well she may ride, requires her horse to be fairly steady to mount), or timid man. And yet nothing is easier than to make, by a few repetitions of the discipline I have indicated, such animals perfectly steady to mount. In all this work, we should endeavour, in the plainest possible manner, to show our pupil that, if he rebels, he will be punished; if he obeys, he will be rewarded; and that, in all cases, he is powerless to resist our commands. My readers may well ask: 'If scientific horse-breaking be so easy and so effective, as it appears to be from your description; how is it that there are so many spoiled horses in existence?' I reply, that the adoption of new methods and new principles in any art, is a slow and gradual process; and that, though very simple, the successful practice of horsebreaking demands an amount of patience, tact and firmness rarely united in one person. On the other hand, I can, with some justifiable pride, point to the fact that a large number of horse owners, especially officers in the army, in in which I have a great following, break-in their animals according to the doctrines I teach.

One of the worst horses I ever handled, was an Australian mare, called Britomarte, and owned by Mr 'Jimmy' M'Leod, a well-known indigo planter, who had promised to get me up a large class if I would come up to his factory in Chumparum. Mr M'Leod is one of the old style of princely planters, who keeps open house and a stable of sixty or seventy horses for the use of his friends as much as for himself. If you go to stay with him, he will be certain to get up a 'pigstick,' a shooting party, or a race meeting for your entertainment. Before he got too heavy, he was the finest steeplechase rider in India, and is still uncommonly bad to beat either across country or on the polo ground. When I arrived, I found a class of fifty planters at £5 a piece, and Britomarte awaiting me. Her history during the two years Mr M'Leod had her, was that she would neither be ridden nor driven. She was so clever in the art of getting rid of her would-be riders, that if she could not catapult them off by buck-jumping, she would throw herself over on them. In harness she adopted the policy of passive resistance, and refused to put one foot in front of another, even after she had been put in as a wheeler in a four-in-hand team, and had been dragged along the ground by her three companions for several hundred yards, and until she had been torn and cut so badly that her wounds took months to heal. As Mr M'Leod had had immense experience in the breaking of rough horses, which was a special hobby of his; it can be imagined that all the ordinary methods of discipline had been tried in vain on the bay mare. At eight o'clock in the morning after my arrival, the shapely and untamed Britomarte was led into the ring round which the ladies and gentlemen of the party sat or stood in eager expectation of what was going to be done. I put the long reins on the mare, and tried to move her from side to side by these means; but she played the *rôle* of a cataleptic who was dead to all external impressions. I kept trying to 'bend' her through the heat of that Indian day, still at the end of the two reins, though breakfast had been announced and eaten and lunch was waiting on the table, until I felt mad and fit to cut up and eat the sulky fiend who stood in front of me refusing to move. The hum of expectant conversation had ceased; the ladies looked woefully bored; the men mixed sodas and whiskies and smoked their cheroots as if they were performing a solemn, religious duty; while I kept getting more and more furious, though I dared not betray my rage: for I knew that an angry jerk at the reins or a cut of the whip would bring back into the mare all the old 'devil,' which was fast leaving her. At last, she took two or three steps to the left; one or two to the right; then I managed to induce her to circle to the left; and a little later to the right. Having done this, I soon got her to circle, turn, and move off, by merely feeling the reins or raising my hand as a signal for her to go on. I, then, put a saddle on her, and got her soon as quiet as an old gentleman's hack. Her driving instruction occupied only a comparatively short time, after which time she went 'kindly' for the first time in her life, after having been in my hands for seven hours. 'What a terribly long business' I imagine I hear my readers saying. Seven hours, I may well plead, are not a long time to do a task which experienced horsemen failed to accomplish in a couple of years. As Britomarte had been the victress in many battles, it required an unusual amount of patience and tact to make her take the all-important first step. 'Was that one lesson enough to cure her of her vices for the remainder of her life?' probably asks a reader who has not carefully studied my remarks on horsebreaking. Having heard and answered similar questions many hundreds of times, I reply almost automatically : That repetition of the discipline which obtained the desired control can alone confirm the habit of obedience; that each succeeding lesson will be easier to impart than the one which preceded it ; that the effect of the first lesson, if it were not repeated may, or may not, quickly wear off ; and that one act of injudicious mismanagement, even in punishing the mare with whip or spur, may undo in a moment all the benefit of the previous instruction. All I know about Britomarte's further career, is that I saw her a week later, being ridden about quietly by an indifferent horseman.

Mr John Hubert Moore was the first to impress upon me the futility, as a general rule, of trying to cure vicious horses for other people. Many years ago, before he had arrived at that conclusion, he formed a partnership with the late Lord Combermere to buy up all the cheap, but otherwise good, horses which were troubled with a 'pain in their temper,' to cure them of their respective faults, and then to sell them as reliable conveyances. The frequent cases they had of these supposed reformed characters being returned on their hands for having ' broken out ' again, caused them to abandon the scheme. Profiting by the experience of the great Irish breaker, I have always found it more satisfactory to teach an owner how to break-in a spoiled horse, than to attempt the task myself.

Towards the end of my Indian trip I did some racing, and ought to have made a lot of money on one occasion ; but didn't. It happened in this way. That good sportsman Mr (now Captain) Bates of the King's Dragoon Guards got up at Rawul Pindee a meeting, at which there was some brisk gambling. I had two of my own and a couple of animals belonging to Mr Larpent (now Baron de Hochepied), who, not being able to be present, occupied the most of the time of the local telegraph clerks by wiring to me : ' Go Nap,' or words to that effect. The instructions of the young Peeler (he was then in the Bombay Police) were disastrous ; for by a strange fatality our gees kept running second to the horses of 'The Treasure,' and to those of a Captain Beresford of the Gunners. The races ended, we paid our money, I had my last drink at the hospitable King's Dragoon Guards' mess, and departed to run a 'show' at the next station, and recoup the lost coin. I was hardly well out of the place, when Captain Beresford died of typhoid fever, and on the examination of his papers it turned out that he and 'The Treasure' were racing confederates. As they had neglected to declare that fact before the late meeting was held; the races for which Mr Larpent and I had run second, as well as the bets dependent on them, were awarded to us. Unfortunately, control on up-country Indian meetings was, at that time, slack; 'The Treasure,' instead of 'parting' went to England, and we neither got back the money we had paid, nor did we receive our winnings. Such occurrences were not uncommon in that country. Men with the best intentions got up races; but as they gave their time and trouble for nothing, and as they were not altogether free agents, having generals and colonels over them, they could not enforce payment as promptly as they might have wished. The carrying over of race accounts from one meeting to another was also a fruitful cause of default, which ended, as might have been expected, by the abolition of most of these up-country fixtures which once formed a very pleasant feature in Indian life. After all, the real culprits were the Suez Canal, increased railway communication, and depreciation in the value of the rupee. In the old days, men went to a station, lived, sported, gambled and drank there till most of them died; for the nearest seaport could be reached only by palankeen or *garee dazak*, and after that there was a four months' voyage round the Cape to face. Then, the rupee was worth 2s. 2½d.; now it stands at 1s. 1½d. With the currency at that price, and England within 21 days' journey, it can hardly be wondered at, that most of the young fellows, now, choose marriage and lawn tennis in preference to horses and shooting.

Photo. by Clarence Hailey, St John's Wood and Newmarket.

CHAPTER IX.

Nellie Reid—Sample and his Machine—A Class at Woolwich—Mr Hermann Vezin—Ormonde—Mr John Porter—Breaking at Kingsclere—Schoolwork for Race-horses—Captain Fitzgerald.

HAVING finished my Indian tour, I returned to England to spend the money I had made. Landing at Liverpool, and seeing that Sample was running a show there, I went to the circus he had taken, and found he was having an equine variety entertainment with Nellie Reid, two trick horses called Pet and Daisy, and some clever jumpers, in conjunction with his horse-taming class. Miss Reid was a bold, fine horsewoman, who, two or three years before, had drawn all London to the Westminster Aquarium to see her ride over a reputed 6-foot wall on poor John Wilson's Australian gelding, Union. Cavanagh, a jockey well-known in India and Ceylon, used to ride with her on a clever, long-tailed grey horse.

Miss Nellie Reid.

The obstacle, which was a boarded structure made to resemble a wall, was held in a sloped position by a man at each end, ready to be let down in case the animal struck it. Despite this circus-like method, which detracted from the workman-like appearance of the affair, Miss Reid's performance was of great merit; for Union, night after night, jumped fully 5 feet 3 inches. After the show was over, I had supper with Sample and Miss Reid, and, of course, we had a great talk about horses and business at home and in foreign parts. I was sorry to hear that my old friend had done no 'good' since I last saw him; but he was buoyed up with hope, for he had seething in his active brain a new invention for the training of horses, which, as he expressed it, would lick creation. It consisted, so he informed me, of a machine into which he could put a wild horse, and in a couple of minutes bring him out of it as tame as a mouse! It had lost him in making experiments with it, a lot of money, which he regarded as lent at usurious interest on the safest possible security. He was also going to patent it in all the principal countries in the world. As I admired his pluck, enthusiasm and originality, I was careful to say nothing that was not encouraging to him. Knowing what great experience he had had in horse taming, I felt certain that he would work out his ideas all right in practice; but I could not help thinking that any method of horse taming, however perfect it may be, forms at best only a small portion of the preliminary education of a horse, and that it is not required with one out of fifty horses which are brought up under civilised conditions like those in the United Kingdom. Had he been in the possession of an invention which could with mechanical precision give a horse a good mouth, form his paces, and teach him to jump cleverly, I would have offered him everything I had in the world, and would have begged him to take me into partnership. As it was, I commended his scheme warmly, praised his ingenuity, and parted from him with the best of good wishes on both sides.

During that year, I amused myself principally by going to races. There being no wild horses in England to tame, I did not attempt the farce of a public show, beyond giving, at the invitation of Miss Lindo, a practical lecture on horse control and on riding, in aid of the funds of the Home of Rest for Horses. As a novelty, I demonstrated, with the assistance of my wife, whose fine riding on that occasion was praised in *The Field* and illustrated in *The Graphic*, a method for teaching ladies and men how to ride, especially over fences, without having to hold on by the reins. Although I was the first to put this method into practice, I hardly like to say that I invented it; because it gradually evolved itself in my mind, during my horse-breaking work with the long reins. At the performance in question, Miss Reid and Miss Streeter also helped by some nice riding to render the affair a success.

By the kindness of Colonel 'Sam' Lyons, who was in command of the Horse Artillery Riding Establishment at Woolwich, I held a class at the riding-school there. Colonel Lyons takes a great interest in the training of horses for military purposes. He did everything in his power to help me in my work and to render my visits to Woolwich pleasant. My time was occupied there chiefly in teaching refractory horses to 'passage,' rein back, jump, or to perform other ordinary evolutions at which they had previously rebelled. The only bit of taming I had was with a Commissariat mule, which, for the preceding four or five months, so I was told, would not allow anyone to handle him, and had consequently passed his time in his stall, eating, drinking, and sleeping, without doing any work. Having gone down to where he was stabled, I led him out of his stall and took him up to the riding-school, where within an hour, he became so quiet that he was handled, saddled, and ridden about without giving any trouble. My readers will naturally suppose that the Commissariat officers, whose ignorance of breaking had been the cause of the country having been deprived of the services of this mule for several months, would have come to my class, paid the fees, learned my methods, and have completed the course of instruction which I had commenced, and which I had shown was easy of accomplishment. Not a bit of it! On the contrary, they blamed me; because, by their ignorant mismanagement, they were able after a few days to undo all the good effects of my one lesson, and to make the mule as bad as he was before. I cannot too strongly impress on my readers that, as a rule, it is of but little use attempting to cure a spoiled horse or mule, without at the same time teaching the method of instruction to the animal's owner or caretaker, who can then confirm the habit of obedience by repetition as may be required. When I began teaching my Woolwich friends, I could not help thinking of the last time I was in that *manège*, bumping round and 'making the corners' to the orders of that stern disciplinarian, Sergeant-Major Dann, who is now a major without the 'Non-Com.' title. The fact of my being the only non-official who has ever been received in that exclusive riding-school, was an exceedingly high compliment, which I fully appreciated. On parting, Colonel Lyons and the other members of the class said a lot of very nice things to me about my teaching.

Mr Hermann Vezin, the well-known actor, whom I knew, as he used to teach my wife elocution, had a great fancy for seeing horses broken-in, and accompanied me in the quest on a few occasions. Long ago he had attended Rarey's performances, and seemed to highly approve of my work at Woolwich, where my pupils were always glad to see him. Like many members of my various classes, Mr Vezin knew nothing practically about horses, and never went near one; yet these animals possessed a great attraction for him. Had I had, during my tours, to rely solely on the support of horsey people, I would not have been able to have paid my way. In fact, I often found that men who prided themselves most on their knowledge of horses, thought it derogatory to their local reputation to be taught orally by me; though, luckily, their scruples on this point did not extend to the perusal (when no one was looking) of my books. Others, on the contrary, to whom horse lore could not have been of any possible use, were eager for theoretical instruction, for which they were glad to pay. I certainly could not have made my horse-breaking tours with anything like the ready recognition I received from the public, had not the fame (if I may be pardoned the word) of my books preceded me. Wherever I went, with the exception of South Africa and Berlin, I found that the English-speaking residents knew me through my writings, and were predisposed in my favour. On the other hand, my success in breaking-in horses and in teaching this art to others, has greatly stimulated the sale of my books, which, in their later editions, owe a large part of any merit they may possess, to the practical experience I gained during my travels.

Through the kindness of that good sportsman, Lord Chesham, whom I had the pleasure of knowing in India when he belonged to the 10th Hussars, I obtained permission from the Duke of Westminster to have Ormonde, the horse of all time, photographed; as I wanted his portrait for the book I was writing on the 'make and shape' of horses. With this object, I went to Mr John Porter's place at Kingsclere, and besides getting the horse 'taken,' I gave the great trainer and his people a practical demonstration of how to break-in and mouth young thoroughbreds. To experiment upon, he gave me a high-priced yearling which had never been mounted, and which belonged to the Prince of Wales. In about half an hour, I made the youngster so quiet and handy, that he allowed himself to be quietly ridden about the paddock, and answered the indications of the reins with a fair amount of precision. Mr Porter seemed very pleased with the work, and asked me where he could get the tackle I used, as he wished to put in practice what he had seen me do that afternoon. I was only too glad to present him with the gear

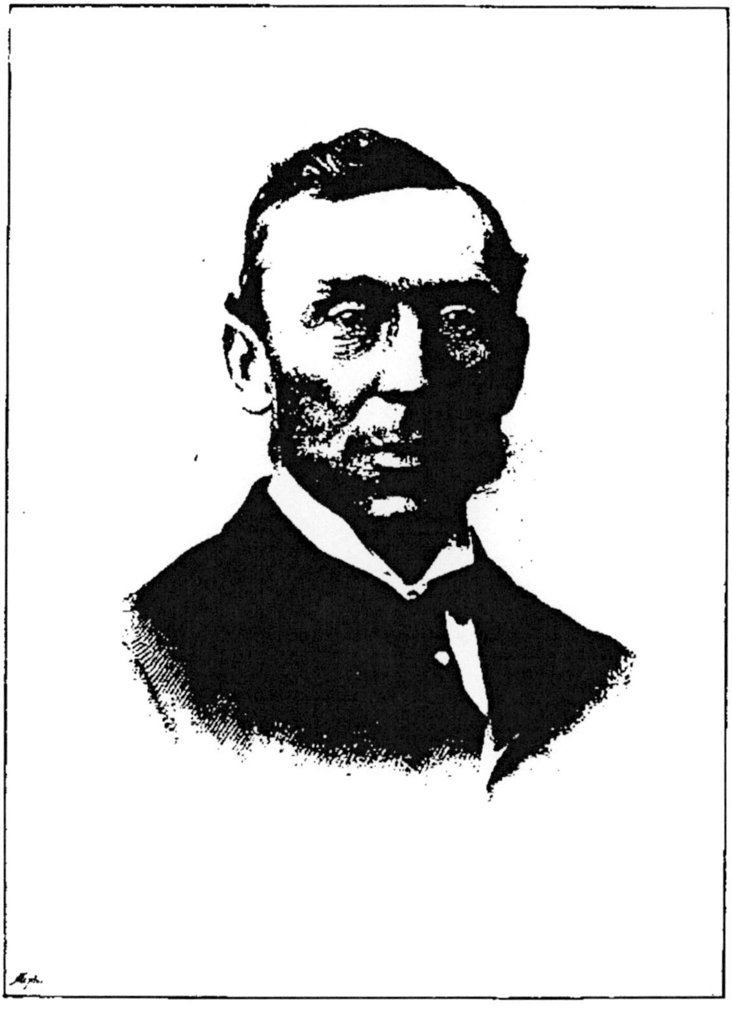

Photo. by Dickinson, 114 New Bond Street.

MR JOHN PORTER.

Porter
1894

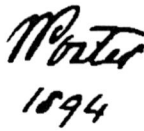

which I had brought with me, and which I hope has proved
useful to him. We had a long talk about breaking-in young
horses for racing, and he thoroughly agreed with me that
yearlings would be greatly benefited by a course of modified
school work, before being ridden in regular exercise. I may
explain that the proportion of weight which the forelegs
have to support will be greater when the horse is mounted
on account of the foreward position of the rider, than when
he is at liberty. Consequently, saddle-horses are apt to 'go
too much on the forehand,' and their forelegs are more liable
to suffer from the injurious effects of work, than are their hind
limbs. The kind of school drill which I have indicated,
would, to a certain extent, correct this tendency to surcharge
the forehand, by teaching the animal to go in a more
'collected' form than he would naturally do. I need hardly
say that a horse as a rule will travel best when the distribution
of the weight borne, respectively, by his fore and hind limbs, is
preserved as nearly as possible in its natural position. We
know from experience that a horse which is constantly ridden
by a competent rider, learns after a time to go in a 'well-
balanced' style ; but, while receiving such tuition, his forelegs
are much more exposed to injury, than if he had not a
weight on his back. Besides, an instructor on foot, can
teach his pupil quicker, more effectively, and with far less
risk to tendon and ligament, than he could do were he in the
saddle.

Mr Porter, I need hardly say, is one of the most famous
trainers of all time ; having brought to the post, among
many hundreds of other winners, such great horses as
Rosicrucian, Blue Gown, Pero Gomez, Isonomy, Bend Or,
Geheimniss, St Blaise, Common, La Flêche, Orme, and
Ormonde, who was undoubtedly the best horse that ever
carried silk or satin. It was a great pleasure to me to meet
him.

During this year, which we spent in England, we saw a
great deal of Captain Fitzgerald (late of the 16th Lancers),

who used to keep the Royal Military Riding School in Gloucester Crescent, Bayswater. He was a most enthusiastic 'school' teacher, and was particularly partial to the instruction of ladies in the various *airs de manège*. Probably, the two best *écuyères* he turned out were Miss Nellie Reid and 'Mlle. Jenny,' who is at present a well-known *haute école* exponent in France. Baron de Vaux says:—'*Miss Jenny est d'origine anglaise ; c'est une fort belle personne qui a obtenu presque autant de succès comme femme que comme écuyère.* He was anxious for me to join him; but the roving fit was strong on me, and I wanted to see new countries and to acquire more knowledge about horses. Besides, I did not think there was much profit to be obtained from keeping a riding-school. The rent is terrible, hay and corn bills and wear and tear of horse flesh are awful, the slack season is appalling, and the fees have been cruelly cut down by competition. Had the financial aspect of the business been promising, I would have gladly co-operated with Captain Fitzgerald; as he is one of the nicest men I have ever met. He has marvellously charming manners, and is consequently a great favourite with ladies, some of whom were inclined to try his good nature as regards his horses and school somewhat too highly. He has since then sold the business, and was lately, I am glad to say, made a Knight of Windsor. My old friend, Mr E. M. Owen, the well-known gentleman rider, now manages the establishment in his usual capable manner; for he has a *main de fer* under a *gant de velours*. They are not likely to put the 'comehether' on him.

Photo by Clarence Hailey, St John's Wood and Newmarket.

CHAPTER X.

Gibraltar—Malta—Duke of York—Duke and Duchess of Edinburgh—Cairo —Colonel Valentine Baker—General Grenfell—Horses in Egypt—Ceylon and its Planters—Breaking a Jibber—The Spanish Mail—Tubbing —Singapore—Mr Harry Abrams—Horses from Western Australia— Horsebreaking—Savage Horses—Wood Flooring for Stables.

TIRED of inaction we packed up the breaking bag, saddle box, and the old trunk, and sailed in the autumn of 1887 to Gibraltar, where I had a class composed of the officers of the garrison waiting for me, thanks to the kindness of Major Crookenden of the Royal Artillery, who had sent a flattering account of my doings at Woolwich to his brother gunners on the Rock. I saw several beautiful Spanish mules at Gibraltar. The horses and ponies were a poor lot, being mostly Barbs, which look like under-bred and weedy Arabs. From careful inquiries made there, at Malta and in Egypt, I would say that the horses of Northern Africa are fully 3 stone inferior to the true Sons of the Desert. Though useful slaves, they are as a rule deficient in spirit. At Malta I had a big class largely composed of naval officers from the flag-ship, Alexandra. These fine young sailors (Mr Colville and Mr Lambton, the brother of the well-known gentleman rider, among others) were enthusiastic lovers of horses, and had a large number of polo ponies, which they generally managed to take with them wherever they went. As I used to hold my breaking classes on The Marsa, a level piece of open ground about a mile and a half outside the city of Valetta, on which polo is played and the races are held, I often saw the Duke of York play polo. He was an enthusiast about the game, rode hard, and was greatly liked by his shipmates, of whom I saw a good deal, both at my class and in the Union Club in the Strada Reale. Among the officers of the fleet, the Duke of Edinburgh was also popular and respected. In the afternoons, I usually saw him and his nephew playing billiards at the club. The young prince seemed full of fun and life, and was well able to take his own part all round. He always seemed to particularly enjoy the fact of his being able to beat his uncle at billiards. Both in Malta and at Cairo I was singularly unlucky in being unable to get any wild or vicious horses with which to 'show off' at my classes. I need hardly say that such instruction, however useful it may be, can be greatly brightened up by practical illustrations of an exciting and dangerous kind. My failure to obtain a single good case at Malta, where all the animals were of the 'dead' quiet sort, was very galling to me; for the Duchess and her daughters did me the honour, on three or four occasions, to come to my class on The Marsa. At Alexandria, on the contrary, where my class was only a small one, I had several good show horses and a couple of refractory mules. Such is life! Thanks to the friendly offices of poor Colonel Valentine Baker, 'Bobby' Kekewich of my old regiment and others, I had a large gathering at Cairo, where I saw a good deal of Colonel Baker. He had singularly charming manners, and was loved by everyone who knew him. General Grenfell was also a member of the class. He is a real sportsman as well as a fine soldier. Captain Astley tells me that General Grenfell was a subaltern in the 60th Rifles, with thirteen years' service, when he went home with him in 1871. Since then he has made up a lot of lost time in promotion.

The horses in Egypt are mostly Syrian Arabs, which are about intermediate in merit between Desert Arabs and Barbs. Animals bred in Egypt from Arab sires and dames, lose a good deal of the Arab type, in that they tend to become long on the leg and 'weedy.' About ten years before the time of which I am writing, I had the pleasure of being introduced by Artin Bey to that great lover of horses, Ali Pasha Shereef, who showed me over his stables. From their inspection, and from what Colonel Baker and other good judges have told me, I am convinced that very few good Arabs go to Egypt, where their average price is about £22.

From Egypt we went on to Ceylon, where, practically, no horses are bred; those that are used being imported from India or Australia. Within the tropics, at altitudes but little higher than the sea level, it is impossible to rear good riding or driving animals. As regards the raising of stock, increased height above the sea has the same effect as increased distance from the equator. Thus, on the mountains of northern Sumatra, which is close to that imaginary line, are to be found a breed of ponies unsurpassed for strength and endurance. The hill country of Ceylon is too small in extent, and too ill provided with pasture, to allow on it the production of useful horses or ponies. I had a pleasant and profitable tour among the planters of that island; as they are extremely hospitable and are devoted to horses. They are as good in work as in sport, and have proved their pluck by the successful battle they have fought against many difficulties. Up to about the year 1867 the growing of coffee was to them like the working of Robinson's good mine in South Africa. They lived like princes and raced with thoroughbreds specially imported from England and Australia. And then the crash came and all but ruined them. As a remedy, they seized upon cinchona, which under their diligent hands produced so much quinine that that valuable antiperiodic fell in price from ten shillings to two shillings an ounce, and had then to be all but abandoned. Cocoanuts and cocoa brought, in a few instances, relief to financial strain: till tea, in an incredibly short time, has made them prosperous. The abundant moisture and warmth in the Ceylon planting districts, render the ground eminently fitted for the production of 'leaf': even more so than for that of berry. The fear, which I sincerely trust is unfounded, hangs over these fine fellows that the light soil of their land may in time become exhausted, and that 'red spider' and blight may ruin their tea industry. If that day does come, which I fervently pray may be long postponed, it will find the brave planters full of resource and courage. I have sojourned among planters in Tirhoot, Chumparun, Assam, Cachar, Kangra, Wynaad, and Ceylon, and have carried away only one impression about them, and that is, that for hospitality, sporting feeling, and entire absence of 'side,' they are not to be surpassed.

The only breaking incident worthy of notice which I can recall in connection with Ceylon, was that of a bad jibber whose owner, at one of my classes, insisted on seeing if I could make his animal start kindly in harness. As this gentleman was the superintendent of several tea-gardens, I could not very well refuse his request to be served first. On ordinary occasions, I was always allowed my own discretion in choosing the order of taking the horses which were brought to me to experiment upon, and naturally liked to commence with a frisky one or two, so as to give some zest to the proceedings, and to keep the sulky ones to the end, by which time I would have had an opportunity of winning the confidence and goodwill of my audience. As this gentleman appeared to 'fancy himself' a good deal about his knowledge of horses, I thought of a way to pay him out and at the same time to utilise his influence in increasing the numbers of my class. Accordingly

A Jibber.

I said I would take his horse as my first subject, and that I would handle no other until I had driven it all over the place, which was a feat that had never been done before. I begged the gentlemen present to bear patiently with me; for the breaking of such a determined jibber, as this one was, could not be accomplished in a hurry; and then I commenced the job. As horses have extremely retentive memories, I knew that it would be hopeless trying to get this one to start by using any of the signals with which he was only too well acquainted. Hence I carefully refrained from hitting him with the whip, 'clicking' to him with my tongue, or speaking to him. I put on him an 'open' bridle (one without blinkers), attached to it a pair of long reins, and commenced to turn, circle him and rein him back. Whenever I wanted him to start, I slightly raised my right hand as a signal, which he readily learned to obey, as it was new to him, and was consequently unconnected in his mind with any idea of punishment or of contest between him and his driver. Contrary to my usual practice, I did not vouchsafe a word of explanation to my class, but kept on mutely doing my best to break the horse according to my own way. After an hour or so, I got into the dog-cart to which I had harnessed the horse, started him off, pulled him up, started him again, and drove him in every direction I was asked. The owner was delighted; he thanked me warmly, and allowed me to go on with the class in the way I thought best. Next morning when I came down at the appointed hour to the breaking-ground, I saw my pupils all assembled with the owner of the jibber looking as if he was in a particularly sulky mood. I asked him how his horse was, and hoped he had had a pleasant drive. 'He is just as bad as ever,' he replied. I accordingly went up to the horse, which had been led up to our place of meeting, changed his usual harness-bridle for an open one, took hold of the reins, got on to the box-seat, slightly raised my right hand, and off he started as 'kindly' as possible. Thereupon the owner's face beamed with pleasure, and he called out to me to let him take the ribbons; for he saw, so he said, that he had made the mistake of using a bridle with blinkers. I made no reply; but got down and handed him the reins. He jumped up, 'clicked' to him, gave him a job in the mouth with the reins, and was surprised beyond measure that the animal stuck his fore legs out in front and refused to move a yard. To make matters worse, he cut the horse with the whip, and after trying in vain every-thing he knew to make him start, he relinquished the attempt and began to blame *me!* My reply was again to take the reins, get into the trap, and start the horse off as easily as I had done before. 'You see,' I said to my class, 'how unreasonable this gentleman is. I have shown him the correct method of accomplishing the task he set me. Instead of adopting it, he tries to make the horse start according to his own way, and because it fails, he blames me.' I then explained how I had attained my end with the horse, for no one had observed the slight signal I had given to the animal with my right hand; and pointed out how much more useful it would be for me to be allowed to teach, than to exhibit proof of my own skill. I then had all the class on my side, including my late task-master. With hardly an exception, my pupils have met me in the most generous spirit, and have been inclined to give me more credit than was my due. I would not have mentioned the foregoing incident, had it not been one which is always apt to occur to a teacher of breaking, and which illustrates certain useful points about horses.

Ceylon is an intensely interesting country to a miner-alogist who, like myself, is fond of the study of precious stones. As that science is not within the scope of this book, I must not write about it here.

We left Ceylon, bound for Singapore, on the Spanish mail boat, *Isla de Mindanao*. This fine and well-appointed steamer carried forty-five first-class passengers, all Spaniards except ourselves, and including about a dozen priests. The food, cooked *à l'Espagnole*, was excellent. At meals there was un unlimited supply of free wine, of good quality and of various kinds. Contrary to hearsay and tradition, there was not on board a single guitar, or any resemblance to one, with the exception of my wife's banjo! Our fellow-passengers appeared an amiable lot of people; but as only one or two of them knew French, and only one of them spoke English, and as we knew only a few words of Spanish, our conversations with them were naturally short. Having learned at Gibraltar something about the ways of the inhabitants of the Peninsula, I bargained, before taking our passage, that there was to be no extra charge for baths, for which the others were liable to be charged three *pesetas;* a sum equivalent to half-a-crown. This was high, considering that the material used was simply cold sea water, without any hot water or steam thrown in. The Spaniards treated the extortion with admirable forbearance; for, with only one recorded exception, they refrained from bathing during the voyage. In fact, they were quite as dirty in this respect as were English people of good birth a hundred years ago. We roving Englishmen and Irishmen, having adopted from the Hindus the practice of daily ablutions, are accustomed to boast about it as a national characteristic. This tubbing custom has not been adopted very willingly by us, else we would not flourish our bathing-towel and big sponge as obtrusively as we do in the face of less Indianised foreigners. The chaste and brave are not those who respectively talk most about their virtue and their courage. Leaving out such bold innovators as soldiers, sailors, 'varsity and public school men, I venture to say that the average lower middle-class Briton does not have a bath oftener than once a month, and the ordinary British workman not more frequently than once a quarter. There is a good deal of truth in the old story about two workmen who, during the annual excursion given by their employer to his people, went bathing. One, observing the state of his companion's skin, made a remark about its being dirty. 'That's nothing,' replied the other, 'I missed last year's outing.' Then again, there is the ancient retort that persons who tub every day must be very filthy to require so much washing. In that respect, women seem to be the greatest sinners, as we can have ample proof if we inquire at any of the London vestry baths about the respective proportions of male and female bathers. We of course remember Edmund About's Italian young lady, who being questioned as to her fondness for tubbing, exclaimed, ' What ! I a noble Roman maiden to wash my body with *water !* Never ! I sometimes lave it with milk.' Not long ago, when staying for a few days at the only hotel in the Dutch village of Boxtel, I asked mine host if I could have a bath. He replied that there was no such thing in the place. I inquired as to the procedure adopted by the inhabitants when they desired to wash themselves all over. He answered that they did so in the river, or went without. I followed up by demanding to know if the ladies, also, bathed in the river; to which he exclaimed that Dutch vrows respected themselves too much to be guilty of any such impropriety. I could not help thinking that were I a young bachelor, I would not come to Boxtel for a sweetheart.

The approach to Singapore through the narrow Straits, which open into the China Sea, and which are studded with beautifully-wooded islands, is singularly picturesque. Being close to the equator, the whole face of the undulating land is covered by an extraordinary wealth and variety of tree and plant life : but it is the worst place for a ' show ' I have ever been in. There are a fairly large number of white men who, for the most part, belong to local mercantile houses, in the transaction of the business of which, they spend the greater portion of their forenoons and afternoons, and having done their work, they flit off to their residences, which dot the surrounding country at distances between, say, two to six miles from the city. Consequently, during the evenings and early morning, no one who can afford to sleep out of Singapore remains in it. This custom is delightful from a social and domestic point of view ; but is abominable to a showman, who, to make his

Singapore.

'ex.'s,' must have his audience close at hand. The dismal tales which I heard of companies stranded at this gate of the Far East were quite enough to make me give up the idea of a performance. We stayed on, however, for about ten days to see the place; to eat that most delicious of all Eastern fruits, the mangosteen; and to enjoy the congenial society of Mr Harry Abrams, who keeps a large horse repository at Singapore, and who, in the kindest possible manner, placed all his horses at our disposal; so we had more than enough to ride and drive during our stay. Having graduated in John Dawson's training stable, he is a fine horseman both on the flat and across country, and is the best man I have ever seen at driving a team of 'difficult' horses, such as, for instance, four 'scrubbers' which had never had a bridle on their heads before being yoked to his brake, which he generally succeeded in making them draw after a more or less prolonged fight. Had I held a class, I could have got an abundant supply of unruly subjects upon which to have shown off my skill; for Abrams's yard was full of freshly-landed Western Australians, than whom there are no more sulky brutes in the form of horses. They are bred promiscuously, and are 'taken up' so late that the process of breaking seems to destroy the little scrap of 'heart' they might have originally possessed. They appear to have only two faults, namely, they are very hard to break, and when they are broken they are no good. Tom Sayers or Jem Mace, at his best, was downright slow in 'popping in the left' compared to one of these unhandled brutes.

I may here explain that the vicious Australian horses which I encountered in India, Ceylon, and Singapore, though infinitely more difficult to reduce to obedience than any to be found in the United Kingdom, had all gone through the discipline of a voyage of at least a month on board ship, in which they had to stand in a narrow stall, tied up to the manger. The fact of their having head collars on, in no way proved that they would allow themselves to be bridled or

K

their heads touched without making a desperate resistance ; because, no matter how wild a horse may be, the Australian rough riders easily manage to put a head collar on him by driving him into a 'crush,' in which he can be securely fixed. A crush, I may remark, consists, as a rule, of two rows, seven or eight feet long, and about two and a half feet wide, of strong posts let into the ground, and provided with pieces of wood which can be used to block up both ends. Such an erection may be used for the entrance into one paddock from another, in which case, any of the horses passing through can be detained and tied up. Sometimes the crush is made to open out, so that the captive, after having been forcibly bridled, saddled, and mounted, can be suddenly let free with full permission to kick his rider off, if he is able. Although these imported horses have had some of the 'rough edge' taken off them, they are, on arrival, difficult to manage, and as they are rarely less than four years old when they are caught and put on board, they are naturally inclined to fight on being handled or backed. Being all either geldings or mares, very few of my Colonial pupils had the vice of biting, which is generally confined to entires. I have had a great number of so-called man-eating East-Indian and Arab stallions pass through my hands, as well as horses of all degrees both at home and abroad ; but have never known a single instance of a horse, outside his own stall, actually attacking with his teeth a man who faced him ; although many animals will make a feint of doing so. I will go farther and say that I do not believe that there is a horse in the world which, in any open place, would try his best to 'savage' a man who guarded himself with a stick held in a direction across the animal's face. Although this statement may be received with incredulity by many ; I not alone adhere to it, but am prepared at any time to prove it practically. Naturally, I shall have cited the case of Cruizer, who was secured only by Rarey hiding under a cart loaded with hay, which occupied the animal's attention while the

Wood Flooring for Stables.

American, from his place of security, fixed his hobbles on the horse's fore-legs. But we must remember that Rarey was a showman who studied how best to impress his audience. As a cart and load of hay were too bulky 'properties' to find a place either in my breaking bag or Gladstone, I made a rule in all cases of reputed man-eaters who were brought to me, to turn them loose in the ring and then to catch and halter them unaided by anyone; a process which occupied only a few minutes. Up to the present, I have described the breaking only of horses which, though difficult and dangerous to handle, had been subjected to a certain amount of discipline. When I come to the account of my travels in South Africa, I shall have plenty to say about the breaking-in of horses which, until they had been driven into the enclosure round which my class used to congregate to see the fun, had never been approached, let alone been touched, by man. I beg my readers to understand that I give the unvarnished tale of my adventures, without any attempt to claim the possession of any peculiar power over horses (which I certainly have not), or of pluck superior to that of other people. Wherever I went, I left behind pupils who, after having been taught by me, were quite as capable of successfully handling vicious horses, as I am. The whole question is one of knowledge and experience.

At the Strait's Settlement, I saw, for the first time, boards used for the flooring of stables. This plan, which I have subsequently seen practised in China, Japan, and Natal, appears to me excellent. Wood, from the fact of its being a bad conductor of heat, protects from chill the horse's feet, while he is standing; and his body, when he is lying down. Besides this, the interstices between the boards provide an efficient surface drainage. I may remark that a damp place for standing horses causes thrush and cracked heels; and a cold one, various foot troubles. Chill, as we all know, gives rise to coughs, colds and chest affections. Those of us who have travelled much are well aware of the great difference as far as warmth is concerned, between sleeping on the wooden deck of a ship, and on the ground. Even with straw on stone or earth, we cannot always insure the certainty of the horse's bedding remaining unshifted and dry. It is instructive to note that navicular disease is particularly rife among horses which stand for the most part on cold stones. It is notorious that cavalry horses which have only paving-stones under them during the day, are often affected by this complaint; although their work is of a comparatively light description. I need hardly say that as the custom of the horse, when in a state of nature, is to keep moving about while grazing, the circulation of blood in his feet quickly becomes impeded during confinement, and that this tendency to stagnation of blood in the extremities will be favoured by the contact of the feet with a good conductor of heat, like stone or earth. The effect of cold being to drive the blood away from the chilled part, it will, if unduly prolonged, be apt to give rise to inflammation on the return of the blood to the blood-vessels, especially, if the renewed circulation be strongly stimulated. The fact that blood vessels which have been deprived of their contents for a considerable time, become inflamed by the return of this fluid, is well demonstrated by cases of frost-bite.

A good way to make a wood flooring for a stall or loose box, is, first of all, to put down a layer of smooth concrete, which of course should be waterproof, and to have it slope two or three inches outwards, and also towards its centre, so as to ensure drainage. A slightly-raised ledge, about four inches wide, upon which the planks could rest, might run down each side. The boards might be nine inches wide by three or four inches thick, and should be placed close to each other. It would be well to slightly bevel off the sharp edges of the planks, which, if required, might be saturated with some appropriate preservative application, such as creosote. Drainage between the boards might be provided for by notches on their sides, if necessary. When the animal leaves the stall, the planks should be taken up, and the concrete flooring thoroughly cleaned. Straw used for bedding lasts much longer on these planks, than on ordinary floors; as it remains longer clean, and does not get cut up so much.

LEEN KWANG, A CHINA RACING PONY.

CHAPTER XI.

The Blue Funnel Line—'We have never lost a Passenger'—Lascar Crews—Steering on Land—Chinese Boatmen—Hong Kong—China Ponies—Racing in China -Buckstone and Tim Whiffler— Mr Fraser Smith—Bandmann—Shanghai—Mongolian Ponies—Mr Kelly Maitland—Small Feet -Society in Shanghai—Shanghai Race Club—Horsebreaking at Shanghai—Rickshaws—Gambling for Food—Tientsin—Mr Butler Mafoos The French Mail—Japan—Hotels and Food.

HAVING been rendered thoughtful by our failure to organise a performance in Singapore, and having a new country before us, we took tickets by the ss. *Jason* of the Blue Funnel Line, the fares of which are cheap, and the boats though small and slow, are well-manned by white crews, and are carefully navigated. This cannot be said of some of the steamers on that coast. By the evidence given in the *Aratoon Apcar* and *Hebe* collison case, it appeared that the man in charge of the latter, which used to trade between Singapore and Sumatra, was, at the time of the accident, a 'black

The Blue Funnel Line.   151

gunner;' that the steersman did not know the points of the compass, and that the man on the look-out had been only seven months at sea. Mr Holt, the chief owner of the Blue Funnel Line, being a careful man, enacts the adoption of special precautions from his skippers, such as giving other vessels and dangerous land a wide berth, and not entering harbours after dusk or before dawn. An old captain of this line was once severely chaffed at a dinner party, for his cautious style of navigation, by a young manager of a rival line which had adopted close-shaving and go-a-head principles, with somewhat disastrous results ; and was sneeringly asked if he did not know every rock between Singapore and the Taku Forts. 'Long ago,' replied the old mariner, 'I used to think I did; but of late, your ships have knocked them about so much, that they have got mixed up a good deal, and I am unable to recognise many of them.' The old 'shellback' was allowed to finish his dinner in peace.

I like a safe line, and for that reason would prefer the Blue Funnel to many others engaged in the Eastern trade. Feeling secure on board Mr Holt's steamers, we readily attack, with what appetite the sea allows us, the somewhat primitive meals put on the table, and think of the traveller on the Cunard boat who received, it is said, to every complaint made, the invariable excuse : 'We have never lost a passenger.' If he demanded a clean napkin, the steward would blandly reply: 'Sorry we have got none, sir; but we have never lost a passenger.' If a remark was made on the rancidity of the butter, the table attendant would complacently say: 'It is certainly not quite sweet ; but we have never lost a passenger.' And so on.

The only Eastern line, judging from the many journeys I have made, that, to my mind, combines every requirement of safety and comfort, is the *Messageries Maritimes*. The black crews of the P. and O. steamers, largely recruited as they are from boatmen who possess but little knowledge of, or experience in seamanship, do not inspire me with confidence. Even the natives, who navigate their lateen-rigged craft round the Indian coast, are only fair-weather sailors who put into port and strike work when the monsoons commence to blow. The effect of climate on the manufacture of seamen is well shown by the difference between those of the Levant and Scandinavia. The native sailors are cheap; they are amenable to discipline in fine weather; they do not get drunk; in port they keep 'lascar watch' (a continued case of 'all hands') when loading and unloading, without grumbling; and consequently meet the requirements of the shareholders, who evidently regard the matter, principally, from a cargo point of view, which is the best 'paying' one. The man who asserts that in times of danger and in moments when self-sacrifice is demanded for the saving of the lives of women and children, a crew composed of Asiatics, is the equal of an English or Scandinavian one, is either a wilful economiser of the truth, or is wholly ignorant of the literature of shipwrecks. I once asked the captain of an M. M. steamer if their line did not employ, like the Spanish Compania Transatlantica, Scotch or English engineers. 'No,' he replied, 'our country gives us a large subsidy for carrying her mails, and expects in return that we shall employ only Frenchmen.' How differently they manage things in England, I am sorry to say. My seafaring acquaintances who have had long experience with Chinese crews, and with whom I have spoken on the subject of the qualifications of these Asiatics, tell me that these men, like their Indian counterparts, are all right when it is fine; but that they are unreliable and apt to give in to fate, when the weather is bad. I ask my itinerant readers, to whom should they accord their patronage? To lines that regard the saving of money, and the facility of loading and unloading cargo, as more important matters than the lives of passengers? I am convinced that the apathy displayed respecting this subject by travellers, is chiefly due to ignorance, and that if the fact of certain lines employing Lascar crews, and others white men, was prominently put before them, they would soon show to whom they prefer entrusting their own lives, and those of their wives and children.

The fact of experienced owners confiding valuable vessels to Lascar crews, might be advanced as an argument to prove their reliability. It fortunately happens that occasions of extreme peril at sea, to cope with which the Lascar is unfit by reason of his want of dogged pluck, of physical strength, and of capacity to endure cold, occur so rarely, that the pecuniary loss thus entailed is, on an average, less than the money saved by their employment. I need hardly say that this principle is the same as that of habitually working ships short-handed. Were the value of the lost lives debited to the Lascar-loving companies, how long, may I ask, would they be able to run their ships under the present system? Again, the manner in which these Lascars are recruited, is often wholly vicious; for it frequently happens that the native boatswain '*tindal*) ' raises ' the crew, who, having gained their position by his favour, naturally regard him, and not the captain, as their master. Such a practice is open to the most glaring abuses. Besides, in none of the Lascar-carrying lines, not even in the P. and O., is there a test demanded of the captain and officers as to their knowledge of Hindustanee. It would be ridiculous to say that it is sufficient if the *tindal*, who is the supposed mouthpiece of the captain and officers, understands English; for peril at sea does not always approach with such slow and measured steps, as to justify imperative loss of time in summoning the interpreter and in getting him to translate orders? Besides, it is as impossible for him to be ubiquitous, as it is for him to be secure from accident or sickness. I grant that the crew, as a rule, understand the general purport of the usual words of command used in making or shortening sail, and other ordinary evolutions; but nothing further. Is this a satisfactory state of things? I appeal to my readers if any ship which has to fight against wind, water, rocks and fire, can be called efficient, if its respective officers and men cannot make themselves mutually and readily intelligible? The foregoing remarks are made with reference to ocean-going steamers, and not to coasters, which spend almost as much time in port, taking in and discharging cargo, as they do at sea.

After all this talk about nautical matters, I have no doubt that some of my maritime readers will ask: 'What does he know about ships?' Not very much, I grant, except from a passenger's point of view, and of that I have had a lot of experience. Were I to undertake the navigation of a ship in a crowded channel, I might fare no better than did the skipper who, having hired a dog-cart, ran into another conveyance one night when driving down a street. When asked how the collison happened, he explained, that having seen two lights on his starboard bow, he steered right between them. They happened to be carriage lamps.

It was thorough punkah weather when we left Singapore, and continued blazing even to Hong Kong, which has a lovely harbour that appears land-locked on every side, when looking from the town, behind which a steep mountain rises in green and wooded array.

The boatmen of Hong Kong, together with their wives and children, form a large floating population. Each of the open row boats, or *sampans*, which take passengers to and from the shipping in the harbour, has, like a conjuror's box, a false bottom, that on being lifted up will generally reveal a nest of chubby little urchins who play, sleep, eat and have their food cooked in a sort of cockpit, not quite two feet high. The sampan which took us on shore, was handled, as is often the custom, by women. We had not proceeded far before I was surprised at hearing under my feet rippling sounds of laughter, and at seeing thin wreaths of smoke arising from the centre of the boat. I hastily pulled up a plank, and found three or four fat little toddles trying experiments at cooking.

Although a considerable portion of the population of China lives in boats on the rivers and harbours, not one of these wretched heathens will, if his dearest friend tumble into the water by accident, stretch out a hand to save him; for he firmly believes that such a rescued one would infallibly do his saviour a mortal injury on some future occasion. The parents who rear up families in boats, partly get over this difficulty by having their wee bairns secured round the waist to the sampan by a cord, which they regard as a perfectly legitimate article to be manipulated at pleasure. Consequently, if a child happens to be attached to the end of a rope which is being hauled in out of the water, no breach of etiquette will have been committed. Although they are well aware that in case of accident, not one of their own people will attempt to save them, these quaint folk delight to shoot their crafts across the bows of any passing steamer, so that they may escape being run down and swamped by the closest possible shave; not, strange to say, with the understandable object of recovering damages for nervous shock; but because they think it lucky. They played this game on Chiarini without, however, consulting him in the slightest, when attempting to land a couple of performing elephants at Amoy for this well-known circus proprietor. The elephants being uneasy, as they might well be, when handed over to the tender mercies of the Chinese, were chained down to a barge which was to have taken them on shore from a ship that had brought them into the harbour. Just at that time, an outward-bound steamer, which was leaving her moorings, gave the Chinamen a chance which they could not resist, with the result that the barge got run down and the elephants were drowned.

China gives us many proofs of the strong love which Englishmen have for racing. The island of Hong Kong is so hilly that the only place where one can ride, except on the hard roads, is the Happy Valley, which is a level piece of somewhat marshy ground, surrounded, except on the side facing the sea, by high and wooded hills. Around it runs the racecourse, which is about seven furlongs in length. This galloping track consists of good turf and has a slight rise and fall on the far side. The ground in the centre is utilised for cricket and other sports. Although there is in Hong Kong hardly any riding, and the driving is confined to man-carts or jinrickshaws as they are called, there is an annual meeting in February, at which there used to be very heavy betting; wagers of ten thousand dollars being not unknown. I may remark that the population consists of about 3000 'foreigners' (or white men) and a garrison of one regiment of infantry and some heavy artillery. All the races are confined to China ponies, a term that is applied to the Mongolians which are imported from Manchuria, and which are all geldings. Practically speaking there are no horses or ponies bred in China. Almost all the ponies which run in Hong Kong have their permanent quarters in Shanghai, and come down south to train, two or three months before this three days' meeting comes off. The custom used to be, and continues still for all I know to the contrary, for about half-a-dozen of these races to be confined to 'subscription' griffens (recently imported ponies that have never run), which, to the number of thirty or forty, are bought, all round, at one hundred and fifty dollars each from the Shanghai Horse Bazaar Company, on the understanding that all these animals are able to do three-quarters of a mile, with weight for height up, in 1 minute 40 seconds; and are distributed by lot among the subscribers. The weight for height of an animal just under 14 hands (fractions of inches do not count in China) would be 11 st. 6 lbs. Such a test, though quite severe enough for China, would be a ridiculously moderate one for English, Australian, Arab, or Indian ponies.

Sir Robert Jardine, who subsequently won a large number of races in England, played 'the great game' in China, where he was a partner of the house of Jardine Matheson more than a quarter of a century ago. He gave four thousand guineas for Buckstone just after this horse won the Ascot Cup in 1863, and had him brought out to run in China; for in those days the races were open to all horses, and there was extremely keen rivalry between the great houses of Dent and Jardine. Buckstone, who was bound for Shanghai, did not go beyond Hong Kong; for soon after his arrival, he got twist of the intestines and died. Bob Sherwood, at that time, used to train and ride for the Jardines in China. Since then he has become famous as the trainer of St Gatien, Florence, Goldstone (remembered by Mr Barnard), Merry Prince, who no doubt lingers in the memory of Mr John Hammond, and many others. As the giving of thousands of pounds for racehorses was beyond the ability of all except a select few in China, and as the house of Dent fell from its high estate, horse racing gave way to pony racing, which was within the reach of all, with the remarkable result that the Shanghai sportsmen are able to have three days' racing of eight events a day, with large fields, and without a single handicap or selling race. The fact that the secretary receives for each meeting entries for about two hundred ponies, about three-fourths of which are griffens, satisfactorily accounts for this most desirable state of things.

The mention of Buckstone's name reminds me of his great rival Tim Whiffler, who was trained by William Martin, with whom, while we strolled over Newmarket Heath, I have had, more than once, a talk about Tim, whose defeat, with Sam Rogers up, by Buckstone was a terrible disappointment to the Fitzroy House trainer. Rogers did not ride to orders; but lay out of his ground, instead of making the running, as he ought to have done, and as he was told to do, with this marvellous stayer. Edwin Martin, the trainer, was riding another horse in the race, and, having been early beaten, entreated Rogers, as he dropt back, to put on more steam; but all to no avail. The Martins are confident that the race was 'all wrong,' and that Tim Whiffler was much the better horse.

Mr J. D. Humphreys is a Hong Kong sportsman whom I greatly admire. He loves to play the great game, and to back his opinion in thousands, not of 'chopped' Mexican dollars; but of golden sovereigns. He is a genuine, big-hearted man, with any amount of life and 'go,' and he is a first-rate loser. While at Hong Kong, I tried him somewhat highly in his last-mentioned character. As I wanted to show my class the easiest manner in which to make a pony lie down, I took one belonging to Mr Humphreys; selected a soft piece of deep sand on which to conduct the experiment; tied up one foreleg; pulled his head gently round to the other side; and down he went without a struggle, never to get up again; for he happened in some mysterious way to break his back. Mr Humphreys took the accident in as good part, as if he regarded it as a portion of the programme. I may mention that this is the only accident I have ever had in making a horse lie down.

Mr R. Fraser Smith, who, in the beginning of the seventies, was a well-known athlete and member of the London Athletic Club and other metropolitian associations, is a prominent figure in the society of the 'model colony,' as the editor of *Hong Kong Telegraph*. He is independent, honest, and a good hater; consequently, he has become, from conducting his own cases, the best authority in the Far East on the law of libel. His experience has been bought not very cheaply, either in the matter of fines or of imprisonment. On one occasion he was sentenced, most unjustly I think, to two months for libelling Bandmann, who, though a great actor, had an extraordinary faculty for getting himself disliked. The last I heard of him was that he was conducting a dime show in New York. Mr Smith seems to have profited by his experience in the cinder path, for he is the best trainer of ponies in Hong Kong.

A run of a day and a half by steamer took us to Amoy, which in old days was a favourite place of resort for Chinese pirates, who now happily confine their raids to the junks of their own countrymen; and three days more brought us into the mouth of the Yangtse, which carries into the ocean a larger volume of water than any other river of the Old World.

During the summer it is navigable for more than 1000

Shanghai. 159

miles by ships of any tonnage. After steaming up the Yangtse for nearly forty miles, we came to the bar of the Wangpoo or Shanghai river, where we waited a few hours for the tide. Near at hand, we saw the Red Buoy, the famous point from which the tea clippers used to start for their annual race to the London docks. That was the great sporting event of the year; but is now a thing of the past. Then, the winner got from £5 to £6 a ton, with no bill of coals, and no wear and tear to machinery. Steamers, at the time of my visit, were taking tea from Hankow at a pound a ton, which is twelve shillings net, after deducting eight shillings a ton for Suez Canal dues; that is, at the rate of about a shilling a ton per thousand miles. Hankow, I may explain, is nearly 700 miles up the Yangtse river. It is the great centre of the tea trade, and is the place at which the tea steamers take in their cargoes of leaf. Shanghai is about twelve miles above the bar at Woosung. The chief business part of Shanghai consists of a line of fine buildings nearly three-quarters of a mile long, on the left bank of the Wangpoo. A broad and well-kept road, called the Bund, runs between the line of houses and the river, which is well supplied with jetties and quays. The Bund forms the front of the English settlement, which occupies about a square mile of ground. The Soochow Creek, which is about 100 yards broad, is on the left of the Bund. and separates the English and American concessions from each other. The Yang King Pang, which is a broad ditch, performs a like office on the right, for the French and English possessions. One of the principal streets in the Ma Loo (Horse Road), which begins about the centre of the Bund, and which extends to the rear, at right angles to the Bund, for a mile, up to the bridge over the Defence Creek, after crossing which we see the racecourse on our left and a row of detached villas on our right. After passing the entrance to the enclosure of the Grand Stand, we find both sides of the road occupied by charmingly-built country houses, with tastefully laid-out grounds and gardens; until, on going for about a mile further, we reach the Bubbling Well, which receives its name from the fact of its being in a constant, though mild state of effervescence. There the road branches off to the right and left; to return to the city, by the former; to be lost to view in the distance among well-tilled fields, by the latter route. Riding excursions and paper chasing are extensively indulged in during the cold weather in the open country.

We were not longer in Shanghai than three hours before Mr Barnes Dallas, the very courteous secretary of the Shanghai Turf Club, called on us, and, in the name of his club, hoped I would consider myself an honorary member, and gave us invitations to the sumptuous luncheons which were to be prepared for the stewards and their friends at the races that were about to come off. We felt deeply touched by the kindness of these gentlemen, and by the generous and friendly manner in which they received us. Our experience of the Shanghai folk, during our month's stay among them, was that they were the most hospitable and charming people we have ever met. They all own ponies, and nearly all race. Their Mongolian ponies are reared under very rough conditions, in their native steppes, having frequently, during the long winter of that Siberian climate, to scrape away the snow with their feet in order to get a mouthful of grass. Like Himalayan and Tibet ponies, they show they are wild and not domestic animals, by, when first brought down, their habit of shying. I have frequently noticed this vice in Hill ponies when riding through the Himalayas on shooting excursions; and was much impressed by the fact that, although my mount might plunge forward, or pirouette round without the slightest warning, at the sight of a falling leaf or rolling stone; the abrupt movement was always made with due regard to the animal's personal safety; and was quite different from the dangerous shy caused by defective sight, or the light-hearted one due to 'beans.' In fact, it was the instinctive action of a wild animal whose only means of security from foes, land-slips,

China Ponies. 161

and other dangers, is flight. As the Manchu Tartars do not catch them until they think they are fit for hard work, they are, when first taken in hand, extremely impatient of control 'a term which is more applicable to them than that of 'vicious', and are consequently difficult to break.

With their natural advantages of great bone and muscle, and hardy bringing-up, these Tartar ponies are grand animals for carrying weight, going long distances, and enduring hardships in a cold climate. I can see no difference between them, as far as type is concerned, and the ponies of the Himalayas, Tibet, and Yarkund. I remember, many years ago at Nainee Tal, winning flat and hurdle races on a Bhootiah pony, called Trooper, who was the 'dead image' of Teen Kwang (the Eclipse of the Celestial Empire), and who I feel certain was quite as good for his size. These Mongolians have, of course, no pretensions to racing form: neither have the Arab horses about which Bombay sportsmen are enthusiastic, if we are to judge them by a Newmarket, or even an Alexandra Park standard. Yet the China and Bombay men get large fields, close finishes, and excellent sport, all of which most desirable objects would have to be sacrificed, were speed alone sought for, by throwing open the races to faster classes of animals.

The 'griffens' are brought down in the spring of the year from Manchuria in large droves, thoroughly in the rough, fresh from their native snows, and wild as the metaphorical hawk. The Tartar importers, keen about their own interests, abstain, unless tempted beyond endurance, from selling any of their crowd on their way down, say, at Tientsin ; and shortly after arrival at Shanghai, put the ponies up to auction, at which the likely ones fetch prices varying from about £10 to £100. Were trials given, and the supposed pick of the basket taken out before the raising of the hammer, the remainder would fetch such small prices that the average would be much below that which would be obtained by putting up the entire lot. On rare occasions, some very 'fancy' prices are given,

L

the highest of which, within my knowledge, has been 3000 *taels* (which, at the time of purchase, was equivalent to 600 guineas!) by Mr D. E. Sassoon for the dun pony Harbinger, an animal that was easily beaten for the Champion Stakes by Mr Galles' Susewind. In England or in India, Harbinger would not have been worth more than £40.

In the early sixties, when Shanghai had an English garrison and Indian cavalry regiments, there were fairly well-filled races for Arabs and also for 'All Horses,' which class was chiefly represented by Australians. The Arab pony (I presume it was he who was meant) must have early established his claim to superiority; for I find that the race for the Imperial Cup, in April 1864, was 'for all ponies, Indians excluded; Manila and Straits ponies 14 lbs. extra.' Later on, the two last-mentioned classes were warned off the course; and from about 1868, the races have been confined, with the best results, to China ponies. When Anglo-Chinese sportsmen of but local experience wax enthusiastic over the racecourse performances of their sturdy Mongolian favourites, and assert, as I have heard them do, that their animals could hold their own, under the weight they have got to carry, and over the distance they are required to run, with ponies of any class; it is clear that they have not studied the history of their own turf.

Mention of old time racing in China naturally recalls to my mind the name of Mr R. Kelly Maitland, who, during the sixties, was one of the most prominent gentleman riders and owners in the Celestial Empire, and is now a well-known owner of racehorses in Australia. He was able to ride without wasting, the wonderfully nice weight for a G. R., of 8 st., or even 7 st. 12 lbs. As I was coming one day out of Jardine, Matheson's place in Shanghai, I knocked up by accident against a gentleman with grey hair, fresh complexion, and a pleasant face. As I stopped to apologise, he looked at me and asked with a smile, 'Aren't you Captain Hayes?' On hearing my 'yes,' he introduced himself as Mr Bush, who had been Mr Maitland's business partner in China. Going in the same direction as I was, and knowing that I had been acquainted with Mr Maitland in India, he began to talk about his old fellow-broker. 'Maitland and I,' he said, 'made lots of money. Twenty-five years ago I could have retired with £50,000, but nothing would do for Kelly but to be a millionaire; so I too kept on. While I was home for a short trip, he made several heavy speculations with such disastrous results that we both lost nearly all we had. He went to India, and I got stuck in that out-of-the-way spot Newchwang, where I shall be delighted to put you up, if ever you come that way. It was not Maitland's fault that we came to grief; it was only his ambition. Ah! you should have seen him in those days. What a swell he was! How he used to make the money fly! During all the years we were together, I always found him "straight."' And then the true-hearted, kind fellow gave me a clasp of the hand, a cheery nod, and walked off with as springy a step and as gay an air, as he no doubt had, while Kelly was manufacturing ducks and drakes out of that half million dollars.

Subsequently Mr Bush told me the following incident, which has been so unfairly misrepresented to Mr Maitland's detriment, that I am glad of this opportunity of giving its correct version.

Mr Maitland went to the Hong Kong races from Shanghai in 1863, with a lot of ponies, and was so successful that he and his party won about £10,000. Being unable to get the better of the little man in a fair game, some of the losers determined to vent their spite on him by means which were not above board. Seeing that Maitland had been enjoying the privileges of a visitor at the Hong Kong Club, his enemies managed to get a rule passed, apparently, only on general grounds, that a visitor could not be an honorary member for longer than six weeks, and that, if he desired to frequent the club after that period, he should be put up and balloted for in the usual manner. When Maitland's time of honorary membership was finished, his friends suspecting nothing and consequently taking no precautions, allowed him to be balloted for, as, so they thought, a mere matter of form, with the astounding result to them, that he was blackballed. Had his proposer and seconder any idea that the ballot would have gone against him, there is no doubt but that they would have got a sufficient number of favourable votes to have had him elected. In any case, they could have withdrawn his name and have saved him and themselves from the slight caused by their inadvertence. Mr Bush and other gentlemen assured me that this was the only approach to any 'unpleasantness' ever connected with Mr Maitland during his long career on the China turf. I may mention that he still retains the privilege of resuming his membership of the Shanghai Club, whenever he chooses to return.

Mr Maitland arrived in Calcutta from China with a couple of horses about the year 1870, and he continued to hold his own at 'the great game' with the best of them till 1880, when he departed for Australia. He was a very peppery little fellow, and took no trouble to conciliate the Indian brass gods by bowing down before them. Consequently, he was most unjustly treated on several occasions by the jacks in office. Although I took his part more than once, I had no sympathy for him in his rows; for by the employment of a very small amount of tact he might have had the said officials his devoted friends instead of his bitter enemies. If these bigwigs were asses for acting the part of piqued children, Mr Maitland was a still greater donkey for annoying them, especially as his part of the show was to make money.

At the races in China, the starting is horrible; because, as all the riders are amateurs, the club official does not like to assert his authority. This of course is utterly wrong. The story is told of Kelly Maitland going on at the start in a race in Australia, with some antics which he had, no doubt, often practised at Shanghai and Hong Kong. Mr Watson, who held the flag, did not at all approve of Kelly attempting 'to jump off in front,' or to come up from behind at a gallop while the others were walking. 'What are you doing, Mr Maitland?' asked the gentleman from Carlow. 'I can't hold my horse, sir,' was the reply. 'Then I'll fine you £10 for bringing a horse to me which you cannot hold,' was the starter's retort, which had an instantaneously good effect on Mr Maitland's mount. I may remark that under the Australian rules of racing, the starter has the summary power to fine up to £50 for disobedience (intentional or otherwise) at the post. This, to my thinking, is a most excellent ordinance.

The North China custom of women having small feet, causes much inconvenience to foreigners when out for a drive; for these crippled ladies, with the combined perversity of their race and sex, always select their time of crossing a street, at the moment when a trap is approaching There is then no alternative but to pull up sharp and wait until Mrs or Miss Ah Sin has finished rocking and floundering about on her heels, during her devious passage across the road. These poor slaves of fashion have their feet so crumpled up and atrophied that, in extreme cases, they can walk only by means of the high heels of their shoes, which they use as stilts. This painful and disgusting sight naturally suggests the thought that their legs must be in a miserably wasted condition. And yet there are Englishmen who marry—yes, actually marry—these wretched cripples. The distortion in question is produced by tight bandaging at an early age; the object being to render the leg as straight as possible from the knee to the toes; so that the foot assumes a near approach to that of a goat. This plastic operation may be seen in all degrees. The stilted lady whom I have already mentioned, may take her seat (goodness knows she wants one!) at the top of the class. Others, not quite so deformed, get their toes on the ground. My eyes, ever ready to note a horsey 'point,' fell one day on the foot of a Chinese woman; and, to my astonishment, I saw in it the principle of a 'rocker' shoe, with which English veterinary surgeons try to alleviate the pain of *laminitis*, in full working order at the end of a female leg. Its ground surface, like that of its iron counterpart, was curved, so that the sufferer could keep constantly changing the seat of pain.

The fact of there being a Government House in Hong Kong, causes, like in Calcutta, a line of social demarcation to be drawn between retail and wholesale tradesmen. In Shanghai, there is no Governor to set the exiles by the ears; consequently the white men of the 'Model Settlement' live in harmony and social equality. In fact, I never met a body of men who pulled so well together, and were so helpful to each other. For instance, there is that genial companion and good sportsman, Tom Fourinhand, who went home some years ago to have a twelve months' holiday, hunting in the shires, racing during the summer, and doing himself well, at the rate of £20 a day. When he returned full of health and spirits, he found that his father-in-law and partner had, during his absence, burst up the firm in a vain attempt to improve the breed of herrings on the China coast. Did Tom set his face as a flint, and start afresh as a junior clerk, with the undaunted purpose in his heart of becoming the head of the house before he was two hundred years of age? Or did he sit down, wring his hands, and drink himself slowly but pleasantly to death? Neither the one nor the other alternative did he accept; but like a proper member of the Hong (*Anglice*, place) he went to the Club at the orthodox hour of twelve to have a cocktail with one, a 'pint' with another, and so on, until he had all his old pals around him. They, being practical men, at once set their remaining wits to work in the endeavour to help their old friend, and, before the merry meeting broke up, they had settled that he was to be made official handicapper of the Race Club, the programmes of which never contain a weight-alloted race, on a stipend that now keeps him going at a very fair rate of speed. Besides enjoying this sinecure, Tom does a bit of brokering, a business

Shanghai.

which has a peculiar meaning of its own in China. There, everything has to be bought through a supposititious broker, who gets a percentage in right of his intermediate position. That being the case, the good, though needy fellows, are naturally selected as the recipients. Thus, if I wanted to buy 1000 shares of the Lie Foo gold mines, I would go to the agent of the company and state my wants. When we had agreed as to the price, he would ask : 'To whom shall I credit the brokerage?' I would then think of the friend of mine who wanted it most, and would, for instance, reply : 'Put it down to Dick Finisher ; he had a bad time during the last races, and wants a lift.'

Although the China limit of height is just under 15 hands, the best ponies for racing purposes are under 13 hands 3 inches. For Arab horses, the limit at which height ceases to be useful, is about 14 hands 2 inches ; and for English racehorses about 16 hands. By this I mean that, generally speaking, the fact of horses exceeding these respective heights is no advantage to them from a galloping point of view.

The Shanghai race stand is a fine large building, which is provided with offices and a coffee-room capable of holding over a hundred people, in which the members of the Race Club meet every morning during the training season, to talk, read the papers, and refresh themselves. The Race Club is a very flourishing institution to which everyone interested in horses is given ready admission without any ridiculous class distinctions being made. Shopkeepers, tradesmen and merchant princes meet there during life on the same terms of equality on the turf, as they will do under it, when they die. The Club owns all the ground occupied by the racecourse, which is about 1¼ miles in length, and the extensive enclosures ; so it keeps this fine breathing space clear from all building encroachments. Although the ground is immensely valuable, it could ill be spared ; for it is a potent means for promoting health and sport, especially, as members only are allowed to ride. This busy commercial community marks the importance it attaches to these considerations, by keeping, as bank holidays, the days upon which the races are held.

The stand is the great early morning rendezvous for the local sportsmen, all of whom are devotees of the 'time test.' During the training season, on the two days a week on which the course is thrown open for work, all the Shanghai racing men crowd against the rails on the inside of the course, close to the winning post, with centre second watches of most elaborate construction, to take the time of the various ponies. The course, I may mention, is as flat as a billiard table, and each furlong on it is marked by an upright post. These gentlemen think that they have their task of 'spotting winners' immensely simplified by the adoption of the maxim that weight makes no difference to a China pony; and that all they have to do in order to ascertain the form of an animal is to take his time, which an onlooker can do just as accurately as the owner. My dislike to this eternal clocking is that its arguments are so plausible that they fill the mind of the hearer thereof, to the exclusion of the far more valuable lessons to be learned from the study of the animal's action and general style of going. Although there are nearly 1000 ponies in the Settlement, there is not a veterinary surgeon in the place. Had there been a demand for professional advice, the want no doubt would have been supplied. As a man can buy there a serviceable pony for about £10, he will, in the event of the animal going wrong, naturally prefer to sell it for what it will fetch and buy another at an equally moderate price, than to go to the delay and expense of having it treated by a veterinary surgeon. Members of my profession can expect good fees only in places where high prices are paid for horses.

The races, which are well filled and spiritedly contested, are the great social event of the year. It did us good to be among people who were as enthusiastic about our favourite subject, as are the Shanghai ladies and gentlemen.

The horsebreaking class which I held close to the racecourse, was largely attended, especially as I made it known that my wife would ride any pony brought to us. Before our visit, the English residents had an idea that obstreperous China ponies, of which there were many, could be handled only by Chinamen. The *mafoos* (native grooms), who regularly 'did *jos*' for my destruction, were naturally the chief originators of this absurd opinion. If an owner wanted to inspect his pony's feet, the *mafoo* promptly applied some appropriate devilment which made the animal kick and bite so badly as to prevent the near approach of the so-called proprietor. If the white man was persevering enough to order Mr Pigtail to 'catchee this side leg,' Mr John would instantly reply: 'No can catchee.' Thus, in the large majority of cases, the *mafoo* groomed the pony just as much, or as little, as he liked; being without fear of inspection. Under such a state of things, it was natural to find a great number of reputed man-eaters and demons of ponies, whose supposed foibles made stable work more of a pleasure than a toil to the attendant *mafoos*. I had the satisfaction of demonstrating to the residents of Shanghai, Hong Kong and Tientsin, that the China pony had not yet been bred, which a white man could not handle, and an English lady could not ride, with safety. My success in these experiments with vicious biters, was greatly enhanced by the adoption of the very simple plan of opening a biter's mouth by means of a stick gently insinuated between the lips, and not by the fingers.

The word *jos*, which I used in the preceding paragraph, means God; and 'doing *jos*,' worshipping God. If we are to believe the old saying that man makes God in his own image, what dolts Chinamen must be! They look upon *jos* as a simpleton that can be beguiled by the most transparent artifices; so, when they want to propitiate him, they are wont to present unto him imitation bricks of silver, made of paper. Although these cardboard structures are as little like the real article as the bit of tin on the top of the cork of a soda-water bottle is to a silver sixpence, confiding *jos* is supposed to be thoroughly taken in, and proportionately delighted with these offerings.

The breaking I had to do in China was almost entirely for saddle, as there are very few carriages; the well-to-do classes affecting the jinrickshaw, the poorer people the wheelbarrow. When I first saw a 'rickshaw, I vowed that I would never get into this Eastern bath-chair. But it was always at hand, and appeared so convenient, that my scruples gradually gave way, and I at last consented to be pulled along in this go-cart. At Simla, it takes four men to trot along on level ground, with a 'ricksaw containing one lady. At Colombo, a single man undertakes the feat; but cannot keep up the accelerated gait beyond two hundred yards, without breaking into a walk. At Singapore, the 'rickshaw coolies never think of walking, unless against a strong wind. At Shanghai, they go half as fast again as at the Straits, and think nothing of a double load. In Japan, which is the home of this man-cart, the coolies step out like match trotters, and instead, as at other places, of confining their runs to borough limits, they think nothing of drawing, in tandem, a 200 lb. man, 50 miles up hill and down dale in a day. Although pedestrianism is not cultivated in China, either as a sport or as a means of keeping in good health; the indigenous coolie quickly learned the 'rickshaw business from the Japs. At first the unaccustomed and ill-regulated exercise manifested its bad effects on the majority of its takers by causing diseases of the heart, lungs and other internal organs, which were fatal to many. On hearing this fact, the natural query would be: 'Why did the coolie work so hard?' The answer is, that if the 'rickshaw man did not keep running at a fair pace the entire journey, the 'foreigner,' as a rule, would get out and walk, or call another conveyance; and the tardy one would be left lamenting his lost fare. Besides this, the writings of Confucius contained no information about athletic training; so the almond-eyed ones committed many errors, and steadily smoked opium. I have been told that this rapid breaking down was, years ago, specially noticeable among the 'rickshaw men who used to occupy the rank in front of the Club; for the members of that institution stimulated record breaking by liberal payment, to a much greater extent than did the more sedate frequenters of other parts of the town. At this club work, a coolie, in the early days, rarely lasted more than six months. Since then, new pigtail generations, trained on improved principles from their youth upwards, have appeared, and the mortality from this special cause has greatly decreased. The distressed breathing, from heart disease, of some of these coolies is most painful to hear.

The Chinaman is nothing, if not a gambler. In the streets, the peripatetic vendor of various kinds of food carries in his hand a cylindrical wooden box about nine inches long, three inches in diameter, and open at one end, out of which project the tops of about twenty thin sticks that look like knitting needles. During all his spare moments, he shakes them up and down in the box, and thus produces a rattling sound which can be heard at some distance off. As the click of the ivory balls is to the billiard player, the rattle of dice to the lover of hazard, and the roar of the bookmaker to the punter, so is the tinkle of the ends of the sticks on the bottom of the bamboo box to the hungry Chinaman, who, on depositing the sum of one cash 'about the tenth part of a farthing' in the hands of the banker, has the privilege of drawing out of the box, three sticks, on the outside of which, near the lower end, are pips somewhat like those on dominoes. If they contain a winning number, the investor gets his cake, piece of pig, morsel of dog, or other dainty. If he loses, he puts down another cash, and so on, until he obtains the object of his desire, or gets 'broke'; just as we do when we try to 'pick' a winner.

After a most enjoyable stay for nearly a month in Shanghai, we went to Tientsin, where I had an invitation to teach a class the art of giving horses good manners and snaffle mouths. The steamers which ply between Shanghai and Tientsin are expensive, but the food is good and the liquor unstinted. The captains do the catering and are paid at the rate of three dollars a day for every passenger by the company. As they provide brandies and sodas all day long, beer and claret during meals, and excellent port wine after dinner, as did that charming skipper of the *Wuchang;* the wonder is how they can possibly afford to be so liberal. With the best of free drinks, any amount of ice, delicious fresh butter, new milk, fish, prawns, vegetables, fruit, and no better meat out of England, combined with admirable cooking and smart attendance, I had on the *Wuchang*, the best four days I have ever spent on board ship. At the Taku Forts, the steamer enters the narrow Pekin river, up which it goes for fifty miles to Tientsin, which is a small, low-lying English settlement, full of good sportsmen. We arrived just in time for the races, which were well supported. Among the local jockeys, two German gentlemen, Messrs Kruger and Lehmann, were the most distinguished. The natural sociableness of the residents of Tientsin is no doubt increased by its isolated position, and by the fact that, owing to the freezing up of the river, business is suspended for nearly three months, which time is given up to poker, dancing, theatricals and general festivity. To show that they have no 'nonsense' about them, I may mention that at the race ball we had the pleasure of meeting a real princess, a couple of live barons, several *freiherren*, and the young man who, that morning, sold me a hat, a pair of boots and a bundle of cigars in the local 'store.' Among many other good sportsmen at Tientsin, we had the pleasure of meeting Dr Irving, Mr Detring, Mr Michie, Mr Fitz Henry and Captain Axen von Brixen.

During our stay at Tientsin, I had many a discussion on the subject of *l'équitation savante* with two of its learned exponents, Captain Lehmann, who is an old pupil of Holleufer of Hanover, and Mr G. A. Butler, the late private secretary to the Marquis of Tseng, the former Chinese Ambassador in England. I tried my best to profit by their instruction; but being incapable of learning any art except by answers to my constant 'why?' I did not make much progress. The explanations of the professors of the high school are so loaded with arbitrary and obscure terms, that I am inclined to think that the large majority of them are empirics—clever, I admit, but still followers of routine and not of reasoned-out principles. Mr Butler, who was an American 'gentleman of colour,' was a man of rare talent and as discreet as William the Silent. He had need to be; for he had plunged deeply into Chinese politics. During the Franco-Chinese War, having negotiated for his masters a loan of several million dollars, he had, on duty connected with this matter, to proceed one night in a steam-launch down the Min River, which was full of torpedoes that had been placed in carefully-concealed positions to obstruct the navigation. As the most rapid possible dispatch was the order, he gave the word, 'Steam ahead full speed'; trusting solely to luck to carry him safely through the terrible dangers that lay in his path. Thinking that the bow would be the first part of the boat which would strike any torpedo, he took his seat on the extreme end of the stern, in the hope that if an explosion did occur, he might contrive to tumble alive into the water, where he would have had to trust to the clemency of the sharks and crocodiles to let him swim to land. The mental agony which he endured through that night of anxiety, was trebled by the fact that he was suffering at the time from a severe attack of fever. Morning, however, broke without an accident having occurred, and the traveller arrived in due course, safe at his destination. After the conclusion of the war, he happened by chance to be again on the Min River, at a time when the Chinese were taking up the torpedoes. When these machines were all landed, they were opened to see the condition of their contents, which were found to be powdered coal, instead of gunpowder. The official who had them filled, evidently understood the advantage which his position gave him to make money.

One day, when at Tientsin, my wife met with a bad accident, by the pony which she was riding, rearing up, coming over, and then kicking her repeatedly while she was on the ground. During this performance, the animal's *mafoo* and a comrade of his looked on, without making the slightest attempt to save her, which they might easily have done by catching the pony, and turning him round. They conscientiously refrained from interfering with, what they were pleased to term, 'jos pidgin.' The accident made us relinquish the idea of going to Pekin, which was only about fifty miles distant; and we decided to spend our holidays in Japan. While staying in Tientsin, I became acquainted with a funny custom of the Chinese, by hearing, on the first night of our arrival, outside our window, a noise as if someone were ringing a cracked bell, or beating a tin can. As it soon faded away in the distance, I did not mind it at first, and being tired, I had just dropped off into a doze, when the same inharmonious tinkle, tinkle, came nearer and nearer. I bore with it for a time; but was at last roused to fury by its infernal repetition, as it went round the house, dived off into the stable, and then returned to its old place under our window. I ran out with a big whip and a volley of 'language,' which must have frightened the delinquent; for he ceased performing during the remainder of the night. In the morning I learned that he was the hotel watchman, whose function is to go about the premises rattling a stone in an old tin pot in order to frighten, not thieves, with whom he has no concern, but the devil.

At Tientsin, we saw for the first time in China, several very fine mules, which in height and substance, almost equal those of Spain. We also met on the road from time to time, Tartar horsemen who proudly 'show off' by making their hardy little ponies amble at a great rate, to the terror of the sober-minded Chinese, to whom rapidity of action, as well as of thought, is an abomination. My only regret was that we were unable to find time for a tour among these ardent lovers of horses, to whose country we were then very near. When

Tea in China. 175

the railway is complete in a few years, you and I, my adventurous reader, may some day stroll into Mr Thomas Cook's office in Ludgate Circus, take an excursion ticket, get out at Vladivostock, and have lots of big-game shooting in Manchu Tartary. Were I to make such a trip, I think I should keep a sharp look-out for all the likely galloping ponies, and having selected the best, embark with them for Shanghai; being quite certain of an average of £50 a piece from my sporting friends in the 'Model Settlement.'

One must never say that anything is new until one has been to China. To my amazement, I saw, one day at Tientsin, the principle of one of my favourite appliances used by a Manchu Tartar in a bridle on his mule. It has probably been employed by these horsemen from time immemorial.

The country round Tientsin is flat, low-lying, is subject to frequent inundations from the river, and is a general burial-ground for the Chinese, who plant their dead wherever they think fit; consequently, the surface water is strongly impregnated with a flavour of pigtail. The Chinese adapt the wise precaution of drinking water only in the form of weak tea, which is dispensed for a very moderate sum by numerous peripatetic venders. They, as we all know, use neither milk nor sugar with their favourite decoction. As they consume large quantities of this fluid, they have it of a strength akin to what ladies are pleased to call 'husband's tea'; although they never commit the atrocity of 'watering the pot,' after it has been exhausted. The Chinaman does not wash out his tea-pot. He simply throws out the used leaves, makes a fresh brew, and so on, until the interior of the utensil has such a fine old crust on it, that, if required, he could get a fairly good cup of tea out of it, by merely adding water.

We returned to Shanghai in June 1888, and started for Yokohama by the French mail steamer. A passenger's life on board one of these boats is the perfection of comfort at sea. The food is excellent, you are given plenty of time to eat it, and the wine is pure, not *fabriqué*. The dilution of *vin rouge*, I may mention, should be accomplished, not with water, but with St Galmier, the slight alkalinity of which corrects any acidity there may be in the wine.

The short run to Kobe, and through the beautiful Inland Sea, was far too brief. We had not been half an hour in Yokohama before I recognised the fact that it would be useless to try to do anything in the horsebreaking line in Japan; for the ponies were too miserable a lot to experiment upon. They are flat-sided, weedy, spiritless brutes, although hardy and good workers at a very slow pace. So we gave up the idea of paying our expenses, and devoted ourselves to sightseeing.

The Yokohama racecourse, which is a mile and twenty yards in length, is about three miles from the city on the Negishi Hill, from which a charming view of hill and valley, field and forest, land and water can be seen. The course is undulating, well kept, and is on excellent turf. The racing which is confined to ponies of China and Japan, is very poor; for the estimable little Japs have far too much of the monkey strain in them to be sportsmen, and the white inhabitants are poor and lacking in enterprise. Grass sandals, which last one day and are then replaced by new ones, are frequently used in place of shoes with ponies in Japan. Whether the men are so fast, or the ponies are so slow, I cannot say; but a *bettoe* (native groom) starting fair on foot with his master on horseback, will always be the first to arrive at their destination.

I utilised my short stay in Japan to the best advantage, in the study of wood and ivory carvings, satsuma, cloisonné work, kakimonas, and other branches of Japanese art, which is too vast and profound a subject for me to touch with the insolence of ignorance. I shall say something about eating, with which I am well acquainted, as I have been practising it regularly two or three times a day for half a century. The climate of Japan is too moist for sheep, though excellent for horned cattle. Prawns, mackerel, and the true black sole are to be had in abundance. The American chad is to be found there, and also in north China, under the name of *samli*. It is, I believe, the same fish as the Indian *hilsa*. The fruit, vegetables, milk, cream, and butter are like unto those of England. The climate is similar to that of France, without the great cold in winter. The people are hospitable, and show strangers plainly that it gives them pleasure to be obliging and civil; consequently, they are incapable business men, and have no moral backbone. Freemasons in Japan have recognised the volatile character of the inhabitants, in that they refrain from admitting any Japanese into their order; although they make no objection to Chinese, whose socialistic training and traditions eminently fit them for keeping their own secrets. With very few exceptions, the native clerks in all the banks and mercantile houses in Japan are Chinamen.

Of all the hotels I have known east of the Suez Canal, the Grand at Yokohama is the best, with the Hong Kong Hotel a good second. The profusion of fruit and vegetables to be found in Japan, is most acceptable to the western traveller. Every morning at early breakfast in the Grand we used to have, without extra charge, an unlimited supply of strawberries, which, I might suggest, taste better with Burgundy (Corton, perhaps, for choice) and a little kirsch (the flavour of curacoa is too pronounced for some), than with cream. I need hardly say that the *kirsch wasser* to which I refer, is the spirit distilled from cherries, and not the sickly mess which goes by the name of cherry brandy. In Yokohama, Shanghai, Hong Kong and Amoy, there are excellently managed dairy farms. The milk, as a rule, costs fivepence a pint, which is two and a half times as dear as in London. On the other hand, it is richer than the English product; for the food given to the cows is drier.

Photo. by H. R. Sherborn, Newmarket.

CHAPTER XII.

Return to India—Starting a Newspaper—Society in India—The Counter Test—Planters—Life in Calcutta—Public Opinion in India—Indian Officials—Amateur Actors—Miss Amy Sherwin—Mr Rudyard Kipling as a Flatterer.

WHEN we got tired of buying curios and studying Japanese life, we asked ourselves the important question: 'What next?' I was for going to California or Australia; but my wife, like all ladies who have ever been to India, longed to return to the country of mangos, curry, 'bow-wows,' ride-where-you-like-and-no-law-of-trespass, supremacy of women, and *kala jugahs*, declared for Calcutta. She, knowing my love for new sensations, represented that I had never run a newspaper, and that there was room for a smart one, on sporting lines, in the City of Palaces. The novelty of the idea charmed me, especially as I knew that in India I had, for my books, a large reading public, many of which, I argued, would be glad to take my paper. We accordingly went to Calcutta, *via* Hong Kong (where I held a large class), Singapore and Penang. Within a couple of months after we had returned from Japan to India, our venture, under the title of *Hayes' Sporting News*, was launched. We burned our metaphorical ships, and entered on our literary campaign with high hopes and a firm resolve to make our paper a success. With the help of a strong outside staff, consisting of Skrene of the Bengal Civil Service, Lloyd of the Opium Department, Beatty of the Bombay Police, Shipley of the Madras Civil Service, 'The Dwarf of Blood,' and many other brilliant and able writers, our *Sporting News* won support and favour from readers all over India. Like thorough Bohemians who would eat no dirt, and who would not bow the knee to brass gods, we took our own line and published that what we thought right. I may explain that Indian society is governed on bureaucratic principles. First comes the army, the subalterns of which stand in awe of their captains; the captains, of their senior majors; the senior majors, of their colonels; the colonels, of their generals; the generals, of their commander-in-chief; the commander-in-chief, of the viceroy; the viceroy, of the home authorities, who continue the chain of responsibility up to King Demos. The Indian Civil Service and all the various 'non-covenanted' departments are ruled by a similar fear. The non-official element may be divided into the mercantile community and planters. As the only social recognition (in India) to non-officials who do not hold titles in their own right, is the *entrée* to Government House, those traders who can obtain the much-coveted invitation are, as a rule, anxious to avoid giving offence to the military secretary or other bigwig who, at a stroke of his pen, can convert Mr Plantagenet-Smith, in the eyes of the local society, from a gentleman into a cad, and, worse still, can thus degrade Mrs Plantagenet. The test of respectability consists in the manner in which the trader sells his wares. If he, like the great house of Henry S. King & Company, will consent to part with, say, a box of cigars only out of a warehouse, he is eligible ; but if, like Pisti and Pelicano, he hands his hundred weeds across a counter, he is damned. The unsuccessful candidate for admission to Government House is debarred not alone from dancing, eating and drinking there; but is actually a social pariah ; for such exclusion practically prevents him from belonging to any of the best local clubs, which do much to mitigate the discomforts of Indian life. The traders who cannot pass the counter test, either willingly accept their position as social outsiders, or so order their life that they may, in the near future, obtain the coveted invitation. In any case, as they, for the most part, make their livelihood out of the officials ; they are careful not to wound the susceptibilities of their customers. The planters, God bless them, care for none of these things. When visitors go to them, they give them to eat and drink of the best, lend them horses to ride, get up shooting and pig-sticking meets, and treat them with that fine old Indian hospitality which, except in the indigo and tea districts, is now almost unknown, and which has become such an anachronism that it is generally its own reward. Hospitality given in Tirhoot or Assam is not always reciprocated in Calcutta, and still less when the quondam guest meets his former host in Piccadilly, and passes by on the other side. Though I do not commend such practice, I cannot wonder at its existence. The isolated planter was glad of the society of the new-comer, out of whom amusement, if not instruction, might be extracted. When the traveller, not alone appropriated the free meals, drink and bed, but also annexes the fun in the form of 'copy,' as has been done by some globe trotters and itinerant journalists, I grant that his conduct is indefensible.

Having placed ourselves in the centre of a public constituted as I have just described, we ought, in the opinion of our well-wishers, to have made capital out of its follies,

Calcutta.

meannesses and prejudices. On the contrary, we called a spade a spade, whether in the case of a horse being 'pulled' or a public institution being mismanaged. We had hosts of secret admirers who longed to extract roasted chestnuts out of the fire by means of our paws; but who were unwilling to expose their own tender skins to the heat of official or social wrath. Besides the record and review of sport, our paper contained valuable articles on popular veterinary surgery, riding, horsebreaking and other kindred subjects which made it useful to a horse-loving public; and it was brightened up by original stories, essays, sketches and *vers de société* which I constantly received from my literary friends. The high quality of the paper killed it; for the keeping it up to the standard we had fixed, necessitated my always remaining in Calcutta. It is true that, besides my journalistic work, I had ample employment in horse-dealing and racing. The trainers, jockeys, dealers, stable-keepers, and rough riders were our friends to a man. But the men whom I knew, when in the Service, as equals, looked upon me more or less as an outsider, so that the dreams which my wife had of a pleasant life in India remained unfulfilled, and, after a three years' struggle, we began to ask ourselves the question: Does the pleasure of 'running' the paper make up for the discomforts of living in Calcutta? I had seen so much of the world, that it was absolutely immaterial to me whether my associates were private soldiers or generals, or men who sold whisky or cigars over counters or out of 'godowns.' The Viceroy of India could confer on me no social position equal to that I held in my own right as an author. I was on friendly terms with all the people in India whose opinions on horses, sport, or literature were worth having. As I had never once availed myself of the right I had of entering Government House, during the sixteen years I spent in India as an officer of the army; it was not likely that I would want to go there in my old age. But my wife is twenty years younger than I am. She could not share with me the amusements I had, knocking about at race-meetings with all sorts of sporting characters, getting up boxing and athletic matches, and other 'divarsions' dear to the heart of an Irishman. She is musical, a clever actress, and born to shine in society. The weather was getting dreadfully hot. The best racing pony I ever possessed died. Our treasure of a cook, whose Roman punch and prawn cutlets were divine, disappeared with another man's wife; and my London publishers kept writing to me every mail, that new editions of my books were required. My editorial work allowed me no time to bring them out, and one of the best of good fellows in the shape of Mr Harry Abbott made an offer to buy our paper for a fair sum; so what could I do, under the pressure of all these circumstances, than accept it?

Among the English residents in India, public opinion does not exist. Such a thing would be too absurd in a society in which the juniors are dependent on the seniors for promotion, leave, and all the small privileges which make life bearable. The continued state of pupilage in which all but the few lucky ones remain, knocks the manhood out of those who dare not call their souls their own. The Indian official, whether military, civilian, or departmental, is consequential, infallible in his own eyes, and intolerant of outside criticism. He regards as a gross personal insult the mention, however well founded, in a newspaper, of any fault in the working of the machinery over which he is the director. This gentleman of the *l'état c'est moi* order maintains that if anything goes wrong in his province, a report might be laid before him, but should on no account be sent to a newspaper. In this contention of his, which advocates the principle that every man should be the sole judge of his own actions and those of his subordinates, there is a large amount of human nature. If his infallibility be acknowledged, he will rarely exhibit any undue amount of insolence of office. Though narrow-minded, on account of the routine nature of his training, he is kind-hearted, generous, and hospitable in his social circle. Being a bird of passage, he lacks sympathy, and does not see why he should worry himself about the misery with which he is surrounded, when his thoughts are fully occupied in trying to get some better post, or in preparing for leave, furlough, or retirement. If a civilian, he has to make a show of public philanthropy, agreeably to the expressed or understood wishes of Government. As he has really a great deal of work to do, and as the climate makes the visiting of the poor and sick an irksome labour, our typical official generally deputes the duty to some understrapper who thoroughly understands the combined service of God and Mammon. If some busybody who absurdly thinks that it is the duty of all of us to minister to the wants of the sick and helpless, dares to call attention to the mismanagement of public charity, the official, fearing that the vicarious nature of his philanthropy may be brought to light, will naturally do everything he possibly can to whitewash his peccant subordinates. Remembering his many good points, among which incorruptibility and kindness of heart are the most prominent; we may well forgive the Indian official for his self-sufficiency and airs of authority. Life is not all beer and skittles with him, any more than it is with the majority of us. A long residence in India unfits him, as a rule, both mentally and physically, to take when he retires, a prominent part among his fellow men in England. As official rank is his sole claim to respect, he carefully chooses the society of men situated like himself; for they are the only persons who would acknowledge such a claim.

Amateur actors and singers and amateur actresses and songstresses are prominent personages in Indian society. They are very exclusive. They refuse to consort with non-professionals connected with trade. Under occasional fits of liberality, they will play with professionals on the consideration of lots of 'fat,' suppers, and clothes. If the legitimate mummers wish to run their own show, the amateurs will let them severely alone, and will try to induce their friends to do the same. We all know and admire that accomplished artist Miss Amy Sherwin. On one occasion, she went to Calcutta with a thoroughly capable concert company. The local amateurs approached her with offers of assistance, which she gracefully declined, on the plea that her company was composed of thoroughly capable professionals, whom she was unwilling to slight by replacing them with outsiders. The spite of the amateurs at this very natural rebuff had such a venomous effect through the weak-kneed Calcutta community, that Miss Sherwin 'opened' to an audience of about two dozen in number, most of whom were 'paper.' Rendered sage by this reverse, she consented to allow the pick of the amateur basket to sing at her next concert. The chosen lady, as amateurs will do, attacked one of Sullivan's most difficult songs, and, probably, to show her thorough mastery of it, sang it through her teeth, with the result that the majority of the audience almost rolled off their seats in fits of laughter. As Miss Sherwin was unwilling to continue this comic business, she packed up her properties and went to Shanghai, where she and her company had a most enthusiastic reception. Not content with loading her with dollars, the good people of 'The Model Settlement' presented her with a very handsome testimonial. The Indian amateur does not usually believe in acting for charity beyond his or her home. And yet, when they deliberately 'go for the pieces' in the shape of drinks, suppers and dresses, they are insulted beyond measure if their *pseudo* amateur status be not regarded by the press as a bar against adverse criticism. Even the thickest layer of butter is sometimes insufficient to satisfy the hunger after praise which afflicts the Indian amateur. As an instance of this, I may mention that Mr Rudyard Kipling told me that wishing to make things pleasant in a report he was writing on some amateur theatricals for an Indian paper, he, trying how far he could go, said that the leading lady (who really was a 'stick' of the most wooden sort), by her marvellously fine acting, reminded him of Miss Ellen Terry.

On the evening of the day in which his report appeared, he met the extravagantly praised-up one, who, instead of being annoyed with him for having chaffed her, said : ' I am very cross with you, Mr Kipling, for having compared me to Miss Ellen Terry, who is much older than I am. Don't you think that I am far more like Miss Mary Anderson?' 'I am very sorry,' replied the gallant Mr Kipling, 'that I made such a stupid mistake. I ought to have said that you reminded me of Miss Mary Anderson.' 'Of course, that was what you meant,' added the lady, who graciously signified her acceptance of the journalist's *amende*. 'After that,' said Mr Kipling to me, ' I gave up reporting amateur theatricals.'

CHAPTER XIII.

Importation of Colonial Horses into India—Horse Dealing at Calcutta—The Saddle selling the Horse—Horses on Board Ship—Mr More on Lord Combermere—Saddles—Colonial Horse Dealers—Mr John Stevens—Maoris—Teddy Weeks—Kerouse—Treatment of Sprains in Horses—Racing in India—The Apcars—Lord William Beresford—Paper-Chasing—A Jingle—India as a School for Riding.

BESIDES the paper, I had horse dealing, veterinary practice, and training to occupy my time; the first two, all the year round; the last mentioned, for about seven months out of the twelve. I may explain that the large majority of superior saddle and harness horses used in India come from Australia and New Zealand; 2500 to 3000 being yearly imported into Calcutta, and about 1000 to 1500 into Madras. Few are sent to Bombay, which imports annually about 1200 Arabs and Persians. Out of the Calcutta lot, 600, more or less, are taken by the Government Remount Department for army purposes; and say, half that number, by the Madras authorities. Though inclined to have plain heads and drooping croups, the Autralasian horses have, as a rule, remarkably good legs and feet, and capital shoulders for saddle work. The dealers, such as Macklin, Hunter, Stevens, Gascard, Ralli, Cavanagh, Dirom, Margarett, Gidney, Madden, Green, Hastie, Hegarty, Hawkins, Gove, MacIntosh, Macaulay and others, bring them over in batches of from 50 to 400. The horses are mostly four or five years old, and average in cost about £15 a piece, to which must be added £10 or £12 for freight and expenses, and, say, £3 or £4 for casualties. They can therefore be landed for about £30 or thirty guineas a head. As Government gives from £40 to £45 a piece for its remounts, and as it buys without imposing any harassing delay or expense, the 'shippers' are generally anxious to submit their new arrivals to the Remount Agent, who reserves to himself the right of selecting for army purposes as many or as few as he likes; the dealer being allowed to reserve some for private sale. This system has been found to act admirably in the hands of poor 'Bill' Thacker, 'Ben' Roberts, 'Tommy' St Quintin, and P. K. Beaver, who, as Remount Agents, have been singularly moderate in using their influence to get horses 'on the cheap' for either themselves or their friends. As the Government purchases are, as a rule, made in October, the majority of these shipments arrive in that month. After the Remount Agent has had his pick, the shipper submits the remainder to the private market, and often, while waiting for it, loses a good deal of time and money. He, probably, has to hang on to the end of February, by which time, the weather is becoming hot, the residents are making preparations to flit to the Hills or to England, and the tired-out dealer wants to get back to the Colonies to see about getting together another importation for the following October. On the principle of the first loss being the least, he will generally sell those that are left at a very small price, or, failing an offer, will put them up to auction to the highest bidder. From among these 'culls' as they are called, I have bought many useful horses, about 100 of which I afterwards sold, at different times, to Native cavalry regiments, whose top price was 350 rupees, say, £20. Neither mouths nor manners were of course guaranteed at that price. The horses I usually bought for chargers and hacks, generally cost me from £30 to £100 a piece. Though capable of breaking-in almost any horse for my own use, I always kept in remembrance the fact that although 'difficult' horses may be reclaimed for the time being, and kept under control by a capable man; they are always liable, at little or no provocation, to revert to their evil courses. Hence I took special care, which of course was not always infallible, to buy quiet horses. The majority of men ride so very badly, that when selling a riding horse, I always put on him a particular saddle which is the most comfortable one I have ever seen. Time after time I have had men who had bought a horse from me, come on the following day and entreat me to sell them my saddle, which, some of them were shrewd enough to observe, had been the means of selling the horse. It certainly was not my fault if men failed to provide themselves with saddles, out of which they could fall with difficulty.

As horses are apt to suffer a good deal from the sea voyage between Australia and India, they often arrive in wretched condition, and can consequently be bought very cheaply. If I have heard one man, I have heard five hundred remark, as if they were making a valuable and original observation, that they like to buy fresh animals thin; for they can then best see their 'make and shape.' My experience, on the contrary, is all in favour of making selections from those which are in good condition on arrival; for the fact that they are 'big,' goes a long way to prove that they must have had good constitutions to have 'stood' the journey so well. Besides this, horses which land very 'poor,' have often suffered so much by, for instance, having been placed in some ill-ventilated position, that their lungs or general health

Shipping Horses.

receive some permanent injury. My advice is, don't have anything to say to such 'wasters.'

The voyage from the Colonies takes from twenty-five to fifty days, according as it is direct, or *viâ* Singapore and Penang. Unless in the case of animals of considerable value, the horses have to stand the whole time, and when the entire vessel is given up to them, they occupy the lower deck, main deck, and upper deck. An ordinary cargo steamer, called in nautical language a 'tramp,' could carry from three hundred and fifty to four hundred horses. The chartering of vessels from the Colonies to Calcutta, is greatly facilitated by the fact that the tonnage of the imports into Australasia greatly exceeds that of the exports, and that there are large shipments of grain and other 'country produce' from Calcutta to England. Hence, there are always a fair number of vessels at Melbourne, Sydney, Adelaide, and other Colonial ports, which, having come out with a full cargo are unable to get one on the homeward voyage, and consequently their owners or agents are glad to hire them to take horses at a cheap rate to Calcutta, at which port they will be certain to get a cargo for England. Sooner than send them home empty, the agents, acting for the owners, often advance the money to a dealer for the purchase of a shipload of horses, which they consign to one of the Calcutta firms to whom the account of the sales is duly rendered, or the agents may advance a portion of the money. Only a few of the shippers work with their own money; although they all naturally like to appear before their customers as men of independent property.

When shipping valuable horses singly, I have found that the chief requisites to their comfort is a flooring of thick coir matting with long fibres projecting upwards (of the door-mat pattern); a roomy box, at least 7½ feet by 5 feet, placed athwart ships to live in; good ventilation; and protection from heavy seas coming on board. The coir matting not alone affords firm foothold, but also gives the frogs of the feet that evenly distributed pressure which is indispensable to their health. No matter how badly a ship may pitch and roll, a horse with this matting under him can remain in security, either standing up or lying down; although he would be knocked to pieces on wood flooring, even if it were provided with battens and straw. Some ignorant persons — among which class I had to number myself, the first time I took a horse on a long sea voyage—imagine that slings are a good thing to put under a horse during rough weather. On the contrary, their employment has the direct effect of taking him off his legs and getting him dashed from side to side in his box. In fine weather they are useful, if the box be too small for the animal to lie down in, and if they be put on slackly, to enable him to rest on them when he chooses. As an improvement, I would suggest that the coir matting, which should have a thick 'pile' on it, be made a little larger than the bottom of the box, so that it may be built up into the sides when the box is being constructed. Then, as long as the box holds together, the coir matting cannot become displaced. The attendant on a valuable horse at sea would do well to provide himself with an equine strait-jacket, which is fully described in my book, *Illustrated Horse-Breaking;* for if there be any chance of the horse getting frightened on account of bad weather, and knocking himself about, all the man will have to do to keep the animal safe and sound, is to slip on the strait-jacket, and adjust it as may be required. I cannot help thinking that few, if any, of the persons who have been in charge of horses which, like Blue Gown, Ossary who was own brother to Ormonde, Prince Io and scores of other valuable animals, have been lost from stress of weather when crossing the Atlantic, knew much about the virtues of thick 'pily' coir matting and strait-jackets for horses. The two great dangers to which a boxed horse is specially exposed on board ship are: having the box knocked to pieces or carried away by heavy seas coming over the side; and the horse getting tossed, during rough weather, from side to side in his box on account of his not being able to retain his foothold, and becoming thus more or less seriously injured. On such unfortunate occasions, the horse will almost invariably become dreadfully frightened, and in his frantic efforts to escape, will dash himself about wholly regardless of the fearful injuries which he may inflict upon himself. With respect to the loss of Ossory and Prince Io, I read in *The Spirit of the Times* that Mr Brett (I wonder if he was any relation of my Newmarket acquaintance, Joshua, of that name, who got into trouble for running over a country as a maiden, an old steeple-chaser and well-known winner?) who had charge of these horses, said that he could not keep either straw or sawdust under them; as it got washed away by the water which was shipped. I need hardly say that no amount of washing would have been able to have removed the coir matting. Besides, straw from its slippery nature, is one of the worst things which could be put under a horse during bad weather at sea. When horses get killed in this outrageous manner, any insurance company which had taken the risk on them, would be right to resist all claim for compensation on account of the fact that proper precautions had not been taken for their safety.

I cannot let the subject of saddles pass, without saying that comfort is the first thing I look for in a saddle. To have 'good hands,' we must, I need hardly say, have a firm seat. In the riding of raw and skittish horses, at which game I am as good as most of my neighbours, I find that, at times, I require all the 'gum' at my command, and more if I could get it, to avoid 'hanging on' to the reins. Hence, I go in for a comfortable saddle in which I can get a good grip. For this work, I do not believe in a plain flap saddle, unless it has 'false rolls,' or unless some extra stuffing is put into the panel at the front part of the flaps; for if this be not done, the rider's knees will have a tendency to go forward, on account of all well-made saddle horses being broader at the spot where the knees grip the flaps, than they are towards the shoulders. This is an anatomical fact which we must not ignore. My experience is that the worse men ride, the more do they affect slippery saddles. Australian horsemen will understand me when I say that the large majority of saddles used in England are unfit to ride in on account of being too wide in the 'twist' or 'waist,' a fault which prevents the rider from sitting close to the horse. This clumsy pattern has been handed down from the days when men rode cart horses, whose broad backs required the bars of a saddle-tree to be wide apart. As Australasian horses are more or less well bred, and as many of them are difficult to ride, only saddles narrow in the 'twist' or 'grip' are used in those Colonies. I may mention that the trees of all these saddles come from Walsall; for no saddle-trees are made in Australia, although many get 'covered' there.

I was on the best of terms with all the Australian and New Zealand horse shippers, from whom I received the greatest civility and kindness. They were always delighted to 'pull out,' and let me try any of their horses; for they knew that I would never think of troubling them, and of losing my own time unless I meant to buy. What these men and all other dealers rightly detest, is a 'messer,' namely, a person who cannot make up his mind, or who, with the idea of giving himself importance, pretends to want to purchase a horse, but who has not the remotest intention of doing so. When I had a good order on hand, I dealt liberally with them; and as they knew that I did not want to keep all the profit myself, they were ready to 'meet me,' if they could possibly do so, when there was not much to be made at the price. They are good judges of horses, and have to work very hard, with a continually sinking rupee to make a livelihood. Mr John Stevens, who was a horse importer and a captain in the New Zealand Cavalry, was a great friend of ours. He had been a Government interpreter among the Maoris, and had many stories to tell about those people. On one occasion, a native chief, who was under cross-examination in court, on being asked why he had not brought a certain man with him, replied, 'I have brought him.' 'But,' said the barrister, looking in vain round the court, 'I don't see him. Where is he?' 'He is *here*,' chuckled the Maori proudly, stroking his own well-filled abdomen. According to Mr Stevens, who is one of the greatest authorities on all Maori questions, these dusky islanders imagine that they can absorb into themselves all the good qualities of those whom they eat. No doubt it was this general idea that prompted his postman, on one occasion, to chew and swallow the newspaper which it was his duty to fetch from a distant post office. The man, not having any conception of the operation of reading, could not imagine how his master became acquainted with its contents, except on the supposition that Mr Stevens ate it; so he accordingly transferred it from his bag to his stomach. When he arrived with an empty post bag and a full stomach, Mr Stevens asked him where was the paper. The Maori explained that he had eaten it, and that he would tell him all the news as soon as he had digested it.

The greatest 'character' among all the shippers, was Teddy Weekes, who died a few years ago. He had an extraordinary number of failings, which are luckily buried with him. His 'language' was loud, copious and foul, and his habits were horrible; but he had the redeeming point of being a thorough sportsman. He was not necessarily one, because he lived only for horses and gambling, or because the dearest spot on earth to him was a racecourse; but he well merited that name for the stoical manner in which he met reverses of fortune in the backing of horses. His losses seemed to act like a powerful tonic on the little, fat, bloated man. One night about five years ago he took a plunge to the amount of £1200, and lost it in the following afternoon by the horse which he had backed getting beaten. It is only fair to him to say that he would not have risked losing a sum he was unable to pay, had he not dined too well. Instead of being cast down or attempting to shirk his liabilities, he brightened himself up, returned to Australia, worked like a slave, brought back a shipload of horses, sold them, paid his debts, and returned to the betting ring beaming with delight to find himself again in his old paradise. He was the only one of his low class of racing men whom I have ever met that loved a genuine straight-away match, for its own sake more than for the money dependent on it. Of the many occasions I have seen him 'lead in' a winner, I have never seen poor Teddy so pleased, although he did not gain a farthing on the transaction, as when my wife won a jumping prize against all comers in Calcutta four years ago on his clever pony mare, Mamma. His joy was on account of his pony having defeated the best horses which his rival dealers could bring against it. Teddy, who had been a fine horseman before he became inordinately fat from too free living, liked, during a sale of his horses, to get the leaping bar put up to a respectable height, and having mounted one of the animals with more assumed than real difficulty, would take the obstacle in good style, to show the people, as he would explain, how clever his horses must be to jump with a fat old man like himself. And then he would describe in a manner few could resist, how marvellously the animal would perform over a country with any of the on-looking *jeunesse dorée* on its back.

The most of the older shippers had come from England or Ireland in their youth, and had worked their way on in the Colonies. The only regular London dealer in the whole lot was Kerouse, whose people kept a livery and commission stable in Edgeware Road. He used to bring out cart horses from England to New Zealand and Australia, and then used to work back *viâ* Calcutta or Madras, with a shipment of Colonial horses. He was certainly the cleverest man in that trade at inducing a shy man to part with his money; but then we must recollect that he had a London training. He had not a thought in the world except for horses, pure and simple. 'It was as good as a play' listening to him when he was explaining to would-be purchasers how his 'five-year-

Sprains of the Forelegs.

olds' had lost all the 'marks' in their teeth by grazing on pasturage the sand of which used to grind down the teeth, so he said, in less than no time; and how the absence of hair on the knees of some of his animals was merely the temporary result of their sleeping in stalls which had not a sufficiency of straw bedding. The poor fellow died miserably from cancer in the throat; yet so strong was his ruling passion even in the presence of death, that when the friend who was tending him wanted to send, on the day before he died, a servant to stop the noise of some horsebreaking that was going on in the yard below the sick man's room, poor Kerouse, overhearing what was said, feebly whispered: 'Let them be. I love to hear the sound of the horses.'

In India, practically, the whole of the heavy cart work is done with bullocks, and in a few cases with buffaloes. There is little or no van work, and carriage horses are not put to any great toil. Consequently, the bulk of serious veterinary cases are those of sprain to tendon and ligament in saddle horses and especially among racehorses. Acting on the advice of Dr Henderson of Shanghai, I had great success during my stay at Calcutta, in the treatment of these injuries to the forelegs, by means of cotton-wool bandaging, an account of which will be found in my *Veterinary Notes*. I positively assert that out of the hundreds of cases of sprain to the back tendons, suspensory ligaments and check ligaments of the forelegs treated in the supposed orthodox method by warm water fomentations, cold water applications, and the use of liniments, blisters, etc., I have not seen a single instance of a return to soundness, which implies entire absence of perceptible alteration of structure, as would be shown by 'thickening.' I may go further and say that I have never seen any permanent good result from the application of either hot or cold water to a sprained part. The experience of every trainer is that such sprains are the beginning of the end; and that their treatment in the old style is, at best, the temporary patching up of a permanently weak spot. I have found, on the contrary, that properly applied cotton-wool bandaging in connection with well-regulated massage will, as a rule, if employed early, restore such sprained parts to a sound condition. A large number of trainers and owners in India have adopted with great success this method of treating such sprains. In course of time, it will, no doubt, become popular in England. Prior to meeting Dr Henderson, I often utilised, with good results, the effect of pressure on sprained parts by means of a combined bandage and 'charge,' with which, however, I was unable to massage the injured structure. One great beauty of this cotton-wool treatment is that instead of keeping men up all night or employed all day bathing, fomenting, irrigating, or applying lotions, liniments or embrocations to a bad leg; not more than a quarter of an hour is required to massage the part and to put on the bandage, after which the horse may be left, without any fear of ill results accruing, for twenty-four or even forty-eight hours. The good effects of this treatment for injuries which form the large majority of those that unfit saddle horses for work, manifest themselves in a surprisingly short time. I need hardly say that this method of bandaging cannot cure a sprain; but it can place the injured parts in the best possible position to become cured by the various reparatory functions of the body. Cotton-wool has no mysterious curative power; but is merely a convenient agent for distributing the effects of pressure.

Besides horse-dealing and occasional breaking, I trained several horses with a fair share of success. At Calcutta, which is the great Indian turf metropolis, the racing is well managed, and liberal prizes are given. Having confidence in the capacity and rectitude of the stewards, the public attend the meetings with all their spare cash in their pockets to back their fancy; and, accordingly, to supply the demand men like Bob Topping, Miller and Brittain, who 'field' during the summer in Italy, Archer, Crouch, who is well-known on French racecourses, and several other 'layers' come to Calcutta for the racing season which begins about the 1st December and finishes about the end of February. The legitimate part of the programmes is varied with pony events, which are probably the most important feature of Indian racing. There are some hurdle races, and two or three days are devoted to chasing. As I have discussed in *The Points of the Horse* the respective racing merits of English and Colonial animals; I need here only briefly remark that English ponies have shown a marked superiority over Colonial ones on the Indian turf. As to the horses, the question is somewhat more difficult to decide. I may state, however, with confidence, that for equal sums, say, up to £1500, which would be about the usual Indian limit, better horses can be bought in Australia than in England. Besides this, it is easier and cheaper to bring horses to India from the former country than from the latter. Furthermore, Colonial horses have, as a rule, better legs and feet than English animals. Considering the care that is taken of valuable horses, I do not think that there is any appreciable difference between the way these two classes stand the Indian climate. Lord William Beresford, who has been a prominent figure on the Indian turf for several years, has generally relied on English horses; because, I presume, his brother Lord Marcus, was in a good position to supply him with the required sort of cattle. His great rivals, the Armenian house of Apcar, 'go in' almost exclusively for Australians; because, I venture to think, their trainers are generally Colonials. Lord William is an admirable business man and on account of his capacity for arranging functions of various kinds, was retained as Military Secretary many years beyond the usual allowance. He has always had a dusky Baron Hirsch or two in training, and has supplied more horses to the native princes, than all the other dealers put together. He is a strange anomaly. Generous, brave and with a 'heart as big as a house,' he sometimes does such funny things at racing that he might be thought, even out of India, grasping, if not 'thick'; and yet, a moment after, he would be ready to give the money thus won and more besides, if an appeal for any deserving object were made to his good-nature. The explanation of these seeming contradictions in his character, appear to be that the spirit of rivalry is so strong in him that he is apt to take the readiest means to be first in every contest.

The paper-chasing which is carried on at Calcutta during the cold weather furnishes good sport. The country is a 'made' one, and the jumps, which are principally stiff mud walls, and hurdles about twenty in number, varying in height from 3 feet 6 inches to 4 feet 4 inches. The distance is from 3 to 4 miles, and the pace is as fast as the horses can go. From this description my readers will see that this paper-hunting is a close imitation of steeple-chasing. The horses are almost all well bred or thoroughbred Colonials. There are big fields, often from forty to fifty starters, of whom there is always a fair proportion of ladies. At Lucknow, under the management of the 16th Lancers and 18th Royal Irish, the paper chasing was conducted on the same lines, except that the course was flagged out, instead of paper being laid down. I very rarely attended any of these events; for my time in the early mornings was always occupied by the horses I had in training. My wife, however, was a very keen paper-chaser. On the mornings of the meet she used to be up at five o'clock, and having dressed and had her cup of tea and slice of hot buttered toast, went off in her dog-cart to find her horse ready saddled at the starting-post. The word 'go' was uttered not later than seven o'clock, and then ensued an amount of hard and zealous riding which would genuinely surprise many an old fox-hunter, could he but see it. These Australasian horses, even when only lately landed, are wonderful jumpers, principally, I think, from the lightness and obliquity of their shoulders. It certainly appears to me that the fact of the large majority of them being allowed to wander over large tracts of country in a state of perfect liberty during their youth, say, up to four years of age, confers on them great freedom of shoulder as well as soundness of limb. I am also under the impression that horses brought up on hilly ground have better shoulders than those reared on level soil.

Calcutta affords to its inhabitants unrivalled facilities for breaking horses either to saddle or harness; for it has, between the English part of the town and the river Hooghly, a level plain of about three square miles in area, over which everyone is free to ride; and there is an ample space set off for the breaking of horses to harness. For making animals quiet to carriage work, some of my Colonial dealer friends used to employ an ingeniously-constructed trap, called a 'jingle,' which had such long shafts that if the horse which was harnessed to it began to kick, he could not reach either the splinter bar or the body of it with his heels. I need hardly tell any experienced breaker that few things make a horse stop kicking so soon and so effectively, as finding that he has nothing to kick against. Another great beauty in it is that the weight put on the animal's back by the shafts can be easily regulated. Here again, the well-taught breaksman will agree with me that the unaccustomed feeling of weight on the back is a strong provocation to a young one to kick or plunge. A third excellence in the jingle, which should not be despised, is that, in the event of an accident or of the horse becoming unmanageable, the driver can readily get out from the rear part of the conveyance! I have been told that the jingle is an American invention.

In India, everybody who, so to speak, is anybody, keeps horses and rides at least once if not twice a day all the year round. There, one's friends are always ready to lend one horses. There is no law of trespass, and, consequently hacking along the road is the exception instead of the rule. These are the causes, no doubt, which make the percentage of capable horsewomen and horsemen larger in India than in England, where not more than one in twenty even out of the few who go hunting ride 'straight.' In fact, the difference is entirely one of practice. Very few of the young fellows who come out to India, know anything about riding on their first arrival, or, indeed, have ever been on a horse except in a riding-school; but after they have served their year's 'griffinage,' we shall find that the majority of them own ponies or horses, play polo, pigstick, paper-chase, race, chase, or at least take their part in the station gymkhanas.

Photo. by H. R. Sherborn, Newmarket.

CHAPTER XIV.

Frank Fillis—Bill Hayes—Mickey Miley—Horse Photography—Journalism in India—Shows in India—Mr Woodyear—Arthur Hancock—Captain Astley, 'The Mates'' Brother.

DURING the last season we spent in Calcutta, we saw a good deal of Frank Fillis who had recently come with his circus from South Africa, where he had made two or three fortunes, and lost them in the crash which took place after the mining boom. He is nephew of the famous James Fillis, who is the greatest living exponent of the French high school of riding, and who happens to be a Londoner. Frank Fillis is a capital circus rider, does the 'jockey act' to perfection, is a good trainer, fine horseman, and is a wonderfully hard-working fellow. He is a man of big ideas, and never counts the cost so long as he can give the public a good show. He had a great deal to tell me about South Africa, where he advised us to go, especially after he had seen a couple of performances which we gave in his circus. His accounts of the fondness of Africanders for horses and of the numbers of wild ones to be found on the *veldt* decided us on making a trip to the land of the Boers.

Our house in Calcutta was a place of call for all poor and distressed sportsmen. One day a bright-looking lad of about twenty came in during morning stables. He told me that he had worked his passage out from England as a fireman on board a steamer; that he had been in a racing stable and had ridden some races on the Continent; and that he wanted a job. As he was a nice light weight and looked a smart, cheery boy, I told him that he could find a room, bed, knife and fork in the house, and that we would go for a ride in the evening; for of course I wanted to see how he 'shaped' on a horse. What a boy that was! Fine, strong horseman, with a heart that knew no fear, and a feeling on the reins as light, yet firm as that of Jack Roberts on a billiard cue. Bill, who happened to have the same surname as I, showed in every possible way his gratitude for the small kindness I had done him, and was so willing and devoted that he quite won my heart. I managed to give him a winning mount in a hurdle race, and with that start, he got several other mounts, and saved £50 or £60 in the first month. At that time a great friend of mine, a New Zealand shipper, Mr John Stevens, asked me to let Bill go up country with him to ride his horses. Knowing that the lad would do anything I told him, I felt greatly tempted to keep him with me; but as it was to his interest to go with Mr Stevens, I consented with a heavy heart; for the boy was so fearless that I was afraid to let him out of my sight. I begged him not to ride anything over hurdles or across country that he was not certain had been well schooled; for I knew that many owners of unsafe horses are cruelly indifferent to the risks men run in riding their brutes. The promise was lightly given. Poor Bill, knowing no fear, got a mount on a manslayer in a chase, with the assurance that 'he is as safe as the bank.' The clumsy, treacherous cur fell at a fence. Bill was picked up badly shaken; but he struggled against his pain. He tried to ride at exercise and do his work as usual; but he caught cold and got worse. Mr Stevens wished him to 'lay up'; but he made light of his trouble. One morning he kept so very still that a servant who was passing through the room looked at him, and found that the boy was dead. We were terribly shocked at the news, the bitterness of which I had felt in anticipation when I said good-bye to him. The worst of it was that he had told me his mother was living; but I forgot to get her address. I have told his story here in the sad hope that she may at least know that in the strange land where he died, he had warm and attached friends who deeply mourned his loss.

My jockeys were inclined to be unlucky. One of them, poor Mickey Miley, whose father used to train on the Curragh, and who was formerly well known in Ireland as a clever light weight, went 'on the spree,' got small-pox and died. Mick belonged to a lovable, easy-going type of Irishman. 'He wouldn't hurt a fly'; 'he would give you the coat off his back'; he had nice manners; was anxious to oblige; and would do anything one asked him, except to look after his own interests. Young Mr Malitte, who was on the staff of my paper, and who also lived with us, was one of the best non-professionals in India, and could ride 7 st. 10 lbs. without wasting. He got killed by accident when riding a training gallop. Geo. Gooch, a famous old-time Indian jockey, on whom I tried various infallible systems for the cure of inebrity, at last 'broke out' again. When he came to himself, he showed his repentance by taking poison; but was brought round sufficiently to enable him to spend the remainder of his days in a workhouse. In India, any fairly good jockey who can ride 8 stone will do well; provided he keeps steady; but that's the difficulty. As a rule, to quote the old wheeze: they eat, and they drink, and they die, and then they write home and say that it is the climate that kills them.

As I had learned a little about photography soon after I

had made the acquaintance of Mr Oswald Brown in Newmarket; I diligently applied myself during our residence in Calcutta to obtaining photographs for illustrating my book, *The Points of the Horse*, with which I had long threatened the reading public. Getting characteristic horses and animals with the required 'points,' bad and good, is a very difficult matter, especially, as exaggeration in many of such 'points' would suggest caricature, which would of course be out of place in a serious work. Being on the best of terms with the 'shippers,' local dealers, officers commanding cavalry regiments and other horse owners, I was enabled to 'run my eye' over, literally, thousands of horses from which to select specimens for my camera. In England, men are as chary of allowing one to take such liberties with their horses, as they would be with their wives; but in India and the Colonies, they are less suspicious and more obliging. As regards the portraiture of animals for purposes of comparison, I had long got hold of the correct idea, namely, that they should be in profile. The broad *Maidan* or plain of Calcutta, with its tropical wealth of sunshine, afforded me unsurpassed opportunities for photographing horses. On this level ground and with a far distant horizon but little broken by trees or buildings, I could hardly help 'taking' my subjects against the sky, and having done this, once or twice, I could still less resist arriving at the conclusion that a horse looks best in a photograph, standing out boldly from his surroundings, when thus posed. Contrary to my expectation, I found that even white horses appeared to most advantage with the background arranged in this manner. I also learned that by placing, in the centre of a plain, a horse which one wanted to photograph; the gregarious animal would instinctively look out in all directions for members of his own species, and would consequently hold himself prouder than if he were standing close to his own stable, or at some accustomed halting-place. In all these cases, I tried to obtain a photograph of the horse and not one of his surroundings, which appears to be the object of those sun artists who subordinate the animal to the hall door or porch against which he is placed, and to the friends and relations who desire to be included in the group. I soon rejected a fixed camera in favour of a hand one, with which I could move about, and thus suit my position to that taken by the horse. This ability was specially necessary to me in my endeavour to get all the portraits in as exact profile as possible, in which attempt, a foot or two, one way or the other, might make all the difference between a failure and a success. Besides, with a hand camera, one can, as one may see fit, lower or raise the machine, for instance, to clear the animal's head from a distant tree or other object. In the class of work which I had on hand, the superior mobility of the hand camera greatly outweighs, as far as my experience goes, any advantages over it which the fixed one may possess. We must remember that a horse retains only for a few seconds any position he may take up, when he is in an attentive, if not excited mood, in which he alone looks well; and that, for him to appear to advantage, he must have his ears pricked forward, which he will continue to do only for a brief period of time.

My progress, which I am afraid was not very considerable, in the study of photography, was greatly facilitated by the fact of my belonging to the Photographic Association of India, the members of which are always ready to lend a helping-hand to their weaker brethren. To the local members, this, as all such associations should be, is, essentially, a darkroom club, at which the student is almost always certain to meet one or more of his *confrères* from whom to obtain practical as well as theoretical help and advice.

Although the English residents in India are very small in number, and are widely distributed through that vast empire, they are, as a rule, well educated, and consequently the local English journals have a high standard of literary excellence. The leading daily papers are the *Times of India*, *The Pioneer*,

The Civil and Military Gazette, *The Englishman*, *The Bombay Gazette*, and *The Madras Mail*. All these journals cater for the decided taste which their readers have for horses and sport. *The Asian* is not an unworthy Indian *Field*, and *The Indian Planters' Gazette* is a bright record of sport and of the doings of Calcutta society, as well as an able mouthpiece of the class which it represents.

India is a favourite hunting ground for showmen. The Indian public being a small one, luckily does not demand large companies and expensive staging. Being composed chiefly of well-read men and women, it is fastidious; but if there be merit in a show, it will not object to the performance being short; for it does not finish its dinner before nine o'clock, and likes to get home by eleven, so as to be up by daybreak for a ride or drive. Among capable showmen, I may mention the names of Tommy Hudson, Frank Lincoln, George Milne and Charlie Harding. The play-going requirements of the natives are best met by a circus. Poor Woodyear, who had been doing big business at Hong Kong when we met him there, brought his circus to Calcutta, but died from cholera not long after his arrival. Having been in the show line myself, I went with a heavy heart to the funeral. As the Calcutta people do not trouble themselves much about funerals, only one of them, besides my sub-editor and myself, was present. When the sad-faced procession had formed up on the road in front of the cemetery, the black professional mutes proceeded to take down the coffin from the hearse and to bear it to the grave, while the real mourners unused to the scene and place looked helplessly on. Though a comparative stranger, I thought I might render to the dead, respectful homage which might be acceptable to those that wept for their dear friend and master, and accordingly gave the lead to have the poor fellow carried to his last resting-place on the shoulders of white men. There was not a dry eye among the ladies and gentlemen of the troupe who stood round the grave. I hope, though cannot expect, that I may have at my funeral as sincere mourners as the clowns, athletes, trick riders and ring men who stood with tearful faces and bowed heads that December afternoon, while the clergymen read the Burial Service over the remains of poor William Woodyear. The scene was very, very sad.

One morning about this time, three travel-stained and thirsty-looking men called at my office. I offered them chairs, the usual whisky and soda, and asked them to tell me their tale, which was as follows: They had just come from Natal, and on landing that morning from their steamer in search of what my friends of 52 Fleet Street would call the 'oof bird,' they inquired if there was anyone who would help them in their designs, and were accordingly directed on to me. Two were jockeys out of work; the other was Arthur Hancock, the once famous walker. One of the knights of the pigskin, Joe Hardy, stayed in India, had good 'chances' and has done fairly well. The other, Martin, went, I believe, to England. I got up two or three contests for Hancock, who, acting on the principle that money earned in a country should be spent in it, paid over the bar of the nearest public house, the £100 or more he might have taken away with him from Calcutta. I was very sorry for Hancock; but he was quite 'impossible.' The decay of those athletes who only think of the present, is almost as sad as that of improvident *demi-mondaines*. Hancock was a grand walker; but had as much capacity for making money out of his long-distance powers as a racehorse would have of 'working' a commission. The only chance such men have of doing any 'good,' is to put themselves in the hands of a 'gaffer,' who would treat and train them as if they were dogs or horses, and who on making a *coup* by their assistance would probably pocket the entire proceeds with the exception, perhaps, of enough to buy a hand-me-down suit of clothes and a couple of bottles of whisky. Hancock had tried America, South Africa, and, I believe, Australia and New Zealand, without materially benefiting himself. Goodness only knows what made him pitch on India, in which country the very thought of walking gives one prickly heat. Finding that a little of it went a long way in Calcutta, I passed Hancock on to my friend, Captain Astley, 'the Mates'' brother, who, like a true sportsman, is always ready to help a lame dog over a stile.

Captain Astley remains absolutely unspoiled by the snobishness and slavish regard to conventional ideas which surround us on every side; and is consequently refreshingly different from ordinary 'sealed-pattern' men, who remind me of the story told about the last joined subaltern that altogether failed to learn the names of his company; because, so he pleaded to his captain, they were all dressed so much alike. 'The Mates'' brother is the greatest living authority on cock-fighting. For many years he has kept in India hundreds of 'war birds,' with which he spends most of his spare time fighting matches and mains at Lucknow and other great centres of cocking, against the birds of Native princes and fanciers, who justly regard him as the grandmaster of their craft. He is an enemy of humbug; is no respecter of persons; has a marvellous fund of quaint and original anecdote; and has been a kind friend to me, and to many more deserving objects.

Captain Astley, who is now in the Pay Department, is an old 11th Foot man. He is a slight, rather tall, active-looking man, with greyish hair, clean-cut, well-bred features, pleasant smile, and an upright, distinguished bearing. When he first went to Meerut, where his regiment was stationed, he arrived with about 500 fighting cocks, the noise of whose crowing was so loud, that the inquisitive ladies of the place sent emissaries to find out what Captain Astley wanted with such an enormous poultry yard. He gravely informed his questioners that he kept it, so as to have a constant supply of fresh eggs, which were the only food allowed to him by his doctor. The ladies thereupon intimated that they, too, would like to eat fresh eggs; but he explained that his hens (which were all cocks) laid only just enough for his own requirements, especially as he was learning to crow, and consequently needed a vast quantity of eggs from which to obtain the proper tone of voice. This news greatly excited the interest of the ladies, who did everything they could to watch the movements of Captain Astley, as they expected at any moment to see him draw himself up on tip-toe, flap his arms and play the part of loud-voiced chanticleer. To him the best part of the joke, which soon leaked out, was that of his being supposed to eat game fowl eggs, which were as forbidden to him as the flesh of a cow to a Brahmin.

I received from Captain Astley the following interesting recollections of Cremorne's Derby:—

'My cousin John Astley had an unnamed one called Brother-to-Flurry, or the Makeshift Colt, that had never run in public up to the Derby of 1872. He was trained by the astute Alec Taylor, and I defy contradiction when I say that nobody knew, or ever will know, how good he was, except George Payne, John Astley and Alec Taylor. All I know is that he ought to have easily beaten Cremorne, if he had but properly come round Tattenham Corner. The first bet laid against him was 1000 to 8 at old Tattersall's; and then the commission was executed with uncommon secrecy and very gradually.

' On the morning of the race, somehow or other, the *Sportsman* got an idea about his form and advised its readers to back him for a place. His starting price of 40 to 1 would have been much longer only for the *Sportsman*. What excitement there was on arrival at Epsom! I hid away in the Durdans to avoid being badgered. At length I emerged from my retreat, and rushing at dear old George Payne and my cousin John, told them how anxious I was that Brother-to-Flurry would win. John Astley remarked, "Nothing but Cremorne can possibly beat him, and I have backed him for £1500 for a place."

'Coming round Tattenham Corner, up went Brother-to-Flurry's head, whereas Cremorne swept beautifully round it.

The unnamed one consequently lost a lot of ground, and was fully fifty yards behind Cremorne when he began to make up the lost distance in a way which baffles description. Just at the last he was "there" but not *quite* "all there." Cremorne beat him by a short head, and a stride past the winning-post he was in front of Cremorne. "What difference does that make to you?" said someone to George Payne. "A hundred thousand, my boy," coolly remarked dear old George as serene as the moon.

'Brother-to-Flurry, who was afterwards named Pell Mell, was fat when he ran at Ascot, so did not win, though they laid odds on him. Cousin John would not run him in the Cesarewitch, being afraid that some lightly-weighted thing would beat him and so spoil his reputation.

'My cousin has owned several good horses, notably Arbury, given him by Newdegate, and called after his place. Arbury ran second for the Grand National. Cousin John then turned him into a hunter, and didn't he show them the way across Leicestershire!'

Photo. by H. R. Sherborn, Newmarket.

CHAPTER XV.

Dan Kingsland—Argentine Horses—Sample's Second Show in London—Another Frost—Colonel Pole Carew—Taming Horses by Machinery—The Love of Englishmen for Horses—Lecturing at the Polytechnic—Mr Frank Haes—The Veterinary Fellowship Degree—Bound for South Africa—Mr Edwin Ashe—Mr W. W. Reade's Cricket Team—Miss Genevieve Ward and Mr Vernon.

WE returned to England in 1891, and I set to work to bring out new editions of some books of mine which were out of print. Among other men I met was Dan Kingsland, who had brought over a shipment of horses from the Argentine Republic to sell in London. He was formerly a driver of a coach in Victoria and seemed glad to meet me and have a talk about his old Australian friends, Teddy Weekes, Macklin and other Colonial dealers whom I had known in India. He had been at Buenos Ayres for about three years.

and was working for the rich firm of Caseres. I went two or three times to Palmer's Green where he was staying, and took a careful survey of his horses. They were for the most part, fairly strong, under-bred animals, averaging about 14.3 high. They had good bone and sufficient substance; but had plain heads and a tendency to be goose-rumped. Although they were well suited to light cart work, they did not fetch at auction more than about £14 apiece; for they were almost all unbroken and could not be handled by the ordinary run of men with safety. People in England have a horror—and small blame to them—of wild brutes that try to knock the brains out of anyone rash enough to come within reach of their hind or fore feet; and will, consequently, give but very small prices for horses fresh off the scrub, pampas, or veldt. In England, above all places, manners make the horse. The South American half breeds whom Kingsland brought over to look after the horses, did not seem a very capable lot. Had he had rough riders like my Australian friends, Doolan, Steve Margarett, Alfred Praetz, or M'Cracken, they would have put the animals straight in a very short time. In such a case, the employment of quick methods of breaking means the saving of time and money. For instance, I would engage, with the help of two good assistants, to make in a fortnight (I might almost say in a week), a hundred such horses, quiet to handle and capable of being ridden about by a lady. They are the type of the useful, medium-sized horse which would suit the Indian cavalry, and other purposes in which 'plainness' might be compensated for cheapness. The question of their importation to India is entirely one of freight, which I believe would be higher between Buenos Ayres and Calcutta, than between Melbourne and Calcutta.

I may anticipate events a little by saying that since that time Kingsland, in later shipments, has brought over horses of much improved class, and has consequently obtained a proportionately enhanced average. The last I saw fetched £23 a piece for tramway work, at which they have given great satisfaction. While I am writing there are a couple of thoroughbred South American fillies imported by him in my paddock. They are good-looking, smart animals with first-rate shoulders, and were sent to me to break and train by Mr F. Pritchard. They give so much 'promise' that there is every probability of the experiment being repeated on a large scale in the near future.

We were not long in London before we met our old friend, Sample, who had perfected and patented in all countries his invention for taming horses by machinery, and was then showing it at Hengler's Circus, with Mr Blundell Williams, who was financing the speculation, as manager. The show, as might have been expected, was even a worse 'frost' than that of 1885; for it was all machine and no amusement. I remember once meeting in town Colonel Pole Carew, who was military secretary to Lord Roberts and who had attended one of my classes abroad, 'Come to teach the Cockneys how to break-in their horses?' asked the cheery guardsman. 'No,' I replied, 'I have come to England only to bring out books.' 'You are quite right,' he said, 'Londoners do not want to learn anything; they only wish to be amused.' I felt the truth of Colonel Carew's remarks, as I sat in the almost empty circus and watched Sample's dreary performance; and thought how different it would be, if he had in the ring a wild South American broncho or two, which he might have easily procured, and a brave man to be bucked off. He could then reduce the 'terror' to obedience, teach him to jump, put up a young lady who would ride the animal about the place, hop him over some hurdles, and 'draw' all London. That was the programme my wife and I would have adopted had we been in Sample's place. Had he not been infatuated with this infernal machine, he might have extracted a few jokes out of it; but he *would* treat it seriously, at a time when his audience were pining to be made laugh. The show soon came to an end, and he and his machine were left stranded.

He was very anxious to go abroad on tour with us, but he and my wife could not agree; for they held totally different views on the manner in which a show ought to be run, and they *would* say what they thought, especially, when they had waxed warm in argument. As defeat had not altered the opinion of Sample as to the correctness of his own ideas, I felt that if I took him with me he might jib at any suggestion that did not tally with his 'system.' Besides, as sailors say, standing rigging makes bad running gear. I grant that I am quite as pig-headed as Sample or anyone else; but, as I had the money to pay the piper, I thought that I had the right to call the tune. Giving up the idea of taking Sample with me, I proposed to hire his machine; but he would hear of nothing except selling a 'territory,' as he called and pronounced the right to use the invention in any particular district. As I was not taking any 'territories' just then, I relinquished the thought of utilising the machine for my own benefit, as well as for that of its patentee.

That machine had cost Sample five years' work and about £3000 in hard cash; for while the idea was growing in his mind he neglected all other business in the endeavour to give it material form. With the mechanical skill which comes naturally to an American, he had devised it in a very ingenious manner. It consisted of a platform which could be rotated by steam or hand, and which supported a 'crush,' or kind of horse box, in which the patient was to be placed, secured, and then spun round, at any required velocity until all the 'starch' and 'stuffing' had been extracted out of him. He was then taken out and used for exhibition purposes. With inexplicable fatuity, the mistake of the first show was repeated. No sufficient proof was given that the animals to be experimented upon, had any 'devil' in them, and when they were released, the audience was supposed to take for granted that their manifest tameness was entirely due to the efficacy of the machine. My experience with horses convinced me that, from a practical point of view, Sample's machine admirably fulfilled the intentions of its inventor; but its working was neither amusing nor exciting, and consequently it was useless for show purposes. As one might think at first glance, there would have been no real difficulty in getting into it any wild or violent horse that had been provided with a strong head stall and rope with which to hold him. By its aid and that of three or four assistants, one could have tamed (not broken in) three or four wild bronchos or 'scrubbers' an hour, and with but little danger and exertion. I was not alone in the favourable opinion I held about this machine; for Dr Fleming, late Principal Veterinary Surgeon of the Army and ex-President of the R.C.V.S., to whom I showed it and explained its merits, considered it such a useful adjunct to the ordinary means of breaking-in horses, that he gave Sample a flattering testimonial in its favour.

Horse training, unless there is a good supply of genuinely wild animals, or unless the performance is strongly supplimented by riding and jumping, makes, as I have already pointed out, a terribly 'thin' show for an ordinary English audience, which from lack of practical experience with horses, is incapable of understanding many of the good or bad points of what is being done. It is ridiculous to imagine that people can take any real interest in a subject which they have never studied, and of the knowledge of which they have experienced no want. The idea that all Englishmen are devoted to horses, is, doubtless, the relic of a tradition handed down from a time when their ancestors lived a more or less country life. No doubt, the effect of such a wholesome tradition is to stimulate sporting feeling, and, if opportunity offers, to convert a mere sentiment into a healthy reality. But in the vast majority of cases, the ordinary Englishman's love for horses is mere love for gambling. If this were not so, we would find that horse shows would be far better attended than race meetings; for, as a rule, the numbers and varieties of horses are far greater at the former than at the latter. Also, the peculiarities of conformation and action of the animals at a race meeting would be more carefully studied than the state of the odds. We all know that racing cannot be carried on without betting; for if that were stopped, the British public would withdraw their patronage, and there would be no 'gate' from which to give the added money. 'What I likes about racing,' said a young so-called sporting publican, who was a devoted student of the turf from a 'tape' and 'price list' point of view, 'is to see my two "quid" coming into the straight, a dozen lengths in front of everything, and all the rest pulling up.' I may point out that other sports connected with horses, such as hunting, polo, pigsticking, and Indian paper-chasing are carried on without either betting or money prizes; but the interest taken in them is confined to horse owners, or, at least, to persons who have some practical connection with horses. Journalists know the tastes of those for whom they write; so, if we desire to learn what sort of horse talk is most pleasing to the average Englishman, we need only peruse the reports of race meetings in our daily and weekly papers. In them we find the gambling aspect of the case analysed with the most minute care, but not a word is said about the horses themselves, beyond general expressions of praise or disapproval. The very selection of the reporters is enough to point out that exact knowledge of horse flesh is not expected from them. Then again, let us take the few of the average Englishmen who have enough money to keep horses; do they, I may ask, as a rule, buy horses to break-in, ride, school, hunt, and make companions of? Not once in a thousand times. If they do spend their money on horses, they, in the vast majority of cases, keep them for show, hand them over to the care of their grooms, coachmen, or trainers, and then pose as lovers (?) of horses. I have seen a great deal of true love for horses among impecunious subalterns abroad, who often had to practise rigid economy on their mess bills and other expenses in order to keep their ponies, which they looked after like a hen would her chickens: but not among non-riders. On the other hand, if we inspect the very small minority of Englishmen who practically interest themselves in horses, we shall find men of marvellous enthusiasm for and devotion to the subject in which their lives are wrapped up. No detail connected with horses is too trivial for them; and no information too dry. But we don't meet them every day, or in every crowd.

About this time I went up for the veterinary fellowship examination, and obtained the right to put F.R.C.V.S. after my name. Members of the Royal College of Veterinary Surgeons are eligible for this examination after they have been in practice for at least five years.

In the autumn of this year I gave, in the Regent Street Polytechnic Institute, a lecture on Animal Photography, which I illustrated, principally, by magic lantern slides of the photographs which have since appeared in *The Points of the Horse;* and had a large and interested audience. When I had done my talk and was about to depart, a gentleman came up to me, and introduced himself as a photographer who had devoted a great deal of his time to the portraiture of horses. He said a lot of flattering things about my work, and, as I had mentioned that I was going to bring out a book on equine conformation, he, in the kindest possible manner, offered to give me the use of any or all of his extensive collection. Since that evening, Mr Frank Haes, for that is his name, and I have been fast friends. I found that he had preceded me in the adoption of the idea, that, for the sake of comparison, animals should be 'taken' in strict profile; although I believe I was the first to insist that, as a rule, a horse looks best in a photograph when he is more or less placed against the sky. Mr Haes was certainly the pioneer of animal photography and the fine work which he did in that line, during the old wet-plate days, testifies to his great technical skill, and true artistic feeling. I got from him, among other subjects, photographs of Diophantus, winner of the Two Thousand Guineas in 1861; of Caractacus, winner of the

Derby of 1862; of Hannah, the heroine of the Oaks and St Leger in 1871; of Favonius, who won the Derby in 1871; of Cremorne, the winner of the Derby in the following year; and of a specimen of the now extinct quagga. I need hardly point to the immense value of such historical portraits. Mr Frank Haes is a prominent figure in the photographic world, by whom he is greatly respected and liked. The two Mr Dixons (father and son), Mr Clarence Hailey, Major J. Fortune Nott, Mr Sherborn, and Mr Gambier Bolton have done much to encourage the public taste for the photography of animals. Mr Medland has been very happy in his instantaneous work in the same direction. In Germany, the name of Anschütz is best known; in France, that of Delton.

As the winter was coming on apace, and as neither of us cared to become laid up with influenza or any of the other seasonable complaints, we completed our arrangements for our long talked-of trip to South Africa, took our passage in the good ship *Dunottar Castle*, and left Southampton towards the end of November 1891, bound for Cape Town. As an old traveller by the P. and O., French Mail, and many other lines, I must say that the accommodation and food on this Castle steamer left nothing to be desired. We had a pleasant lot of passengers, including the Ward-Vernon theatrical troupe, and an English cricket team, 'run' by Mr Edwin Ashe of Richmond and Mr W. W. Read, the well-known Surrey amateur. The team consisted of Messrs Reid, Murdoch, Ferris, and Brann, and the professionals, Alec Hearne, G. G. Hearne, J. Hearne, Chatterton, Brockwell, Harry Wood, Martin, Pougher, Ayres, and Leeney. As this tour was managed on purely commercial lines, and as all the members of the team came out first class, it was understood that Jack was as good as his master. Read, Murdoch, and Ferris naturally tried to draw, between promateurs and pros., that imaginary line of social demarcation which is recognised only in the cricket world. Relations would have been over-strained on several occasions, had not Mr Ashe, with the consummate tact of which he is a master, been present to restore harmony. He was the real, though vicarious, leader of the party, the members of which were so influenced by his unselfish kindness and winning manners that they treated his suggestions as orders. He was led into this speculation in a round-about manner. Being well and favourably known at the Cape as he is in England, he, out of pure good nature and with the desire to promote sport, allowed his name to be used in arranging the terms of the trip with the South African cricket authorities. Within a few days of the time appointed for starting, the gentleman who was to have financed the team failed to produce the passage money, so Mr Ashe, feeling that he had unwittingly bound himself to the engagements made, joined in with Mr Read. Though the team won all its matches in South Africa, it was not, as might have been expected, a success. The Ward-Vernon troupe were, on the whole, a capable lot. Miss Genevieve Ward is a Jewess of romantic history. She has a grand style and has a rich, deep musical voice to aid it. Years ago she made a great sensation in London by her playing in *Forget-me-not*. Old playgoers consider that since the days of Mrs Siddons no actress has played the part of Queen Catherine, the hapless wife of Henry VIII., so powerfully as Miss Ward has done. Her last success was at the Lyceum as Queen Eleanor in Tennyson's Becket. She reminds me a good deal of that great tragic actress, the late Miss Glynn. Mr Vernon and his fellow player and passenger, Mr Gofton, are clever, and have no 'side.'

CHAPTER XVI.

Horsebreaking in Cape Town—Englishmen in South Africa—Social Equality—No Style—Sir Henry Loch—Port Elizabeth—A Stranded White Man—A Cockney and a Mule—A Real Showman—'Outside of the Ring, please'—Killing Horses—Rockwell—Driving Tandem without Reins or Traces — A *Café au lait* funker — October, the Basuto Kafir — Mr Hilton Barber—South African Farmers—Cauliflowers Three Shillings a Piece—South African Horses—Horse Sickness—Defeated by a Mare—Bloemfontein — Orange Free State Boers —Colesberg—Candlemas and Belladrum—Roaring.

SLEEPY, old, semi-Dutch Cape Town looked a terribly unpromising place in which to start a horse show. Like at Singapore, all the residents (to use an Irishism) lived out of it. During the day, they worked in their offices, like bees in their hives; but by six o'clock in the evening, they had flitted to their homes miles away in the picturesque surrounding country, leaving the streets empty of carriage and rider. Their horses were mostly of the uncomplaining, spiritless slave sort. Very few of the owners of these animals rode, and those who went in traps preferred, as a rule, to entrust the reins to a black groom than to steer the conveyance themselves. To meet them at the City Club, they were a charming set of fellows: hospitable, 'good company,' and always ready for a game of pool or poker; but horses were not much in their line. In my ignorance I imagined Cape Town was the capital of South Africa, and thought it incumbent on me to give a show there, so as to advertise myself for the remaining towns in that part of the continent. But I could not see how I was to make a start. From the date of our arrival in the beginning of December, up to Christmas, the attention of the inhabitants was centered by day on the doings of the cricketers, and by night, on the performances of the actors. We sat 'tight' and 'suffered,' as the jockeys say. When Yuletide arrived, every man and boy gave themselves wholly up to its celebration, which they merged into that of the New Year; and then took a fortnight's holiday for the effects of the liquor to die out. By the end of that time, our purse was so light that we could brook no more delay. By the kind assistance of H.E. Sir Henry Loch, *The Cape Times*, *Cape Argus*, Colonel O'Callaghan of the Gunners, Major Garnet of the York and Lancaster Regiment, and other horse enthusiasts, we got up a class at the Fort and at Wynberg camp. As all the gentlemen who attended came with the idea that they were going to learn a lot about horses, they went away thoroughly satisfied; and I feel certain that we left a good impression behind. On one occasion, to enliven the proceedings for Sir Henry Loch and his party from Government House, I let my wife get on a buck-jumping pony that had disposed of all the young men of the place who had been rash enough to mount him. Though the little fellow did his best, he could not stir her in the saddle. This good performance was very warmly applauded. I may remark that if a lady will ride in the way we teach, her seat will be far stronger than that of any man in a hunting saddle, and quite as firm as that of a practised rider in a buck-jumping saddle.

'British workmen' or their descendants form the large majority of the English residents in South Africa. In their struggle after wealth, they do not appear to have had the inclination or opportunity to advance in education or culture beyond the standard of their ancestors. Their reading is chiefly confined to periodical literature and novels. Fluctuations of wealth have been so common among this essentially gambling community, that the possession or want of money makes but little difference as regards social distinction. The well-born and well-educated are so few in number that they either form a 'negligable' quantity by remaining apart, or become merged in the crowd. In England, men are 'gentlemen' by birth, education, or money. In South Africa, the only 'guinea stamp' is the fact of being a white man. Consequently every English colonist regards himself as the social equal of everyone else, and is no more puffed up by that idea than he would be by the thought of there being practically no difference between his flesh, blood and bones, and those of any of his neighbours. If he happens to earn his bread by the sweat of his face, he will make no blatant claim, as a working man, to superiority over those who have been born with the proverbial silver spoon in their mouths; for he considers that he is their equal; and they his equal. He will be a kind and helpful friend to you, so long as you treat him as he treats you; but no patronising airs please, or there will be a coolness, if not a fight. If you ask him to have a drink, he will consent with pleasure; and, when the fluid has disappeared, he will return the compliment. If you do not want to drink any more, have a cigar instead of the whisky or beer, or say that you will only be too glad to let him 'shout' next time you and he meet; but, unless you want to insult him, don't play the *rôle* of the superior person by expressing your wish to pay for him. I need hardly say that the average workman in England would take many such insults without getting angry. Not so the South African son of toil, whose independence of mind is above all praise. As regards education and the observances which are current in what is called 'good society,' he is certainly not worse, even if he is but little better than the members of his class in England.

In Australia, where there is practically no admixture of black and white blood, the rising generation are proud to call themselves Colonials or Australians, and would resent being termed Englishmen. In South Africa, where miscegenation is not unknown, the English-speaking inhabitants will brook no other name but that of Englishmen. To style them Colonists would be an indignity; to allude to them as Africanders, an insult.

Sir Henry Loch, who is a man of tact, as well as an aristocrat and a soldier, keeps his people in good humour by playing to their social equality ideas. He invites all the shopkeepers in the place to his garden parties; and they, in their turn, allow him the honour of being governor over them without having the slightest power in their government. This amiable fooling serves to keep both sides in good humour. We brought letters of introduction to Sir Henry from our good friends, General and Mrs Monty Turnbull. Both he and General Turnbull had fought side by side in the old Sikh war of 1847-9.

From Cape Town we went to Port Elizabeth, which is a thriving commercial city. The newspapers had prepared our way so effectively that all I had to do was to give a lecture in the town hall. The mayor, Mr MacIlwaith, kindly took the chair, while I explained my programme, told yarns, amused my audience, and got up a big class, the members of which being all riding men, like those of Cape Town, took an intelligent interest in the work, which was gratifying to me. With the approval of keen horsemen like Mr Wimble, Mr Miles, Mr Guthrie, Dr Edwards, Mr Lyons and others, I felt that all we had now to do in South Africa was to go on and prosper. We had a pleasant week's breaking among men of the same sort at Grahamstown, and after that I held, by invitation, a second class at Port

Elizabeth, where I left my wife, when I went to hold a class at Craddock.

My assistant up to that time had been a young Londoner of the clerk class, which is the worst of all for getting on in foreign countries. He wrote a much better hand than I did. He was well-educated, sober, honest, respectful in his manner, punctual, attentive to buisness; and yet for want of a certain amount of 'devil' and physical energy, he was only fit to be put behind a counter or at a desk, at neither of which kinds of work are there any vacancies in the Cape. Dalston (which will do as a name for him as well as any other) not being a hard-handed, resolute style of chap, was in a 'stranded' state when I first met him. He could get no employment at Cape Town, and his prospects of suitable work up country, even if he had the money to go there, were even worse. I could not help wondering what on earth had ever induced him and hundreds like him to come to South Africa, for which they are as suitable as a one-legged man would be for sprinting. At the time I engaged Dalston, I was patiently waiting at Cape Town for the completion of existing functions before starting our show, and hoped that, when it would be ready, my coadjutor would have learned to clean leather and steel work, and to know the names of the various portions of my saddle and bridle gear. This he did with alacrity, and displayed great intelligence in the manufacture of oxygen gas for our magic lantern. He understood the chemistry of the process quite as well as I did, and used to stop up half the night studying that portion of optics which refers to lenses and condensers. I was careful to explain to Dalston that the magic-lantern lectures I gave were merely a bit of by-play to the serious business of horsebreaking. I trusted that he would not become discouraged during the period of our enforced idleness, and promised to make him as expert as I was in the art of giving horses good manners and snaffle bridle mouths. I advised him not to be too venturesome with the horses in my forthcoming classes, and told him that when they 'came off,' I would allow him only to hand me the gear which I required, so that he might have every advantage in observing the manner in which I 'went about' difficult horses. One day while holding my class at Port Elizabeth, I explained the wrong and the right way of lifting up a horse's hind leg, and to give Dalston some encouragement, I granted him, as I considered, the great favour of showing the assembled gentlemen how an expert would 'pick up' the near hind leg of a vicious mule which stood in the centre of the ring, as a subject for experiment. Dalston apparently misconstruing my meaning, acted to perfection the part of the typical novice, for the enlightenment of whose ignorance I had come to South Africa—so I had declared in lecture and on hand-bill. The mule did not enter into the joke; for the moment he put his hand on her fetlock (instead of on her hamstring, as he ought to have done), she 'let fly' and knocked him down with admirable precision. To turn the mishap to good account, I ran forward, gathered up Dalston under one arm, and sawed the air with the other, while I explained that although I had always advised my assistant to observe the principle of *point de zèle*, his youthful enthusiasm had outrun his prudence and that, wishing to demonstrate the wrong method of lifting up a mule's hind leg, he had played his part in too realistic a manner. I lifted him on his feet, whispered an encouraging word or two, looked imploringly at him to see if I dared tell the gentlemen present that he would now show them the right way of picking up the mule's hind leg; but as I saw the poor fellow was in a state of abject fear, I did the job myself, and passed off the mishap as best I could. When the class was over for that day and while we were returning to our hotel, I explained to Dalston what a chance he had missed in not turning the accident to good account as any true showman would have done. He replied that he was not a showman. I pointed out that according to the text beloved of John Hubert Moore, that they who take by the sword, shall perish by the sword. Dalston answered very meekly that he did not feel at all inclined to die, and that he would be very grateful if I would help him to go to Durban where he knew a publican who would give him a job in his bar. I paid his passage, and as I said good-bye to him on board the steamer, I was delighted to see that the 'hunted' look which had of late become habitual to his face, was replaced by a happy, thankful expression of deliverance. We met again at the close of my tour at Natal. He was behind a bar and doing well. 'Dalston,' I said, 'you ought to take up my game and run a show in a lot of places I have left out. You would make heaps of money; as you know all the business.' 'Serving drink at a bar is good enough for me,' he replied. 'I would not go near a horse if you gave me a £1000.' I laughed at this, as it reminded me of the mule; and to show I was friendly with him, I gave him a ticket for our show, and hoped he would come. He promised he would do so: but he was probably afraid that he might tumble up against another mule; for he gave his ticket to someone else and stayed away.

To illustrate the way in which a real showman would endeavour to turn disaster into profit, I may recount the two following incidents which befell Sample. On one occasion, the great American tamer, while holding a class, got into a light trap to which a horse that he had put through his system was harnessed. It seems that all the 'stuffing' had not been taken out of the animal; for, as it was being driven round the ring, it kicked, plunged, and finally upset the cart on top of Sample. Horror-stricken, the members of the class rushed into the ring to extricate their teacher from his perilous position. 'Keep outside of the ring, gentlemen, please!' called out Sample from under the cart, 'I am just showing you how *not* to do it.' He then hailed Joe, who pulled him out of harm's way. Sample adjusted his gear, gave the horse another dose of the 'system', and drove it round in his usual fine style to the immense delight and admiration of his audience.

Another time, when holding a class in America, the animal with which Sample was doing the head and tail trick, fell down the wrong way by accident, and broke its neck. Thereupon, he called out to the irate owner: 'How much did you value that horse at?' 'Forty dollars' was the reply. 'Here's the money,' said the showman, handing him that amount. 'Now gentlemen,' continued Sample, 'if you have got any more vicious horses to be killed, bring them along and I'll settle them up.' His open-handed action of paying and looking pleasant, made him a host of friends, and quickly brought back the forty dollars with liberal interest.

To be a good showman, a man requires not alone to be clever, ingenious and resourceful; but must also be ready to utilise flukes as much as well-played strokes. Some of my readers have no doubt heard of Rockwell, the famous American horse tamer and trick teacher. This great expert had broken a pair of horses so admirably to harness, that he was able to drive them about in a town, and make them walk, trot, turn corners, and pull up, without reins; their entire guidance being accomplished with almost imperceptible movements of the whip. To bring horses, in the open and at liberty, to such a high state of training as this, required an extraordinary amount of skill, patience and time from the teacher. Marvellous as this feat was, Sample accomplished by pure accident the still greater one of driving in tandem a leader which had neither reins nor traces. While touring through Australia, he was asked to break into harness a horse that used to persistently refuse to pull between the shafts. Wishing to take the animal with him to the place at which he was staying, he was going to hitch him to the back of his trap, when the horse becoming frightened by something or the other, broke loose, and successfully resisted all efforts at recapture. Sample, tired of the pursuit, and wishing to proceed home, got into the cart and drove off. He had gone only a little way, when to his surprise, he saw the loose horse range itself in front of the harnessed one, and act as if it was in tandem. It quickened its pace, 'slowed down,' turned or pulled up in exact accordance with the wheeler. Sample kept the knowledge of this incident to himself; bought the horse; and, by its means, acquired a reputation for skill in breaking to harness, even exceeding that of Rockwell, who, sad to relate, went down with his entire circus and troupe in a steamer which foundered at sea.

In place of Dalston, I took with me to Craddock a light-weight lad who had been riding horses at exercise for one of the local trainers. He, like the majority of other Africanders or 'Cape boys,' was a sort of Anglo-Hottentot-Dutchman. As he knew the country and could speak English and Dutch, I hoped he would be useful. While I was holding my first class at Craddock, I broke in a very bad buckjumper, and having fixed him up with a saddle on his back in such a manner that he could not buck, I told my *café au lait* friend to mount, while I held the horse. My nominal assistant begged to be excused, as he did not want to have his neck broken. Not wishing to argue out the subject before my pupils, I turned to a group of Kafir boys who were standing by and offered 10s. to anyone who would get on the horse. Hardly were the words out of my mouth, before a tall, strapping Basuto with a pleasant, ugly face, which reminded me of that of a favourite bull dog I once owned, strode up to me and said with a cheery smile and a light-hearted toss of his head, 'Baas! I'll ride him.' Pocketing the half-sovereign I gave him, he threw his long legs across the animal and immensely enjoyed the futile efforts it made to break loose from my grasp. When, after about ten minutes, it had 'given in,' I unfixed it, and gave the reins to October (that was the Basuto's name), who rode the animal quietly about the ring. These half-civilised Kafirs, I may remark, are great users of second-hand clothing, and especially of cast-off uniforms ; for they dearly love a bit of colour. October, at that time, affected a garb which was a cross between that of a cowboy and of a costermonger. He had on an enormous slouch hat, smart jacket brightened up with bits of gay ribbon, scarlet sash round his waist, moleskin trousers, tight down to the knee, and from that opened out like bells over his No. 19 boots. After the breaking was over, I took him back with me to the hotel, and engaged him as my servant at £6 a month. It was not likely that I should miss securing such a treasure as I recognised him to be. Brave, big-hearted October was destined to be my faithful companion through many adventures. He was always the same willing, devoted helper. Nothing that I could do or say would make the slightest difference in his dog-like affection for the ' baas' he loved. Of all the men I have ever met, had I to choose one to be my companion in danger against man or beast, I would select October ; for he knew no fear, and would do anything I told him. He was a man of simple tastes, and needed for amusement, after the day's work was done, only a bottle of *dop* (Cape brandy), which he would drink with one of his *vrows*, of whom he appeared to keep a relay at every place we went to. Not wanting the whitey-brown boy for ornament, I paid him up, and saw him no more.

At Craddock, I met a fine specimen of an English Cape farmer in Mr Hilton Barber. He has a farm of over 100,000 acres, on which, among other things, he raises ostriches and racehorses. He is fond of the great game and is a good sportsman. The custom in South Africa is to have immense farms ; anything under 50,000 acres being considered a small one. A Boer does not feel comfortable if he can see from his own house the smoke from any other man's chimney. Fortunately, the ambition to be a large landed proprietor in that part of the world can be easily gratified ; for land can be bought right out for from half-a-crown an acre, and upwards. Owing to want of water, much of the land is unproductive, and the high price of labour restricts the amount of tillage within very narrow limits. Despite high protective duties, the most of the corn, and even of the flour, is imported. So backward is the practice of agriculture, that market gardening is almost unknown, except in Natal, where it is assiduously and profitably carried on by natives of India. The most of the vegetables eaten by white men are imported in tins! So scarce are fresh vegetables in up-country towns, that, as a rule, those which come into the market, are auctioned off singly. It is nothing uncommon to see a cauliflower which in England would cost twopence, knocked down to the highest bidder at three shillings. Throughout Cape Colony, Natal, the Orange Free State and the Transvaal, there are lots of well-watered ground admirably suited for market gardening, which land might be cheaply purchased; but no one seems anxious to enter into such a sound speculation. 'They are too lazy or too well-off,' you, my readers, will possibly remark. Neither alternative, I think, quite explains the case, which is, more probably, one arising out of the unsettled state of men's minds in South Africa, where booms and collapses have followed each other in demoralisingly rapid succession. The farmers have few wants. A suit of clothes lasts them for years. They don't buy books, back horses, smoke any tobacco which they don't grow, drink any liquor which they don't make, or eat any food which their farms do not produce. They don't keep fast society, gamble, go to theatres, or 'take any delight out of themselves,' as we say in Ireland. With a minimum of trouble, they make more than they can spend with raising cattle, Angora goats, merino sheep and ostriches. It is not likely that they should bother about anything which cannot propagate and develop itself without assistance. I am afraid that some of them are just a little lazy; for I have known several instances of these gentlemen buying harness horses, when they had hundreds of animals running wild on their land;

but did not care to take the trouble of catching those they required and breaking them in.

Among the South African farmers' sources of income I have not mentioned horses, which, though they abound throughout the country, do not bring in much money to their breeders. The Cape horse of thirty years ago, was a strong serviceable animal that was well up to remount form, and was prized in cavalry regiments in India. At present he is as extinct as the quagga. His place is now taken by a weedy slave, who, though sound and hard-working, is singularly deficient in spirit and strength. Colonel Swaine who commanded the 11th Hussars when I met that regiment in Natal, told me that is was impossible to get horses which had speed enough for purposes of manœuvre. The South African troopers of his regiment were a very 'scratch' lot, and cost about £40 apiece. The average unbroken Cape horse fetches about £7. The farmers have not alone to contend against scarcity of grass from want of water; but are menaced every season by that awful equine scourge, 'horse sickness,' which slays an average of, probably, 20,000 horses a year. With the fear of this terrible plague over them, it is no wonder that the breeding of horses is neglected. The well-watered parts of South Africa are admirably suited to this purpose; not alone as regards ordinary requirements, but even for racing, if we may judge by the capable way such horses as Prosecutor, Goschen, Stockwell and others, have held their own against imported thoroughbreds.

'Horse sickness' is a specific fever, the symptoms of which more or less resemble those of anthrax, from which it is entirely distinct in its nature. It runs a rapid course and is always fatal. It is, I believe, peculiar to South Africa.

Having to struggle against the want of water and the frequent occurrence of horse sickness, it is greatly to the credit of the farmers that they endeavour to improve the breed of their horses as much as they do, by the importation of fresh blood and by the establishment of agricultural shows. As I was asked to judge at several of these shows (Bloemfontein, Colesberg, Pretoria, Petermaritzburg, etc.), I can testify to their good management.

Throughout South Africa there are an immense number of horses raised in a semi-wild state on the various farms. Very few of these animals would be from an English, Australian, or Indian point of view, worth breaking; for the privations they have to undergo from want of grass, make them weak and listless. Four of them harnessed to a two-wheeled Cape cart or a dozen of them attached to a coach, serve their purpose admirably; for, when their work is done, they need no further attention than to be turned out into the *veldt* to cater for themselves; though the owner may at times pamper them up with a little Indian corn and some oat hay. Such horses, even if they could be obtained for nothing, would not be worth exporting to India or to any other country. The really serviceable horses, say, those up to light cavalry remount form, would fetch more money in South Africa than in India. Consequently, we may regard the exportation of horses from Africa as a thing of the past; at least, for many years to come, and until a preventive to horse sickness has been discovered.

While I was at Craddock, Mr Hilton Barber sent me over, to experiment on, a five-year-old mare which had never been handled, and which, from having been allowed her liberty so long, had become very artful. Expecting to see the mare led into the ring, I was greatly surprised to see her driven into an adjoining yard in company with two or three other loose horses. This was my first experience of having to tackle an absolutely wild loose horse. Though she hit out all round, and was cunning and quick, I put on a halter by means of a long stick without much difficulty. My real trouble now began; for nothing would induce her to 'lead.' She fought and struggled and when she found that she could not get away, she threw herself so violently on the ground that I thought she would kill herself. As often as I forced her on her legs, so often would she throw herself down, the moment I tried to put any restraint on her. Seeing that this was a determined case of 'sulks' which would be tedious to cure, and not knowing how to get her into the breaking ring without injury to her, I passed her over, and took another subject, which, I thought, would make a better show. I frankly confess that this mare defeated me; for I had never before met any animal quite of her sort. I may plead, as some excuse, that the flooring of this yard was so hard that any attempt to break her on it was quite out of the question. As my breaking ring was in an open field, I could not catch her in it. On the other hand, although I was able to halter her in the yard, I could not induce her to lead out of it without the risk of her injuring herself against the trees and stones which were in it.

From Craddock, October and I went to Bloemfontein, which is the capital of the Orange Free State. There I met some very kind friends in Mr Rietz the President, Mr Williams of Tempe, Mr Raafe the High Sheriff, and others. I was now with the Boers, among whom news travels so slowly that I thought it advisable to give a free show to His Honour the President, Mrs Rietz, and a few representative gentlemen. To test my skill, they brought me a horse which no one had previously been able to handle, and which had been given up as a bad job by the best Boer breakers. It was driven in loose into the showyard, and I haltered it as soon as I got it into a corner. It showed plenty of fight without any sulking, and accordingly gave in after a short time, so that October and also one of the local grooms could ride it about quietly. As my audience were thorough horsemen, they greatly appreciated the quickness and efficacy of my methods of breaking. I got up a good class, which gave me a flattering testimonial in Dutch.

Although the Free State Boers helped their cousins of the subsequently formed South African Republic, during the

Transvaal war, they have very friendly feelings towards the English. They are fond of horses and pay a good deal of attention to breeding.

From Bloemfontein I went to Colesberg, which, though only a village, is the capital of the best horse-breeding district in Cape Colony. Hearing that my teaching was well worth the two guineas a head I was charging for it, all the young farmers of the place trooped in and paid their money. I had lots of good subjects, and left behind me a large number of expert horsebreakers, who, I know, will remember their old instructor with kindly feelings for many a year. I must say that I have never met men more anxious to learn sound, practical work about horses than these young South African farmers. Having been outrageously swindled time after time by so-called Englishmen, who are mostly east-end Jews, the Boers naturally regard every man who speaks English as a thief. But if one is fortunate enough to gain their confidence, they will give it entirely without reserve.

At Colesberg I had the pleasure of meeting the Van Zeils, who are wealthy landowners and great lovers of horses, and Alec Robertson of Stormfontein, who goes in largely for the breeding of thoroughbreds, and with capital results. He and Mr Homan, another rare good sportsman, owned Candlemas, who is full brother of St Blaise. Although Candlemas was a terribly bad roarer, all his stock are sound in their wind. The same can be said of the 'noisy' Belladrum, who after winning the Two Thousand Guineas was sent out to the Cape for breeding purposes. His produce did no good; as they almost all turned out light in bone and were weedy. I may remark that roaring, although common in damp, cold climates, is practically unknown in dry warm ones like South Africa, India, and Arabia. It is far less frequent in Australasia than at home. Big horses are more liable to it than small ones; and grain-fed animals, than those which are restricted to grass. From Colesberg I went to Kimberley, at which place I had arranged for my wife to meet me.

CHAPTER XVII.

The Diamond Fields—Lecturing at Kimberley—Badly reported—The De Beers Company—'Squaring' Governments—'Trapping'—'I. D. B.'—Taking the 'Sulk' out of a Horse—The Horse and the Goat—Equine Friendships—'Wasters' and 'Remittance Men'—Captain Goodwood—Broken-down Officers—Manners and Customs in South Africa—The Kimberley Exhibition.

AS I had a letter of introduction from my fellow clubsman, Captain Gordon Hughes, the well-known pigeon shot, to Captain R. E. Wallace, who is one of the chief diamond valuers to the De Beers Company, and as our names by that time were well known through the country, we got to know all the good people at Kimberley very quickly. At that time the inhabitants were enjoying the calm before the storm which Mr Rhodes was preparing for them. Knowing that Kimberley was the hot-bed of I. D. B., he had issued orders that it was to be destroyed by removing all the employés of the De Beers Company from it and locating them in the new town of Kenilworth entirely by themselves. He arranged that their wants should be supplied by company's stores on terms against which no private individual in Kimberley could compete, and gave them every facility for recreation and amusement. The streets of smart shops, the broad roads with fine trees on each side, the luxuriously built villas, the large hotels, the best club in South Africa were all doomed to decay in the near future. Yet a short respite was given; for the South African Exhibition was to be held at Kimberley in four or five months' time. Many of the residents deeming the first loss the least, had disposed of their property for what it would fetch and had departed, in the majority of instances, to Johannesburg, or the Randt as it is familiarly called. But others held on in the hope of making a fortune during the three months of exhibition time. These men are so accustomed to take the rough with the smooth, the lean with the fat of life, that they seemed to be but little affected by their impending financial doom. Anyhow, the tightness of money, about which I had heard and read a good deal, luckily did not prevent them from coming to my class.

In order to explain my programme and to put myself *en rapport* with the people, I gave a lecture one evening in the Town Hall on horsebreaking, and Mr Lawrence, the mayor, very kindly took the chair. I felt myself in good form, told lots of yarns, made the audience laugh, and must have spoken well; for after my talk was over, I had a large number of applicants to join my class. Although I may carefully think over what I am going to say, and may even jot down a few short notes to be used while I am speaking, I always find that when I begin to talk about horses from a platform, the subject carries me away, so that I am guided neither by notes nor by any pre-arranged plan. In this I believe I am no loser; for if I were to pay more attention than I do to the choice of my words and to the construction of my sentences, I would weaken the interest of the audience in the subject-matter of the discourse. Besides, when a man is thinking of his words (as when reading from a book, or when repeating by heart) or of himself, more than of his subject, he can rarely help pitching his voice in too high a key, and, consequently, in an unnatural tone of voice, which, however beautiful the words or admirable the reasoning, will fail to impress the hearer. During the forenoon of the day on which I was to lecture at Kimberley, Mr Wilson, the editor of the *Diamond Fields' Advertiser*, came to see me at the Grand Hotel and asked me to give his reporter before I went on the platform a copy of the address I was going to deliver, so that it might appear to the best possible advantage in the newspaper next morning, and would thus be free from any errors the shorthand man might make. I gratefully thanked him, and promised compliance; but was so occupied with visitors that day, that I forgot all about the promised manuscript. As I was dressing for dinner before going up to the Town Hall, I suddenly remembered that I was to give a copy of my lecture to the reporter. As there was then no time to write it, I thought I might utilise an article which I had very carefully written on the same subject for another paper; but which I had kept back for some reason or the other. This I handed to the reporter on my arrival at the hall, with the uncomfortable feeling that my audience would, after reading their paper on the following morning, conclude that the local proof reader had outrageously embellished my discourse of the preceding evening. When I saw Mr Wilson on the next night he laughingly told me that I had unwittingly placed him in a very awkward position; for several of his subscribers who had heard my yarn and who had read its supposed reproduction in the newspaper, had written to him saying that it was a disgrace to Kimberley that such an admirable lecture should have been so badly reported.

The great success of the De Beers Company is due to their having been able to buy up the mines of their rivals, and to hold I. D. B. (illicit diamond buying) in check.

In both these immense undertakings the genius of Mr Rhodes has helped them greatly. To make a 'corner' in diamonds, he had to be strong; but to keep I. D. B. in control, he had also to work on the fine old principle that every man has his price. As English law supposes that everyone is innocent until proved guilty, and that the burden of proof lies on the person who asserts the affirmative, it was manifestly inadequate to grapple with this contraband trade. The De Beers people accordingly drafted out laws which, they considered, would meet their difficulty; and by judicious 'squaring' induced the Cape Parliament to put them into force. It would be preposterous to suppose that if the House of Assembly had not been 'squared,' and very well 'squared,' too, it would have enacted that anyone found in possession of an uncut diamond could, without further evidence, be sent to penal servitude, unless that he or she could conclusively prove that the stone had been lawfully obtained; that conviction would follow such detected possession, even if the accused person could prove that he or she had innocently obtained the diamond from police officers of the company who had given it with the deliberate intention of betraying the receiver; and that all such convictions were summary, without any trial by jury. The company make no secret about this system of 'trapping,' which they try to excuse on the plea that it is essential to their existence, and aver that it is never put in force, except against those whom they have good reason to know are engaged in the illicit traffic. As their detectives obtain rewards for convictions, innocent people are, of course, now and then trapped. The victims, however have the consolation of knowing that although it is naturally a hardship to have to 'do time' on the 'breakwater' at Cape Town, where they are sent for I. D. B., it is not much of a disgrace in the eyes of the South African public, who, directly or indirectly, have had a fairly large connection with the game. Not alone was the policy of 'squaring'

I. D. B. 239

legislative assemblies successful in the Cape Colony, in which the possessions of the De Beers Company lie; but it was also extended with equally facile results to the neighbouring, though foreign, Governments of the Transvaal and Orange Free State. Viewed from purely a commercial point of view, I do not see that the De Beers people are either to be praised or blamed for their handling of the I. D. B. question. If they have adopted discreditable means to accomplish their ends; their enemies, who had begun the battle, fought even more unfairly.

I. D. B. is a subject around which a great deal of romance has centered in the minds of emotional people in South Africa. We have had pointed out to us the Jew millionaire whose prolific *chère amie* used to go to England every year for her annual interesting event. On one particular important occasion, having her feet firmly planted on English ground, she refused to deliver up the burden she carried until her 'friend' had made her an 'honest woman.' This he did with the best grace he could; for he regarded her as a lesser evil than the loss of his uncut diamonds. There were the Africander or native 'runners,' who, before the 'squaring' of the Orange Free State, used to carry 'parcels' across the frontier on specially-trained racehorses. These 'boys' took a pride in their hazardous calling, and used to swagger about Kimberley in the smartest of riding toggery, drinking champagne at a guinea a bottle, smoking half-crown cigars and generally misconducting themselves. The female detectives of course made a point to 'trap' their rivals in love. A policemen who had been censured for 'slackness' for not obtaining convictions, induced, after a great deal of persuasion, a friend, who was far from well off, to lend him five pounds, and after insisting on his benefactor keeping in pledge an uncut stone which he gave him, informed on him, with the result that the unfortunate friend got three years penal servitude. Another policeman put two of his friends, with whom he used to go on short trips across the frontier to shoot, into a serious predicament by, when he was over the 'line' one day, bidding his friends good-bye and riding off towards Natal with, of course, a 'parcel' concealed somewhere about him. There were lots of stories about the detectives who used to fish along the roads by means of uncut stones which they laid down as ground bait, and when, from their place of concealment, they saw a verdant passer-by pick up the diamond and go on as if nothing particular had occurred, they would sally forth, seize him, and bear him off to summary injustice. As many of the female's 'tees' were also *demi-mondaines*, they had unusually good facilities, which they fully utilised, for 'trapping' their lovers.

One of the first horses given to me to break-in at Kimberley was a black stallion that was driven along with his harem of about a dozen mares into the enclosure in which I was holding my class. He was about six years old, and was so wild and violent that although he had been caught once or twice, he had successfully resisted all efforts which had been made to secure him. In a short time I had him saddled, and gave October the signal to mount. The hitherto untamed one carried his black burden quietly round the ring, and allowed the Basuto to dismount and mount again without making any attempt at 'playing up.' Not alone had all idea of active hostility against his captors been removed out of his mind; but the far more difficult task of 'taking the sulk out of him' had been accomplished for the time being. His education was now so far advanced, that he would require only a few more lessons of far less severity than the first, to confirm the habit of obedience.

Almost all the horses that were brought to me at Kimberley were semi-wild ones which were driven in off the *veldt*. One of these subjects was followed into the ring by a goat, which tried to butt everyone who attempted to make him quit his equine friend. The goat appeared to take an intelligent interest in the proceedings, and as soon as I had finished with his companion, and had driven him out of the enclosure, the goat followed him, and the strange pair went off at full gallop to the distant pasturage, from which they had been taken. It is worthy of remark that this friendship had been cemented while these animals were in a practically wild state. While at Cape Town I noticed the existence of a friendship between a horse and a cow, both of whom, by keeping constantly together, showed that they valued each other's society. On more than one occasion, I have known amicable relations to be entertained between a cat and a horse. In such instances the love of puss appeared to me to be wholly selfish, and that she liked to lie on the horse's back, because it supplied her with a warm couch, from which this inveterate lover of ease and pleasure could watch the movements of the mice that came out in search of the grains of corn which had fallen from the manger. A racing pony mare which I owned, and which was barren, indulged in the kindly freak, when she had been turned out to grass in her old age, of adopting a motherless foal, and was never happy unless it was close to her side. Captain Beresford of the Royal Artillery once had in India a racing pony called Potboy, who would go nowhere unless he was accompanied by a particularly ugly and worthless pony mare, who accordingly spent her time walking about training grounds and attending race meetings, at which her friend Potboy was engaged to run. If she did not go down with him to the starting-post, he would persistently refuse to go forward when the flag was dropped.

A man who has seen the world, and especially if he has been a soldier, is certain to meet with in South Africa some of his companions of former days and of different scenes. The majority of these exiles are 'wasters,' as a rule, from 'drink,' though in a few cases absolute incapacity for business is their only fault. One in twenty, to take a liberal estimate, makes money, and attains to a good position. In all 'foreign parts' are to be found a class of Englishmen, who, to use a New Zealand expression, we may call 'remittance men,' on account of their always averring, when seeking temporary assistance, that they are waiting for a remittance from home. Such folk, as a rule, are no good either to themselves or to the colony in which they reside; for with few exceptions they prefer to 'cadge' and 'loaf' on anyone who is good-natured enough to listen to their tale of woe, than to pull off their coats, roll up their sleeves, and work. However graphically they may 'tell the tale' about the love which their rich relations in England bear to them, the fact remains that the said 'friends' are delighted to have seen the last of them, and would on no account send them money to return and annoy the family. Making them 'shift' for themselves is the truest kindness. To give a case in point, I may relate that of Captain Goodwood (which is not far from his name), who was in the service when I knew him in India. He was then a tall, smart, good-looking fellow, fond of horses, hospitable, 'good company,' member of a very old family, and close to the succession of an earldom; but volatile. In fact, so much so that he took no pleasure in doing anything that was staid. On account of his connections and pleasant manners, his colonel 'stood' him as long as he could, and then gave him the best possible advice. The next place I met him was at a horse show at a country town where he was a local magnate on account of having married a charming young lady of great wealth, every penny of which her guardians, knowing their man, had insisted on putting under her entire control. I lost sight of him for a year, and then met him in London, looking as *débonnaire* and well dressed as ever, though with a slight suspicion of anxiety in his eyes. He appeared overjoyed to see me—why I could not just then tell—and begged me to come that evening to supper at his rooms; the address of which he gave me. I went there, and met, besides my host, his brother, and a couple of men who had that undefinable something about them which indicated more the bird of prey than the homely pigeon or goose. We sat down to play a game of cards called Marmora, in which three cards are placed face downwards on the table in front of each player, and one card is turned up as the trump. A pool having been formed, the player on the left of the dealer is asked how much he will 'go'; his chance of winning being that one of his three cards, none of which he has as yet seen, will be of the same suit and of higher value than the turned-up card. Naturally, if a two or a three of, for instance, hearts has been exposed, the player will feel justified in thinking that he has among his three cards a heart which will beat it, and will 'go the lot,' or a good part of it. Having declared the amount of his bet, he will turn up his three cards, whether he has to draw the money from the pool, or in the event of his losing, to pay an equal amount into it. The next player will then be asked how much he will 'go,' and so on. The amount in the pool will naturally fluctuate greatly; for it may have to be frequently made up by general subscription, or it may increase to a very high value by a rapid succession of bold though unlucky declarations. My host's brother and myself played the game in a way which even Cavendish would have admired, and went 'the lot' only when a two or a three was turned up, which was frequently; but fortune or skill proved monotonously unkind. The strangers on the contrary played with seemingly the most deplorable recklessness, and went 'the lot' even when a knave or a ten was against them, and always won when the pool was big. I did not continue this game long; but quite long enough to lose a considerable sum, as it was very 'warm' while it lasted. Although from the peculiar and remarkably skilful manner in which the strangers manipulated the cards, I thought I had reason to suspect that they had played with what Mr Labouchere calls 'the advantages;' I payed up and went away, vowing that I would have nothing further to do with a gentleman who cultivated the acquaintance of such highly-gifted card-players. Sometime afterwards, I was glad to hear that Captain Goodwood's friends, not being satisfied with his ways, had renounced him and all his works, and with commendable fortitude had decided that he should never again spend a single penny of their money. I heard no further tidings of him for several years, and concluded that he had had the good taste to die, until I happened one day in South Africa to go into a wayside bar to have a drink. As I laid down the glass my eyes fell on a well-known face, sodden with bad brandy and worse whisky, yet having in it a few traces of those of a soldier and a gentleman. I felt sorry enough for the poor waif, in whom I recognised the once handsome and brilliant Captain Goodwood, to take him into lunch, and give him as much food as he could eat, and as much liquor as I thought good for him to drink. When he had lighted a cigar, and had poured out his second or third glass of Benedictine, I threw off the *rôle* of stranger which I had assumed, and addressing him by name, asked him in a cheery way how he had been getting on. In his old light-hearted way he described his adventures, and how he had at last settled down as a simple member of the Cape Mounted Police on the inclusive pay of five shillings a day, out of which he had to keep his horse, and to feed, lodge and clothe himself. I could not help thinking that he was much better thus than at his old games in town, after which his soul hankered day and night.

Another old acquaintance I met was one of the good-natured fool sort. He had been second in command of a smart Hussar regiment, had left the service, and had drifted out to South Africa, where his too readily made friends had robbed him of all his ready money, and left him in the old, old way, waiting for remittances. Another man whom I knew slightly, and who had commanded a distinguished infantry regiment, hawks milk round Johannesburg. I am afraid that soldiering is not a very good training for life in South Africa.

Literary globe trotters who come out to South Africa and publish their *impressions de voyage*, have viewed, as a rule, the manners and customs of the people from a wrong standpoint. Having, generally, been accustomed to the society of people of good education and of sufficient leisure to cultivate the refinements of comfort, if not of luxury ; they do not realise the fact that the moneyed people with whom they associate in South Africa are the representatives of the artisans and tradesmen of England and Holland. Consequently, it is unfair to apply to them a standard of culture which is not appropriate to their class. In the education which is to be derived from social intercourse as well as from books, South Africa has of late years made rapid strides, and there is no doubt but that in the near future, when society has settled down, the most of the relics of barbarism, which either amuse or annoy the visitor, will be removed, even before they are things of the past in the parent countries. The member of the Athenæum, Carlton, or Army and Navy Club who comes out, probably remarks that the ordinary man whom he meets, cares but little for art, science or literature ; that he pronounces the words 'clerk' and 'Derby' as they are spelt ; that when speaking of his wife, he calls her Mrs (whatever her surname may be); that he considers a lady a fine musician if she can play a waltz on the piano ; that when comfortably seated he is not particularly inclined to jump up and offer his seat to a lady who is obliged to stand for want of a place to sit on ; that when ladies are present, he sometimes thinks it superfluous to ask their permission if he wishes to light his pipe or cigar ; and that he sees no harm in cleaning his nails in public and even at meals. The visitor will also be surprised to find that at hotels the waiter invariably brings him cold instead of hot milk with his coffee ; and that the horrible cesspool system of sanitation is almost universal up country. If, however, he be a man of the wide, and not only of his own narrow, world, he will know that in similar grades of life in Holland and in England, the people are equally, if not more, deficient in education and refinement. As regards any want there may be of studied courtesy towards women, we must remember that South African ideas on that important subject are, to a certain extent, those of the Dutch farmers, who look upon their womankind more as useful household drudges than as intellectual equals. At the same time, I must say that if these colonists do not make a great parade of their politeness to ladies, it is not for want of goodness of heart; for they could not possibly be kinder or more obliging than they are to them in any time of need. The one thing which they do not go in for is 'style.' Their saddlery is the commonest stuff which comes out of England, and is rarely cleaned. Their bits and stirrup-irons are never touched with a burnisher; and their horses are seldom groomed. No doubt it is better to have them as they are, than to burden their minds with refinements of culture which would be of no use to them in their rough life. The rising generation in South Africa are to be admired for their independence and readiness of resource.

My wife's pluck and skill in riding bad horses and those that had never been previously bridled or saddled were immensely admired, especially by the Kimberley ladies, whom I had put on the free list; as they were all either wives, daughters, or sisters of the members of my class. As almost all the men had a great deal to do practically with horses, they were never tired of listening to me while I held forth on my favourite subject, or of watching me handling, mouthing, and teaching to jump the animals they brought me. Needless to say that my cup of happiness was full. Our work here was so warmly appreciated, that the committee of the South African Exhibition, which was to be held four months later in Kimberley, invited me to hold performances during the three months of the Exhibition time. They offered me seventy-five per cent. of the 'gate' and promised that they would pay all expenses for advertising, seating, and lighting. The offering of these liberal terms was a good proof that they considered that our show would be a big 'draw.' Unfortunately, I was unable to fulfil this engagement; for the rough work through which we subsequently went, injuriously affected my wife's health so much, that she felt it would be impossible for her to bear the fatigue of riding day after day at the Exhibition. As I would have to run the affair entirely as a show and not as a class, I felt that I could not work it properly single-handed. I had intended to have gone home and to have brought out some big jumping horses ; but the time was too short to make these arrangements. So, greatly to our regret, we were unable to return to Kimberley.

Photo by M. H. Hayes.

CHAPTER XVIII.

DIAMONDS.

THESE precious stones form such a large industry in South Africa, that it may not be inappropriate if I give them a short chapter to themselves.

They are obtained either by mining or by surface washing. The former operation is incomparably the more important one of the two, and as it requires a large capital, it is worked by companies. The latter is the sole kind of diamond hunting open to private enterprise, and is pursued, principally, on the Vaal River, with financial results which are not as a rule very satisfactory. Although the diamonds found there are inclined to be small and of not very frequent occurence, they are generally of fine colour.

A diamond mine appears to occupy the site of some old volcanic eruption, during which a mass of liquid material burst through the overlying strata on its way towards the surface, and, on cooling, assumed the appearance of a slaty-coloured hardened earth, known technically as 'blue ground.' This formation does not appear usually to have reached the surface, at which it is generally covered by a bed of 'yellow ground.' The 'blue' is the essentially diamond-bearing deposit; although there is a certain but small proportion of diamonds scattered through the yellow ground. The pretty translucent stones with which children used to play on the *veldt* now possessed by the De Beers' syndicate, and which, on being recognised by a passing traveller as diamonds, gave the first hint of the enormous wealth that lay beneath the surface, doubtless came from yellow ground. When a main shaft of blue ground has been tapped, there appears to be practically no limit to its depth. The increased expense due to the continued sinking of the mine, is often more than compensated for by the proportionate richness, in diamonds, of the 'blue,' the further it lies from the surface. I feel that I must omit all detailed mention of the manner in which the diamonds are extracted from their matrix, and of the extraordinary precautions which are taken to prevent the stealing of these stones; for it would take me too far away from the main subject of this book.

The De Beers Company have obtained control not only over all the South African mines, but also over all those that are worth working in other countries. Finding that the world will spend yearly not more than £4,000,000 sterling on diamonds for himself and his wife, the company regulate its output, so, that without seriously depreciating the value of these precious stones, it will issue just enough of them and no more, to secure the £4,000,000. The output necessary to attain this object, forms only a small part—probably not a twentieth—of the diamonds that it would be possible to dig up year after year. Any attempt to glut this narrowly restricted market would not only fail to extract more money from the public, but would almost certainly have the evil effect of rendering these stones unfashionable from their cheapness. Had the companies which the De Beers' people 'bought up,' continued to work in rivalry, this result e'er now would have come to pass, and diamonds might, perhaps, have ceased to merit the name of 'precious stones.' I may mention that a stone to be 'precious,' must be rare, beautiful, and permanent enough in its nature to stand wear. With the exception of the Kimberley and Jagersfontein mines, all the others have been closed, so as to keep down the superabundant supply. The Kimberley mine is remarkable for its extraordinary richness; though the stones extracted from it, are, as a rule, of inferior quality. The Jagersfontein mine, though not nearly as productive as the other, turns out diamonds of great purity. As regards quality, we may divide diamonds into 'white' stones, 'off colour' stones, and 'fancy' stones. A stone to be 'white' should be free from the slightest trace of yellow (the besetting sin of these minerals), brown, red, or any other colour except blue, of which a faint shade greatly adds to its value. 'Off colour' stones are those which are slightly though manifestly tinged with any colour except blue. They are worth comparatively little, even when the shade is perceptible only to trained eyes, and even when the diamond, thus discounted, might have finer lustre than an ordinary white stone. Diamonds which are decidedly off colour find a market chiefly among the native princes of India. When, however, the colour is deep without affecting the lustre, the stone is called a 'fancy' stone, and might fetch, per carat, even a higher price than the most beautiful blue white stone. As such a diamond is not 'every man's money,' the owner of one, if he wished to sell it, might have to wait a long time before he got a customer. The commonest off colour and fancy stones in South Africa, are yellow, amber, brown, and reddish brown. Some of the deep yellow ones look very well, and closely resemble yellow rubies; but are more brilliant, and far more costly. Deep amber is a favourite shade, in which I can see but little beauty. I met with no pure red diamonds in Kimberley. As far as I know,

Diamonds. 251

the only blue diamonds of fair size in existence are the historic Hope Diamond, and one which is supposed to be a broken-off portion of the Hope. Before the discovery of diamonds in South Africa, the value of a diamond was reckoned to increase according to the square of its weight. Thus, if a white brilliant of one carat was worth £8, a similar one of two carats would have been worth £32; of three carats, £72; and so on. This enhanced price was due to the extreme rarity of large stones in those days. This scarceness disappeared with the advent of South African diamonds, among which there are so many of a not easily saleable size, that the big ones are often cut into two or more pieces, so that they may be sold separately. As a rule, the public do not care to buy diamonds of a greater weight than four carats. If a diamond exceeds that limit, it will cost too much and will be too obtrusive in appearance for ordinary people. It is altogether a mistaken idea that South Africa does not produce as good diamonds as ever came out of Galconda or Brazil. There is nothing in any high-class white cut diamond to indicate from what country it came. In the majority of cases, an expert can tell not alone from what country, but also from what mine an uncut stone was produced. I may remark that a white uncut stone looks not much unlike a lump of alum which has been subjected to the action of water.

By the kindness of Captain Wallace I had while at Kimberley several opportunities of visiting the De Beers' sorting-room, in which scores of thousands of pounds worth of uncut diamonds were laid out on separate sheets of paper according to their colour and other peculiarities. Their crystalline form, in many cases, was wonderfully perfect, and was specially interesting to a mineralogist.

CHAPTER XIX.

South African Railways—Coaching across the Veldt—Driving Twelve in Hand—Driver and Guard—Food for Horses—Oat Hay—Temper of South African Horses—South African Method of Horsebreaking—Horsemanship in South Africa and Australia—Tying Horses to Post in the Streets—Knee Haltering—The Veldt.

AS the journey from Kimberley to Johannesburg, where I had arranged to go, was rough and costly, I thought it best to leave my wife at Kimberley, where we had several pleasant friends, and to attack the Randt alone. After a wearisome journey of two nights and a day in a most uncomfortable train service, I arrived in Kronstadt, which is a small town in the Orange Free State, and had then to travel twenty-four hours in a coach before arriving at Johannesburg, the capital of the gold fields.

The way in which the railways, a Government monopoly, are managed in Cape Colony is a disgrace to a civilised country. The fact that the amount of the particular fares are not printed, as they are in England and elsewhere, on the tickets, can be explained only on the supposition that the railway authorities make this strange omission for the good-natured purpose of enabling their ticket clerks to get a 'bit' out of incautious travellers. The *habitués* of these lines of course know the proper fares or can readily find out where the list is displayed; but the stranger who has always been accustomed to take for granted that he has, on the ticket he receives, a record of the amount he paid, can hardly help being swindled the first time he trusts to the honour of the Africander ticket clerk. The cost of the fares far exceed that of any other country in which I have travelled, and no attempt is made to cater for the poorer class of passengers. Consequently, the well-to-do Kafirs prefer, as a rule, to walk than to submit to extortionate charges. I may point out that in India, the people of which are extremely poor, there is an immensely large native third-class traffic; for the railway companies of that Empire, by putting the tariff at less than a farthing a mile, make railway travelling cheaper even for the poorest than walking. Except when starting at one of the main termini by an express train, the separate accommodation for ladies, and the sleeping arrangements for both sexes are very inadequate. Any omission made at these principal places can seldom if ever be rectified at any of the intermediate stations; for the officials seem to consider that their sole duty is to blindly carry out the inflexible orders of their superiors, and that they are in no way bound to study the interests of their real employers, the travelling public. The restrictions put on the carrying of luggage are as severe as they are in Germany, and the charge for excess of luggage is much higher. If the railway authorities were taken to task on the foregoing points, they would, no doubt, plead that as the number of their passengers are small, they have to charge them highly. To this I may reply that by doing so they adopt the most effective means of checking any increase in the number of their patrons. This suicidal policy has had the effect of preventing the Africanders from forfeiting their claim to be considered the most stay-at-home people in the world.

The coaching in South Africa is of a primitive kind, and would not commend itself to old Charlie Ward, or even to his son Frank. Yet for all that it admirably accomplishes its purpose. There are no roads either to speak of, or to see. After saying that the country is an open one and not fenced in, I have praised the 'going' as far as I may truthfully venture. The coach is of the old American backwoods sort, is hung on leather springs, and is capable of holding twelve closely-packed inside passengers, with a few less hampered ones outside. Having to be very strong to resist the terrible jolts it receives on its cross-country travels, it is heavy, and as the cattle are either weedy ponies, or small mules, their individual deficiency in pulling power has to be made up by an increase in their numbers. Consequently, a team of ten or a dozen has to do the work of four or six ordinary horses. These animals are harnessed two by two, with one pair of reins for the leaders, and another for the wheelers. The intermediate pairs follow the leaders and do not require any special guidance. The man who holds the reins is an unconsidered cypher. The driver, who is the ornamental man of the show, amuses himself with a light fifteen foot pole, from the end of which hangs a long thong, finished off with a lash of gemsbok raw hide. This sportsman prides himself on the dexterity with which he can manipulate this funny-looking whip, and has more tricky ways of 'catching' and 'double thonging' than ever entered into the mind of even poor Jim Selby. With this flail he can reach either the near or off leader, and can, if he likes, cut 'chunks' out of any of his team. He is, however, supposed to show his skill less by punishment, than by describing figures in the air with the thong, and by shrieking in a peculiarly terrifying manner at his horses. Besides the fifteen-footer, he carries

Food for Horses.

a kind of magnified dog-whip for the special benefit of the wheelers. The third and last person of the coaching show is the guard, whose business is to take tips, tell the passengers yarns, and induce them to patronise the halting-place shanties, at which he is on the free list for food and drink.

The ponies, or horses, if I may dignify them by that term, are admirable workers for their weight, and will trot along merrily and pull gamely up hill and down dale over bad ground, a stage of twelve miles, once, and sometimes twice a day. Their sole food is Indian corn, oat hay, and any grass they can pick up on the *veldt*. The 'mealies' are given in a dry state, whole or crushed, or after having been soaked over night in water. The oat hay, or 'forage' as it is called, consists of oats which have been cut before the grains in the ears have lost all their milky character, and which have been dried in the sun like ordinary hay. If the ears were allowed to ripen more than I have stated, the grains would become so much loosened that they would fall out of the ears on too slight provocation to bear transit, or ordinary handling. This 'forage' is an excellent food. Although I have used a good deal of it with horses when I lived in Calcutta, to which city it is often brought from Australia, where it is known as oat hay, in steamers that are loaded with horses. I am unable to decide whether or not it would be a good substitute for English hay. Anyhow, it is a valuable adjunct or change to a horse's food. It is sometimes used in England during years in which there is scarcity of ordinary hay.

In temper, the South African horses more nearly resemble the Barbs I met at Gibraltar and Malta than any other horses I have seen. Both these breeds are, as a rule, very quiet, spiritless, though good slaves, and are inclined to be obstinate. Their lack of 'life' is no doubt due to the fact of their being kept during their youth in a state of semi-starvation. The cause of the tendency to be sulky I attribute, in the case of South Africans, to their being broken-in at a comparatively late period of life. I have no acquaintance with the early bringing-up of the horses of Algeria and Morocco. No fact in horsebreaking is better established than that the longer the inculcation of discipline is delayed, the more stubborn will be the horse. It is just the same with a child.

The way in which horses are broken to saddle in South Africa is one which I have never seen practised in any other country. It is charmingly simple and has its good points as well as its bad ones. It consists of tying the head of the neophyte close up to that of a steady horse by means of a cord connecting the respective headstalls worn by these animals. After they have both been saddled and bridled, the 'schoolmaster' is first mounted, and then another man gets on the young one, who is powerless to buck, rear, or run away, on account of his head being fixed. Besides this, the fact of his being alongside another horse gives him confidence, and no matter how wild he may be, he will learn in a short time to carry his burden and regulate his pace according to that of his companion. As he settles down quietly to work, the connecting cord may be gradually loosened out, until at last it can be taken off altogether. This is a capital plan if one has a good break horse, and if one knows no better way. Its great fault is its tendency to make a horse unwilling to go alone. Of course, it has no pretensions to giving a horse a good mouth.

The extreme quietness of the majority of South African horses is, I think, due to the fact of their being starved on arid pastures, for a considerable portion of each year, and to the non-stimulating quality and quantity of the food given to them when in work.

As Africanders are 'broad in the beam,' and often have to remain several hours on horseback, they like saddles to be particularly wide towards the cantle, and to have a good 'dip' in them. So long as the saddle is comfortable, they don't trouble themselves about its weight. As they do not, as a rule, study the finer points of riding, they do not affect the narrow-waisted saddles which are greatly in vogue in Australia. Their saddles, with few exceptions, are very clumsy affairs ; but they serve their purpose. South Africa being an extremely open country, little attention is paid to jumping. As the young men connect riding chiefly with shooting, they almost all ride with only the left hand on the reins, while the right hand is supposed to be occupied with a rifle. The use of a sharp curb or pelham is a natural consequence of the adoption of their one-handed form of equitation. With the object of being able to carry the rifle comfortably, the most of the saddle horses are taught to amble or 'tripple,' as it is called. Their style of horsemanship and taste in bridles and saddles are entirely different from those of the Australasian colonists, who regard riding as the art of clearing a five-foot post and rails and of sticking to a buckjumper, and who, consequently, like to have both hands on the reins, and to use no other bit but a snaffle. I can only say that both parties are right from their own very different standpoints.

Before I went to South Africa, Frank Fillis used to tell me that the Africanders were wonderful fellows for teaching a horse to stand quietly in any required spot, by taking the reins off his neck and putting them round any convenient post, or even by letting them hang down on the ground. When I heard this, I vowed that if I ever went to the Cape, I would learn how to teach a horse this valuable habit. Having arrived there, I sought instruction on this point from the best horsemen I could find. They all told me that there was no teaching required ; for their animals are naturally so quiet that the difficulty is not to make them stand still, but to go on. When a man rides into a town on business in England, France, Germany, Australia, or other similar country, and wants to dismount, he either deposits his animal in a stable, or gets it held by one of the unemployed who are always ready for an easy and well-paid job ; if in India, China, or Japan he brings along with him his respective *syce*, *mafu*, or *bettoe* to take charge of the horse or pony. In South Africa he troubles himself about none of these things; but simply gets off, draws the reins over the animal's head, puts them on one of the upright posts which are planted in the ground for that purpose in front of every store, and leaves his mount to take care of itself, while he goes off to transact his work; being well assured that no matter how long he may stay away, he will find it in the same spot on his return.

When a South African wants to turn his horse out on the *veldt* to graze, and wishes to prevent it from roaming too far away, and to be able to readily catch it, he usually 'knee halters' it. This is done by taking the leading rein (a piece of raw hide called a *reim* is employed for this purpose) of the headstall and attaching it, at the required length, to a foreleg, either above or below the knee, by means of a clove hitch, and then fastening the loose end of the *reim* to the headstall.

By the term *veldt* is meant the open plain, which is as familiar a feature of the scenery of South Africa, as the *maidan* is of that of India. The *veldt* is singularly free from trees or even shrubs, and one may go for hundreds of miles without seeing on it any larger form of plant life than stunted grass or *karoo*, which is a green-coloured weed that grows to about a foot in height. The *veldt* is not safe ground to ride over at speed; as it is full of holes made by *mereats* (ant cats) and ant bears.

CHAPTER XX.

Arrival at the Gold Fields—Clubs in South Africa—Johannesburg: its Jews, Englishmen, and Boers—Types of John Bull—A Public Performance under Difficulties—A Lady riding Backjumpers—Performances at the Johannesburg Circus—Bad to Mount—The Farce of Horse Taming Shows in England—How to make a Good Impression—J. R. Cooper, the South African Champion—Wolff Bendoff—"The Mates" Son—Mr Grey Rattray—Eggs Sixpence Apiece—Dave Moss and the "Tape"—Johannesburg "Sharps"—The Really Reckoner Story—Justice to "Niggers" in the Transvaal—Vichy, the Winner of the Johannesburg Handicap—English Horses in South Africa.

WEARY, jolted to pieces, and with a pain in my back which had made me wish to die, I arrived one Sunday morning at Johannesburg on the coach that had carried the mails and three or four passengers for twenty-four miserable hours, with only a rest of, say, ten minutes for changing horses about every two hours. After dropping down from the box seat, the first thing I did was to recognise a passing sportsmen who had been a member of my class at Malta: whereupon we simultaneously exclaimed: 'Dear me, what a small world this is!' My friend seeing my state of collapse, led me off to the Randt Club, which was hard by, refreshed me with the best, and got me made an honorary member. The men of the better sort in South Africa are eminently clubable, and even in the small towns, generally manage to form a pleasant retreat for themselves where they can eat, drink, read the papers, and play billiards without being poisoned or fleeced. Their clubs are comfortable, well managed, and afford a stranger an easy means to become acquainted with the members, who, like all South Africans, are only too glad to be kind and hospitable to strangers who can give a 'good account of themselves,' and who do not put on 'side,' which was the stone over which Lord Randolph Churchill stumbled when in those parts. It is the custom in South African clubs to have a bar, similar to those in public houses, at which drinks are dispensed to the members. Such an adjunct to a club in England or India, would naturally render the place liable to be termed a 'pot house'; but in South Africa the case is very different. There, men who belong to clubs, instead of being more or less idle like those in the two countries I have mentioned, have their time fully occupied, and appreciate the convenience of the bar system. Besides, in a country where good waiters are very difficult to be found, it would not always be possible to procure sufficient and suitable attendance for serving liquor only in the various sitting-rooms. When South African society has assumed a more permanent and a more cultured form than it has up to the present attained, and when its ladies have increased in number, and have become less afraid than they are of each other, the club committee men will see the advantage of catering for the amusement of the members' womankind by, for instance, allowing them the entrance into certain club rooms during certain hours of the afternoon or evening, having lawn tennis courts at which they might play, and getting up periodical dances. Such a desirable consummation, outrageously improbable as it may now appear, will no doubt come to pass in time.

Leaving the Randt Club and feeling about five stone better than when I entered it, I walked down the principal street in the direction of the Central Hotel, where I had sent on my luggage. The street was broad, macadamised, and had good masonry houses on each side. Off this main thoroughfare, there was only one or two metalled roads, with straggling streets of ill-assorted houses; some being pretentious; others, paltry. Many of them were of corrugated iron, which is the staple material of which South African houses are constructed up country. The style of architecture and the method in which the bricks and mortar had been put together, denoted that the buildings had been erected in a hurry and under difficulties to meet the requirements of immediate occupation. Remembering that five years previously Johannesburg had been a mere miners' canvas camp, and that at the time of my arrival it housed 60,000 people, my wonder was not that it was lacking in many of the beauties and comforts of old-established cities, but that it was such a flourishing and go-a-head place as it was. The old proverb of money making the mare go, is equally applicable to towns. As a site for a city, Johannesburg has no advantages. It is situated on a desert, the dust of which, when the wind blows, gets into the lungs of the unfortunate inhabitants and afflicts them with various forms of chest disease. There being no natural drainage, sanitation has to be carried on by the 'pail system,' with the consequence of a chronic stench. It is far away from everywhere else; but it has gold in vast quantities under its surface. I believe it is now the third most productive gold field in the world. This precious metal is an immense advantage in stimulating the growth of a city; but alone, and it is alone in this case, it can never make of Johannesburg anything more than a mining camp: a splendidly flourishing one, no doubt; but still nothing more than a place at which to dig up gold, and to fight for its possession.

The term 'the Randt,' which is often applied to Johannesburg, is a contraction of *Wittwatters randt* (the edge of the white waters), which was the name given in former days to the high ground which fringes a few small lakes, and upon which the capital of the Gold Fields now stands. Although Johannesburg is in the territory of the South African Republic, it is essentially an English-speaking city. Writing from the impression left on my mind during a residence of about six weeks, the whole of which time I had unrivalled opportunities for getting to know the people; I would say as a rough guess that of the business men, four-tenths are Jews; three-tenths, English; two-tenths, Germans; and one-tenth, Americans and other nationalities. I have an immense respect for the Jews as a nation, and number among them several valued friends. Originally they were a pastoral and warlike nation, whose virtues and valour have been recorded not only in the Bible; but also by Josephus and others who were in no way prejudiced in their favour. While suffering from bitter persecution and the enactment of shamefully unjust penal laws, many of them have risen to the highest eminence in art, science, literature, politics, and philanthropy. They are warm friends of our Government, and in many cases flatter us in the sincerest possible way, by trying to pass as Christians. Unfortunately, Johannesburg has not recruited her stock of Jews from the better classes of that ancient nation. With a few exceptions, the best of them would pass for members of 'The Den of Lions' in Rathbone Place; and the majority, for the 'boys' who 'follow' racing. They seem to take their tone from their chief leader, who from nothing has risen to be a millionaire many times over. His East End co-religionists worship him for being the incarnation of successful cunning, and for preferring to remain one of themselves, than to become respected and honoured. The example of a man whom the acquisition of immense wealth has failed to improve in manners, education and taste, is in all communities a public misfortune.

Among the English residents, there are several good sportsmen, like Mr Payne Galway and Mr Buckridge, who play polo, race, and are fond of horses. The same may be said of the Germans, who are quite English in this respect. It is an unfortunate circumstance that there is in our language no term to designate the inhabitants of the United Kingdom. That of 'Britishers' will not do; for it does not include the Irish. Without any disloyalty to my native country, I, as a travelled Irishman, see no impropriety in putting them all down as Englishmen, when out of Ireland, where such a broad generalisation might hurt the hypersensitive feelings of those who regard life only from one standpoint. I make this explanation on account of having dubbed Mr Galway a Sassenach. The mention of his name reminds me that when dining one night with him at the Randt Club, I had a striking proof, one among many, of the smallness of the world. As we sat down, he told me that he had just received a letter from his brother, who is a tea planter in Ceylon, telling him that his greatest friend had broken his neck when riding one of his horses at the late Colombo Races. 'You don't mean to tell me,' I said, involuntarily jumping up, 'that poor Waller is dead?' Hearing me repeat the name of his brother's dead friend, without his mentioning it; Mr Galway was naturally surprised, and asked me how I could have guessed it. I explained that both Mr Waller and his brother were friends of mine, that I had stayed with them when in Ceylon, and that I had seen a good deal of Mr Waller, who was a fine gentleman rider, and who always rode for Mr Galway's brother.

Mr Buckridge, who is a Devonshire man, is a type of John Bull for which I have a great respect; although nature has built me on altogether different lines. He is as English in his speech, manner and style, as if he had never left his native land, whose ways and institutions are perfection in his eyes. He likes his horse appointments to be as smart as Wilton, Merry or Soutar can turn them out. His riding boots would be a credit to Peal ; and his breeches, to Tautz. The rest of his attire is just what he would wear among his own good set at home. As South Africans do not particularly affect collars and ties, or the brushing of boots and clothes, and, as a rule, are content to rely on the local hand-me-down man for their wearing apparel ; they are inclined to resent any approach to 'smartness,' which word I use here in its army, and not in its society meaning. Though I am now 'slack' enough, goodness knows, I have very kindly memories of the days when I, too, liked to be as 'smart' as the best of them.

In Johannesburg there was another gentleman who belonged to the same John Bull type as Mr Buckridge, but was not, like him, a good business man. His ideas were solely centered on horses, hunting and chasing. He was a fine horseman, and would ride any 'chancy' brute sooner than sit down and look on while a cross-country event was being decided. He would live on dry bread and water, and sleep on any miserable 'shake-down,' so long as he could be near a horse or a racecourse. He cared nothing for gambling ; but everything for sport. Through all his bad luck and misery in his exile, he was buoyed up with the hope, which never left him, that one day he would ride the winner of the Liverpool Grand National : he could then die happy. I saw him at the Johannesburg Races riding in a chase, with his left arm bound tightly to his side on account of a recently fractured collar bone. Though his horse had not a hundred to one chance, and was but an indifferent jumper, he rode him straight and well, all for sport ; for proud of the name of G. R., he would not get even the fee of a losing mount, which would have come in very handy to him at that time. As he was cantering down to the post, I took off my hat to him with deep respect, though his back was turned to me, and he was far away from where I was standing.

The Dutch are the nominal rulers of the place; but they don't make much show of authority. The Boers come in to market with their *spans* of twelve to twenty oxen (see page 279). Having done their business quietly and inoffensively, they *trek* away home. The Transvaal Government appear disinclined to meddle with the turbulent foreign crowd in their midst. There are several honourable men among the Dutch officials; but a large number, high and low, of them get 'squared'; a fact which the existence of the iniquitous system of 'concessions' amply proves. No wonder that the Transvaalers view with dismay the increase in size of Johannesburg; for they see that in the near future they will have to choose between allowing the foreigners a vote in the management of their country, or of assembling their bullock carts and *treking* further afield. We have harried them out of Cape Colony and out of Natal. Having beaten us in fair fight when we wanted to worry them in the Transvaal, it seems hard lines that we should now attack them in a manner they are powerless to resist. Their quarrel with us has always been about the treatment of the black man. We claim for him equal rights with the white man. The Boers deny the justness of this claim, and sooner than admit it, they would fight, and if beaten, would prefer to clear out of the entire country, than submit to our dictation on that point. As Sir Roger de Coverley used to say: there is a good deal to be said on both sides.

I occupied the first week of my stay in Johannesburg with getting to know, on the polo ground, in the Stock Exchange, and at the club, all the good sportsmen in the place. I found that they had heard from the newspapers about our work at Kimberley and elsewhere, and that they were anxious to see us perform; but there did not appear much chance of getting together a big class, because all those who were interested in horses had their time fully occupied with a fresh boom that had just then sprung up among New Primroses, Jumpers, Robinsons and other mines. All my friends advised me to relinquish the idea of a class, and to give either at the Circus or in the Wanderers' Ground a public performance, to which, they said, everyone would come. This was a very embarrassing dilemma in which I found myself. A class was obviously out of the question, and a public performance presented both dangers and difficulties. As horses are not bred around Johannesburg, I did no know where to procure subjects, and even if I got likely ones, I could not tell if they would 'play up' on the opening night. Giving a show of this kind on the Gold Fields was a very different thing to one in London; for instead of a lot of law-abiding Cockneys who knew nothing about horses, I would have to face an expert audience, largely composed of a rough element that would stand no trifling. Had I had a circus, a theatrical troupe, a collection of performing dogs, or any show, the performers in which I could have been certain would do their 'turns' properly, my mind would have been at rest; but I had to rely on actors who would give me no guarantee that they would play their parts in the required manner. I confided my trouble to Mr Bonamicci, who had formerly been Frank Fillis's manager. I found him intelligent, sympathetic, capable, resourceful, and trustworthy in every way. We scoured the city and came across a stage-coach horse which no one up to then had been able to ride, on account of his being a very bad buckjumper. The owner, Mr Donaldson, very kindly promised to lend me this animal and another that was equally bad, so I was told. Mr Butters, who is one of the chief men in the Robinson mine, and is an American gentleman of the very best type, offered to produce a vicious mule which was warranted to eat up anyone that went near him. After wiring off to my wife at Kimberley to come in hot haste to Johannesburg, I engaged the Athletic Grounds of the Wanderers' Club, which were to be lighted with electricity, and having fixed the evening, I left Bonamicci to fill up the newspapers with advertisements of the most thrilling kind, to get editorial puffs under 'local intelligence,' to placard the town, and to distribute hand-bills broadcast. My wife arrived; the evening came to pass; I had the animals all ready near the ring; the electric light was on, and three turnstiles were opened for admission; but they proved so inadequate to clear the way in front of the ever-increasing crowd which sought admittance, that half an hour before the performance was advertised to take place, the gates yielded to the pressure from behind, and thousands entered on the free list. This was an unforeseen accident for which excess of patronage alone was to blame. As the crowd invaded the ring, October and I hurried through our work as fast as we could. When the throng of miners, Boers, roughs and gentlemen, all mixed up together in a tangled mass, saw a pretty, slight, young woman of middle height and faultlessly attired in riding costume, step into the ring and walk up to the horse that no one had been able to ride, they began cheering and yelling as if they were all mad. Some shouted out words of encouragement; others, entreaties to leave the horse alone; while the Boers loudly encouraged the animal to do his best against the accursed ' Rednecks,' as they are pleased to call the English. In the midst of this row, my wife was hoisted into the saddle, which she had hardly touched, before the horse began to buck and plunge as if he were possessed with an evil spirit. When he was tired of this amusement I gave him a lesson in jumping, and then my wife rode him quietly about the place and made him jump hurdles for the first time in his life. Her fine horsemanship, the like of which had never before been seen in South Africa, created a great sensation. We then did a lot of interesting work with some other horses and the mule, and finished a very trying evening in a satisfactory manner. Despite the giving way of the gates, we did not do very badly; for we took £173, out of which we had about £140 profit. Had the gates stood firm the sum might have run into four figures.

As the majority of the people who had attended the show had been unable, owing to the crowd and row, to see the performance, I engaged the Circus which Fillis had built, and gave in it a couple of breaking exhibitions, which were largely attended, as we were given some very violent horses to handle.

I may explain that after one of these horses had been tried by October or any volunteer, I used to ask the audience if the animal was bad enough to take in hand. If the answer was in the affirmative, I did the breaking, and my wife the riding. But if, on account of the horse failing to buck, or to resist all efforts to mount him, the cry was: 'Quiet horse; let us have another,' I sent him out of the ring and subjected the next one to a similar test. The refusal of the audience to believe in the vicious propensities of these animals was a bitter disappointment to several of their respective owners, who, both for the reward of £2 which I had advertised for the production of each buckjumper and for the 'swagger' of bringing a horse which no one could ride, had fetched their animals from long distances to our show. I need hardly say, that I allowed no injustice to be done, as far as the 40s. were concerned. This policy of offering rewards for vicious horses and of allowing our audience to choose the animals they deemed most suitable to test our powers, gained us hosts of friends; but soon exhausted the supply of wild horses. It was, however, the only way to render a horse-breaking performance a success as a public show. Deprived of this excitement, it would be as thin and flat to the multitude, as would be a lecture on chemistry without plenty of interesting experiments. To show that we were appreciated, I may mention that after we had stopped exhibiting in public from want of raw material to work on, we made £100 with a horsebreaking class for gentlemen, and a riding class for ladies. Remembering these things and the kind of men and horses we met in the Transvaal, it makes me laugh to see so-called horse tamers performing in England, night after night, for weeks together, on the same old cab horse.

Having had numbers of terribly bad shows foisted on them, the South African public are, as I have already said, coy of strangers ; but are very generous with their patronage, when they get a proof that it will not be abused. They are few in number and are scattered over an immense extent of country. Consequently, it does not pay to tour through that country with a large company. Frank Fillis found out this to his cost. He is a man of very big ideas, and is but little inclined to count the cost, if he thinks he can strengthen his programme. He left South Africa with his circus owing £16,000, and bearing the good wishes of his creditors. Their confidence was not misplaced; for before their first season in India was finished, he had remitted to South Africa the whole amount of his debt.

I had, while at Johannesburg, a very helpful friend in Mr George Fotheringhame, who is a Scotchman, and was then a livery stable keeper and horsebreaker on the Randt. I have heard that he has since gone to Mashonaland. He, like the large majority of the Colonists and Boers who attended my classes, took a deep interest in the work and could never see enough of it. He is a manly, honest fellow, and is one of the many fine horsebreakers I have left behind in South Africa. He was the great friend and second of Couper, the South African champion, who is a quiet, well-bred Scotch gentleman, about 5 feet 8 inches high, and about 10 st. 7 lbs. when 'fit.' He had gone out to the Cape as a lad with the love of adventure and travel strong in him. Finding that education availed nothing there and knowing no trade, he conceived the happy idea of teaching boxing, which he had learned in Edinburgh from old Charlie Ball. He is a natural fighter, 'good general,' and has indomitable pluck and the capacity for taking ' punishment.' His first battle of any consequence was for the South African championship against 'The Lady's Pet,' a West Indian negro, who, though about twice the size of his Scotch antagonist, was out of condition and past his prime. Couper won this fight without a mark. After that he had a good time for some years, during which he was patronised by Mr Barney Barnato, who is an ardent lover of the P.R., and was a clever exponent of the noble art in his younger days. For some reason or the other, a coolness sprung up between the two, and to pay the Scotchman out, the Jew imported his co-religionist, Wolf Bendoff, who was a good second-class man in England. The Johannesburg Hebrews thought that their representative had a nice, easy job against an antagonist whom they regarded merely as a good amateur. Couper being a firm believer in hard work as the best means of getting into condition, kept going his 25 to 30 miles day after day, and stepped into the ring full of muscle, clear in wind, and brimful of pluck and vitality. The Jew despising his enemy, took things easy. In the first few rounds, Bendoff hit his man pretty freely; but his blows, which were somewhat lacking in 'steam,' made little impression on his opponent. As soon as he began to get a little slow from fatigue, Couper, who is a terribly hard hitter, knocked his man about so vigorously that Bendoff soon gave up the fight. I believe that on the day of this battle Couper was a better man than we have had in England for the last ten or fifteen years; I mean in the 'old style,' and not at glove-fighting, for which he was too light. My opinion of Couper's excellence is no doubt worthless, and would not be recorded here, did it not coincide with the estimate formed by that admirable judge, Bat Mullins, after he had sparred with Couper, who used to practise with Bat when he was home from South Africa. Couper might have retired with £10,000 or £12,000; but he lost the most of his money speculating in mining shares; his chest became permanently weakened by the irritating dust of Johannesburg; and he had a run of particularly bad luck in other respects. Out of the ring, as well as in in it, he took his punishment like the brave, honest fellow that he is. I may mention that although he was a professional prize fighter, he has always been warmly welcomed as a guest at the Randt Club, and at all other places where gentlemen congregate at Johannesburg. Not long ago he published a novel, which shows a great deal of literary ability, and is specially interesting to those who are acquainted with the persons and scenes in South Africa described by Couper.

While at Johannesburg, I met on different occasions a nice young fellow, a Mr Astley, who is a son of Sir John, and who was in the Barnato office. I was sorry to see him there: for I thought he was as much out of place, as his father had been among the Hurst Park financiers, who, after utilising his name to the utmost, 'shunted' their benefactor. A man of whom I saw a great deal and liked, was Mr Grey Rattray, who, though a kind-hearted and honest fellow, has the strange fancy of wishing people to consider him unscrupulously sharp. He is a bold speculator, and is singularly clear-headed, even for a Scotchman. Speaking to him one day about the high cost of living at Johannesburg, I foolishly remarked that it was monstrous that eggs should cost there sixpence apiece. 'If,' replied he. 'I learned that there was a country in which eggs sold for a guinea each, I'd pack up my portmanteau and go there straight away.' From this accurate view of life taken by him, I learned to estimate at their true value the advantages offered to capable men by South Africa, in the up-country parts of which the coin of least value is a three-penny bit; and the lowest price paid, and paid willingly, by the poorest working man for a shave, is sixpence.

There is a large number of bookmakers, chiefly Jews, at Johannesburg. They are a pleasant lot of fellows out of whom a good deal of fun, if not money, can be extracted. One of these gentlemen, probably, as a delicate compliment to Lady Loch, who is a sister of the late Lord Lytton, called himself by that name, under the idea that it was the English equivalent of his own, Lichtenstadt ('Light town'). Dave Moss, another of the Randt fraternity, was a man for whom I had much sympathy. Instead of spending his spare time in the Beaufort or Albert (he never aspired quite so high as the Victoria), he was eating his heart out on the Gold Fields, and all on account of not having been able to keep his own counsel. Those of my readers who are old enough to remember the introduction of the 'tape,' can no doubt call to mind many occasions on which, instead of an intelligible row of words being presented on the long and narrow strip of paper, the letters and figures came up in a seemingly hopeless state of confusion. While punters at gambling clubs were eagerly waiting for the result of a race, such a joke on the part of the machine, was taken by them in anything but good part, and the interruption instead of being hailed as a respite from the labour of betting, always acted as a stimulant, until the tape had corrected itself and had repeated its lesson correctly. One day when in London, Dave Moss happened to look at the jumbled mess which the tape disclosed at that moment. He continued gazing on it, until at last, by a marvellous inspiration he saw how to make sense out of the confusion. Like unto one of his own prophets in ancient days, the spirit of inspiration waxed so strong in him that he explained the riddle unto the people. And then he went to his tent or his apartments and cursed himself for having been a fool for teaching his brethren to read riddles set them by machines, instead of backing the winner each time to a certainty, without anyone else being the wiser.

The inhabitants of Johannesburg are proud of the sharpness of their 'boys,' and tell the visitor wonderful tales of these practitioners cheating the Boers (the Dutch farmer is the recognised victim) at the three-card trick, faro, and other games of skill. I really must warn those of my readers who intend to go to South Africa, to be prepared for the ready reckoner story, which the new-comer is doomed to hear from ten to a hundred times a day, according to the company he frequents. It runs thus: A Jew (they say it was Ikey Sonnenberg; but in this case I think the *vox populi* is a lying spirit; for my Vryburg friend is incapable of a shabby trick), having concluded the purchase of a number of articles— bullocks, sheep, bags of corn, or it does not matter what— from a Boer, made up the account greatly in his own favour, paid the farmer and dismissed him. The Boer on his way home, thinking he had been defrauded, worked out the sum according to his Dutch almanack in which a ready reckoner is always included. Finding that the total was a good deal more than the amount he had received, the yokel retraced his steps and demanded the difference. The Jew on hearing this claim, asked for its explanation. When he was shown the ready reckoner, he took up the almanack, and after inspecting its title-page, handed it back to its owner with the contemptuous remark that as it had been written for the previous year, it did not hold good for the present one, and that consequently its ready reckoner did not apply to the case in point. The Boer thereupon acknowledged the justice of the plea and departed. If only a tenth of these stories are true, it is no wonder that the Boers hate the English, among whom they include all English-speaking Jews.

People in England pride themselves on the love which they feel for their black brethren, and are willing to let the blood of their officers and soldiers be shed in maintaining equality between the respective descendants of Shem and Ham. I admire the sentiment, although my experience has been that Englishmen abroad do not treat black men any better than do other nations; the Boers, for instance. As a case in point, I may mention that one afternoon while we were staying at Johannesburg, my wife, who was in the hotel, was informed by one of the Kafir servants that some people were beating October in the backyard of the building. Hearing this, she rushed to the spot, and found our Basuto boy struggling with a constable and three or four other white men who were vainly trying to drag him off to the police station. She being a law-abiding Englishwoman, though knowing nothing about the cause of the row, called out to October to go quietly with the constable, which he instantly did. She then drove off in hot haste to fetch me from the circus, where I was breaking-in a horse, and we went off to the police station together. Our first action was to deposit the necessary amount of bail, and we received our Kafir with a broad grin and several cuts and bruises on his good-tempered face. The constable, whom we met on the road, told us that an Englishman and a Jew had given October in charge for having assaulted them and for having been drunk. He said that, in his opinion, the Basuto had not the slightest appearance of being intoxicated, and that he had seen nothing of the alleged assault. In fact, he was so sympathetic that I remarked it was a hot day, and gave him a couple of shillings for the quenching of his thirst. Although I intended to 'remember' him after the case had been settled, I did not think it safe to give him more than a florin, lest he might 'round' on me and say that I had tried to 'square' him. My wife and I then investigated the matter and found that the Englishman and the Jew while riding past the backyard of the hotel, had gone close to the spot where October and one of the hotel servants were beating a carpet. In the usual hectoring style, the 'damned niggers' were ordered to clear out, and to assist them in that movement, the Englishman struck October with the hunting whip which he was carrying in his hand. The fact of October, in order to parry the blow, putting up the light cane with which he had been beating the carpet, enraged the Englishman so much, that he got off his horse, and clubbing his heavy hunting whip, dealt the Kafir several savage blows about the head and face with the butt end. October, who was a real fighter, rushed at his man (a big, powerful one), knocked him down and would have killed him, if some white men who were near had not pulled him off; while the Jew kept at a safe distance from the scrimmage, and contented himself with using bad language. Having fetched a policeman, and laid a false charge of assault and drunkenness against October, the two gentlemen went away. Later on, I met them at the hotel. The Englishman acknowledged that he had struck October in the first instance, and expressed his regret that he did not know that the 'boy' was my servant; for had he been aware of this, he would not have chastised him for want of alacrity in obeying the order to clear out of the road. He said, however, that he intended to get October severely punished for having dared to strike him. I pointed out that as he was the aggressor, he could not blame the Kafir for retaliating. To this he replied that it is an unpardonable offence for a 'nigger' to return the blow of a white man. I urged that Couper had fought 'The Ladies' Pet,' and that Couper was as good a gentleman as he was. He answered that 'The Ladies' Pet' was a West Indian 'nigger' and not a Kafir, who could be admitted to no terms of equality with white men in South Africa. The fat little Jew, being an arrant coward, was loud in the threats of vengeance which he uttered against any 'nigger' who dared to turn on him whenever he choose to beat the black man no matter whose servant he was. Such, my readers, is the style of cad, who, assuming the garb of an Englishman, does much to bring that honoured name into contempt among so-called savages. I of course engaged the best lawyer I could find to defend our servant, with whom we went to the police court. The landrost (magistrate) heard the evidence of the plaintiffs and the policeman, who, to our astonishment, swore in the most unblushing manner that October, at the time of the fray, was outrageously drunk, and had assaulted every-one within reach. My wife, appearing for the defence, swore that October was absolutely sober at the time in question, and I corroborated her statement as regards his condition half an hour after that; and informed the magistrate that I was ready to bring scores of witnesses who would give evidence as to October being a remarkably civil and obliging 'boy.' An Africander who had seen the scrimmage, and who looked something like a half-caste cab-driver, now got into the box. On being asked if he knew the complaining Englishman, he replied that he did, and very good reason he had to do so; for the gentleman was always damning, cursing and threatening to strike every servant whom he met. And then, after very drolly imitating the swagger and offensive manner of the principal plaintiff, he narrated how the whole affair had occurred. The landrost, who no doubt knew far more of the *histoire intime* of the parties, than redounded to their credit, 'told them off' in a mercilessly contemptuous manner. He said that he preferred to believe black men than white men such as they; and that he was determined to stop fellows who considered themselves 'swells' from ill-using the natives. As to the policeman, the magistrate merely asked him, 'What have you been paid for all this?' at which there was such a loud roar of laughter from the people in the court that the answer of the guilty-looking constable was lost. The landrost told him to leave the box. When ordering October to be released, he gave him to understand that he could have his legal remedy. I thought, however, it would be better for me to recompense October in a way he would deem amply sufficient, than to stir up any race hatred, which is a very dangerous form of explosive in the Transvaal; than to institute a counter action on behalf of our servant; so we let the matter drop. Although this trial formed the subject of conversation all over the place, two out of the three Johannesburg daily papers took no notice whatsoever of it, and the third one merely gave the finding, without making any allusion to the evidence or the remarks of the landrost. This example of South African journalistic policy is worthy of note.

At the time of my arrival in Johannesburg, the local sportsmen were busily engaged in preparing for the races, the principal event of which was the Johannesburg Handicap. Knowing that I was a veterinary surgeon and had experience in the training of racehorses, Mr Ben Curtis and his cousin Mr Lay asked my advice about a horse of theirs, called Vichy, who was entered for this race. This son of Hermit had run about fifteen times in England, and had succeeded in winning only a couple of small selling races. He was then sent out to South Africa. When I saw him, he was lame in one foreleg from a sprained suspensory ligament and swollen fetlock joint. The question submitted to me was: could I get the horse sound enough to run for the big handicap? Messrs Ben Curtis and Lay told me that they stood to win a large amount on Vichy, and that they would have to scratch him if I could not help them in getting him well enough to run. As it was one of those cases in which I had frequently proved the immense efficacy of well-regulated pressure (preferably, by means of cotton-wool bandaging) and massage; I gave these gentlemen strong hopes that Vichy would come out on the day of the race free from lameness, and that if he was good enough, his bad leg would not stop him from winning. I put him through the course of bandaging and massage, which reduced the swelling, and had the great satisfaction of seeing him trot down sound to the starting-post, and win his race in easy style.

The all-pervading presence of 'little men' and millionaires with the instincts of East Enders makes racing in South Africa an affair in which there is a considerable amount of dog eating dog. This undesirable state of things will naturally mend as the country becomes more settled and opened up by railways. The Johannesburg racing company is well managed, and has a flat and steeplechase course with stand, paddock, etc., enclosed like at Sandown Park. Although, when I was at the Gold Fields, there was not a single qualified veterinary surgeon at Johannesburg, I did not see the prospect of being able to earn enough to pay my expenses, if I had set up in that capacity at the Randt. The ordinary horses were not worth enough to pay for skilled veterinary attendance, and the treatment of racehorses would come in only in the way of an odd job.

It is a noteworthy fact that English horses which are imported into South Africa take a comparatively long time, probably two years on an average, before they get sufficiently accustomed to life in South Africa, to thrive and show their proper form there. I have often been asked why it is that these animals take so long to become acclimatised, and have always replied that, in my opinion, climate had nothing to say to this fact, which I felt certain was entirely due to the poor quality of South African hay, even when it is supplemented with oat hay. Although the climate of India is far hotter than that of South Africa, we find that newly-imported English horses do much better, as far as their health and condition are concerned, in the former than in the latter country. The grass and hay which are given to valuable horses in India are, however, exceptionally good; better even, I am inclined to think, than what can be got in England. I would advise anyone who intended to send a racehorse to South Africa in order to run there, to make arrangements for exporting good English hay for the animal's use. The small extra expense might be justly regarded as a cheap insurance against loss of condition.

CHAPTER XXI.

Racing in South Africa—Polo—Performances at Pretoria—An Accident—Enthusiasm of the Boers—General Joubert—Breaking-in a Zebra—The Language of the Boers—A Journey by Coach—Prize Fighting in South Africa—Nickless and Kelly—Majuba Hill and Laing's Nek—Harrismith—Hendrik Truter—Maritzburg—Sir Charles Mitchell—Colonel Swaine and the 11th Hussars—Horsebreaking at Durban—Farewell to October—The Climate of South Africa—Return to England.

RACING in South Africa, to which I briefly alluded in the preceding chapter, has a fine future, though a somewhat ignoble present. The 'great game' in order to flourish, requires to be managed by men who are independent of it either for their livelihood or for their recreation, and whose probity and love of fair play are above suspicion. It also needs a public that is wealthy, numerous, and fond of sport. With the opening up of the country, increased population, and improved railway communication, all these things no doubt will come to pass in South Africa.

The well-attended race meetings which were held thirty years ago on the common just outside Cape Town on Sea Point Road, and which were chiefly managed by the officers who garrisoned the colony, now exist only in history. The Dutch and Africander inhabitants would willingly look on at the races, but with few exceptions they did not see the force of paying for entrance into any of the enclosures, when they did not know the difference between the starting-post and the judge's box. By the withdrawal of the troops, the number of owners and supporters of racing have become greatly diminished. The ground was accordingly changed to private land about six miles outside of Cape Town and not far from the camp at Wynberg; but the public is not, as yet, educated up to paying point. The racing, what there is of it, is very poor; not much better than Indian *jymkhanah* form. Mr Graham Cloete, secretary of the City Club and races, and cousin of Mr 'Paradox' Cloete, does his best; but even with contributions levied from 'under and over,' faro, three-card trick, and other 'table' men, racing at Cape Town is in a dying condition, and has but little hope of improvement. The busy commercial town of Port Elizabeth has a flourishing turf club, nice racecourse, and one of the 'straightest' of men and pleasantest of companions, for a bookmaker, in Nobby Clarke. At Kimberley, racing may be regarded as a thing of the past. So much for racing in Cape Colony.

Johannesburg is the only racing centre in the Transvaal. The sport on the Randt, as I have previously said, is well conducted, and good stakes, amounting in some cases to £1,500, are given. There are, however, so few horses and owners that two meetings, the programmes of which have to be strengthened by pony events, chases and hurdle races, are quite enough for the requirements of the place. In the Orange Free State, the sportsmen of Bloemfontein and Harrismith make spasmodic though well-intended efforts at getting up meetings. Racing in Natal, in which colony there are fixtures at Durban and Maritzburg, is at a low ebb. As

Johannesburg is now connected by rail with Port Elizabeth and East London, and will soon be united to Durban, racing in South Africa is bound to improve. Yet I think it will be a long time before it will be worth a stranger's while to take horses out there to race. There are a few English jockeys of moderately fair pretensions and some Africander light weights. The fixtures are so few and as a rule so unimportant, and the distances between them are so enormous, that South Africa is a very poor place for a jockey. The horses are of inferior selling race form. There is no steeplechasing or hurdle racing worth speaking of; and the racing ponies are moderate in the extreme. Again I say, all these things will be changed for the better in the near future. The one great reformation which South African racing sorely needs, is the formation of a central turf club (preferably at Johannesburg) which would legislate for the entire country.

To the best of my belief, Johannesburg is the only place in South Africa at which there is a non-military polo club. The 'soldiers' have a club at Maritzburg and are the chief supporters of the game at Wynberg (Cape Town). Polo can be played in South Africa only under great difficulties ; for the white population is not alone small in number and widely distributed, but there are remarkably few ponies in that country suitable to the game. To me, the strangest thing about the horse flesh of that part of the world, is that although the ordinary horse is a hardy, leggy animal of from 14.2 to 15.1 and has often a manifest dash of the Arab, there are extremely few smart ponies from 13.2 to 14 hands to be met with. There are several hard-working Basuto ponies to be found ; but they are almost all too slow.

Having bade good-bye to our kind friends at Johannesburg, we went to Pretoria, which is about twenty-four miles distant, and which is the capital of the Transvaal. Having had the way well prepared for us by the newspapers, we were well received by the Dutch and English residents, and had the good luck to get the able and courteous Mr Jack Hess to act for us as manager. As a large number of Boers had come in from the country to the Agricultural Show, which was being held at that time, I determined to give a couple of public performances, as well as to hold a class. The first one came off in the Berea Park, which is an enclosed ground, and had I not been particularly thick in the skull, my tour would have abruptly ended on that day. A very vicious horse which I was handling in the ring, struck me with one of his fore feet so hard on the top of the head that I reeled back from the force of the blow. My wife seeing this, rushed into the ring and begged me to stop the performance. Though very dizzy, I had just enough sense left to feel bitterly annoyed that the animal should have got the better of me for the time being; so I told her I was all right, and then hearing the shouts of the Boers who were cheering the horse which was defeating the 'Redneck,' I took off my hat and told them that I was an Irishman, and that my wife would ride the horse in an hour. I must have looked a funny object, speechifying with my hat in my hand and the blood streaming down my face on to my clothes. When the show was over, one of my Dutch friends proudly remarked, that none of the Dutch ladies who saw the accident, fainted, turned pale, went away, or showed the slightest concern, as Englishwomen would have done, had they been present. But to return to the description of the breaking, I need only say that I felt so weak from the effects of the concussion and from loss of blood, that I could get no further on with it, than to make the horse quiet to be saddled and mounted. Although I knew he would buck if he was made to go on, I dared not delay. A glance at my wife informed me that she was ready to pull the show out of the metaphorical fire which was waiting to consume it. On seeing my signal, she walked into the ring, and in the next moment was in the side saddle. As soon as she shortened the reins and touched the horse to make him go on, he 'went to market' (as Australians say) in a style I have seldom seen equalled, and at every buck he gave, he uttered a loud grunt of fury. Not being able to move her in the saddle, he at last 'gave in.' As such a fine riding feat by any man, let alone a lady, had never before been seen by the assembled Boers, their habitual stolidity gave way to enthusiasm, and they warmly cheered and praised the Englishwoman.

The Boers were so well pleased with our first show, that we had more than double the number of them at our second one. As the payment of an entrance fee is a product of civilisation but little understood among these primitive people, the policemen whom I had engaged and I myself had a desperate struggle to keep at bay the army of would-be 'deadheads' who stormed our gate. When the battle was at its height, General Joubert, the hero of Laing's Nek and Majuba Hill, came to my help, and by voice and hand so vigorously aided the defence, that the tumult subsided, and we opened to a paying 'house.' The only part of this performance worth noticing, was the breaking to saddle of a young Burchell's zebra, which I accomplished in a short time without any difficulty. This animal belonged to a Dutch gentleman, a resident of Pretoria, whose name, if I remember rightly, was Mr Ziervogel. A few hours before the show began, he very kindly promised to let me experiment on it. As I knew I could easily break it in, and as I was anxious to take it with me to England, I wanted to buy it then and there; but he put me off by saying that we could settle that afterwards. When the show was concluded and the zebra was quiet to ride, Mr Ziervogel's 'afterwards' became like unto St Patrick's 'to-morrow' which never came to the last snake in Ireland after my patron saint had inveigled him into his strong box.

Several gentlemen attended my class in Pretoria. The most of them had a good deal of experience with horses, and were keen to learn everything about breaking. In the Transvaal, to say nothing of Cape Colony, Orange Free State, or Natal, I certainly left behind me several expert pupils who were capable of breaking-in any Burchell's zebra. Accordingly, I was not at all surprised at reading in the *Field*, about a year after I had quitted South Africa, that a successful attempt had been made to utilise these animals for coach work. I need hardly say that breaking-in horses or zebras for harness is much easier than for saddle. The Burchell's zebra is a far more docile animal than the mountain zebra (*equus zebra*), of which I broke-in a specimen in Calcutta for my wife and myself (see page 186) to ride. There are still large numbers of Burchell's zebras to be found north of the Transvaal; but the mountain zebra is nearly extinct. For further information about these striped asses and the extinct quagga, I may refer my readers to *The Points of the Horse.*

The nickname ' Rooinek ' (Redneck) which the Boers apply to the English, refers to the red or rather reddish-brown appearance which the action of the African sun gives to the comparatively fair skin of our countrymen. The 'touch of the tar-brush,' which has been at work for a few hundred years in South Africa, preserves the epidermis of the Boers from this temporary discoloration. The language spoken by these people is a Dutch *patois*, so much mixed up with Kafir, Hottentot, English and other forms of speech, that it is all but unintelligible to a newly-arrived Hollander. Its grammar is more simple even than that of Persian or Hindustanee; and as it is expressive and easily learnt, it forms a useful *lingua franca.*

As Mr Meiring, who is an officer of the Free State Customs, had kindly guaranteed me a large class at Harrismith; we returned to Johannesburg, which was in our route, and I took seats for ourselves and October in the coach that ran between the Randt and Charlestown, which was then the terminus of the Natal railway.

It was bitterly cold, pitch-dark and raining hard on the May morning when we were called at four o'clock to get up and depart again on our travels. After trudging through the darkness and driving rain for about half a mile, we arrived at the posting office, and found the coach waiting for us. This conveyance was a long four-wheeled box, inside which the passengers sat *vis-à-vis*, and had their luggage tied on outside. We climbed into its dark interior, and tumbling over three other wayfarers, we stowed ourselves in the first convenient corner, shivering with cold and glad to think that if ever we were to travel over this road again, it would be by an express train. October had, in the meantime, wrapped himself in a few horse-rugs, lit his pipe, and deposited himself somewhere on the outside. At last all was ready, the twelve ponies were put in, the driver mounted the box-seat, took his long whip in both hands, cracked it vigorously, gave a few yells, and away the ponies trotted down the dimly-lighted street. In ten or fifteen minutes we were out in the open *veldt*, and soon were jolting through slush, sand and stream, with a few short intervals for refreshments at wayside shanties till eight o'clock in the evening, when we put up for a part of the night at a comparatively comfortable inn. We found our three companions of travel pleasant, obliging fellows. They were itinerant prize fighters who, like ourselves, were trying to run a show. They were not able to give a public performance in the Transvaal; for the Dutch authorities would not allow such exhibitions to take place in their country; and probably they had worn their welcome somewhat threadbare. They were therefore going to try their luck in Natal. The eldest of them was George Stevens, a man of about forty, who had fought some battles in England as a light weight. The next in age was Donovan, who had been defeated for the middle-weight championship of South Africa by Kelly of Maritzburg; and lastly there was Barny Malone, a 9-stone man of about twenty-seven, whose colours had also been lowered by Kelly, to whom he had given away a great deal of weight. Barny had been a clown in Frank Fillis's circus; but after having had an accident, he lost, through want of confidence, the knack of turning summersaults, so he took up prize fighting as the next easiest job. He was, at the time I met him, in the unfortunate predicament of not being able to get on a match with anyone at 9 stone, and of not being good enough to concede 14 lbs. to Kelly. The fight between the Maritzburg lad and Donovan was decided in the Orange Free State, and when the police of that Republic tried to stop it, the backers of Kelly, who saw that their man was winning easily, pulled out their revolvers and declared that they would shoot anyone who interrupted the game. The battle was then continued, and Kelly won. As business was booming merrily along in South Africa at that time, Kelly, who I may mention is a steady young fellow and fond of athletics, netted as a result of his victory a large sum, which I do not think I would be far out by estimating at about £3000. With this in his pocket, he took a pleasure trip to England, and proud of his title of middle-weight champion of South Africa, he got on a match with a then unknown man called Nickless, who knocked him about in such an easy style, that the *Sporting Life* and *Sportsman*, on the supposition that Nickless was a fourth-rate man, made merry over the lamentable ignorance of South African people about boxing, when such a duffer as Kelly could pose as their champion. So Kelly returned to Maritzburg far poorer in money and fame than when he had left it, and recommenced serving drinks over the bar of his patron publican, with a chastened spirit. Time, the healer, at last brought its salve for the lad's wounded vanity; for Nickless soon proved that the mean opinion of his abilities formerly held by the sporting papers was entirely wrong, and he is, at the time I am writing, ready to fight any 10-stone man in the world.

We seemed to have hardly settled to sleep before we were again called at four o'clock in the morning, and had to start before daylight. Tired and stiff from the jolting of the coach, we arrived by noon that day at Charlestown. The Belgrave Hotel in which we put up, was clean and

Majuba Hill.

well provisioned; mine host attentive; the liquors good, the climate delightful; the bright coal fire in the taproom, the first we had seen in South Africa, and above all things, Majuba Hill was within easy reach. Next morning, after a capital breakfast, we found a pair horse ramshakle Stanhope and a guide waiting for us. Our amateur *cicerone* was a Mr Petly of the Natal Mounted Police, who had, at the thoughtful instigation of our landlord, volunteered in the kindest possible manner to show us over the ground. We were indeed lucky to have his courteous and intelligent help; for he had fought at Laing's Nek, and had been with the main body of the troops when General Colley was shot. After a drive of about four miles up the first slopes of the mountain, we got out and walked up the steep hillside which the Boers climbed on the morning of that memorable 27th February 1881. The position of the Transvaal troops was behind Laing's Nek, which is a saddle in a low range of hills, about five miles in extent, between high mountains, which guard its flanks; the left being also secured by the Buffalo River, which runs at the foot of the hills. This neck, through which passed the line of communication between Natal and the Transvaal, is, on a rough guess, about 2000 feet lower than the hills on each side; the higher of the two being precipitous Majuba on the right.

The Majuba mistake appears to have been due to the mad egotism of Sir George Colley, who having been defeated at Laing's Nek and at Ingago, evidently tried to retrieve his reputation by a dash at Majuba during the temporary absence of Sir Evelyn Wood, who had gone to Maritzburg in order to hasten up the arrival of reinforcements. It was the custom of the Boers to occupy Majuba by day with pickets, which were withdrawn at night. On the morning of the 27th February, they were surprised at seeing against the sky line men moving on the crest of the now historical hill. Fearing that their right flank would be turned, they gallantly resolved to make a counter attack, and despatched about 400 men for this purpose to scale the mountain side. In the meantime, General Colley's troops, of about the same number, who had gained the top of the hill before daybreak, found themselves on a piece of ground, which is about 150 yards square, and which is slightly depressed in the centre. It was an ideal position on which to make a stand even against vastly superior numbers; but with an incredible want of foresight, General Colley neglected to properly defend the edge of this basin which faced the enemy. Had he done so, it would have been impossible for a single Transvaaler to have reached the top. Almost the first intimation of danger which was conveyed to our men, was the firing of the Boers who had crept up and taken shelter behind the rocks and boulders which surround the ground that had been occupied by the English. Confusion and then panic ensued, with the result of a blackened page in our military history. These young Dutch farmers were accustomed from their early youth to handle a rifle and stalk game. From the open nature of the *veldt*, they had to shoot—as they did with extraordinary accuracy —springbok and blessbok, often at distances of from 400 to 600 yards. I may mention that our famed Indian *shikaris*, such as Nightingale, Colonel Campbell (*The Old Forest Ranger*), Gunning Campbell, Kennedy, Shakespeare, Forsyth, Kinloch and others, have always held that about 200 yards is the limit of a fair sporting range for black buck or ibex. We have, however, this consolation for our feelings as regards Majuba, that if we come, which God forbid, into collision again with the Boers, that we shall find them far less formidable than they were fourteen years ago; for, owing to the rapid disappearance of game, the young Dutchmen are not nearly such good rifle shots as were their fathers. Happily an appeal to arms is not likely to be again needed; for the attack made by English capital and intellect on the rich gold fields of the Transvaal cannot be resisted by the rough farmers, whose sole ambition is to have a homestead far from the abode of any other man.

Majuba Hill.

Too little credit, I think, has been awarded by the English writers that have described the Majuba affair, to the heroism of the Boers, who finding that their enemy had practically turned their flank, gallantly resolved at all hazards to make an attack up the steep mountain side.

After examining the nature of the ground, we performed the sad duty of visiting the few memorials of our dead countrymen. A whitewashed rough stone, with 'Colley fell' in letters of black paint on it, marks the spot where the English leader was shot. His grave, I may mention, is between two trees which stand out prominently by themselves on the side of Prospect Hill, which is in the centre of the ground that was occupied by the English. A handsome stone cross shows the place where sleeps poor Captain Maud, who after resigning his commission in the Grenadier Guards, joined the 58th Regiment as a volunteer. Some abominable ghoul has knocked off a corner of this cross quite recently. Other low-lived scoundrels have carved their contemptible names on the small wooden cross over the grave of twenty men of the 58th. A woman (!) not to be behind men in shamelessness, has also added her name, or had it added by some depraved companion. It is consoling to know that the creature was too uneducated to spell it properly.

However heartburning to Englishmen may have been the action of Mr Gladstone in staying the avenging hand of General Roberts, we must not forget that our quarrel was an unjust one. By our meddling and oppressive policy, we drove a large number of the Dutch farmers out of Cape Colony, which they had occupied for many years before our arrival. They sought refuge in Natal out of which we pushed them into the country beyond the Vaal River. Not content with having harried them so far, our Government, egged on by the Exeter Hall Brigade, began to worry them in their new location. Their reasonable demand for representation in return for the taxes they were paying was refused, contrary to the wish of Sir Theophilus Shepstone, the British Governor

T

of the Transvaal, who was beloved by the Boers and was in thorough touch with them. His successor, in 1879, Sir Owen Lanyon, was a man void of tact, and had no sympathy with the people over whom he was placed. He, either ignorantly or culpably, misrepresented to his Government that the Transvaalers desired English rule. It is probable that but for his evil influence, our heavy loss in life and honour would not have been incurred.

Had Mr Gladstone not made peace at the time he did, it is all but certain that General Roberts with his 10,000 men, would have come up and beaten the farmers' army. 'Then,' say the Conservatives, 'we could have made peace with honour, and given back with a brave show of generosity, the country we had unjustly seized.' But we must remember that it takes two to make peace as well as war. The sympathies of the Boers in the Orange Free State and those in Cape Colony—hardy, resolute fellows and incomparable riflemen—were becoming stronger every day in favour of their Transvaal countrymen, whom they certainly would have joined in many thousands, had General Joubert's army been sorely pressed. It is doubtful if General Roberts, brave soldier and brilliant leader as he is, could have reduced the Transvaal to subjection with only the troops he had brought along with him. Probably 10,000 more would have been required, and in the meantime the whole of South Africa would have been in a blaze. I may reasonably ask: would all the continental nations have calmly looked on while we carried on this unjust and oppressive war against a people who were fighting for their liberty, and who were closely allied to some of them? When one gets beaten, fairly and squarely, it is only human nature to call out to one's big brother for help. But when one's foe happens to have big brothers of his own, it is perhaps better for one to make up the quarrel, than to allow it to implicate all one's friends and relations.

From Charlestown we went most of the way to Harrismith by train and had only a short distance, over which the trains now run, to go by coach. My class at Harrismith was similar to that at Pretoria and Colesberg, being composed chiefly of farmers who spent a good portion of their lives among horses. The appreciation of these hard, practical men was very flattering to me, especially as they had never heard my name mentioned in connection with books on horses. I could not help thinking that if my wife and I had not been particularly smart at our work, we would not have won the good opinion of the Boers, whose hatred of the English is equalled only by their contempt for us as horsemen. These farmers, I need hardly say, judge Englishmen only by the specimens who go out to South Africa, few of whom have had any previous experience among horses. One of the members of my Harrismith class was Mr Hendrik Truter, who had led the Boers in their attack up Majuba Hill against General Colley's party. Either to pose me or to test my skill, he brought a horse that was extremely difficult to catch when loose, and, if I remember rightly, to ride when caught. I accomplished so easily the task he had set me, in making this animal obedient, that instead of being pleased, he seemed rather annoyed that a 'Rooinek' should be a better breaker than any Boer. Though the 'score' was a paltry one, I was glad to have been able to make it off the redoubtable Boer leader. Mr Truter, who is about fifty years of age, is one of the finest men I have ever seen. He stands about 6 feet 4 inches; is well built; straight as a dart; is of immense breadth of shoulders and depth of chest; and has a hard, resolute, good-looking face. Although the Orange Free State was at peace with us during the Transvaal war, a large number of Free State men, among whom was Truter, joined General Joubert's army. The Majuba storming party, which was led by Truter, consisted, I believe, chiefly of them. I saw a good deal of Mr Oliver Davis—who lives at Harrismith and whose name has been mentioned several times in the London papers in connection with the Matabele war—

at Harrismith, Maritzburg, and Durban. He is a good sportsman, hard to beat across country, an owner of racehorses, and is a great favourite with everyone who knows him. His horse Capsome was for several years by far the best steeplechase horse in South Africa. One of the Days, nephew, I believe, of old William Day, the famous trainer, used to ride and train for Mr Davis. Day is a fine crosscountry rider. Hall is another good man between the flags.

After Harrismith, we went to Maritzburg where the annual agricultural show was being held, and I was asked by the committee to judge horses and jumping. I accepted the invitation with pleasure and did my best to give satisfaction. This show, being a long established fixture, was well attended, and the exhibits proved that agriculture was prosperous in the Colony. I must, however, say that many of the saddle horse sires which I saw exhibited here, at Pretoria, Bloemfontein, and Colesberg, were, to my thinking, utterly unsuitable to the requirements of the country; in that they had heavy shoulders, upright pasterns and the respective direction of their back tendons and cannon bones were far from being as nearly parallel to each other as they ought to have been. I also noted that the baneful system of judging of the goodness of a horse's forelegs by the measurement just below the knee, instead of also taking into consideration the width of the fetlock from front to rear, was too much in vogue. It would have given me great pleasure to have expounded my views on the conformation of horses more widely than I did in South Africa; but I had no time to do so. As it was, I had to refuse invitations to judge at the agricultural shows in Port Elizabeth and Graf Reinet.

Besides a couple of public exhibitions in Maritzburg, at which we did well, I held a class in the town, and another in the camp for the officers of the 11th Hussars and Gunners. Colonel Swaine, who was commanding the 'Cherubims,' was so pleased with my work that he got me to teach all his sergeants, as well as his officers, how to break-in horses. Sir

Charles Mitchell, the Governor, and Lady Mitchell attended our shows, and appeared to take a great deal of interest in them. We had the honour of being invited to the ball they gave on the Queen's Birthday, and had a very pleasant evening. One of the most popular sportsmen in Natal is Mr Phil. Payne, to whom I had a letter of introduction and who was very kind to us. He is a good example of a man who waited too long in the race for wealth. During the 'boom he made a lot of money, and as he knew that the inflated prices could not last for ever, he determined that he would sell out and 'go' when his capital had reached the limit of £200,000, which would yield him the £10,000 a year that he considered sufficient for a nice place in the country and a house in town for the season. When his pile rose to £120,000 he was strongly advised to sell; but it appeared such a pity to miss the chance of affluence for life, that he held on, with the result that the first crash came and down went all the shares. The proper policy now appeared to be to wait for a reaction; but unluckily the shares went lower and lower until many of them disappeared altogether. South Africa is such a wonderful country for changes of fortune that few things would surprise me less or give me greater pleasure than to see Mr Phil. Payne, who is as good a loser as he is a winner, return home in a year or two with that couple of hundred thousand which has so long eluded his grasp. Both at Maritzburg and at Durban I was fortunate to have as my manager, Mr Cuthbert, who treated me more as a friend, than as a mere employer.

The horse which was kept waiting for me at Durban, and whose reputation for untamed vice had been spread all over the Colony, turned out to be a maligned animal, that with ordinary skill and patience might have been converted into a lady's quiet hack. He made no attempt to buck when my wife rode him, and although very nervous at first of being handled, he gave in and got quiet as soon as he found that if he obeyed, no harm would befall him.

Having finished with Durban, we formed ourselves into a committee of ways and means. We might have gone to East London, Queenstown, King Williamstown, Aliwal North, Bloemfontein; have had another turn at Colesberg and Kimberley, and then finished at Vryburg. But we were both very tired of the work and wanted to get back to London. Besides, my wife did not think her health could stand the strain of another trip, and as she had been the best part of the show, I thought it only fair that her interests should be first considered. I was very sorry to say good-bye to dear old October, who had been a faithful and helpful friend to me. He had saved money enough to buy a sufficiency of cattle and wives to keep him well supplied with food and strong drink for the remainder of his life, without working. As he had no higher aspirations than the gratification of his instincts, he was troubled with no longing after more wealth than he possessed. He was happy, and that was all he wanted to be. I offered to take him with me by sea to East London or Port Elizabeth and from thence to send him on to his home in Craddock; but he shook his head, doubled himself up, and laughed long and low, as if he thought my offer excruciatingly funny. I asked him how he intended going to Craddock. He told me that he would travel to Ladysmith by train, and would then march across country on foot. I represented to him that by taking such an overland route he would spend a good deal of money and time; but that if he went with me his journey would cost him nothing. The more I argued with him, the more he laughed and shook his head, till at last the fact began to dawn on me that the fear of my carrying him off and making him a slave, was the cause of October's refusal to go on board a steamer. That evening I saw him off by train, and having been accustomed to the demonstrative forms of grief freely indulged in by well-rewarded Eastern and Western servants when parting from their respective masters, I could not help being somewhat disappointed with October for not weeping or at least showing some signs of emotion on his ugly, honest face, when I took my last look on it, framed in the window of a third-class railway carriage. But he only grinned, happily though affectionately at me. And then I began slowly to understand that I had at last met a man who was not a hypocrite, and the worst of it was that I was obliged to part from him a few seconds after I had made this astounding discovery; for the station-master, at that moment, was waving his flag for the engine-driver to start. 'Good baas; always good baas,' said October, waving his hand to me. And then the train bore him slowly off into the *ewigkeit:* as far as I was concerned. I believe that he was very fond of me, in his own way, and that he bore me no ill-will for my supposed treachery in wanting to carry him off into bondage.

I felt remarkably well after all the hard physical work I had gone through during the six months we had spent in South Africa, the dry, warm climate of which did my chest a great deal of good. For about a year before going out to the Cape I suffered so much from bronchitis, that I had feared that my air passages would become chronically affected. Though more than double that time has elapsed since we left that country, my lungs and their tubes continue to remain in perfect order. When the locality has been judiciously selected, the climate of South Africa, in many cases, offers much benefit to sufferers from chest ailments. If very dry and bracing air be needed, Harrismith (for choice) or Charlestown might be selected; as they are over 5000 feet above the level of the sea. The altitude of Bloemfontein is nearly as great. If a warmer, though also a dry, climate be required, I know no place more suitable or convenient than Craddock.

We had a pleasant journey home on board the Union ss. *Tartar.*

Photo by M. H. Hayes.

CHAPTER XXII.

Homeward Bound—Blazing Weather—'Professor' Norton Smith—The Dublin Horse Show—Jumping—Paris—High School Riding—Baucher—M. Auguste Raux—Gustave—Teaching a Horse to Jump—Horse Taming Competition between Sample and Leon.

OUR trip round the coast from Natal, and then home by Madeira, was delightful. The sea for the portion of the route south of Gibraltar is generally smooth, and there is really no unpleasant heat even when crossing the equator. Either homeward or outward bound we had not had more than two days hot enough to make us wish to change ordinary English summer clothes for those of lighter material; and on the warmest nights we were able to sleep 'down below.' In the tropics, the heat far out in the ocean is much less than close to land, which continues to radiate into the surrounding air the caloric it has received from the sun long after that orb has disappeared below the horizon. When the fierce rays of the tropical sun beat down for some hours on rock or sand, the surface of the ground often becomes so hot that it would be painful to place the palm of the hand or sole of the foot on it, and consequently it causes the air which blows over it to assume more or less the character of a blast from a furnace. On this account, the highest range of the thermometer on board steamers going through the Red Sea, is about 20° F. more than on the Cape boats when crossing the equator. Owing to the land-locked nature of the Persian Gulf, the heat there is exceptionally great, even reaching at times, I have heard from reliable authorities, to 120° F. in the shade. In the Scinde desert I have endured, in the shade, a heat of 125° F. As a good example of the radiating power of arid ground, I may mention that I have known the thermometer, at nine o'clock at night, to register 109° F. at Meean Meer in the Punjab. At that temperature, the sheets and pillow of one's bed had become so hot that one could not lie down on them without having had them first sprinkled with water. Unless the wind is 'dead aft' and blowing at the same rate as the steamer is proceeding, there will be a certain amount of cooling wind made by the ship. During the three voyages I made round the Cape in sailing vessels, we had some very hot weather when becalmed in the 'doldrums,' which is the belt of ocean that extends 10 or 12 degrees north and south of the equator, and, as a rule, is untroubled by the trade winds. If Cape Town was a pleasant place to live in, it would soon become a favourite resort for tourists, who would be naturally attracted by the delightful sea voyage to and from it.

As soon as we arrived in London, we began to put in order, amplify and correct the materials which my wife had collected for a long-threatened book on ladies' riding. Ever anxious to learn something new about horses we went one afternoon to the Crystal Palace to see a "Professor" Norton Smith who had come over from Canada to show, so the advertisements said, a marvellous system of horse taming. I must say that the performance greatly disappointed us, and that there was nothing new in it, except that, instead of tying up one foreleg, in order to throw a horse down, and pulling up the other foot by a rope or strap passing through the surcingle or through a pulley attached to it, as Rarey used to do; both feet were pulled up, with the result that the animal came down on his knees with more or less violence. This way of making a horse lie down appeared to me very much inferior to the method which was first shown in England by Sample, and which was, so Sample tells me, invented by Hamilton the American horse tamer. Norton Smith strictly confined himself to the dreary taming business, and we came away unamused and uninstructed.

Among the people I had left behind, I was glad to see on my return, Mr Vero Shaw, who is one of the few genuine literary Bohemians I have ever met. He is the best all-round judge of a dog in England, especially if the animal be a bull terrier. 'In rain or shine' he is always the same cheery companion, and there would be no difference in his kindly greeting were he to meet me sweeping a crossing, or dispensing hospitality from a well-stocked four-in-hand at Ascot. I have found from experience that one's acquaintances are far more ready to accept one's surroundings than one's self.

I was glad to meet Mr J. Moray Brown, an old 79th and Wellington College man. In India he did a great deal of shooting and pigsticking, especially in the Central Provinces, and had his name bracketted with that of Mr (now Colonel) W. S. Hebbert as the winner of the greatest number of First Spears, including one off a panther, for the Nagpore Hunt Cup of 1870-71. At the end of fourteen years service, and tired with the slowness of promotion, he retired in 1880, had seven years' hunting in the south of England, and then 'took' to journalism and literature. Being an old polo hand, having played the game twenty years ago at Aldershot and Edinburgh, his articles on polo in *Land and Water*, of which he is

Photo by Dickinson, 114 New Bond Street, W.

Mr J. MORAY BROWN.

Hunting Editor, have been an attractive feature in that paper. He is Polo Manager at Ranelagh, and has written several good books, the one of which most takes my fancy is that on *Polo*. This good sportsman puts pigsticking in front of hunting, and polo third. I would give hunting, chasing and pigsticking as the order of preference, and polo fourth, probably because I have not played that game much. But, *quot homines, tot sententiæ*.

As my wife had never been to Ireland, I was glad to have the chance of taking her to the Dublin Horse Show, at which she would have a favourable view of the horses and men of Paddyland. The show of saddle horses at Ball's Bridge was certainly very fine. The most of them were grandly 'topped' and carried their heads, necks and tails well. I could not help thinking that the 'bone' of too many of them had been obtained more by an infusion of cart blood than by judicious selection. Not having been in Ireland since I began the serious study of breaking, I was greatly surprised to see that, with few exceptions, the horses were singularly deficient of either 'manners' or 'mouths.' When cantered round a large ring, it was enough to take the conceit out of an Irishman for his countrymen's knowledge of horses, to see how the animals bored on their riders' hands, led with the wrong leg, went at the speed which each one thought best, and required at least a couple of hundred yards in which to pull up. The necessity for instruction in horse breaking (not horse taming) was obvious, and nothing would have given me greater pleasure than to have gone through the country on a breaking tour, had such a scheme been feasible; but the horse-taming farce had been played so often that had I had any such intention, I would have had, first of all, to live down, for goodness knows how many years, the bad impression made by others. I need hardly say that breeders and owners of horses in the United Kingdom are keenly alive to the advantages of knowing how, quickly and efficiently, to give their horses, which have been reared under civilised conditions, snaffle-bridle mouths, form their paces, and teach them to jump; but mere instruction in the taming of wild horses or of exceptionally vicious ones is, practically, of no use to them; and they naturally resent it being foisted on them as an all-sufficient system of horse instruction.

I thought the judging of the jumping particularly good; for the rule of taking the horses over all the fences at fair hunting speed was insisted on throughout. I must say that the majority of the horses pulled hard; and consequently were badly broken-in. How true the old saying is, that manners make the horse. The jumping course was in the form of a horse-shoe of about 300 yards in extent. The first fence was a low hedge in front of water about 9 feet wide; the second, which was opposite the stand, was a ditch about 4 feet wide in front of a bank about 3 feet high, 4 feet wide on the top, and without a ditch on the landing side; the third, a 4-foot wall, the upper third of which consisted of loose stones; the fourth, an on-and-off, about $5\frac{1}{2}$ feet high, with 4-feet ditches and nearly straight sides; the fifth, a 13-feet water jump with a hedge in front of it; and the sixth and last, a sort of flattering compromise between a hedge and a hurdle. The first fence was, as it ought to have been, of an easy character; the second presented still less difficulty, and could have been negotiated by any ordinary 10-hand Shetland pony; and the last one could be brushed through with immunity. The 4-foot wall, the big bank and the water jump required a clever horse to take them properly. Besides this regular course, there was a 4-foot-9-inch wall, which was capped with loose stones, and which was reserved for special competitions. By the kindness of the committee, I was allowed to come into the jumping enclosure, and while there, one afternoon, I had a short conversation with Lord X, who is considered in Ireland to be a great authority on horses. For information sake, I asked him why there was no gate or posts and rails on the jumping course, and suggested that, for instance the substitution of a gate in front of the stand, for the trivial bank, would add to the variety of the fences, and would consequently improve the course as a means of testing the jumping capabilities of the animals. He informed me that such obstacles were not put up, because they were not met with out hunting in Ireland. I urged that they were often encountered in England, which was a great market for the sale of Irish hunters; that the fact of a hunter being a good timber jumper would add to his price; and that, consequently, a gate or post and rails, say 4 feet high, would be a useful and legitimate test. He said that I talked nonsense, and that if my advice were acted upon, the majority of the horses would break their necks. I pleaded that it was easy to teach any ordinary horse to jump a gate; and that I would be only too happy to show him how it could be done. He replied that he did not want to see; because he knew everything about breaking, and had, in fact, written an article on that subject in a certain book, I congratulated him on being the only man in the world who had ever reached finality in any art; and went away thinking that if such be the kind of instructor, it is no wonder that Irish horses are, as a rule, badly broken.

Although the jumping was good, the two things that pleased us most in the show, were the riding and the great personal interest taken in the leaping competitions by the large majority of the thousands who were present. Almost everyone of the spectators knew some, if not all, of the horses and riders, and keenly and intelligently criticised the good and bad points of the men and animals. I was proud of my countrymen's love of horses, and contrasted it with the lukewarm feeling entertained by the inhabitants of London about that subject, apart from betting. The 'dash' with which the men rode (there were no ladies among the competitors) was in marked contrast to the hold-him-tight-by-the-head style usually adopted at Islington.

After a trip to the county of Cork, we returned to England and went to Paris with the idea of learning all we could about high school riding, and, if possible, buying a well-broken *manège* horse.

Had we not been people of impulse, we would have thought out the matter, made due inquiries, and would have refrained from invading the capital of France at a time when 'everyone' was out of it; but then the great pleasure of yielding to the temptation of the moment would have been lost. We were disappointed chiefly at not being able to see Mr James Fillis, who had gone to Berlin under an engagement to ride in Renz's Circus. We had an obliging and efficient guide in M. Charles Sorel, who being a Parisian, a high school rider, and an assistant at the Cirque d'Été, knew all the places which would be interesting to us. Besides, as he was well acquainted with the English system of riding, having lived in England and also stayed with Captain Fitzgerald at the Royal Military Riding School, Gloucester Crescent; he was able to understand our difficulties, and explain the points of variance between the English methods and those of the high school. In this research I must acknowledge the great assistance I received from the reading of Dr Le Bon's book, *Équitation Actuelle*, in which many instructive and original views of this subject are described. Our experience in Paris taught us the very noteworthy truth, which had hitherto remained unknown to us, that *l'équitation savante* (to adopt the term which French high school professors love to apply to their art) is a system of horse dancing, or horse deportment. However useful it may be as a 'setting-up drill,' it is inapplicable to ordinary and long-continued requirements, on account of progression, according to it, being performed under unusually fatiguing conditions, and because the horse is deprived of the initiative. For a long journey or for cross country work, keeping a horse at the *rassembler* would be as appropriate as attempting to utilise the 'goose step' for a day's march. The required abnormal 'collection' is obtained principally by the spur, one of the chief maxims of *la haute école* being *beaucoup de jambes, et peu de mains.* Hence, when any of the various *airs de manège* is being performed, the spurs have to be kept close to the horse's sides; if not actually with painful effect, with sufficiently vivid remembrance of 'punishment,' to make him keenly anxious to avoid its reinfliction. It is evident that in order to retain these 'aids' in that position, the knee, or knees (according as the rider is a lady or a man) have to be kept away from the flaps of the saddle, with a corresponding decrease of firmness in the seat. In a man's saddle, the knees can be brought back in a moment to the flaps, but in a side-saddle, the stirrup leather, in order to admit of the free use of the spur, has to be lengthened out so much that the pressure against the leaping head, which is all essential for firmness of seat, and which is obtained chiefly by the play of the ankle joint, has to be entirely sacrificed. No wonder then that the *écuyères* whom we saw going over some very small jumps in the Hippodrome at Paris, and later on in Circus Renz at Hamburg looked pictures of discomfort, each one clutching hold tight to her horse's head, and having her left foot drawn so far back, that the sole of the boot was turned upwards. When we visited the Manège Pergolèse, M. Auguste Raux, teacher of high school riding, was kind enough to tell us that English ladies rode shockingly badly; because, so he said, their left leg did not hang down by the horse's side. Although my wife could have easily demonstrated that he was utterly wrong, we did not contradict him; for gratuitous instruction to riding masters, who are the last persons to accept it kindly, was not down in our programme. We saw him two or three times at the Cirque d'Été, where he used to go in order to look after a pupil of his, an *écuyère* who each night did a high school riding act on a handsome, well-bred horse, that was brilliant and *perçant* to an extraordinary degree. His movements were so light that he appeared almost to tread on air (if I may be permitted the use of this threadbare simile): so much so, indeed, that the first time I saw him perform I became anxious to see how the 'fakement' was done. As my wife had been told that the young lady, when mounted, was tied into her saddle, we both determined to satisfy our respective curiosities. On the second night of our attendance at the circus, having taken seats close to the exit from the ring, we agreed to miss a part of the *numéro* preceding the entrance of the lady; so, before it was finished, we slipped out into the promenade which was reserved for those who had tickets for the best seats, and which gave access to the loose boxes and stalls for the performing horses. Greatly to my wife's disappointment, the lady was already mounted; but the object of my search was gained, for we saw M. Raux standing alongside the horse and touching him up with a spur which he held in his hand. Being restrained from going forward by the reins, and being excited by the spur, the irritated animal could expend its energy only by extravagantly lofty movements, which in a few minutes were to win the plaudits of the public. When the Russian clown, if I remember rightly, had gathered together his three performing cats, and had made his exit in a chariot drawn by a pig, with a boar hound, who immensely enjoyed the joke, acting as postilion, a wait of about three minutes was given, before opening the barriers; and then with a flourish of trumpets the lady and the (spur) proud horse made their entrance through two rows of drawn-up attendants. I may mention that the horse before he began his 'turn' was sweating profusely, and seemed fit to jump out of his skin; not from high spirits, but from the 'punishment' he had received. The act was all very nice from a showman's point of view; but to my mind there was nothing in it to please a horseman. The movements performed might no doubt be valuable exercises in the school training of a horse, but at best were only a means and not an end. Baron de Vaux, in his charming book *Écuyers et Écuyères*, with evident reference to James Fillis, says that Auguste Raux *considère les changements qu'a subis l'équitation de cirque depuis Baucher comme une révolution néfaste.*' When we saw Fillis, as I shall describe later on, we were better able to judge of the correctness of these statements than when we were in Paris. This criticism was possibly inspired by Fillis having remarked in his *Principes de Dressage et d'Equitation* that certain French *dresseurs* broke their horses in a manner similar to that adopted with performing poodles.

I may explain to those of my readers who are not well acquainted with the training of horses for circus or high school work, that a high degree of obedience can be obtained from the horse, only by lessons, the number of repetitions of which depend for their efficacy on the effect produced. Hence, when the greatest possible excellence is required, the lessons have not alone to be numerous; but have to be conducted with severity. To the instructed I need hardly say that horses, like ourselves, are so fond of having their own way that fear of punishment, which should be judiciously applied, is the best means for making them submit unconditionally to man. Vanity or love of admiration, which I have not found developed in the horse to any profitable extent, can be largely utilised in the teaching of tricks to the dog, in whose character there are many human traits; but not in the education of horses. We read in Baron de Vaux's work, to which I have previously referred, that 'The horses trained by Laurent Franconi had arrived at such a degree of excellence, that during the school evolutions which he made them perform, his seat remained unaltered, and the use of his aids were imperceptible. It was this fineness in the employment of the aids, to which Guérinière alluded when recalling the delicate feeling (*pincer*) of the spur.

'This delicate touch completed the perfect accord which existed between the rider and his pupil, the latter obeying the slightest indication of the hand and legs, as I have already said. School work under these conditions enabled the rider to maintain his academic seat on horseback.' The public, no doubt, put down the proficiency of the horses to the intelligence of the animals, and not to their remembrance of the prick of the spur, and the touches of the whip.

To obtain the desired precision in school work it is necessary, as previously stated, that the horse should resign the initiative absolutely to his rider, who, consequently, has to continue the application of certain aids, or change them for others as may be required. For instance, if the horse be cantering forward with the off fore leading, and the rider turns him to the left without altering the aids, the animal will continue to lead with the off fore, instead of 'changing' to the near fore. Or if he met in his onward course a dangerous inequality in the ground, he would, instead of avoiding it by going off to one side or the other, go into or on top of it with the chance of injuring himself or his rider, unless, indeed, his fear of an accident was greater than his sense of discipline. It is evident that a horse which would depend solely on his master for guidance, would in time lose to a great extent its instinct of self-preservation when being ridden, and would consequently be an unsafe 'conveyance' over bad ground, or across a 'country.' In fact, the less developed a horse's natural 'cleverness' is, other things being equal, the better school horse he will prove. Again I say that school riding is worthy of practice only as a means and not as an end. Owing to the mechanical condition of mind into which school horses are brought by their training, they are bad for ordinary outdoor work. In fact, they are rarely used outside the *manège*, especially as hacking, hunting, and similar kinds of work tend to unfit them for the business in the school. Fillis told me that Baucher, with whom he had been an assistant for three years, never to his knowledge rode in any other place than a *manège* or circus. On one occasion, so Fillis related to me when I met him in Germany, a nobleman of high rank came into the *manège* belonging to Baucher, who at that moment was riding a beautifully trained horse, on which he performed a number of elaborate evolutions for the benefit of his distinguished visitor. While they were talking together, the nobleman suddenly remembered that he had forgotten to post an important letter which he had in his pocket. Drawing it out he handed it to the great *écuyer*, and asked him, as he was mounted, to kindly take it as quickly as possible to the nearest post office. 'Sir,' replied Baucher, 'I am overwhelmed with regret that I am unable now to obey your request, but if you will wait for three months, in order to give me time to train my horse to go outside, I shall then be delighted to take the letter for you.' Considering that, as a rule, it takes fully two, if not three, years to train a horse properly for high school work, and that by the end of the required time the animal is generally rendered unsound from the abnormal and excessive strain thrown on his joints, tendons and ligaments, we need not be surprised that *la haute école*, except for circus work, has fallen into disrepute both in France and Germany.

I must not omit to say that M. Auguste Raux, whom we saw riding in his *manège, rue* Pergolèse, has a good seat on horseback, is a nice weight for the saddle, and is an excellent *écuyer* and *dresseur*.

My reason for having wanted to buy a well-trained school horse was to utilise him in strengthening our programme during any future tour we might make. I gave up the idea; firstly, for the excellent reason that I could not get a capable one which was sound enough not to do discredit to my repute as a good judge of horses; and secondly, because the more I saw of school work, the less I valued it from a practical point of view. At about the time when I had come to this conclusion, my wife, Sorel and I went for a ride in the Bois on three school nags, which were listless and out of condition from, probably, the hard work they had gone through during the preceding season. The grey gelding ridden by my wife had such capital shoulders and good action that I resolved to buy him and turn him into a jumper, although he was about ten years old. I entrusted Sorel with the offer of 500 francs, which was accepted, and we brought him back with us to London, where I put him up at The Royal Military Riding-School, Gloucester Crescent, Bayswater. I will now let my readers into a little secret, which was that, through all our travels, my wife, notwithstanding the lavish praise she had obtained for her riding from foreign newspapers, had the great sorrow of her London notices being limited to a brief mention in the *Field*, and some sketches in the *Graphic*. Wherever we went, after having ridden at one of our shows, to the enthusiastic delight of the men, she was almost always asked by some lady (of course) if she had ever performed in London. She had then the mortification—which was naturally aggravated each time it was repeated—of explaining that the only occasion on which she had come before the London public in the capacity of a lady rider, was for charity, as I have described on page 130. As we had an idea of going to America later on, she felt that the only press notices which would pass muster across the Atlantic would be those with the London trade mark on them. As soon as I had concluded the purchase of the grey gelding, whom we called Gustave, I told her to cheer up; for, bar accidents, she would have her book full of London 'cuttings' before the year was ended. With this object in view, I commenced to train Gustave so that he would have a perfect snaffle-bridle mouth and become a clever jumper. He was a well-bred horse, with a moderately-sized head, light neck, remarkably flat and sloping shoulders, short back, good loin and barrel, tail set on high, clean forelegs barring a few splints, and with rather sickle hocks.

Gustave had had his mouth spoiled by a long succession of riding-school pupils, whose attacks on the reins he used to try to avoid by throwing up his head in the air, or by jibing. He had only a very faint idea of jumping; he was miserably thin; and the heels of all his feet were contracted, and their frogs were suffering from thrush. The first things to do were, evidently, to get him a nice loose box; give

him plenty of lucerne, carrots, corn and hay; take off his
shoes; 'lower' his heels; treat him for thrush; and exercise
him on the soft ground of the riding-school. I may here
mention the interesting fact, without stopping to offer any
explanation of it in this place, that if the tan which is used
in riding-schools be allowed to remain in a horse's feet, it
will cause their frogs to rot away in a short time. Consequently, the feet of animals which are worked on such soil
should be 'picked out' immediately they come off it. As
I am on the subject of veterinary treatment, it may not be
out of place if I mention that a solution of as much iodoform
and camphor, or of camphor alone, as any required quantity
of oil of turpentine will dissolve, is an admirable application for thrush. I began to put Gustave's mouth in order
by means of the long reins and standing martingale; and
gave him his first lessons in jumping 'at liberty,' for which
work I had the advantage of knowing how to use the lunging whip, which has obtained its name of *chambrière* (house-
maid) in French, from the able manner in which it puts
horses in order. The jumps over which I practised Gustave,
both at liberty, and with the long reins, were a heavy log
and a wall made of wooden planks, neither of which could
be 'chanced' with impunity. As he had to go over them
about a dozen times a day, he soon learned the important
lesson that it was pleasanter to jump than to rap his shins.
I took care that the notion of refusing did not remain long
in his mind. I have no doubt that many of my readers who
have followed me up to this, will think that I adopted
the best possible means of disgusting the horse with jumping,
by giving him so much of it, and that I did not succeed in
spoiling him, solely on account of his marvellous forbearance
and good temper. So far from the grey gelding being of an
ingenuous turn of mind, he was as artful as the proverbial
cart-load of monkeys, and obeyed only because he found
that it was better policy to do so than to resist. The idea
that it disgusts a horse to jump him time after time over

the same fence, holds good only when the act of leaping is connected in his mind with pain, as, for instance, when he has infirm forelegs, or when his mouth gets pulled about by an incompetent rider. In less than a month, I made Gustave so clever that he used to easily jump, on the heavy tan of the riding-school, a bar 5 feet high with my wife on his back; and he did not hesitate to do this when the obstacle had no wings and was only 10 feet long. I also taught him within this period to strike off from the halt into any required pace (walk, trot, canter or gallop), or to change his pace into any desired one, or to halt by the mere application of the leg and slight movement of the body, while the reins were loose on his neck, and while I kept my hands in my coat-pockets. He would do this in the open, as well as in the riding-school. I may state that Gustave had never received any high school training.

A few days after our return to London, we met Professor Sample in the street, looking very thin and dejected. We took him back with us to lunch, told him how we had got on in South Africa, and listened to his story. We were sorry to hear that he had continued in a vein of bad luck ever since he had shown his machine in London. His affairs were then in a desperate condition, and to crown all his misfortunes, his beloved machine was in pawn for debt. He believed firmer than ever in the glorious future that was in store for this child of his brain, if he could only get a chance of bringing it before the public. His one concern for the plight in which he then was, was its influence on the success of his invention. I honoured him for the steadfastness of his faith in the thing that had ruined him, and won his heart for the time being by telling him that the fact of the public not having accepted the machine in no way altered my good opinion of it. He implored me to help him in giving it another chance, and I need hardly say that I promised to aid him. I took lodgings for him near where I was staying, and told him that he would always

A Match.

find a knife and fork ready for him at our 'diggings.' A few days after, he informed us that Leon, who at that time was giving performances at the Aquarium, had challenged him in the *Sporting Life* to a horse-taming contest for £50 a side, and that Leon was willing to let him use his machine; but that he was unable to accept the challenge as he had no money. I said that I would be only too glad to act as his backer, and that I was ready to go, then and there, to the office of the paper and 'cover' the £50 cheque which had been left by Leon with the editor of the *Sporting Life*. On hearing this, Sample seemed so overcome with emotion that his eyes filled with tears; and his throat with sobs. He said a lot of nice things about our kindness to him at a time when no one else would give him a friendly hand. My wife, from womanly sympathy, began to cry, and having got my cheque-book out of my desk, handed it to me, and begged me to go at once to the *Sporting Life* and put Sample's mind at rest. When Sample and I arrived at the office, we explained the reason of our coming, and I paid in my cheque. All the preliminaries were arranged without any trouble; an influential committee was formed; and on the opening night my wife and I went down early to the Aquarium to see that our man was ready for the fray. I may explain that the field of battle was the stage of the Imperial Theatre, which is at the west end of the Aquarium.

When we arrived, we went behind the scenes and found Sample in a great state of excitement on account of there being some hitch in the working of the machine. I begged him to leave the unlucky thing alone, and assured him that a man of his great experience and skill could not possibly lose in a competition against a comparative novice who had never been out of the United Kingdom, and who had taken to horses late in life. He replied that he did not care a button about the match, and that his sole object in making it was to demonstrate to the world the marvellous efficacy of his invention for taming horses by machinery.

I tried to point out that the fact of my having 'found' the £50 entitled me to a voice in the matter. He begged me to let him play his own game, and declared that my money was safe. As the contest was to last a fortnight, the time on each evening being divided equally between the two, and as I felt certain that the old man would sooner die than get beaten; I let him have his own way, and looked on. In the meantime, my wife had found out the dressing-room which had been improvised into a loose-box for several of the supposed man-eaters and equine demons which had been brought to be tamed. Knowing only that they had been led through the streets and through the narrow passage at the back of the stage, and seeing that they looked kindly at her, she gave them carrots, patted each of them on the neck, and made friends with them. When, after they were brought on the stage, she heard their characters traduced in the severest possible manner, instead of smiling, she got quite cross. After her inspection of the country, she told me that the referee, who was the representative of the *Sporting Life*, had got Sample, during my absence, to sign a certain paper. On hearing this I went to Sample and asked him what was the nature of the document which he had signed. He told me it was a private affair of no consequence.

The show commenced by Sample in dress clothes coming forward on the stage and making a speech in a good deal of his old 'taking' style. Greatly to my regret for his own sake, he looked nervous and worried, and consequently lost touch with his audience, which preferred to see something done, than to listen. He at last began operations by getting the machine, which had been mounted on wheels and which contained a horse that was shy of steam-engines, drawn on to the stage. Sample then connected the revolving apparatus of the machine with a small steam-engine which he had at the side, in order to make the horse-box spin round, and to render the imprisoned animal giddy. But as the stage had a considerable downward slope to the front, the tiresome thing would not turn round, except very slowly and at a terrible amount of muscular expenditure on the part of the ever-faithful Joe, who had in his usual kind-hearted way came to help his master. The bad performance of the machine, which was really not to blame for its failure to act properly on this occasion, was greeted with uproarious laughter by the audience. I could have heartily joined in with the merriment, had I not known the agony of mind that the poor inventor was feeling at that time. At last, seeing that he could do nothing on the stage with the machine, which required to be placed on level ground in order to work efficiently; the horse had to be backed out of its confined position, and the machine ignominiously led off. To make up for this failure, Sample took the nervous horse in hand, and in his customary expert manner, after about ten minutes, made the animal stand still while he blew a steam whistle all about it. This feat naturally 'showed up' the unfortunate machine still more.

Leon came on attired in his usual sombrero, Norfolk blouse and fishing-boots, and gave a show of what, as far as I could see, he had learned from Galvayne and Norton Smith, and of what they had respectively learned from Sample and Gleeson. To my thinking, his work was entirely without merit from a horseman's point of view; yet, having an immense amount of self-confidence and self-assertion, he 'went down' fairly well with a certain class.

The second horse, if I remember rightly, which Sample was given to handle, was a reputed man-eater. 'Ladies and gentlemen,' said Sample, coming up to the footlights, 'I am an old man, and this is a very vicious horse. To prove to you the excellence of my system, I shall have him turned loose, and merely by the use of the whip which I hold in my hand, I shall, without hurting him, make him so quiet that he will come up to me to be patted.' The old man—whether he was acting with consummate cleverness, or whether, from having been a long time away from horses, he was really a little nervous, I cannot say—while he was thus speaking, looked so forlorn with his anxious face, grey hair brushed off his forehead, and trembling hand upraised, as if in appeal for pity, drew to him the sympathy of all the spectators, and won their hearty applause when, in less than a quarter of an hour, the savage one finding that it could in no other way escape the constant flicks of the whip on its hind quarters, came up to the Professor and allowed him to stroke its head and neck. Despite the machine fiasco, the large majority of the committee voted for the American. When we three returned home to supper, Sample promised to discard the machine for the remainder of the contest, which in that case was a certainty for him. I tried to get further information out of him respecting the purport of the paper which he had signed, and after some pressure, he acknowledged that it was a secret agreement between him and Leon with the *Sporting Life*, for Leon to get back his own cheque; for Sample to receive my cheque; and for both of them to hold the newspaper free from all responsibility in the matter. On hearing this I got annoyed and refused to listen to what Sample called 'reason.' Believing as I did then, and do now, that a match for returnable, or, as I would call them, bogus cheques is a deception on the public, I naturally resented having been made a participator, even though an innocent one, in any such transaction. Sample said that Leon would not have made the match on any other terms, as it was purely a 'gate money' affair; that the match would have come off whether or not I had 'put up' the money; that he accepted my offer to be his backer, because my name would be a 'draw'; that I had better get my cheque back; and that he would substitute for it his own cheque, which would be handed back to him to tear up at the end of the contest. The editor of the *Sporting Life* returned me my cheque, which, contrary to my expectation, had not been 'presented'; I withdrew altogether from the competition; the committee voted almost unanimously in favour of Sample; the public, probably because they thought it was not a genuine money affair, refused to be drawn to it; Leon left the Aquarium; and Sample disappeared from my sight. In this matter, I need hardly say that I had no grievance against either Leon or the *Sporting Life*, the editor of which arranged matters in the not unusual way, out of pure good nature and from the natural desire to keep his paper before the public as a leader of sport.

During this autumn, at the invitation of General Sir Evelyn Wood and the Committee of the Military Society, I gave a lecture at Aldershot on horses for army purposes. I had a large and attentive audience, and was gratified by gaining the approval of General Sir Baker Russell and other good men; although I could not help feeling depressed by the knowledge that no matter how clearly I might point out defects in our military school system of training horses, and suggest improvements, no words of mine could loosen red-tape bands. Our military breaking has remained unaltered for at least sixty years, and is consequently in an antiquated condition. As this is not the place in which to fully discuss such subjects, I may content myself with saying that the great advance made in school riding and breaking on the Continent during the last few years, has been due to the knowledge of the movements of the horse, as investigated in the first instance by Marey and completed by Muybridge. This is exhaustively shown in Barroil's *L'Art Équestre*. What was good enough for their grandfathers, appears to be regarded by our military riding authorities as excellent beyond the possibility of improvement. The fact is that their sixty or eighty year old system is as much inferior to that of Raabe or Fillis, as a 'Brown Bess' is to the present magazine rifle. I hope within the next year to bring out a book on military riding and breaking; for such a work is greatly needed. Even if it be not adopted by the military authorities, I am certain that it will be largely read by officers in the army, among whom I have a big reading public.

CHAPTER XXIII.

The Horsewoman—Practical Lectures on Side-Saddle Riding—The Wards—Fred Allen—Teaching Ladies to Ride—Riding Masters—Learning from Teaching—Improvements in Side-Saddles—Safety Skirts—The Danger of being 'Dragged'—Saddlers—Walsall—Effect of Cast-iron on the Franco-German War—The Row—Lady Dilke.

ABOUT this time, we brought out *The Horsewoman*, a book on side-saddle riding, written by my wife and edited by me. It received a cordial welcome from the London press, and has had a large sale. After it had appeared, we thought that it would be a good idea to give in London some performances which would prove that my wife knew her subject practically as well as theoretically, and which would procure the long-desired London press notices. Knowing how inefficient are the methods adopted in England, and also abroad, for teaching ladies to ride, and how greatly such instruction is needed, we resolved to give a series of practical lectures on this subject according to an entirely novel manner. With this object, we hired Ward's Riding-School, in Brompton Road, from twelve to two on the required afternoons. I did the talking about bridles, saddles, mounting, dismounting, seat, 'hands,' length of stirrup leather, habits, etc.; and my wife dressed in a Norfolk jacket, breeches and boots illustrated the various points on Gustave, who by that time was beautifully trained, and was able to jump, as I said before, a bar 5 feet with ease in a very small riding-school. The mention of a riding-school reminds me to say that this was the first time my wife had ever ridden in one. To show the most efficient manner by which a lady could be taught to ride in a very short time, I made, by means of the long reins, Gustave circle, turn, leap, refuse, and stop 'dead' while my wife sat unmoved in the saddle, with her hands on her lap holding a light cane. As she had no skirt on, we were able to show in an exact manner how balance and grip could be obtained in the best possible way. I am certain that we threw a great deal of new light on the subject, and we won warm praise from all the representatives of the press who came to see us. The *Queen*, in an extremely kind notice, described our performance as follows :—

'We cannot but recommend all ladies interested in equestrian matters, as well as those who are in special need of really useful hints on riding, to take the earliest opportunity of attending these lectures. It is a real pleasure to see a lady ride as Mrs Hayes does; she combines in an unusual degree an absolutely firm, strong seat with a pretty and graceful one; as much may be learnt by watching her carefully as from Captain Hayes's very practical and useful instructions.

'Mrs Hayes's wide experience qualifies her to speak with authority as to the best methods of training horses; of the newest and most satisfactory kinds of saddles, stirrups, bridles; of ladies' riding costumes; and last, but by no means least, of the novel method adopted by herself and Captain Hayes for teaching a lady to ride well, and especially to gain a firm seat in jumping—that is, by learning to ride without reins. Of this Mrs Hayes gave a practical demonstration. Captain Hayes first explained the proper way of mounting a lady and arranging the habit; also dwelt at length on the proper length of stirrup, the various kinds of safety stirrup, and other preliminary matters; and then mounted Mrs Hayes on her horse, which had on an ordinary snaffle bridle and a standing martingale. The short reins were taken off, and long ones of about 20 feet put in their place. Captain Hayes, on foot, proceeded to drive the horse round, turning it quickly, walking, trotting or cantering, and finally driving it over some big jumps, which were taken in excellent style. One can readily believe that this method is well adapted to give the pupil a really firm seat, as well as to give her confidence; and it makes it impossible for the beginner to acquire the very common, but most insecure and ungraceful trick of holding on by the reins. Much might be said of the large amount of valuable and practical instruction given by Captain Hayes in his lecture, as well as of some of Mrs Hayes's brilliant performances, such as riding a horse without any bridle or reins whatever over some big jumps.'

Riding over fences, especially without reins, in a small school, where one is continually on the turn, is a far severer test of firmness of seat than going over an ordinary 'country.' Also, jumping in cold blood tries the horse's staunchness much more highly than negotiating obstacles under the excitement of company or of the music of the hounds. To show how well both horse and rider knew their work, I used to put up, in the centre of the school, a gate 4 feet 9 inches high and only 9 feet long without wings of any kind. My wife would then canter Gustave up to it, and as he was in the act of taking off, she would drop the reins on his neck, and keep her seat without the slightest movement in the saddle, while the grey gelding cleared the obstacle in his usual clever style. I would recommend any man who wishes to know if he can ride over fences without hanging on by the reins, to try this feat. I need hardly point out the great advantage of teaching a horse to jump in cold blood anything within his compass, to which he may be put by his rider. Hunters, for instance, that will leap kindly only in company or when hounds are running, are not more than half-trained; for in the event of their rider being thrown out of a run, or wishing to join the pack by taking a straight line across country, the reluctant one, when left to himself, might get 'pounded' at any moment. Firm retention of seat by a lady, without holding on by the reins when going over a big fence, is easy, provided she has knowledge and a sufficiency of practice, which, in ordinary cases, need not be more than that which could be obtained in eight or nine lessons given, according to our methods, by a competent teacher. A man's seat, in the usual form of hunting-saddle, is so much weaker than that of a lady in a side-saddle that it would take him as many months, if not years, to attain a like proficiency.

With a book full of flattering press cuttings about her book and her riding, my wife felt quite happy, for the time being.

I think I am right in saying that the Wards are the most accomplished driving family in England. The father, old 'Charlie' Ward, the famous 'Whip of the West,' and his brother Harry are probably the last two representatives of the old 'Mail' coachmen. His first engagement was with the Norwich and Ipswich Mail between London and Colchester, when he was only seventeen years old. For seven years he drove the 'Quicksilver,' the Devonport Mail, which was the fastest one of its time, sixty miles a night without an accident. After that he drove the Brighton Day Mail, the 'Telegraph' between Exeter and Ilminster; another 'Telegraph' between Devonport and London; the 'Tally-Ho!' between London and Truro; and others. Though over eighty years of age, he is as capable a whip as ever. Frank, the eldest son, is a thorough workman, and is unrivalled in showing a four-in-hand team to advantage. During the first horse show at Olympia in 1887 (the Jubilee Year), he was asked by the management to give the Prince of Wales and other members of the Royal Family an exhibition of driving with a team of bays which the Wards had entered. When the ring was cleared, he gave a very fine show, and did several times the figure of eight, which requires a considerable amount of skill to perform properly in a small space. As he passed the Prince of Wales, he raised his hand to the brim of his hat, dropped the point of his whip behind his right shoulder by loosening the grip of the finger, and took off his hat. This neat method of making his bow produced quite as great an impression on the spectators as did his admirable driving. His team got first prize, beating two capital ones which belonged to King, the Piccadilly dealer, and which were tooled by those two crack coachmen, Mr Beckett and Mr M'Adam. The winners were an extraordinary level lot of short-legged cobby bays. They were real coach horses, and fine goers. In 1893, Frank also won the first prize at the Richmond Horse Show with Mr Fred. Gooch's showy team of skewbalds. He gave then an exhibition similar to the one at Olympia. Both at the Hall and at Richmond, Mr Butcher gave a very clever exhibition of tandem-driving. The Wards have a big business in teaching driving. The sons do the most of the work; though some of the pupils, especially those who are Americans, among whom the Wards have a large following, insist on having old Charlie Ward to impart to them the practice and traditions of the road.

Mr Gooch, whose name I have just mentioned, is one of the best known figures in the horse world. He lives at Windsor, where he has a small but select stable of horses and a private riding-school, in which he 'makes' the faultless prize winners, for which he is famous at all the principal horse shows. At Dublin in 1893 he was first in the Hacks and Roadsters; first in double harness, tandem and single harness; and first and second in the Champion Class. He

Mr F. V. GOOCH.
(From a Painting by James Miley.)

trains his jumpers on the same ground at Ascot as Ben Land used to train. He well deserves the reputation of being the best dressed and best 'turned out' man either on a horse or on the box seat of a coach in England, and is consequently an object of envy to all the young Guardsmen who follow the Windsor Drag Hounds, with which he always takes a prominent place. He is a fine horseman 'between the flags,' as well as in the hunting field, and is particularly good in showing high-class park hacks of his own breaking. One of his last wins was the Drag Hunt Cup this year at Windsor on May Morn. His first love was pony racing, in the days when Sally Brass and Deuce of Diamonds were unrivalled in their class. Coming home from hunting about eighteen years ago poor George Fordham, who was very fond of a good pony, offered to back a pony he had against any other little one in the world. Mr Gooch, who was present, accepted the challenge for three matches, at £25 each on the flat, over a country and over hurdles, on behalf of Deuce of Diamonds, who made such an example of Fordham's pony in the first race, that Mr Gooch received forfeit for the other two. Among all the good ponies I have known, such as Gamecock, Skittles, Lord Clyde, Maythorn and Sylvia, I have never met any I liked so much as Deuce of Diamonds. Mr Gooch has owned Jack Frost, Papyrus, Red Enamel, Bringari, Wisdom, May Morn, and many others.

Among the gentlemen who came to our lectures on side-saddle riding, was Mr Fred. Allen, who used to own the large riding-school which is in Seymour Place, W., and which he sold to Mr Haines. Mr Allen's father, Mr John Allen, built this *manège*, and also wrote, in 1825, *Modern Riding*, in which the system of side-saddle equitation, before M. Pellier invented the third crutch, is described. In those days, high school riding was diligently cultivated in England, and as Mr John Allen was at the head of his profession in London, his *manège* was attended by all the best people, and he made, by his great ability as a teacher, an ample fortune.

After his death, his son proved to be a worthy successor, and has certainly been one of the most distinguished riding-masters we have had in England for the last fifty years. He had the honour of teaching the Empress of Austria and a great number of royal and imperial princes and princesses. Although he has retired from active work now, he is often called to instruct members of the imperial family in Austria, where he is a great favourite. He is a thorough good horseman, and is a man of charming manners and great tact.

After we had finished our series of lectures, we received so many applications from ladies for lessons, that we thought it advisable to make an arrangement with the Wards for the hire of their school at the hours required. As we charged a guinea a lesson, our *clientèle* was composed chiefly of wealthy people. The progress made by our pupils under our novel method of instruction was so remarkable that I would not venture to say how fast it was, if I were not able to give supporting evidence, which is furnished by the following extract from the *Queen* (17th June, 1893): 'I made the acquaintance of the authoress of *The Horsewoman* one morning in Ward's *manège*, where I went to see two little friends taking their riding lesson from her. It was a novel and pretty sight. Mrs Hayes has inaugurated a method of instruction hitherto unpractised, and which must recommend itself to anyone who sees the extraordinary progress which accompanies it. The children are dressed in gymnastic costume, and it was the third time only that they had been put on a horse—a large horse it was too, and as patient and kindly as it is possible to be. The first thing Mrs Hayes teaches is how to sit. By the pupils wearing no skirt, she can see at a glance whether the position of the legs is right, and this is all important.

'By the time I saw the children they were galloping gaily round and round, with radiant faces and flying hair, sitting better into the saddle, even at this early stage, than many a woman who considers herself a complete rider. They are not allowed to hold the reins; the hands lie in the lap, holding the whip across the knees, which accustoms them from the first to keep their hands low, besides teaching them to keep their seat without "riding the bridle" as so many people do. The horse is driven with long reins, like those used in breaking by Captain Hayes, and managed by him with the dexterity of a circus master. After a few turns at a canter, wicker hurdles are put up, and to my astonishment, the children, without the slightest fear or hesitation, settled themselves down, leaned well back, and popped over without raising their hands or altering the position of their legs. They had been over the same hurdles at the second lesson, and too much can hardly be said in praise of a system that has such results to offer in so short a space of time.'

When we got our pupils secure in their seat by balance and grip alone, we used to give them the reins, and teach them how to manage the horse. For any average young lady who had never been on a horse before, we found a dozen lessons amply sufficient to make her ride in a graceful and workmanlike manner on the flat or over fences, of course without any 'bumping,' 'screwing' or hanging on to the horse's head. We had several young and married ladies who had been given up as hopeless by riding-masters. They were, naturally, nervous and were painfully wanting in confidence. As soon as they understood that I had entire command of their mount, and that it was absolutely under my control, they felt relieved of the serious responsibility of managing the horse, and were then able to devote all their attention to acquiring a strong seat. Having obtained that great requisite for success in the saddle, they readily learned the use of the reins and the whip (as an aid). As one cannot manage the reins properly without having a good seat, and as the temptation to hang on by the reins is well nigh irresistible so long as the seat is insecure, it is surely advisable to prevent the pupil acquiring the fatal habit of 'riding the bridle,' by not allowing her to touch the reins, until she feels absolutely confident that nothing, except the bursting of the girths and surcingle can displace her from the saddle. I need hardly remind my readers that I am here referring to pupils who wish to learn in a short time to ride, and not to girls that can acquire the art by years of practice. At the same time, I confidently assert that my wife and I could teach in a fortnight young ladies to ride a great deal better than those who have ridden all their lives without any special training. We must remember that ladies, unlike men, ride the saddle and not the horse, and as their side seat is a wholly artificial one, practice alone is not sufficient to obtain grace and skill. To explain my meaning with reference to artificial and natural exercises, I may point to the fact that a sprinter may be an exceedingly graceful and fast runner without teaching; but that no one has ever become a dancer of great merit, without long and serious training. Hunting ladies might say that my pupil of fourteen days, however well she might stick on her horse and handle him, would be certain to make a poor show in the hunting field from lack of an instructed 'eye for a country,' and from not understanding 'pace.' To this I may reply that riding is only one of the component parts of hunting, and that many good men and women to hounds have been extremely poor riders. In the same way, some of our best jockeys, and even some good chase riders, have been indifferent horsemen. I may here remind my readers of the old saying that we should ride to hunt, and not hunt to ride.

In London, as I believe, elsewhere, competition has reduced school charges so much, that there is but little profit to be gained from the teaching of riding. As a rule, the proprietors are content, for a slight increase for the hire of the horse or horses, to add the services of the riding-master, who has to act the part of groom as well as instructor on from 30s. to two guineas a week. These men have been usually army rough-riders, and rarely know anything beyond what they have been taught at Canterbury or Woolwich. Consequently they teach ladies and civilians to ride with one hand; for the very funny reason that soldiers, who are supposed to have their right hand occupied in holding a weapon, ride in that manner. If our finest steeplechase riders find that they need the use of both hands on the reins, how much more would ladies require that assistance. Besides, it is easier for a woman to sit square, when she has both hands on the reins, than when she has only one. All the riding-masters I have met, firmly believe that they are competent to teach riding to ladies in every stage of proficiency; and yet we never encounter riding-mistresses who assert their ability to instruct men in the art of sitting on a horse. After the lady pupil has got over the first difficulties about her seat, length of stirrup, position and action of her legs, etc., she will be ready to learn from a man how to manage her horse, regulate his paces, and make him obey her wishes with precision and intelligence; but up to that point his counsels are of but little value compared to those of a competent woman, who knows from personal experience what he, in most cases, talks about theoretically, or at second hand. For outside work, a riding-mistress has the disadvantage of her professional brother, in not being able to help her pupil in difficulty as well as he could do. Therefore, for thorough efficiency, the staff of every riding-school in which ladies are taught, should include a riding-mistress as well as a riding-master. Here again comes the question of cost. If, however, persons object to pay a fair price for good instruction, they have only themselves to blame, when they or their children fail to learn properly. This parsimony, as regards riding, is idiotic in one's own case, and culpable in that of one's children, who from ignorance or wrong teaching, will be far more liable to suffer from accidents than if they had been instructed in a capable manner. This miserable economy, which also extends to horses, saddle gear, and habits, has been the cause of many a young lady losing her life.

My readers may, not unlikely, ask why I have dwelt so exclusively on riding from a woman's point of view? My reason for having done so is that it is far less understood than cross-saddle riding, about which there is but little new to be said. Although from the artificial nature of a woman's seat, improvements in side-saddles and consequently in feminine equitation are constantly being made, no great advance has been wrought by men in riding during the last half century. I do not think that if Allen M'Donogh, Frank Butler, and Baucher came to earth again, they would have much to learn in their respective styles of riding, from the best professionals of the present day.

I am aware that many persons hold in contempt all work done in a riding-school. While fully admitting that the final and crucial test of the training of a man, woman, or horse, is his performance in the open, and, I would almost add, over a country; I must say that the first lessons can be given far more effectively in a *manège* than outside, where the pupil, whether human or equine, is far less under the instructor's control and guidance than in a school.

Although London riding-masters are no doubt well acquainted with military riding, according to the English red book, I have never yet met one of the ex-rough-rider class (I am not referring to men like Captain Fitzgerald or Mr Fred Allen) who understood anything about high school riding, steeplechase or flat race riding, or horsebreaking, which is an art that, in my opinion, every riding-master ought to know. Nothing looks, or is, more incompetent than the exhibition of ignorance, by such a teacher, of the proper way to make a horse steady or obedient, there and then, when the animal 'plays up' with a pupil. But what can you expect from a 35s.-a-week man? Baron de Curnieu in his *Leçons Hippiques* says:—'*Il nous faudrait un professeur d'équitation qui peut nous enseigner en même temps l'anatomie comparée.*' That's all very well; but one would have to pay him accordingly. This puts me in mind of a reply which a Mahammadan servant of mine made to me when I found fault with him for having failed to exercise special forethought respecting some business which I had given him to do. 'Sir,' said he, 'you should remember that I am only a £2-a-month servant. If I were as clever as you expect me to be, you would have to pay me at least £30 a month.'

The craze for cheap riding lessons is not confined to England. James Fillis told me that on one occasion when he had created a very favourable impression by his high school riding in Berlin, several ladies of the Prussian capital asked him to give them riding lessons; but that on his mentioning that his terms were eight marks (shillings) a lesson, they all with one accord expressed their sorrow and went away.

Although our riding lessons did not bring us in much money, for only a few people will pay highly for good quality after having been accustomed to obtain an inferior article cheaply; they taught both of us a great deal. Long before we commenced them, I was aware of the truth of the old saying that one never knows a subject well, until one has had some experience in teaching it. We were of course delighted to get this opportunity of increasing our knowledge, and we stored up the results of our observations for use in new editions, as well as on future occasions. One morning in the riding-school, I remarked that my wife, while going over some jumps and, consequently, while pressing her leg against the leaping-head of her saddle, kept the flat of her knee away from the flap of the saddle, instead of close against it. I could see this, because she was riding without a skirt at the time. When she had finished, I asked her why she rode in this manner, and remarked that she would be firmer and 'squarer' in her seat, if she would bring her knee close to the horse's side. She replied that what I said was quite true; but that the curve of the leaping-head forced the knee away from the flap of the saddle, when the leg was pressed against the leaping-head, and that this was a failing inherent in all leaping-heads. I told her that I would try to remedy this defect, and by a good deal of thinking, many experiments and the aid of that admirable mechanician, Mr Weston, I brought out a new kind of leaping-head, which I have patented and which I believe has a big future. I need only say that it answers its purpose, and that it greatly increases the rider's strength of grip, without any disadvantage to neutralise in the slightest its usefulness. Having fully tested it, my wife thinks that it quite doubles a rider's firmness in the saddle. It is as much my wife's invention as mine; for without her counsel I could not have thought it out. I may explain to those of my readers who are not conversant with saddle gear, that the leaping-head is the horn or crutch which is made to take the pressure off the rider's left leg, just above the knee. Not to be behind hand in the inventing line, my wife devised an admirable safety skirt, which she has had patented, and has given it to Messrs E. Tautz & Sons, of 485 Oxford Street, to sell. It possesses the great advantage of looking like an ordinary skirt when the wearer is on foot, and being absolutely safe when the lady is in the saddle. She and I thought, at first, that its graceful and decent appearance when on foot would be a great charm in the eyes of ladies. We begin to doubt this on seeing the popularity enjoyed by certain safety skirts which, when the wearer is dismounted, give a very liberal view of the limbs, especially, when viewed from behind. Can it be that there are ladies who like to afford this gratuitous show to the public? My wife, in conjunction with Messrs Hampson & Scott, who are large wholesale manufacturers of bits, stirrup-irons, saddles and harness at Walsall, has also patented a saddle with a movable upper crutch, over which the right leg is placed. The invention was the result of my wife's idea and of Mr Scott's mechanical skill. As there is only one place in which a rider can sit comfortably in a side-saddle; it follows that the length of the rider's leg will determine the distance of the upper crutch from it. Hence, a saddle that will fit a tall woman, will be uncomfortable or altogether unsuitable for a small one, and *vice versâ*. In England it is easy to get a saddle made to order; but as saddle-trees are not constructed in India, China, or any of our colonies, I feel certain that in these countries, saddles of this movable upper crutch type have a great future before them; for, by a very simple arrangement, the crutch is made to move forward or backward and to be clamped at any required distance from the cantle, which, I need hardly say, is the rearmost portion of the saddle-tree. In the 'trade,' the crutch to which I have given the name of upper crutch, is called the 'near head;' and the now obsolete one which used to be on the off side, the 'off head.' As the leaping-head is also on the near side, I think the term 'upper crutch,' or 'upright crutch' is less liable to cause confusion than the trade expression. Some persons use the word 'pommel' for 'crutch,' which is in no way a pommel, according to the modern use of that part. Although the word 'horn' is quite as suitable as 'crutch,' it is rarely employed. I may mention that it is the German equivalent for the crutch of a side-saddle.

While I am on the subject of side-saddles, I cannot help alluding to the terribly dangerous practice of ladies riding with a man's ordinary stirrup or, worse still, with a padded 'Victoria stirrup' which is unconnected with a safety bar. Not long ago, there was a case, one of many others, in which a young lady on being thrown from her horse was fatally injured by being dragged by the stirrup. At the coroner's inquest, there was a good deal of evidence taken as to the pony she was riding being quiet or not; but no one at the inquest made any inquiry as to the nature of the stirrup, which was the cause of a very ordinary accident having had such a horrible result. The best rider in the world mounted on the quietest horse in existence, might by accident get a fall; but the danger of being dragged is absolutely preventable. The precautions which ought to have been taken for the young lady's safety had evidently been neglected; probably through ignorance.

We were fortunate to make the acquaintance of Mr

Wilton, who is by far the largest manufacturer of side-saddles in England. He greatly helped us by the experiments he was always ready to carry out for us, and by giving us the results of his unrivalled experience. He is the fourth generation of saddlers in his family; and, although he has made an ample fortune, he has determined that his two sons will be the fifth generation in this trade. It is a pleasure to meet a man like him who knows his business and takes a pride in it.

Very long ago it used to be a mystery to me how a saddler who had no workshop was able to execute orders which required the employment of skilled labour. I subsequently found out these men have their work done for them, except trifling repairs, by wholesale houses, which in, probably, nineteen out of twenty cases, belong to Walsall. As the flaunting of a scarlet rag infuriates the proverbial bull, so does the mention, by a layman, of the name of the busy Staffordshire city make mad the ordinary workshopless saddler. Honestly speaking, the surmise would be a compliment; for wholesale houses like Hampson & Scott, Barnsby, and Christie turn out far finer work than any ordinary retailer could produce, even if he had men under him. The saddler without a workshop, if in London, will, as a rule, admit that he sends his work 'out'; but not to Walsall. He airily explains that his workpeople prefer to labour in their homes than to toil at a bench in his shop. He concedes them this privilege, and states that they work under his personal supervision. '*His* workmen' are of course those of the wholesale house. Owing to their immense facilities, the large Walsall firms work with extraordinary economy and expedition. For instance, they can supply the retailer with a saddle complete, for less money than he could cover and stuff it in his own shop. Besides this, an order received by the morning post for, say, a hundred sets of harness can be executed during the day and the goods dispatched the same evening! I have no intention of 'giving away' the retail saddler who is workshopless ; but if he charges me for a job as much as Champion & Wilton, Whippy & Steggles, Langdon, Harries of Shrewsbury or any other saddler who gets his work done in his own premises would do, I would, not unnaturally, feel aggrieved. I would certainly prefer to give an order to a firm whose manager would have my work done under his own eyes, than to trust to a man who would have to write to someone else and tell him what I wanted. When it is a question of buying a ready-made saddle, bridle or set of harness, I don't care where it has been manufactured, so long as it suits me.

While on a visit to Mr Scott of Messrs Hampson & Scott, we spent three very pleasant days at Walsall, where we had the best possible opportunities of seeing leather, bits, buckles, hooks, stirrup-irons, hames, clipping machines, saddles, harness, etc., in every stage of preparation. What struck me most was the excellence of the work turned out ; although economy was closely observed as far as could be done legitimately. One of the greatest labour-saving inventions ever discovered is that of annealing, which is a process of gradually cooling iron castings which have been heated, so that their texture becomes greatly toughened. I may mention that ordinary cast iron is so brittle that it is liable to break almost like glass if it is struck by, or let fall on, a hard substance. After being annealed it is called malleable iron, and then occupies, as regards toughness, a position which is about midway between cast iron and wrought iron. Before the process of annealing was known, iron buckles had to be made of wrought iron, and were consequently very expensive. Now they are all, practically speaking, of malleable iron, which fairly meets the requirements of the case in this instance. During the Franco-German war, very large orders for girth buckles for the French cavalry were sent to Walsall by men who were so unscrupulous that to obtain all possible profit out of their speculation, they contracted only for cast-iron buckles, the large majority of which must have broken in two the first time any strain was put on them. The Walsall men believe that much of the inefficiency of the French cavalry during that war was owing to the bursting of these wretched buckles. Although the process of annealing greatly adds to the strength of cast iron, it cannot diminish the liability of cast iron to contain bubbles, formed by escaping gas, distributed through its substance. This tendency to contract these bubbles, from the weakening effect of their presence, renders even annealed iron wholly unsuitable for bits. It is however largely used for their manufacture, especially for Liverpool bits, curbs and Pelhams, and with many deplorable accidents as results of this policy of 'cutting down' prices. Cast nickel bits are for this reason also unsafe. No bit which will not stand being well hammered when in a cold state, is fit to trust one's life to when on or behind a horse. In cheap side-saddles, the leaping-head iron is usually made of malleable, instead of wrought, iron. This is another terribly dangerous economy which should be made penal.

Being in town during the season, we rode a good deal in the Row, and saw there the worst broken horses and the feeblest riders, probably, in the world. Among other nice people, we made the acquaintance of Lady Dilke, who, on the appearance of my wife's book, *The Horsewoman*, wrote from France, where she was staying, a very kind letter of encouragement, and hoped that we would call on her when she returned to London. Lady Dilke rides well and dearly loves horses, especially, her handsome Arab, Shihab. With all her fondness for a horse, her sympathies are, as they ought to be, even more strongly enlisted in the cause of suffering humanity.

Among many other horse enthusiasts to whom our lectures on riding made us known, were Mr and Mrs Norman. As he is assistant editor of the *Daily Chronicle*, that paper is particularly sound in its reviews of books on horses. Mrs Norman, as Miss Dowie, the authoress of *A*

Riding-School Work. 337

Girl in the Carpathians, is, like her husband, well known as a clever and original writer.

All through this winter and spring I industriously availed myself of the use of a riding-school, to increase my knowledge of school breaking and riding.

Photo. by W. Till, Melton Mowbray.

CHAPTER XXIV.

Accident to Gustave—Ranelagh—Richmond—The Duke of Cambridge—Management of Horse Shows—Apathy of Londoners to Horse Shows—A Libel Action—Berlin—Berliner Tattersall—German Riding and Breaking—The Thiergarten—Riding in Berlin—*The Points of the Horse*—Fillis and Germinal—Circus Renz—Melton Mowbray—Lectures—Rugby—Yorkshire—Leicestershire—End.

WE had hoped to have Gustave ready for the jumping competitions at the Agricultural Hall; but about a month before that event came off, when practising him over a broad water jump, he overreached badly on account of the landing side being so soft from the infiltration of water, that he could not get his forefeet quick enough out of the sticky ground to avoid an accident. I freely admit that this was due entirely to my carelessness; for no one knew better than I did, that horses should never be schooled over water, or over any kind of fence in heavy ground, without having proper boots on their legs. In fact, I had always prided myself on having devised an admirable schooling boot for jumpers; but as I had mislaid the pair I had generally in use, I neglected to get another pair, or to employ a bandage with a strip of felt to protect the back tendons. I may mention that it is a good plan to lay down on the far side of a water jump of this kind, strong wicker hurdles or screens covered with earth, so as to prevent the animal's feet sinking into the ground on landing. Although the wound was an ugly one a little above the fetlock, Gustave made a rapid and complete recovery, thanks to dry dressing with iodoform, and pressure by means of cotton-wool bandaging. He appeared for the first time in a jumping competition at the Ranelagh Club Horse Show, where, ridden by my wife in a field of over twenty competitors, he was second to Lufra, who has been one of the most successful show jumpers in England. I may mention that Lufra belongs to Mr Fred. Horton, who takes a great deal of interest in show jumping, Mr Irving, F.R.C.V.S., and Mr Landsley, both of whom are fine horsemen, ride for him at competitions. On the first day at the Richmond Show, Gustave was footsore, and accordingly jumped reluctantly. Being all right on the second day, he fenced in beautifully clever and temperate style; but the water jump was so short (laterally), that the old gelding, seeing the turf on each side of him, leaped sideways (as any intelligent horse would have done, and got disqualified. For this reverse, my wife had the consolation of being personally complimented on her seat and hands by the Duke of Cambridge, who came up to where she had halted Gustave, and told her that he had never seen a lady ride better over fences than she did, and that he was greatly pleased with the way she handled her horse, and with her method of giving him a loose rein when jumping, instead of hanging on to his head, as many riders do. The Duke admired Gustave, especially for his good mouth; and remarked to her that it was always a pleasant sight to see a lady riding a nice, temperate horse in a snaffle, and particularly over fences.

To my thinking, the management of the jumping competitions both at the Agricultural Hall and at Richmond left much to be desired. The first blot on both programmes was the rule that the jumpers had to be entered for some of the other classes, so as to qualify them to take part in the leaping events. This was nothing less than an attempt at trading on the sporting feeling of the owners of the jumpers, instead of trying to encourage it. The only excuse which could be put forward in defence of this unjust tax is that it tends to keep out horses which are not of sufficient quality to compete in non-jumping classes. If this were really the reason for fining an owner for wanting his horse to jump, the committee would much more effectively accomplish their supposed desire, if they were to exclude from the jumping competitions all horses which did not come up to their standard of excellence, whether as hunters or hacks, for instance. Of course they would not adopt such a plan; for they are well aware that the leaping is their biggest 'draw.' To be consistent, they should force all horses entered for non-jumping prizes, to be also entered for the 'leps'; but for that flight of arbitrariness they have not as yet attained sufficient hardihood. At the most of these shows, the entrance money for the jumping competitions is so high, as compared to the value of the prizes, that the horses which attract nineteen-twentieths of the gate money, compete as a rule only for their own entry fees.

The second point which I disliked in the management of the leaping events at Islington and at Richmond was the absence of system in the judging. We all know that even a bad system is better than no system at all. No hint was given to the competitors as to the necessary requirements for a prize winner. Not the slightest regard was paid by the judges at either place to manners or style. Jibing brutes which had to be led out, took prizes. Impetuous beasts which had to be pulled up into a walk between the fences, obtained ribbons. Even refusers got placed. And yet the slightest touch, such as many of the cleverest and safest hunters that ever looked through a bridle would always give to a wall, if followed by the displacement of even a wooden brick, entailed instant disqualification. In all these competitions, except, of course, when there was only one obstacle, as at the big stone wall event in the Dublin Horse Show, no horse should be given a prize, unless he had been taken round at a canter or well-collected slow gallop, and without a refusal. I am here assuming, as I think I have a right to do, that all such jumping enclosures are mimic hunting fields. I may add that the rule against pulling horses up between the jumps is strictly observed at Ball's Bridge. The 'rapping' of a gate by a horse is such a dangerous experiment, especially if the gate happened to be unfastened, that it ought, I think, to be a bar to success. But a wall is different. Other things being equal; the horse which jumped everything clean ought undoubtedly to be awarded the prize in preference to one that chanced any of the fences, even in a manner that could cause no danger. As horses have to carry a rider over fences, and are not judged by their powers of jumping when at liberty; the first requirement of a jumper is a good mouth; the second cleverness.

The awarding of prizes to so-called hunters which have never been over a fence is funny. An equally striking anomaly is that of judging cart-horses without seeing how they pull when between the shafts. It seems to me hardly right that a horse should obtain a prize as a hunter unless he was able to jump; or as a cart-horse, unless he could draw a load. The respective tests need not be very severe; but at least they should ensure the fact that prize winners are entitled to the designation under which they were entered. I need hardly mention that hacks and harness horses are put through their 'facings': why, then, should hunters and cart-horses be exempt? Having asked this question, I shall try to answer it as regards hunters. The usual method of teaching a horse to jump by getting on his back and riding him at fences, is so uncertain in its results, so apt to give rise to an accident, and so liable to make a horse fidgety, if not dangerously impetuous, that owners, especially if they be breeders and dealers, naturally object to incurring risks which they can avoid, or which they can make over to the purchasers of their animals. The addition of a jumping test would therefore greatly decrease the number of exhibits in the hunter classes, which are accordingly judged solely by their conformation, looks, action and manners. We find, even among old horses which are exhibited as hunters, total ignorance of one of the most essential parts of their work. I feel confident that if the method to which I have previously alluded, of teaching horses to jump cleverly before they were mounted were well known, the objection of exhibitors to a jumping test would speedily vanish. These remarks concerning horse shows in no way apply to young horses sold as hunters at Irish fairs, such as those of Ballinasloe or Cahirmee, where sellers are always ready to demonstrate the ability of their animals to 'throw a lep.' Without going into any details, I may remark that the jumping education of hunters should begin before they are older than two years.

Remembering the intense interest with which the Horse Show at Ball's Bridge was regarded by all classes of persons in Dublin, I could not help being struck with the apathy displayed by Londoners about the May Horse Show of the Royal Agricultural Society at Islington. This great annual event in the English horse world had less space devoted to it in the advertisement columns of the daily and evening papers than any of the theatres or principal music halls; and those organs of public opinion reported its proceedings more poorly than they did the doings of any of the nightly places of amusement. As far as I could judge, the majority of the small number of people who went to the Agricultural Hall were chiefly country visitors. And yet this was the one grand yearly occasion afforded to Londoners to inspect a large variety of some of the finest horses in the world. I am again forced to the conclusion that the great body of Londoners, and I might add, or people who neither ride nor drive, care nothing about horses. The newsboys who run in and out among the crowd, hawking their evening papers, show their knowledge of their customers by shouting 'Winner! Winner!!' Imagine what would be the disgust of the average purchaser if, instead of the results of races, he were to find only a list of the winners at the Agricultural Hall!

In country parts of England, great interest is taken in horse shows. Judging by the familiar faces which invariably turn up at the Hall, Cambridge, Peterborough, Liverpool, Leicester and other places, we may conclude that there is a small body of enthusiasts who spend all their time at horse shows, or in looking to these functions. These are the people whom I like to get among, and talk 'horse' with them.

During the preceding winter, I had, greatly to my surprise, been served with a writ for a libel action, which Mr Sexton, *alias* 'Professor' Leon, had instituted against my wife for her comments, in an Indian newspaper for which she used to write, on Sexton's horse-taming show at the Aquarium. She had listened seriously to the statements made concerning the awful depravity and wildness of the 'crocks' which were brought on the stage, and knowing what wild and vicious horses really were, she got mad, and wrote what was certainly a libel. Had she known that 'Leon, the Mexican horse-tamer' was only a *rôm de théâtre*; that instead of being a Mexican horseman, he, Sexton, was, as he stated at the trial, an English printer's clerk who had never been out of the United Kingdom; and that he had learned the 'system' from his brother-in-law, Galvayne, she would have smiled at the hyperbole used, and would have applauded Sexton for not giving a worse show than he did. The weak point about ladies is that they are so practical that when a man says a thing, they believe him. To me the strange thing about this trial was that I, who was as ignorant as the child unborn about what my wife had written, should, by the law of *tort* (cursed be the inventor of it), also be made liable. The principle seems wrong; although, personally, I regard the obligation thus imposed as an honour.

In order to get the money to pay the 'damages,' we took Gustave to Berlin with the intention of making it by horse-breaking; but the time of our arrival (beginning of July) was out of the season, and I could find no one who took any interest in the art of giving horses good manners and snaffle-bridle mouths. To test whether there was any chance of being able to get up a class, I gave a free performance to some of the officers of the 2d Uhlan Regiment at their barracks. I took in hand a horse of theirs which had up to that time always refused to jump, and after about a quarter of an hour's work with the long reins, I made him obey so effectually that when ridden by one of the gentlemen present, he jumped kindly several obstacles which were in the open school. They warmly commended this way of driving a horse on foot, and said that it was infinitely better than their own manner of lunging a horse; but they had no desire to learn. I then showed them how I had trained Gustave to walk, trot, canter, gallop, turn and halt by signal, while I sat on his back with my hands in my pockets. This performance on the part of the grey gelding delighted them beyond measure, and they all said: '*Er geht wie ein mensch*' (He goes like a man), which is the highest compliment a German can pay to a horse's style of movement. I may mention that I sold Gustave to Graf Magnis of this regiment for a great deal more than I had paid for him. I am glad that the Count, who is a fine rider and greatly admires English horse methods, got Gustave; for he can both ride and appreciate a clever jumper. The transformation from an over-worked and under-fed livery hack in Paris, into one of the most-admired and best-cared-for horses in Berlin, must have been a happy event in the life of the amiable grey gelding.

Berliner Tattersall, at which I put up Gustave at the very moderate livery of 3s. a day, is, no country excepted, the best livery stables I have ever seen. The feeding and grooming is very good, and the owners of horses which are put up there, are allowed the use of two immense covered riding-schools in which to exercise them. There is a restaurant attached to the larger *manège*, round which there is a low gallery capable of holding at least 300 people. The existence of these *tribunes*, which are free to the public, gives to dealers admirable opportunities for 'showing' horses to intending purchasers.

The German seat on horseback, according to the precepts of the *Vaterland*, is, to my thinking, singularly artificial and stiff, and is consequently insecure for the rider and fatiguing for the horse ; but, by their methods, they obtain great control over their animals. Different to the Germans, the English cavalry ride well ; but break-in their horses badly. If any of my readers desire a proof of the inefficiency of our military school training, they will obtain a striking one if they attend a cavalry review and observe the length of time it takes a regiment to reform after a charge.

The Thiergarten, which is just outside Berlin, is an extensive wood and pleasure ground through which there are miles upon miles of beautifully kept drives and well laid down rides. It has also, near the Zoological Gardens, a large open space, called the Hippodrome, round which are placed a few small fences for the use of the hard-riding public. The Thiergarten confers on Berlin immense facilities for riding, superior even to those which are enjoyed by Paris, and consequently this exercise is extremely popular among the residents of the Prussian capital. Knowing the equestrian scenes which may be daily witnessed in his own familiar Rotten Row, an Englishman might think that the riders in the Thiergarten are equally wayward. For nearly four weeks my wife and I rode every day, except Sunday, for a couple of hours in the Thiergarten, and although we met on each occasion a large number of riders, we never once saw a horse pulling hard or playing up in any way. A very bad place, you, my readers, will observe, for a horsebreaker to go to. That is quite true; although, had I been given a chance, I cannot help thinking that the plan of doing in a month what it takes German breakers two or three years to accomplish, would have been appreciated. The credit of the good manners displayed by the horses in the Thiergarten was due to the excellence of their training, for the ordinary Berliner would as soon think of mounting a tiger, as one of the hard-mouthed brutes which we are accustomed to see in the Row. Hence, to sell well in Berlin, a saddle horse must be absolutely 'confidential.' I must say that in this respect Germans display a large amount of sense which is uncommon in England. On the day we arrived at Berlin, we met Herr Freitag, who is a German horse dealer. On the following morning, when he saw my wife ride and jump Gustave in the *manège*, he conceived a great respect for us, and as he had five or six Irish horses which he had lately imported, he placed them at our disposal. He even offered to pay half our expenses if we would stay in Berlin and ride his horses every morning; but as we were staying only a short time in the place, we told him we would be glad to do the work without payment, as long as we remained in Berlin. The people of the stable were greatly surprised to see us ride these comparatively raw horses in the open, without their having had any school training. We had a lot of pleasant rides with Korn, Freitag's rough-rider, in the Thiergarten, and we three always made a point of taking the youngsters over the jumps in the Hippodrome. In this we had our amusement and exercise; and Freitag was able to sell a couple of the animals by reason of my wife having been seen on their back. The purchaser would not have considered this a guarantee of docility, if he only knew the class of horse my wife had been accustomed to mount during our breaking expeditions.

While we were in Berlin my book, *The Points of the Horse*, was published. With its appearance, fifteen years of work came to an end. I am content to have, at last, a book upon which I can rest my reputation, and am thankful that I had the many hundreds of pounds which I spent in getting up material for it. Its merits have had very generous recognition from the press and also from the public. The Prince of Wales was graciously pleased to accept a copy, and I have had from the Continent several applications to purchase the right of translating it.

When going to Berlin we made the mistake of travelling by the Flushing route, which is both inconvenient and expensive for horses. The best way would have been by Hamburg; for though the sea voyage from London is rather long, it is cheap, and the rail journey from thence to Berlin is only about 80 miles long. We returned by Hamburg; as we wished to meet Fillis, who was performing there in Circus Renz. The thin, little old man was very chatty. He showed us his great school horse Germinal, and another which he had in training. His good opinion of himself was amusing, though it was no doubt to a large extent well deserved. His contempt was great for all other school riders, of whom, so he told us, he was the god in public opinion. I must say that as far as I know and have heard, he is easily first. Even Baucher, as I have previously described, was not sacred to this *sapeur*. The mention of the name of M. Barroil, author of *L'Art Équestre*, made him mad. 'What can he know about a horse?' said Fillis. 'He weighs 80 kilos.' Alas! I thought, how prone we mortals are to take credit to ourselves for natural advantages. Treading still further on dangerous ground, I asked him about Baron de Vaux, who, I believe, is the horse critic of *Gil Blas*. 'He abused me in his *Écuyers et Écuyères*,' replied the famous Londoner; 'because I would not let him help me in writing my book. I wrote it all myself.' I have always understood that M. Clémanceau, the late French deputy, put Fillis's ideas into words; and think so still. Anyhow, *Les Principes de Dressage et d'Équitation* is a book to be proud of; although it would be in better taste if Fillis had avoided adversely criticising in its pages, the books of other authors on *équitation savante*, to wit, those of Baucher and Barroil. *Écuyers* who are not particularly friendly with Fillis, retort that in his actual breaking, he largely employs, to obtain many of his *airs*, the whip, against the use of which he is particularly severe in *Les Principes*. Fillis, in his own estimation, is infallible and has obtained finality in his art.

When we saw Fillis enter the circus on the back of the handsome and well-bred Germinal, we forgot his faults of phrase and manner, and reverently acknowledged that we were in the presence of a great master. What I liked most about him was that the horse walked into and round the ring in ordinary style, and without a trace of excitement or exaggerated collection, until he began his particular turn or act. As soon as he had finished his *numéro*, he resumed his placid way of going, which showed that his brilliancy was not the result of his having been recently tortured. Germinal was supple, light, and executed all his movements with admirable precision, and with entire absence of fretfulness. In fact, he appeared to work by the indications of the hand and leg and not by the irritation of the spur. Fillis was more 'starred' on the programme than any other performer; a fact which shows how highly esteemed clever circus riders are on the Continent. The points which I did not like about his riding were as follows :—(1) His seat was inelegant; because he humped his back and worked his body, arms and legs with far too evident effort to obtain effect on his horse. (2) He held his hands too close together on the reins. In the position he kept them, they had the appearance of those of a man who is trying to steer a boat with both hands on the tiller. (3) He held his hands too

Photo. by A. F. MacKenzie, Birnam, N.B.

Rutland.

high, and consequently there was too much weight on the hind legs of the horse. Yet for all this, he made his horse do more than I have ever seen any other high school animal perform.

The lightness and freedom of Germinal was in singular contrast to the wooden movements of the horses ridden by Herr Wulff when I saw him in his circus at Hengler's. The Germans seem, in obtaining control over their riding horses, to deprive them of all their spirit, and their animals, as a rule, go through their work in a dead, mechanical manner. The French, on the contrary, do all they can to preserve the fire of their animals. Among the former, the control is that of the breaker; among the latter, that of the rider.

Fillis did each night about ten *airs*, which were put down in the programme, so that one could follow each evolution. I cannot understand why those high school riders who perform in circuses in England do not grant this favour to their audience, few of whom have any acquaintance with this system of equitation.

Although Circus Renz is the best one I have ever seen, its programme had the objectionable item of two rearers each carrying a lady on an ordinary side-saddle, while these two horses walked about on their hind legs. The feat itself is not alone opposed to all principles of true horsemanship; but its performance, in this case, was nothing short of a crime, in that it placed two women in a position of danger out of which they could not escape if anything went wrong. Herr Renz is no doubt aware that poor Emilie Loisset, an exceptionally brilliant *écuyère*, was killed at the Cirque d'Hiver in 1882 by a rearer falling back on her.

After staying a few days at Hamburg in order to study Fillis and Germinal, we returned to England, where I finished this book; gave a lecture to the Society of Arts on the Horse from an Artistic Point of View, and one to the Walsall Chamber of Commerce on Horses and Saddles; showed my photographs of horses to the Photographic Society of Great Britain and at the Royal Institution, and settled down at Melton Mowbray.

On a recent trip to Rugby in search of a smart pony for a friend, I had the good fortune to meet Mr E. D. Miller, whom I knew in India when he was in the 17th Lancers. He and his brother keep a large stable of polo ponies for sale at Spring Hill and break them in their riding-school and polo ground. They generally have about fifty ponies of the highest class. I may mention that the ideal pony is a dwarf-hunter and as well bred as possible. Practically speaking these animals are to be found only in Ireland. Mr Miller played in the winning team at Meerut for the Cavalry Cup in 1888 and 1889, and also at the Calcutta Tournament in the same years. Finding on the return of the 17th Lancers that 'soldiering' was not as pleasant at home as in India, he joined his brother, who in 1891 had started the Spring Hill business. They began by trying a little dealing in hunters; but soon gave it up in favour of polo ponies. Their great success has been due to careful selection and thorough good breaking. Two years ago they started a polo club and had last year a polo tournament in which eight teams competed, among them being those of the 14th Hussars, Inniskilling Dragoons, and county teams. Since the 31st of last March, they have been playing three days a week. Their busiest months for play are April, July, August and September, when the London season is not on and people are not playing at Hurlingham. Rugby is so centrally placed that they get players from all parts. Lord Shrewsbury and Captain Daly come from Stafford; Lord Harrington and Mr Gerald Hardy, from Derby; Captain Renton, from Liverpool; Mr Nichalls (17th Lancers), from Preston; Mr Burnaby, from Leicester; Mr Cartland, from Birmingham; and many others from different places. They have consequently made Rugby the great Midland centre for polo.

Thanks to the kindness of Mr Scarth Dixon, the author

of that delightful book *In The North Countrie*, I have lately had an instructive and pleasant trip to Yorkshire, where I went with 'The British Yeoman' of *The Sporting Times* to study Cleveland bays, Yorkshire coach horses, and Yorkshire hackneys, and to take photographs of the best types for *The Points of the Horse*. Among other good men, I was lucky to meet Mr John Lett of Rillington and Mr Mitchell of Eccleshill. Mr Lett is a large breeder of all classes of horses; is a well-known judge at horse shows; a great exporter; and was the pioneer of the American trade in Cleveland bays. Mr Mitchell devotes himself chiefly to Yorkshire hackneys, and is the owner of that beautiful horse and champion, Ganymede, for whom he paid 2000 guineas. He is also a great breeder, judge, and exporter. Mr Dixon initiated the movement that resulted in the formation of the Cleveland Bay Society, for which he was secretary for ten years. He, like his friends Mr Lett and Mr Mitchell, is an enthusiastic fox-hunter. It was not their fault if I came away from Yorkshire without knowing something about the horses of the 'county of broad acres.'

Under the difficulty of having to ride anything we could get without money, in exchange for the risky work of 'making' 'green' horses clever, we had enough of hunting last season to show us that the sport in Leicestershire cannot be surpassed. A Friday with Lord Lonsdale and Tom Firr will satisfy the hardest man to hounds; and Lord Edward Manners and Gillard may be safely trusted not to lead the ladies into danger. Lord Lonsdale on behalf of the Quorn and the Duke of Rutland with respect to the Belvoir, foster the true interests of hunting by their kindness and consideration to the farmers, even more than by their profuse liberality. The Cottesmore, hunted by Mr Baird, has a corner of its district, like the Quorn and Belvoir, touching Melton Mowbray, which is consequently the best hunting centre in England. The 'hunting people' are wealthy birds of passage, among whom there is a small percentage of fine horsemen. This proportion is of course lowered by the fact that hunting at Melton Mowbray is a fashionable function. Being a stranger without friends to puff or foes to ignore I would in no way wish to make invidious distinctions; but cannot help saying that the man who wins my admiration by the way in which he gets over a big country is Colonel Forester, who, well on in the seventies, goes as straight as the best of them. The riding of the ladies is beyond all praise. For their numbers, there are far fewer 'hard funkers' among them, than among the men. My readers will think that I ought at last to be happy. Well, I don't quite know about that. English people in their own country are so different to the soldiers, sailors, planters and colonials among whom I have spent the best years of my life, that I catch myself every now and then regretfully looking at the old breaking-bag, saddle-box and trunk, and thinking of foreign lands where we have always found a welcome. Melton Mowbray is a bad place for a veterinary surgeon to invade; for it already possesses an admirable one in Mr Goodall, who is also a fine horseman, and a very pleasant companion. After we have brought out some fresh editions and two or three new books we have in preparation, I think we shall flit once again to a country where the people, to accept us, will not require us to have been born in the place and to have at least as much money as themselves. If we do so, I may be able to narrate some further experiences among men and horses.

INDEX TO NAMES.

ABBOTT, Mr Harry, 182
Abdool Rayman, 60
Abrams, Mr Harry, 145
Ali bin Abdoola, 60
Ali Pasha Shereef, 139
Allen, Mr, 71, 72
Allen, Mr Fred., 325
Anderson, Colonel Joe, 63
Artin Bey, 139
Ashe, Mr Edwin, 218
Astley, Captain, 208, 209
—— Mr, 271
—— Mr John, 209
—— Sir John, 15
Ayres (the cricketer), 218

BAILEY, Charlie, 56
Baird, Mr, 353
Baker, Colonel Valentine, 138, 139
Barber, Mr Hilton, 229
Barnato, Mr Barny, 269
Barroil, M., 27, 347
Barry, Mr Dick, 12
Bates, Captain, 126
Baucher, 27, 308
Bayley, Captain John, 23
Beatty, Mr, 179
Beaver, Colonel P. K., 187
Bedford, Duke of, 121
Bendoff, Wolf, 270
Benson, Colonel, 116
Beresford, Captain, 127
—— Lord Marcus, 66
—— Lord William, 119, 197
Berkeley, Mr Stanley, 68
Blaine, Sir Seymour, 91
Blew, Mr, 74
Bon, Dr Le, 304
Bonamicci, Mr, 266
Bradford, Sir Edward, 47
Brann, Mr, 218
Brett, Mr, 191
Brine, General Fred., 19
Brixen, Captain Axen von, 172

Brockwell (the cricketer), 218
Brown, General 'Begorra,' 24
—— Mr J. H. Oswald, 95, 97
—— J. Moray, 298
—— Mr Tom, 87
—— Professor, 73
Buckridge, Mr, 263
Buffalo Bill, 45
Burnaby, Mr, 352
Bush, Mr, 162
Butler, Mr, 172
Butters, Mr, 266

CAMBRIDGE, Duke of, 339
Carew, Colonel Pole, 213
Cartland, Mr, 352
Cartouche, 48
Charlton, Mr John, 96
Chatterton (the cricketer), 218
Chesham, Lord, 132
Clémanceau, M., 348
Cole, Mr Comyns, 74
Coleman, Mr Fatty, 69
Colley, General, 287
Colville, Mr, 138
Cumbermere, Lord, 126
Cooke, Colonel, 115
Corlett, Mr John, 88
Couper, J. R., 269
Crookenden, Major, 137
Curtis, Mr Ben, 276
Cuthbert, Mr, 293

DALLAS, Mr Barnes, 160
Daly, Captain, 352
Dann, Major, 131
Davis, Mr Oliver, 291
Deerfoot, 18
Detring, Mr, 172
Dilke, Lady, 336
Dirom, Mr, 187
Dixon, Mr Scarth, 352
Donaldson, Mr, 266
Dowie, Miss, 336

356 *Index to Names.*

Dubarry, Madame, 48
Dufferin, Lady, 120
—— Lord, 119, 120
Dwarf of Blood, 179

EDINBURGH, Duchess of, 138
—— Duke of, 138
Edwards, Dr, 223
Elliott, Colonel Locke, 114

FALLON, 109
Fermoy, Lord, 11
Ferris, Mr J., 218
Fillis, Frank, 116, 201, 257
—— James, 304, 308, 331, 347-351
Firr, Tom, 353
Fitzgerald, Captain, 136
Fitz Henry, Mr, 172
Fleming, Dr, 63, 215
Fordham, George, 325
Forester, Colonel, 353
Fotheringhame, Mr George, 269
Frank, 110
Freitag, Herr, 346

GALVAYNE, Mr, 101
Galway, Mr Payne, 263
Garnet, Major, 221
Gascard, Mr, 187
Gérard, Balthazar, 48
Gidney, Mr, 187
Gillard, 353
Goater, Jim, 88
Gofton, Mr, 219
Gooch, Mr F. V., 322
—— George, 203
Goodall, Mr, 354
Goss, Joe, 31
Grey, Mr Cecil, 112
Grenfell, General, 138
Gubbins, Mr Nathaniel, 88
Guthrie, Mr, 223

HAES, Mr Frank, 217
Hailey, Mr Clarence, 218
Hammond, Mr John, 87
Hampson and Scott, 332
Hancock, Arthur, 207
Harboard, The Hon. Walter, 91
Harding, Charlie, 206
Hardy, Joe, 207
- Mr Gerald, 352
   Mr Haywood, 96
Harrington, Lord, 352
Hawkes, Mr George, 3
- - - Mr Quail, 4
Hayes, Bill, 202

Hayes, George, 12
—— James, 12
Hearne, Alec., 218
—— G. G., 218
—— Jack, 218
Henderson, Dr, 195
Hess, Mr Jack, 281
Homan, Mr, 234
Horgan, Mr Dan, 21
Horton, Mr Fred, 339
Hudson, Mr Tommy, 206
Hughes, Captain Gordon, 235
Humphries, Mr J. D., 157

IRVING, Dr, 172
—— Jack, 41
—— Mr, 339

JACKSON, the American Deer, 18
Jardine, Sir Robert, 156
Jarvis, Mr W., 87
Jenny, Mlle., 136
Joe, 110, 315
Jones, Captain, 69
Joubert, General, 283
Joy, Captain George, 91

KEKEWICH, Major, 138
Kelly, 285
Kerouse, Mr, 194
Kinchant, Colonel, 76
King, Mr Harold, 112
Kingsland, Dan, 211
Kipling, Mr Rudyard, 121, 184
Knolles, Mr Tom, 6
Korn, 346
Kruger, Mr, 172

LAMBTON, Mr, 138
Landsley, Mr, 339
Lansdown, Lord, 43
Lanyon, Sir Owen, 290
Larpent, Mr, 126
Lead, Jack, 31
Lehmann, Mr, 172
Leon, 313, 343
Lett, Mr John, 353
Levitt, Jack, 17
Lincoln, Frank, 206
Lindo, Miss, 130
Livingstone, 47
Lloyd, Mr, 179
Loch, Sir Henry, 221
Loisset, Emilie, 351
Lonsdale, Lord, 353
Lynx, Captain, 66
Lyons, Colonel Sam, 130

Index to Names. 357

Lyons, Mr, 223

MACDOUGAL, Major 'Ding,' 116
Machell, Captain, 15
Macklin, Mr, 187
Maitland, Mr Kelly, 162-164
Malitte, Mr, 203
Malone, Barney, 285
Manners, Lord Edward, 353
Margarett, Steve, 43, 187
Marryatt, Captain, 15
Martin, Edwin, 74
—— George, 18
—— William, 74, 157
—— (the cricketer), 218
Maud, Captain, 289
M'Leod, Mr Jimmy, 124
Medland, Mr, 218
Meiring, Mr, 284
Michie, Mr, 172
Miles, Mr, 223
Miley, Mickie, 203
Miller, Mr E. D., 352
Mitchell, Mr, 353
—— Sir Charles and Lady, 293
Moore, Mr Garratt, 79, 81
—— Mr J. H., 79, 81, 126,
—— Mr W. H., 79, 81
Morley, Colonel, 65
Morton, Colonel, 115
—— Mr, 74
Moss, Dave, 271
Mullins, Bat, 33
Murdoch, Mr W., 218
Myers, Mr, 23

NICHALLS, Mr, 352
Nickless, 286
Nolan, Joe, 29
Norman, Mr and Mrs Henry, 336
Nott, Major, 218

O'CALLAGHAN, Colonel, 221
O'Connor, Mr T. P., 22
October, 228, 273, 294
Orellana, Mr, 77
Owen, Mr E. M., 136

PATTON, Captain Aubrey, 16
Payne, Mr George, 210
—— Mr Phil., 293
Petly, Mr, 287
Playfair, Sir Lyon, 46
Porter, Mr John, 132
Pougher (the cricketer), 218
Prince of Wales, 132, 347
Pritchard, Rev. Mr, 77

Pudney, Jim, 31

QUAIN, Mr, 19

RAABE, Captain, 27
Raafe, Mr, 233
Radcliff, Mr Joe, 70
Rarey, 100, 101, 119, 146
Raux, M., 305, 309
Rattray, Mr Grey, 271
Reid, Miss Nellie, 128, 129
—— Mr W. W.,
—— Young, 20
Remmington, Mr, 112
Renton, Captain, 352
Rhodes, Mr Cecil, 235
Richardson, Bill, 29
Rietz, Mr, 233
Rivière, Mr Briton, 96
Roberts, Colonel Ben, 56
—— Lord, 119, 120, 289
Robertson, Mr Alec., 234
—— Professor, 63
Robinson, Mr Kay, 71, 72
—— Mr Phil., 71
Roche, The Hon. Ulick, 11
—— Miss Johanna, 12
Rockwell, 227
Russell, General Sir Baker, 317
—— Lord Herbrand, 121
Rustem Pasha, 47
Rutland, Duke of, 353

SADLER, Joe, 31
—— Mr Alf, 87
Sample, Professor, 100, 128, 213, 226, 312
Sampson, Colonel, 111
Sanson, 48
Sar Firaz Hussain, 123
Scott, Mr, 335
Sassoon, Mr D. E., 162
Sealy, Mr Allen, 96
Shaw, Captain Barnard, 12
—— Mr Vero, 298
Sheikh Esa bin Curtas, 60, 61
Shepstone, Sir Theophilus, 289
Sherwin, Miss Amy, 184
Sherwood, Mr R., 157
Shifter, The, 91
Shipley, Mr, 179
Shrewsbury, Lord, 352
Sinnet, Mr A. P., 71
Skrene, Mr, 179
Smith, C., 19
—— Mr Fraser, 158
—— 'Professor' Norton, 297

Sonnenberg, Mr, 272
Sorel, M. Charles, 304
Stevens, Mr John, 187, 192
St Quintin, Colonel, 187
Streeter, Miss, 130
Sturgess, Mr John, 81
Swaine, Colonel, 231, 292
Symonds, Tom, 29

Tanner, Dr, 21
—— Major, 21
Tautz, Messrs E., 332
Taylor, Mr John, 15
Thou, De, 48
Townsend, Mr, 94
Travers, Bob, 31
Treasure, The, 127
Truter, Mr Hendrik, 291
Turnbull, General Monty, 60

Vaux, Baron de, 347
Vernon, Mr, 219
Vezin, Mr Hermann, 131
Vikar ul Umra, 123

Wales, Prince of, 132, 347
Wallace, Captain, 235
Waller, Mr Sam, 96
Warburton, Colonel Fred., 22
Ward, Charlie, 321
—— Frank, 321
—— Miss Genevieve, 219
Wardropp, General, 116
Watson, Mr Alfred, 68
Webling, Mr, 68
Weekes, Teddy, 193
Westminster, Duke of, 132
White, Sir George, 121
Williams, Mr Blundell, 213
—— of Tempe, Mr, 233
—— Professor, 61, 63, 64
Wilson, Mr, 237
Wilton, Mr, 334
Wimble, Mr Fleming, 223
Wood, General Sir Evelyn, 287, 317
—— Harry (cricketer), 218
Woodyear, Mr, 206
Wulff, Herr, 351

York, Duke of, 138

Ziervogel, Mr. 283

THE END.

Lightning Source UK Ltd.
Milton Keynes UK
UKOW04f1055230315

248329UK00001B/110/P